TOWN
TM
image

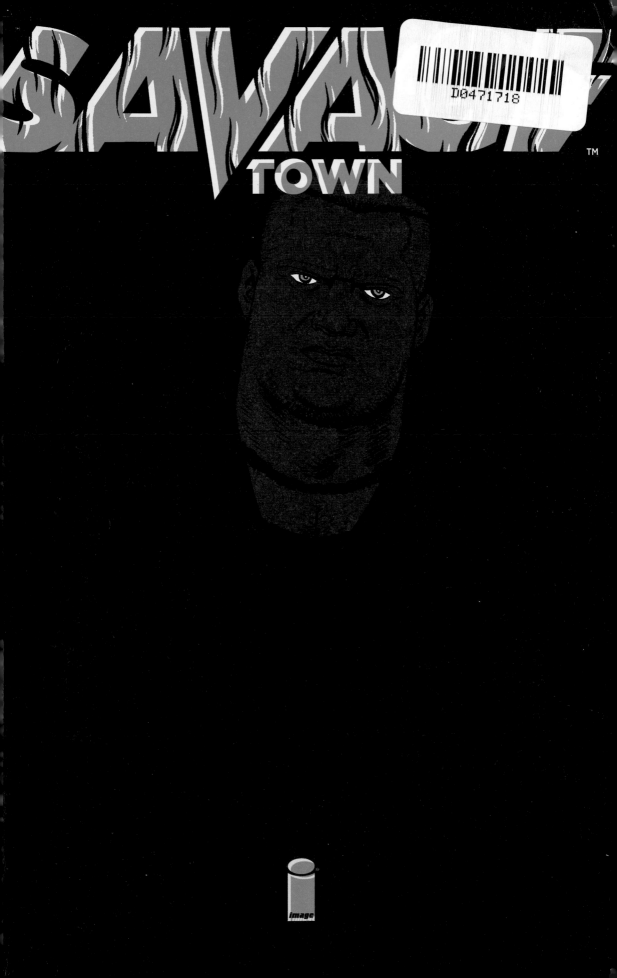

IMAGE COMICS, INC.
Robert Kirkman—Chief Operating Officer
Erik Larsen—Chief Financial Officer
Todd McFarlane—President
Marc Silvestri—Chief Executive Officer
Jim Valentino—Vice President

Eric Stephenson—Publisher
Corey Murphy—Director of Sales
Jeff Boison—Director of Publishing Planning & Book Trade Sales
Chris Ross—Director of Digital Sales
Jeff Stang—Director of Specialty Sales
Kat Salazar—Director of PR & Marketing
Branwyn Bigglestone—Controller
Kali Dugan—Senior Accounting Manager
Sue Korpela—Accounting & HR Manager
Drew Gill—Art Director
Heather Doornink—Production Director
Leigh Thomas—Print Manager
Tricia Ramos—Traffic Manager
Briah Skelly—Publicist
Aly Hoffman—Events & Conventions Coordinator
Sasha Head—Sales & Marketing Production Designer
David Brothers—Branding Manager
Melissa Gifford—Content Manager
Drew Fitzgerald—Publicity Assistant
Vincent Kukua—Production Artist
Erika Schnatz—Production Artist
Ryan Brewer—Production Artist
Shanna Matuszak—Production Artist
Carey Hall—Production Artist
Esther Kim—Direct Market Sales Representative
Emilio Bautista—Digital Sales Representative
Leanna Caunter—Accounting Analyst
Chloe Ramos-Peterson—Library Market Sales Representative
Maria Eizik—Administrative Assistant
IMAGECOMICS.COM

SAVAGE TOWN™

Declan SHALVEY Wrote it
Philip BARRETT Drew it
Jordie BELLAIRE Coloured it in
Clayton COWLES Put the letters in

Emma PRICE Made it look nice
Sebastian GIRNER Edited all around it

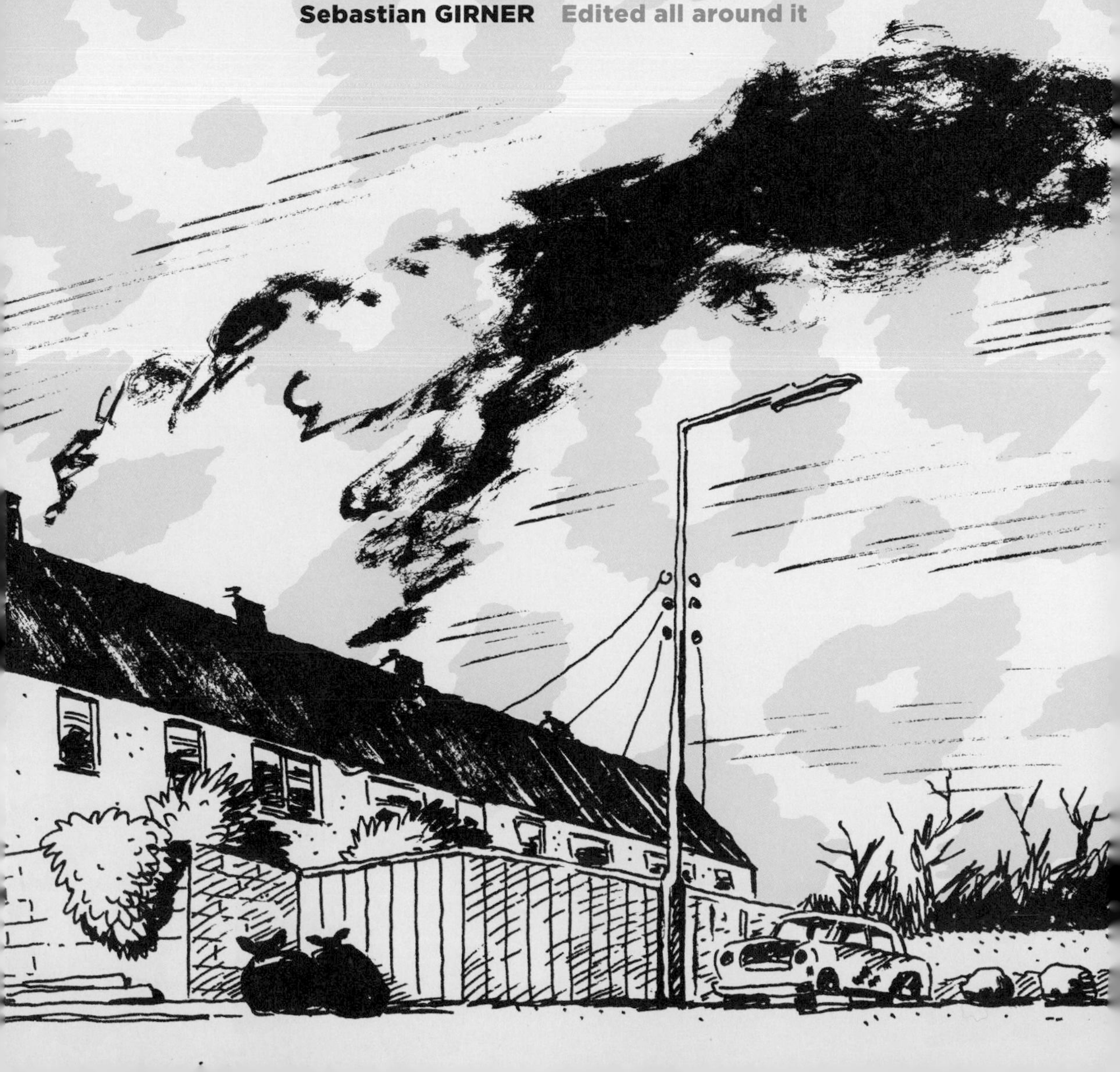

For Steve Dillon

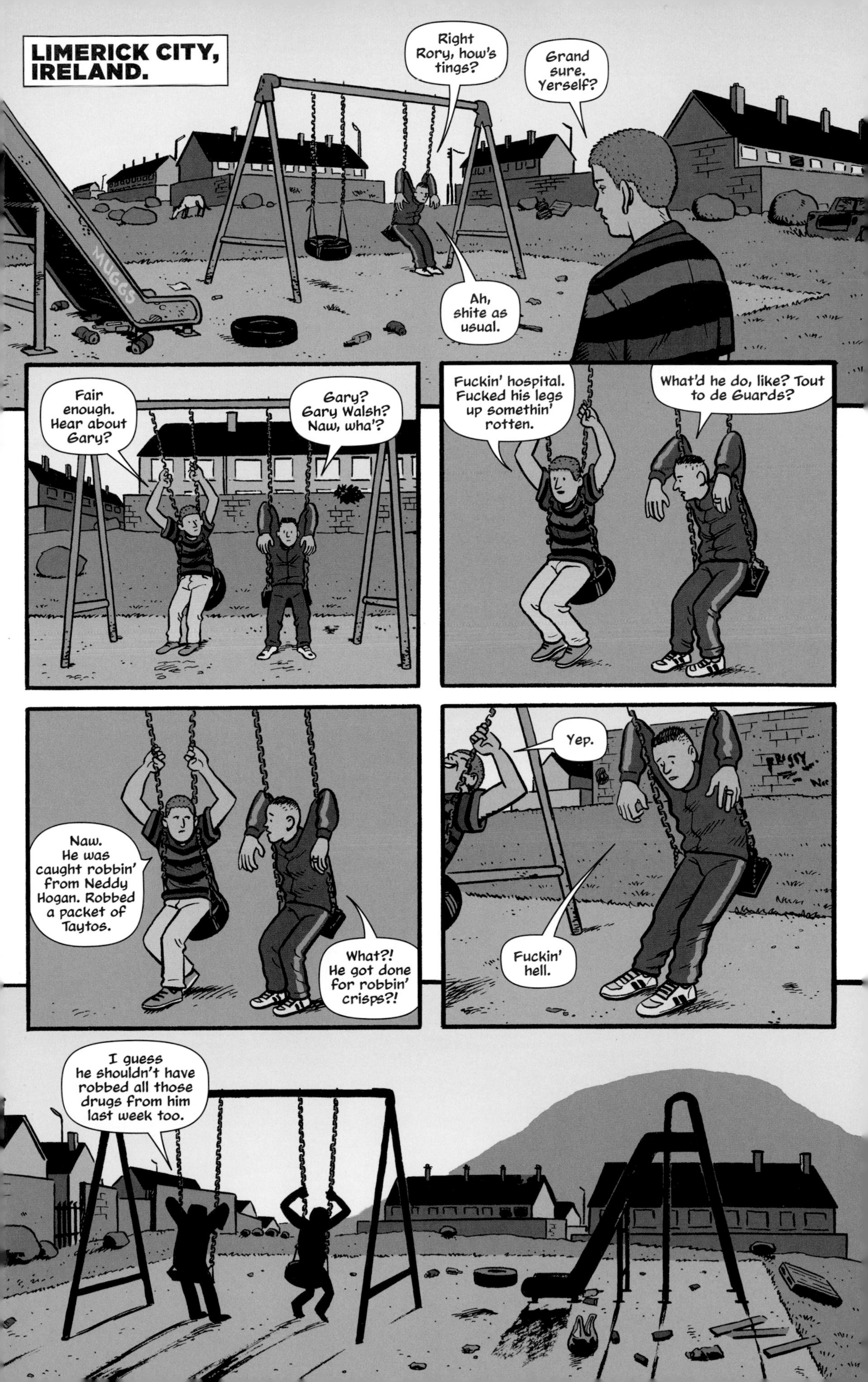
LIMERICK CITY, IRELAND.
Right Rory, how's tings?
Grand sure. Yerself?
Ah, shite as usual.
MUGGS
Fair enough. Hear about Gary?
Gary? Gary Walsh? Naw, wha'?
Fuckin' hospital. Fucked his legs up somethin' rotten.
What'd he do, like? Tout to de Guards?
Naw. He was caught robbin' from Neddy Hogan. Robbed a packet of Taytos.
What?! He got done for robbin' crisps?!
Yep.
Fuckin' hell.
I guess he shouldn't have robbed all those drugs from him last week too.

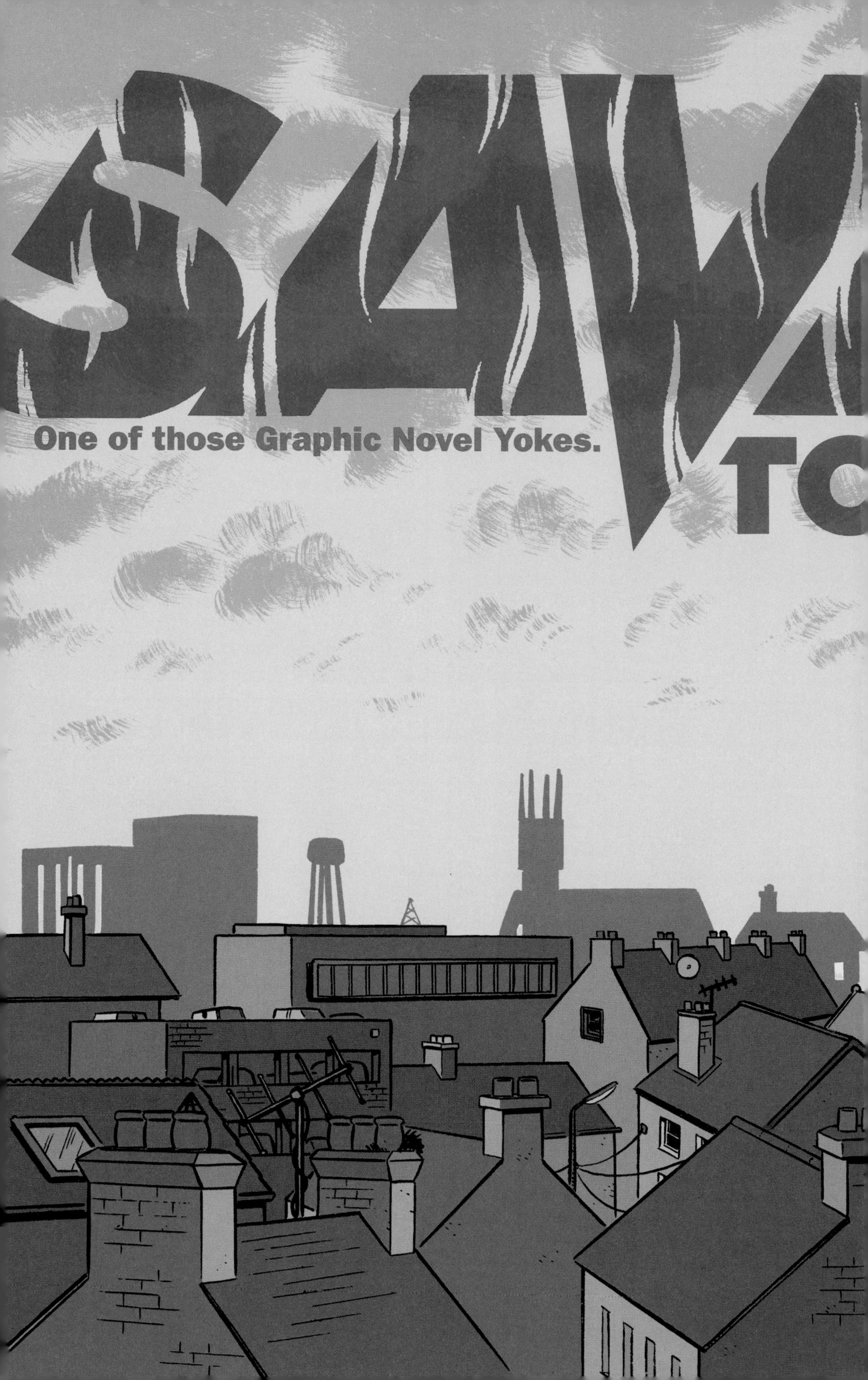

SAV
One of those Graphic Novel Yokes.
TO

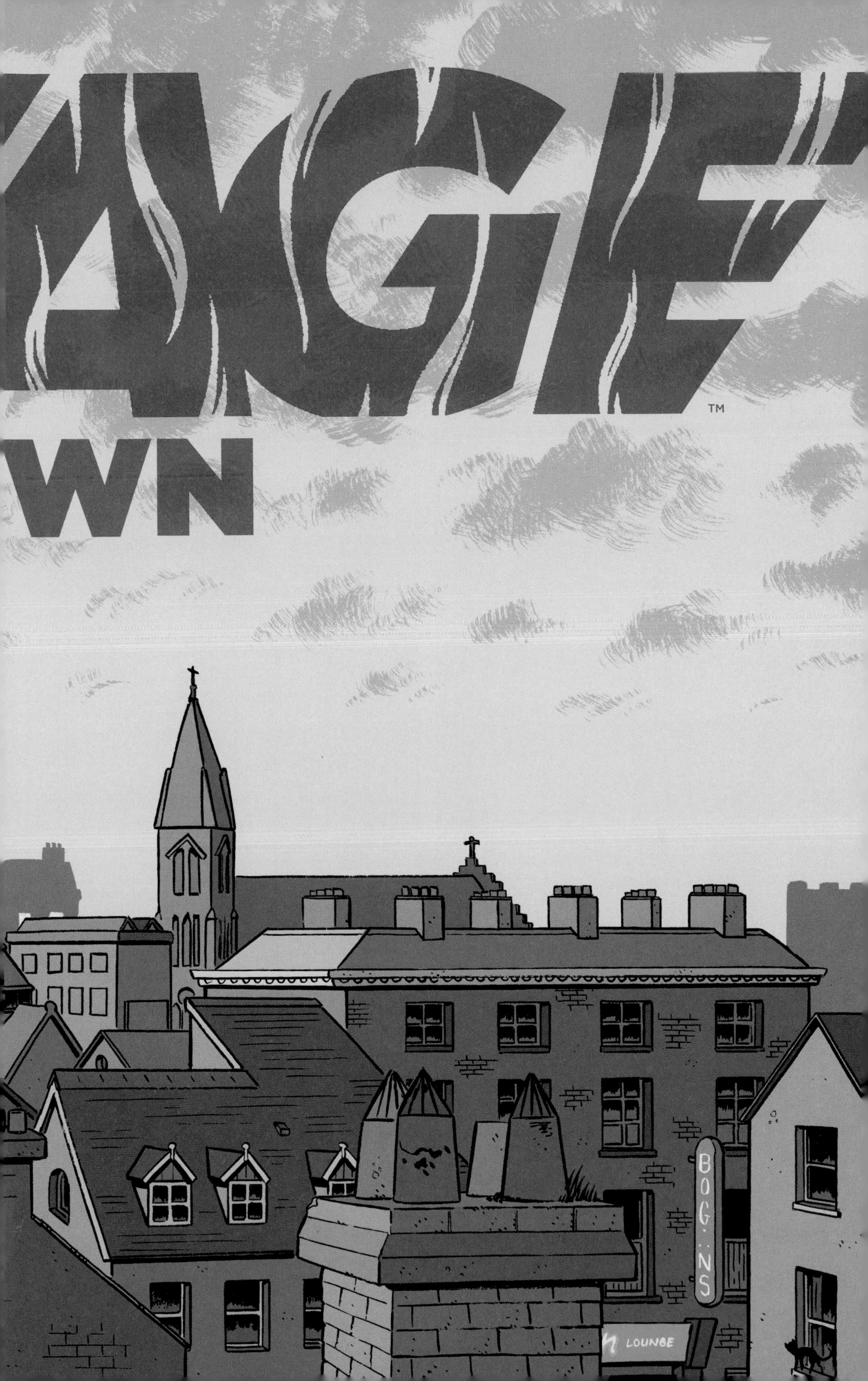
AGE
™
WN
BOG:NS
LOUNGE

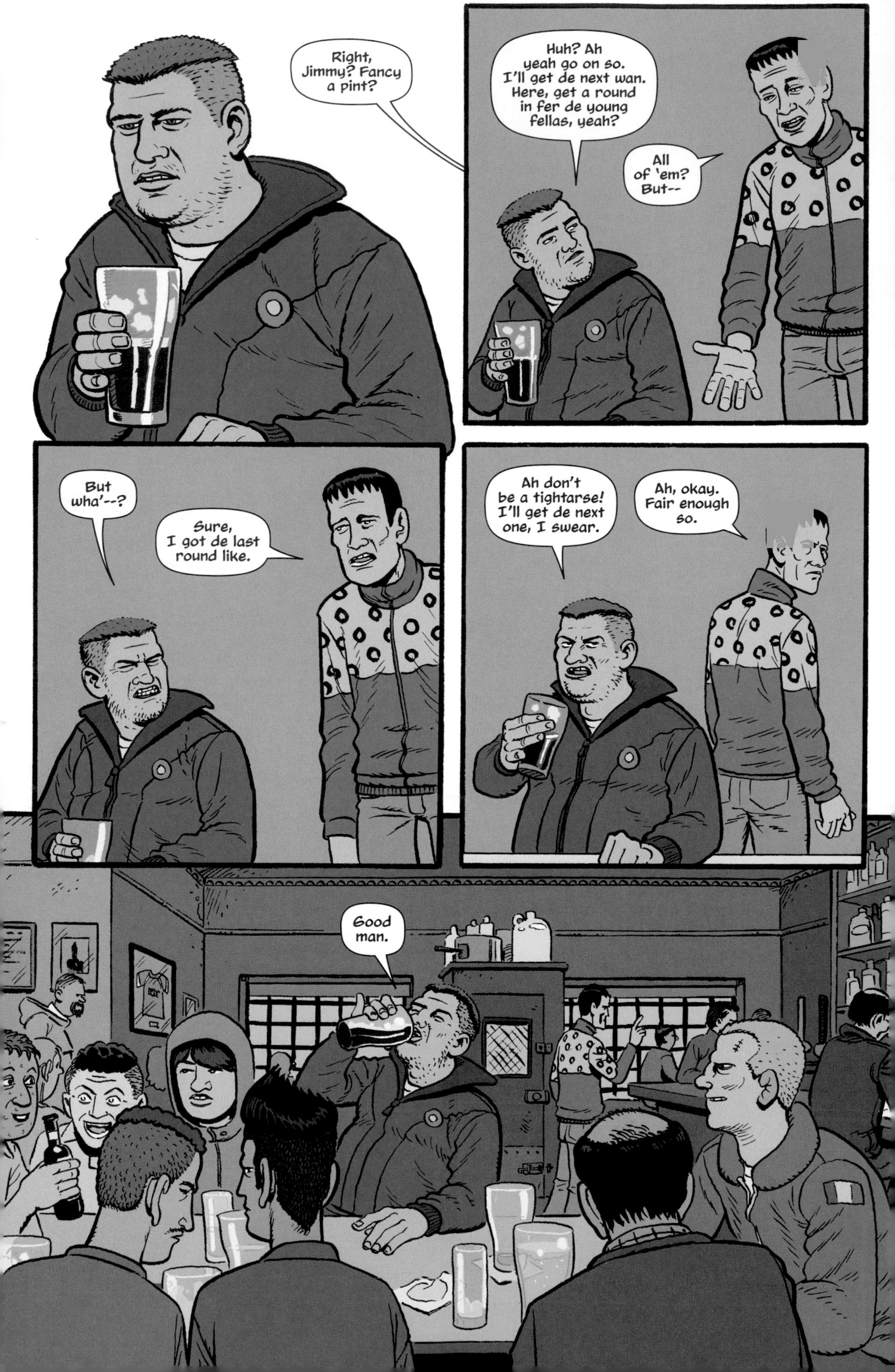
Right, Jimmy? Fancy a pint?
Huh? Ah yeah go on so. I'll get de next wan. Here, get a round in fer de young fellas, yeah?
All of 'em? But--
But wha'--?
Sure, I got de last round like.
Ah don't be a tightarse! I'll get de next one, I swear.
Ah, okay. Fair enough so.
Good man.

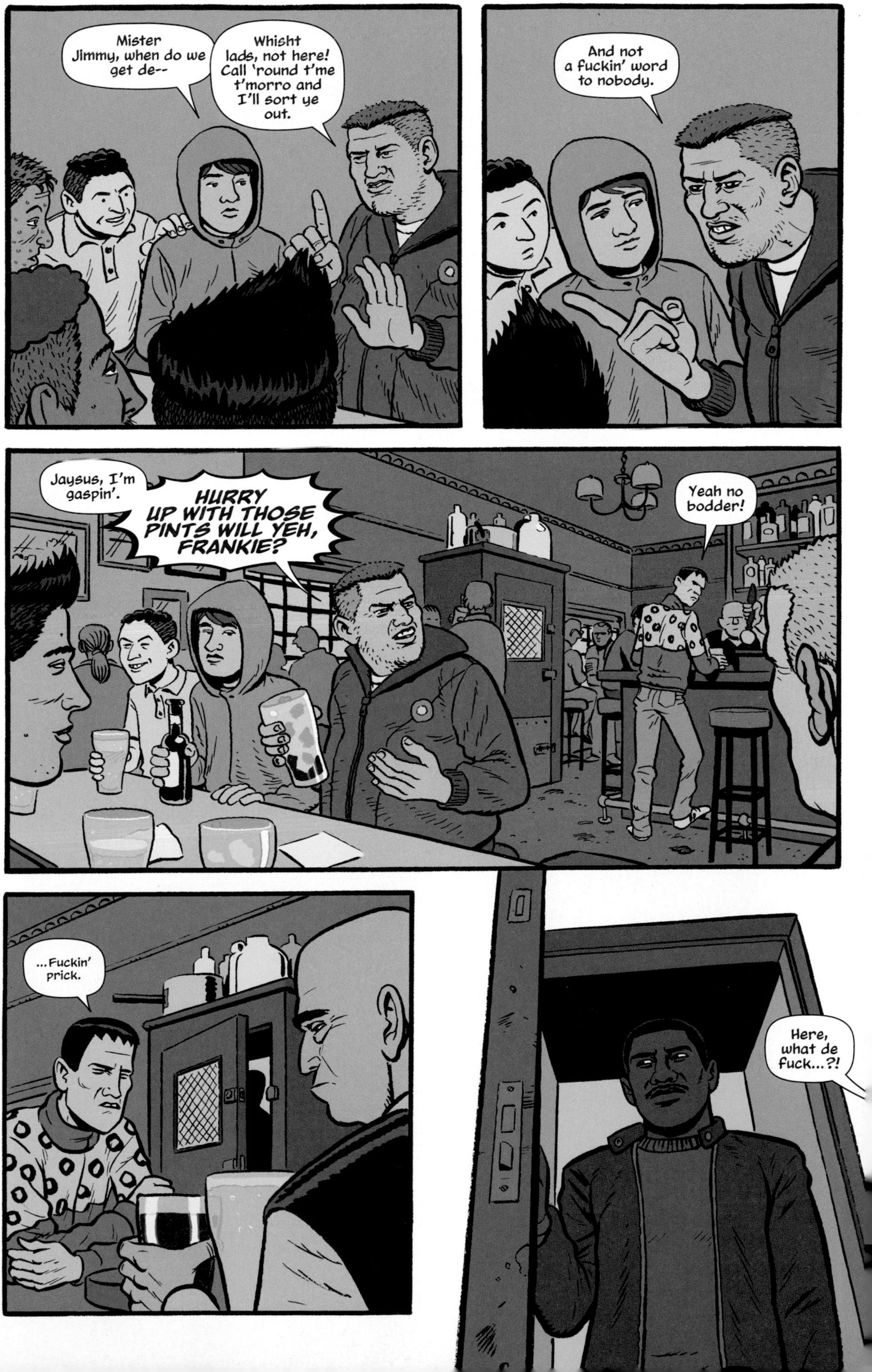
Mister Jimmy, when do we get de--
Whisht lads, not here! Call 'round t'me t'morro and I'll sort ye out.
And not a fuckin' word to nobody.
Jaysus, I'm gaspin'.
HURRY UP WITH THOSE PINTS WILL YEH, FRANKIE?
Yeah no bodder!
...Fuckin' prick.
Here, what de fuck...?!

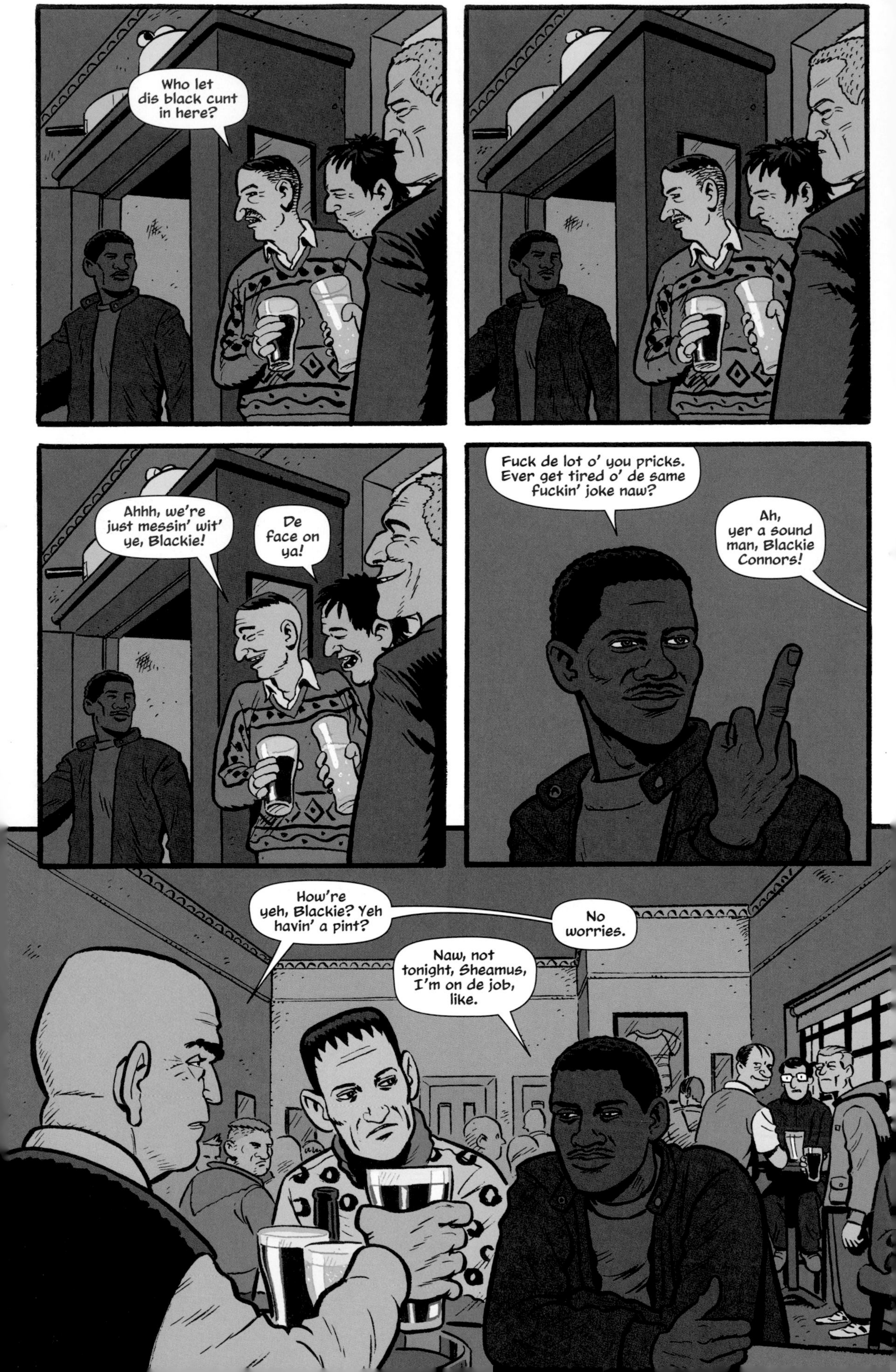
Who let dis black cunt in here?
Ahhh, we're just messin' wit' ye, Blackie!
De face on ya!
Fuck de lot o' you pricks. Ever get tired o' de same fuckin' joke naw?
Ah, yer a sound man, Blackie Connors!
How're yeh, Blackie? Yeh havin' a pint?
No worries.
Naw, not tonight, Sheamus, I'm on de job, like.

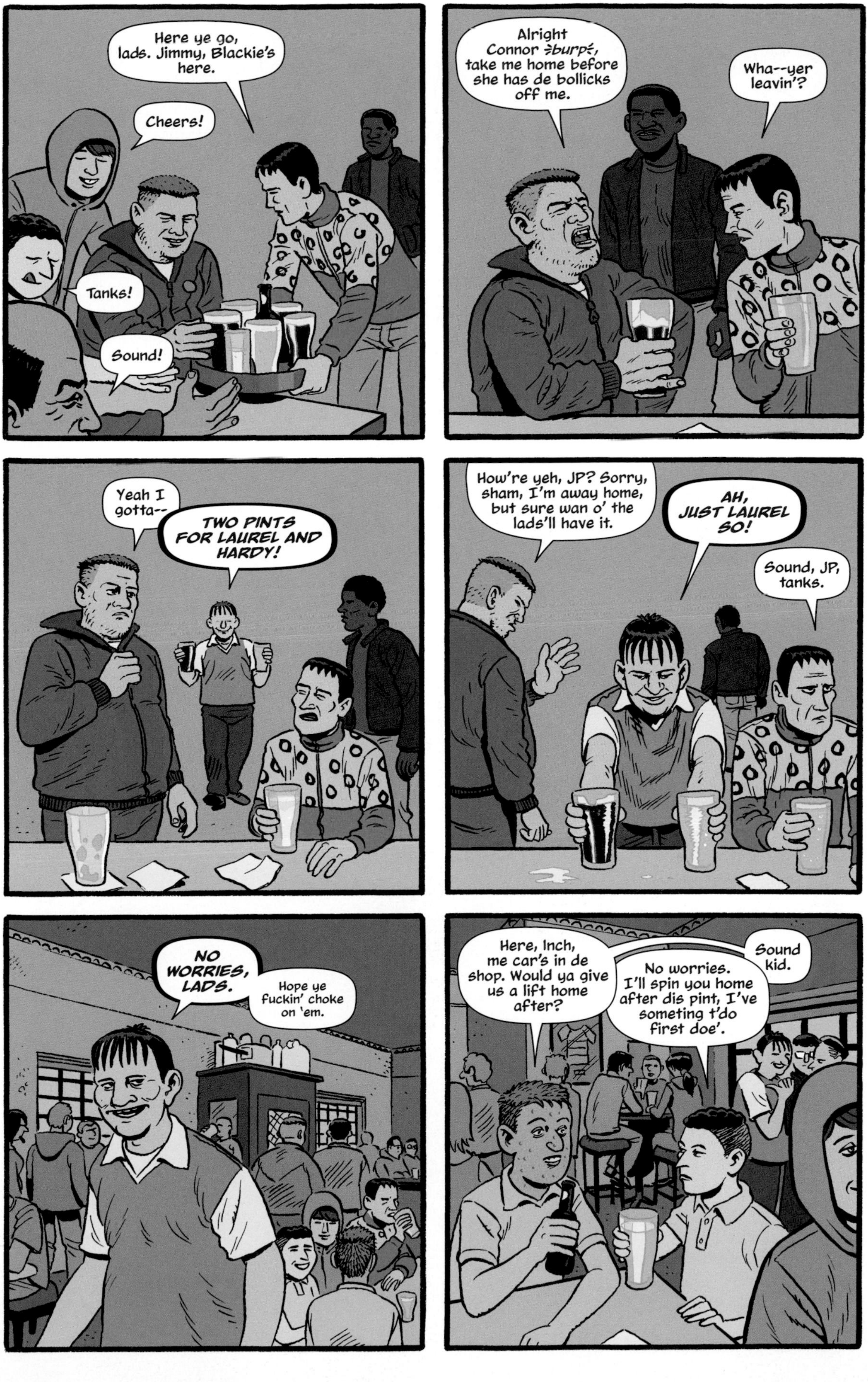
Here ye go, lads. Jimmy, Blackie's here.
Cheers!
Tanks!
Sound!
Alright Connor =burp=, take me home before she has de bollicks off me.
Wha--yer leavin'?
Yeah I gotta--
TWO PINTS FOR LAUREL AND HARDY!
How're yeh, JP? Sorry, sham, I'm away home, but sure wan o' the lads'll have it.
AH, JUST LAUREL SO!
Sound, JP, tanks.
NO WORRIES, LADS.
Hope ye fuckin' choke on 'em.
Here, Inch, me car's in de shop. Would ya give us a lift home after?
Sound kid.
No worries. I'll spin you home after dis pint, I've someting t'do first doe'.

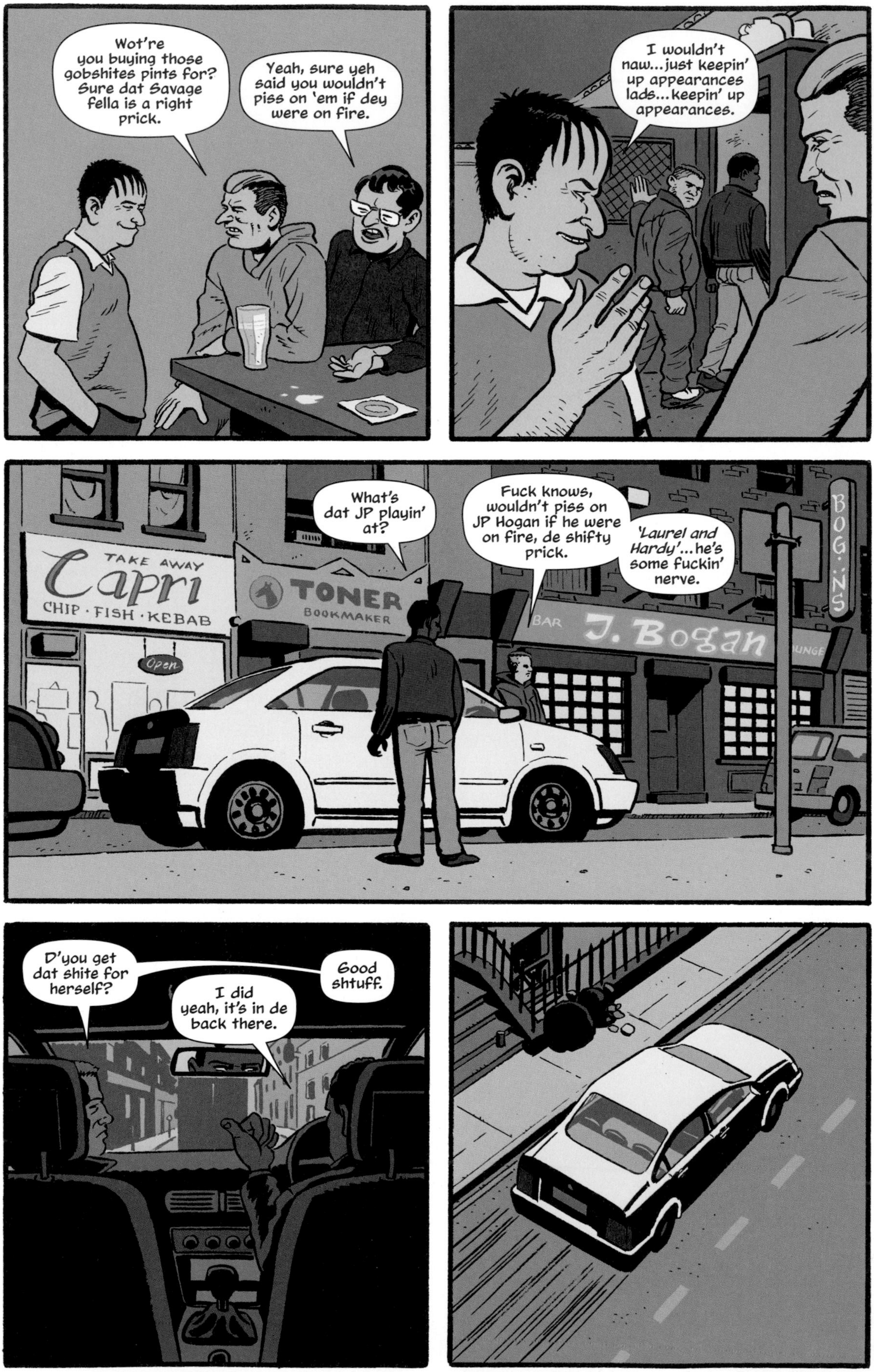
Wot're you buying those gobshites pints for? Sure dat Savage fella is a right prick.
Yeah, sure yeh said you wouldn't piss on 'em if dey were on fire.
I wouldn't naw...just keepin' up appearances lads...keepin' up appearances.
TAKE AWAY Capri
CHIP · FISH · KEBAB
Open
TONER
BOOKMAKER
BAR J. Bogan
What's dat JP playin' at?
Fuck knows, wouldn't piss on JP Hogan if he were on fire, de shifty prick.
'Laurel and Hardy'...he's some fuckin' nerve.
D'you get dat shite for herself?
I did yeah, it's in de back there.
Good shtuff.

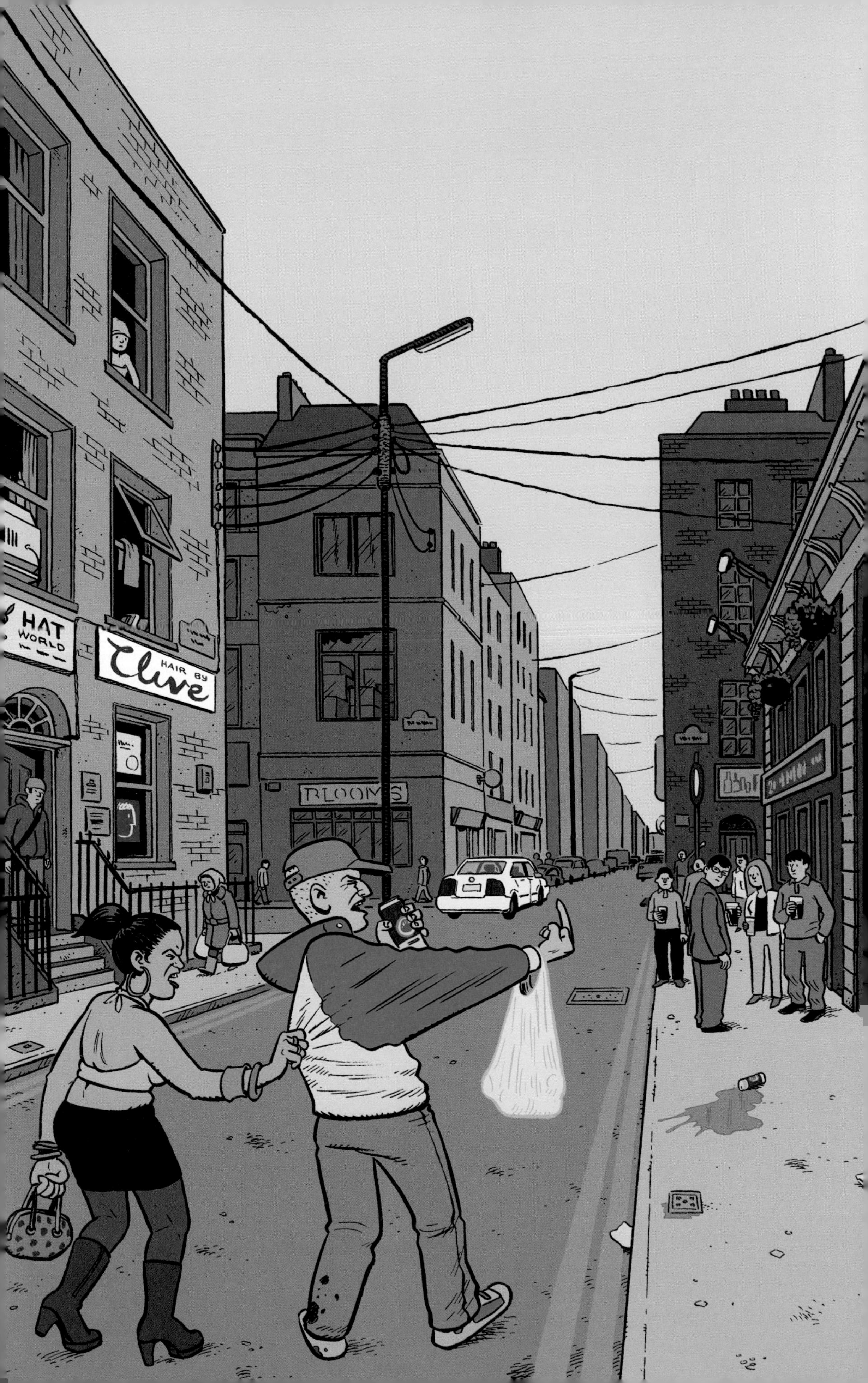
HAT WORLD
HAIR BY Clive
BLOOMS

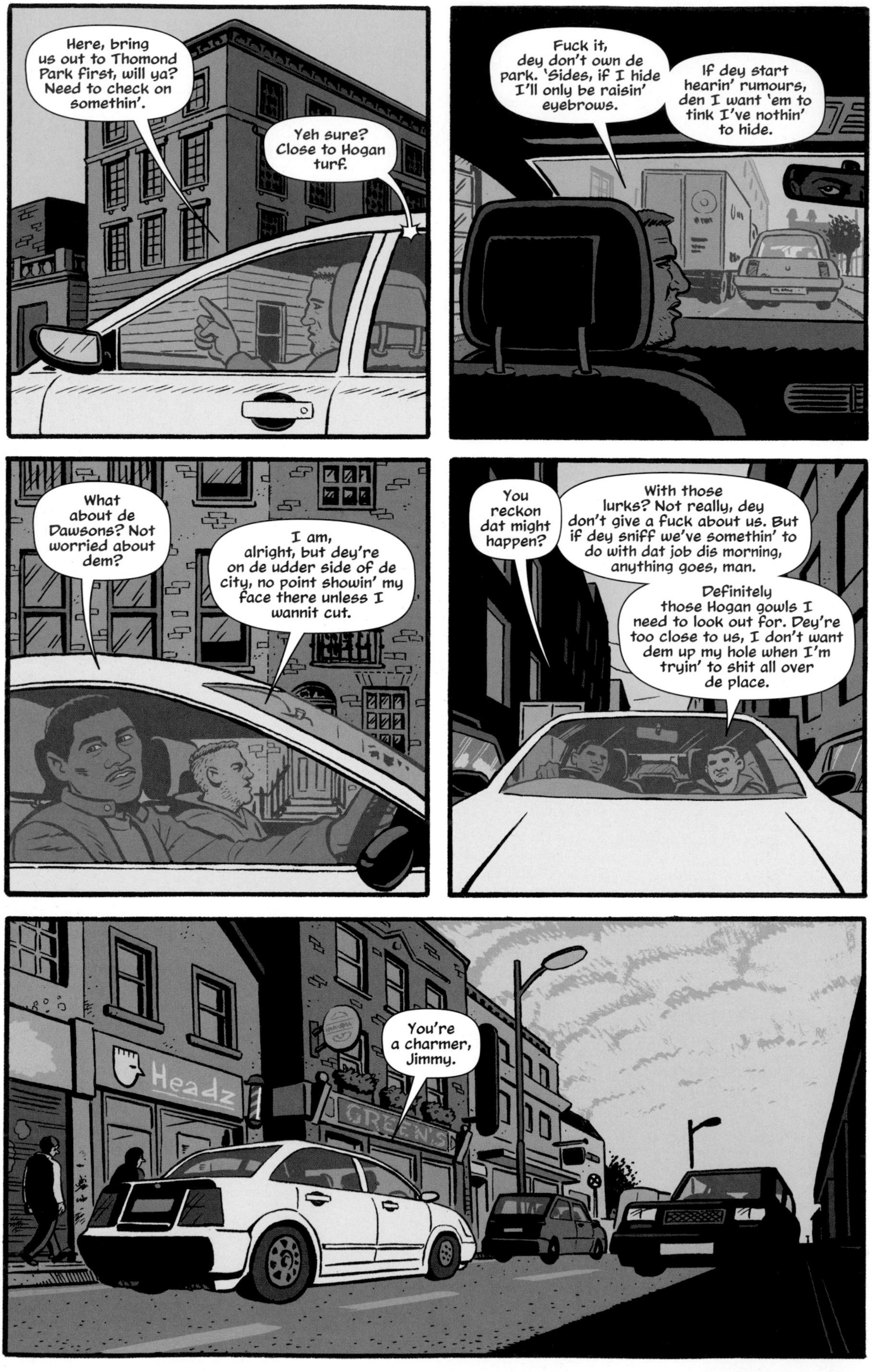
Here, bring us out to Thomond Park first, will ya? Need to check on somethin'.
Yeh sure? Close to Hogan turf.
Fuck it, dey don't own de park. 'Sides, if I hide I'll only be raisin' eyebrows.
If dey start hearin' rumours, den I want 'em to tink I've nothin' to hide.
What about de Dawsons? Not worried about dem?
I am, alright, but dey're on de udder side of de city, no point showin' my face there unless I wannit cut.
You reckon dat might happen?
With those lurks? Not really, dey don't give a fuck about us. But if dey sniff we've somethin' to do with dat job dis morning, anything goes, man.
Definitely those Hogan gowls I need to look out for. Dey're too close to us, I don't want dem up my hole when I'm tryin' to shit all over de place.
You're a charmer, Jimmy.
Headz
GREEN'S

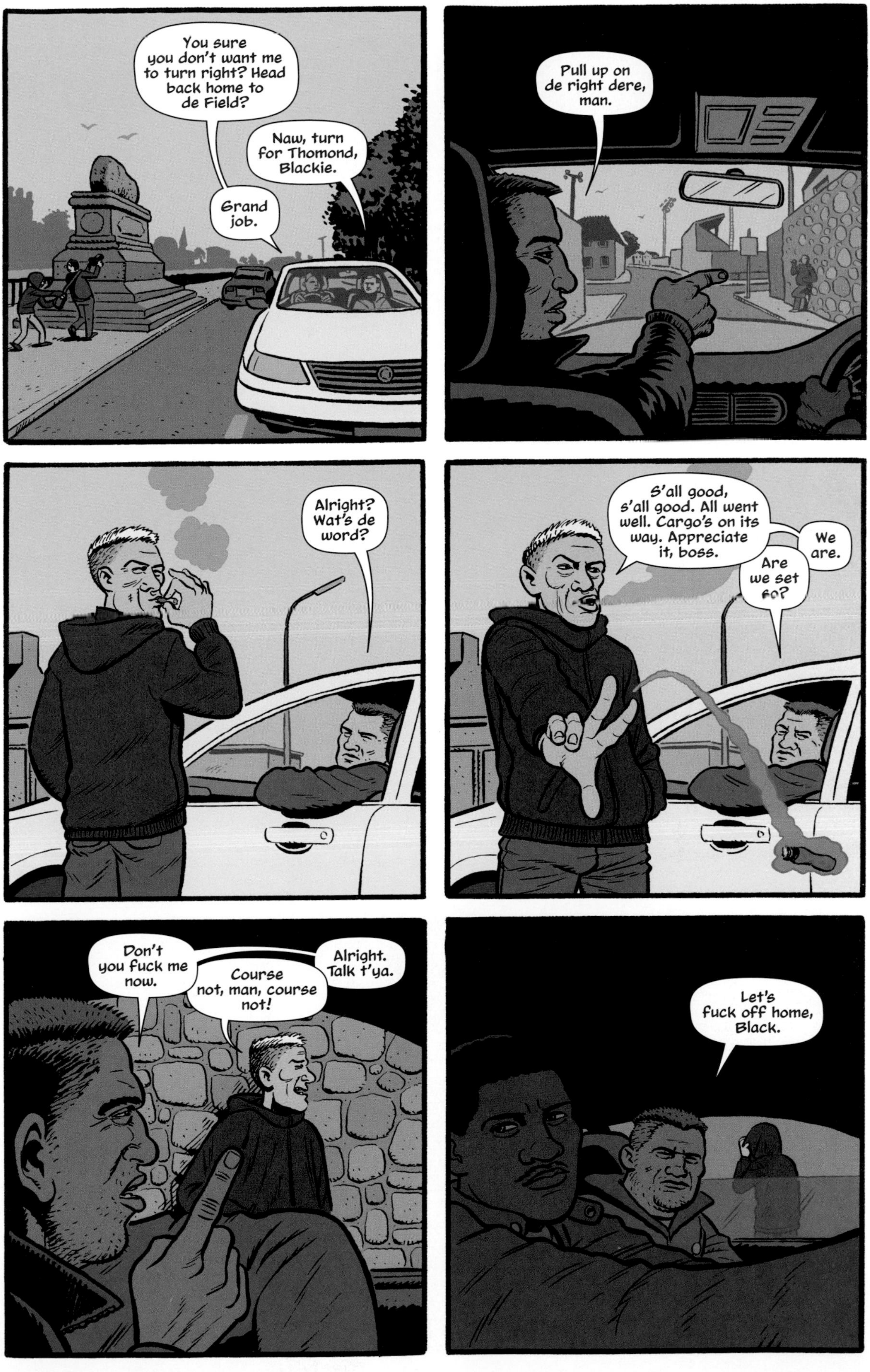
You sure you don't want me to turn right? Head back home to de Field?
Naw, turn for Thomond, Blackie.
Grand job.
Pull up on de right dere, man.
Alright? Wat's de word?
S'all good, s'all good. All went well. Cargo's on its way. Appreciate it, boss.
Are we set so?
We are.
Don't you fuck me now.
Course not, man, course not!
Alright. Talk t'ya.
Let's fuck off home, Black.

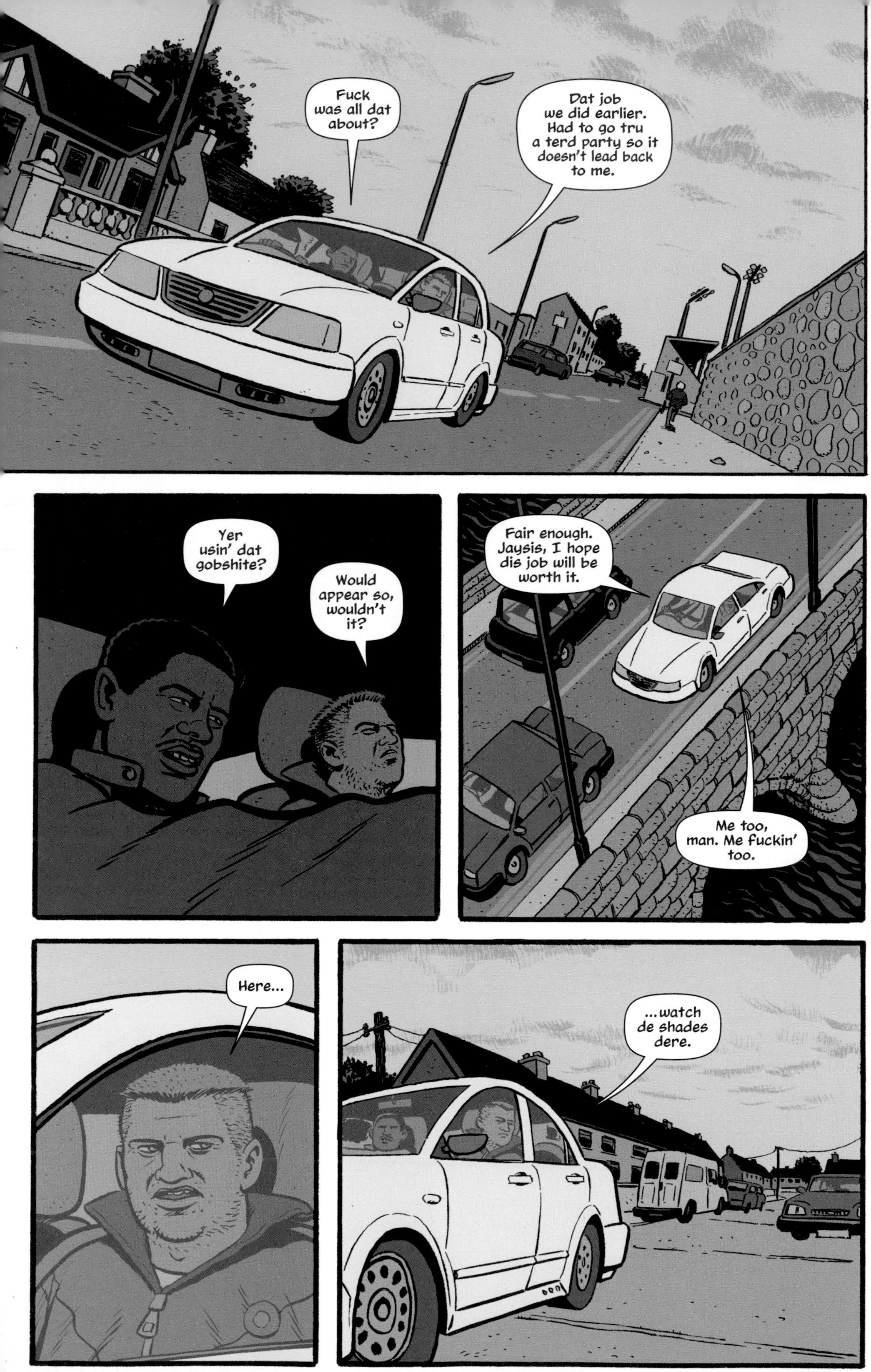
Fuck was all dat about?
Dat job we did earlier. Had to go tru a terd party so it doesn't lead back to me.
Yer usin' dat gobshite?
Would appear so, wouldn't it?
Fair enough. Jaysis, I hope dis job will be worth it.
Me too, man. Me fuckin' too.
Here...
...watch de shades dere.

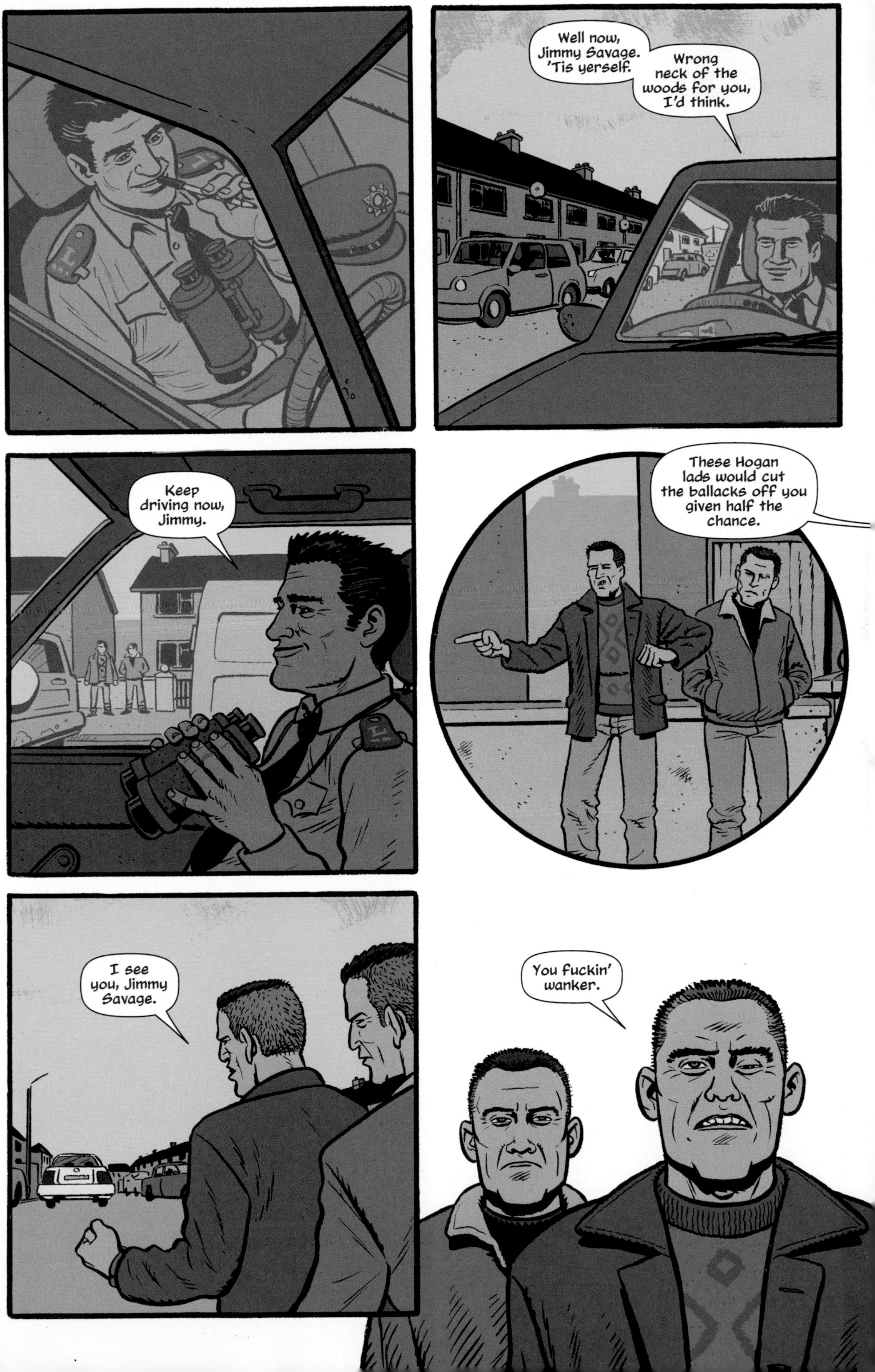
Well now, Jimmy Savage. 'Tis yerself.
Wrong neck of the woods for you, I'd think.
Keep driving now, Jimmy.
These Hogan lads would cut the ballacks off you given half the chance.
I see you, Jimmy Savage.
You fuckin' wanker.

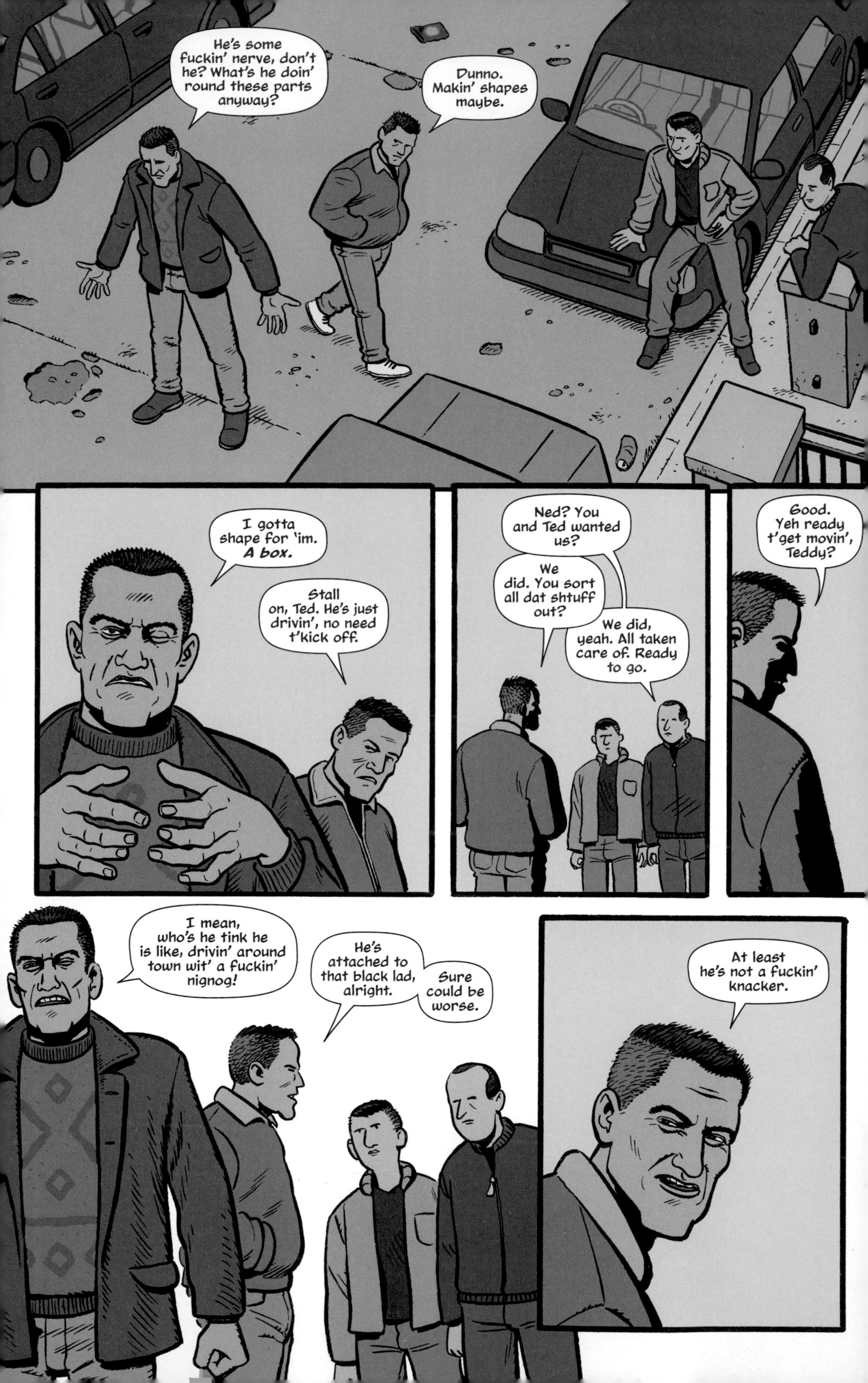
He's some fuckin' nerve, don't he? What's he doin' round these parts anyway?
Dunno. Makin' shapes maybe.
I gotta shape for 'im. *A box.*
Stall on, Ted. He's just drivin', no need t'kick off.
Ned? You and Ted wanted us?
We did. You sort all dat shtuff out?
We did, yeah. All taken care of. Ready to go.
Good. Yeh ready t'get movin', Teddy?
I mean, who's he tink he is like, drivin' around town wit' a fuckin' nignog!
He's attached to that black lad, alright.
Sure could be worse.
At least he's not a fuckin' knacker.

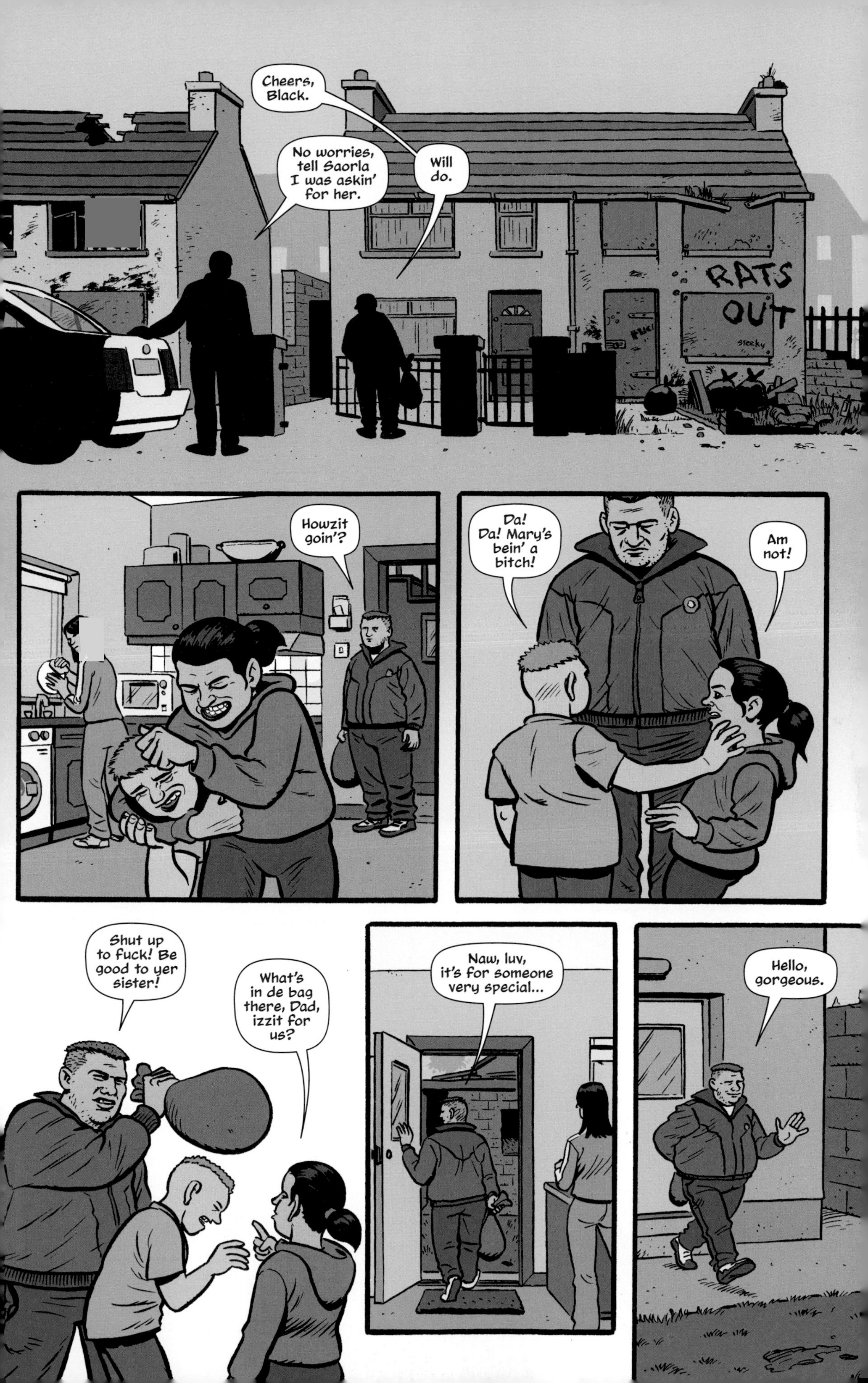
Cheers, Black.
No worries, tell Saorla I was askin' for her.
Will do.
RATS OUT
Howzit goin'?
Da! Da! Mary's bein' a bitch!
Am not!
Shut up to fuck! Be good to yer sister!
What's in de bag there, Dad, izzit for us?
Naw, luv, it's for someone very special...
Hello, gorgeous.

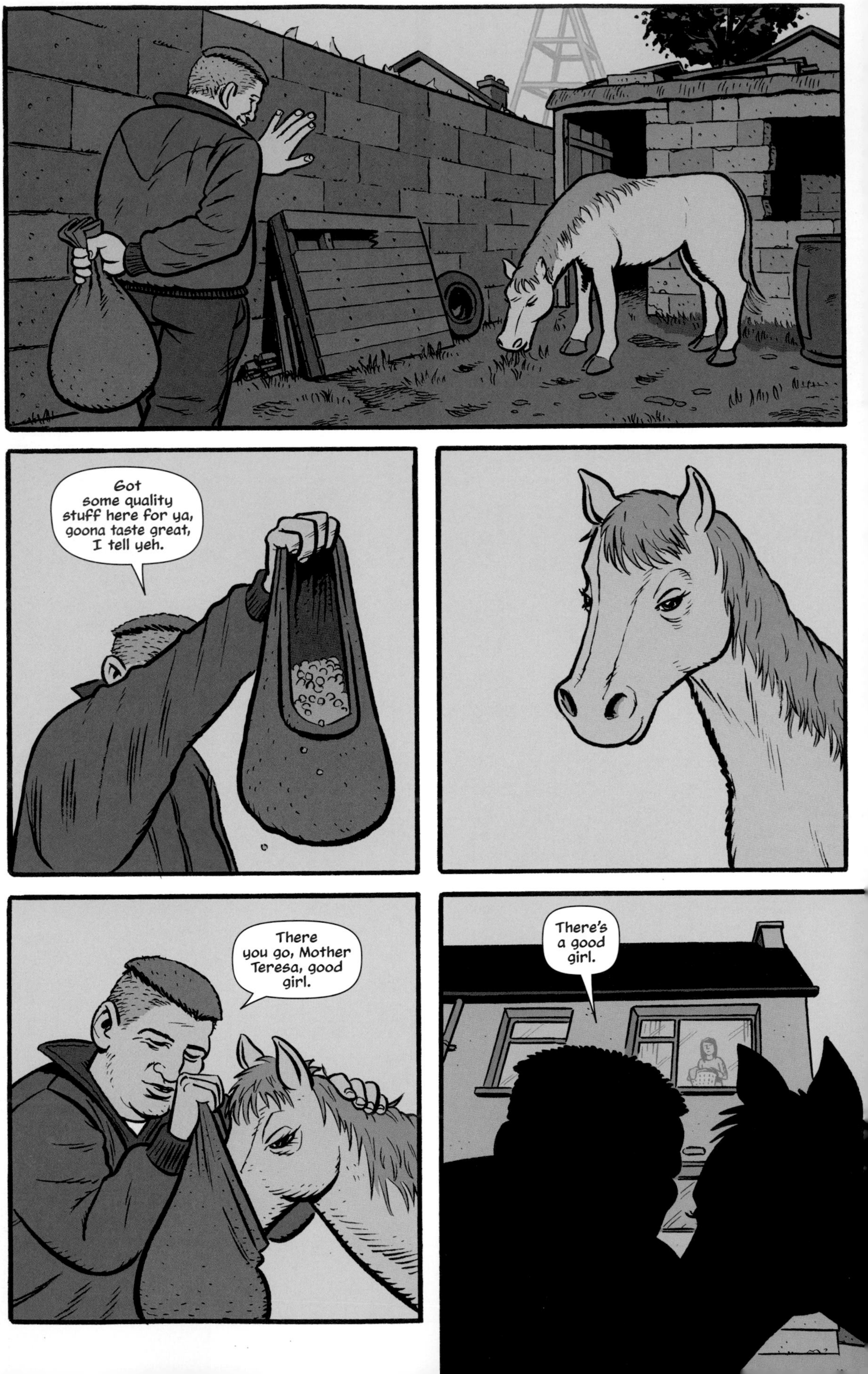
Got some quality stuff here for ya, goona taste great, I tell yeh.
There you go, Mother Teresa, good girl.
There's a good girl.

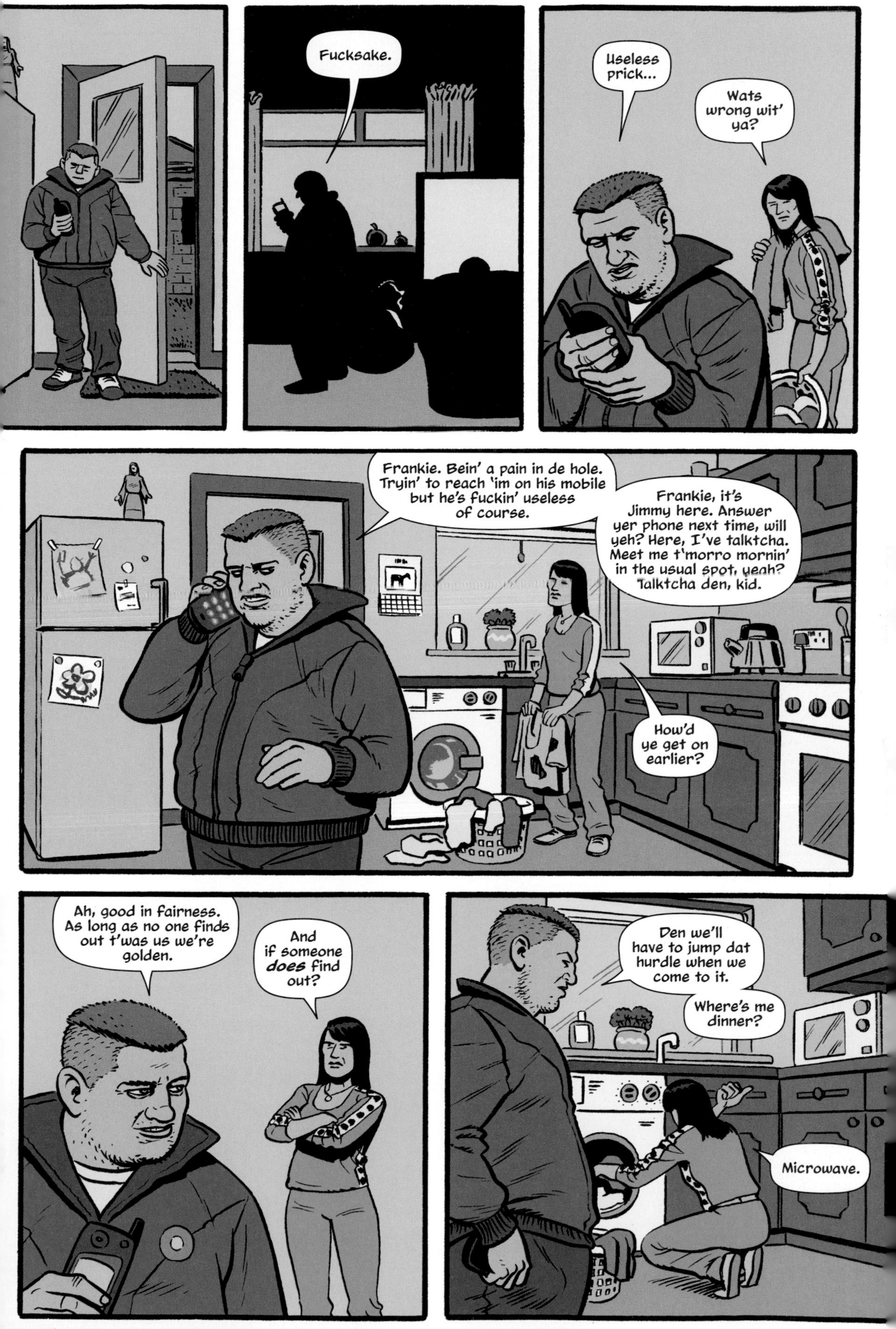

Fucksake.
Useless prick...
Wats wrong wit' ya?
Frankie. Bein' a pain in de hole. Tryin' to reach 'im on his mobile but he's fuckin' useless of course.
Frankie, it's Jimmy here. Answer yer phone next time, will yeh? Here, I've talktcha. Meet me t'morro mornin' in the usual spot, yeah? Talktcha den, kid.
How'd ye get on earlier?
Ah, good in fairness. As long as no one finds out t'was us we're golden.
And if someone *does* find out?
Den we'll have to jump dat hurdle when we come to it.
Where's me dinner?
Microwave.

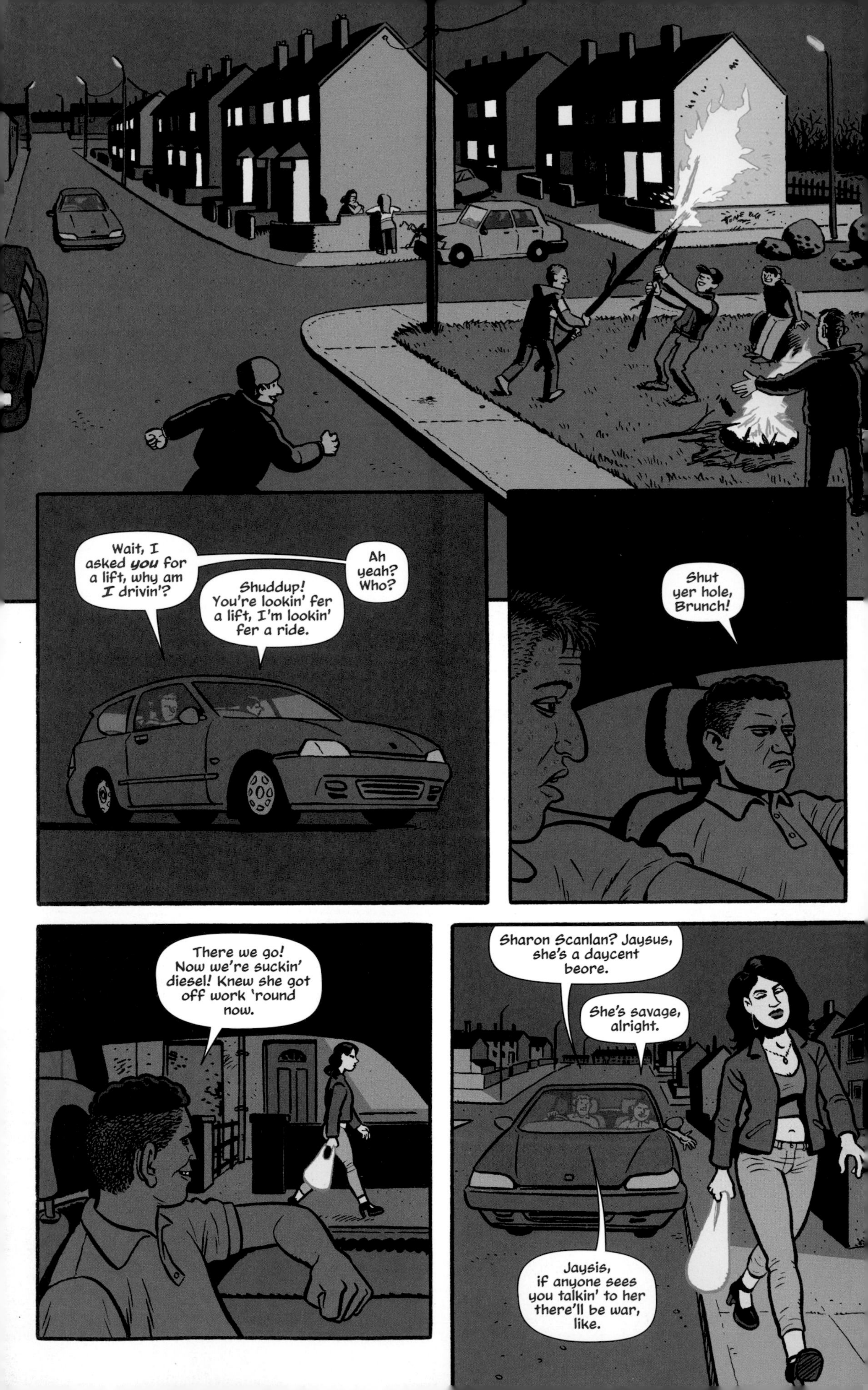

Wait, I asked *you* for a lift, why am *I* drivin'?
Ah yeah? Who?
Shuddup! You're lookin' fer a lift, I'm lookin' fer a ride.
Shut yer hole, Brunch!
There we go! Now we're suckin' diesel! Knew she got off work 'round now.
Sharon Scanlan? Jaysus, she's a daycent beore.
She's savage, alright.
Jaysis, if anyone sees you talkin' to her there'll be war, like.

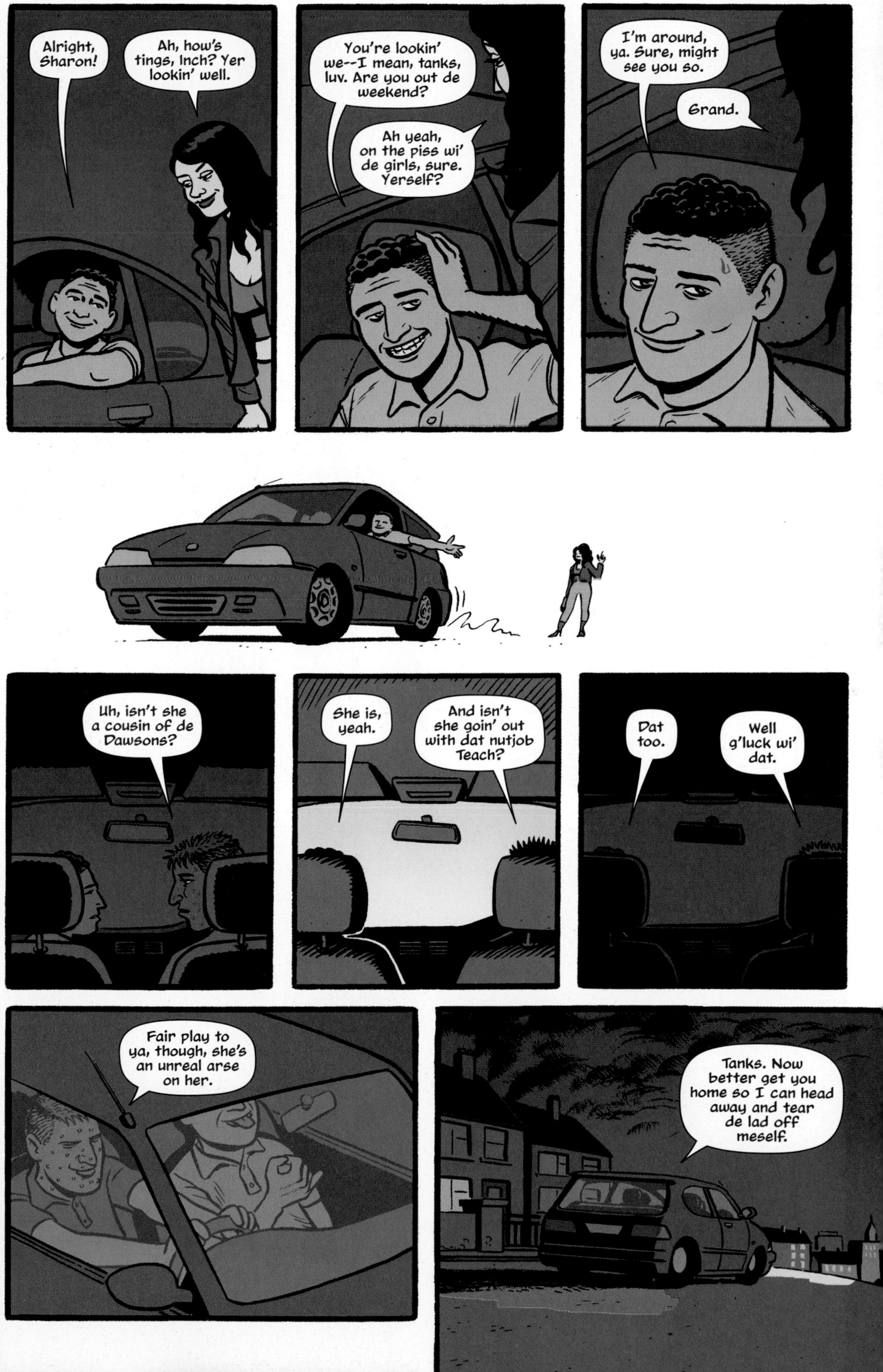
Alright, Sharon!
Ah, how's tings, Inch? Yer lookin' well.
You're lookin' we--I mean, tanks, luv. Are you out de weekend?
Ah yeah, on the piss wi' de girls, sure. Yerself?
I'm around, ya. Sure, might see you so.
Grand.
Uh, isn't she a cousin of de Dawsons?
She is, yeah.
And isn't she goin' out with dat nutjob Teach?
Dat too.
Well g'luck wi' dat.
Fair play to ya, though, she's an unreal arse on her.
Tanks. Now better get you home so I can head away and tear de lad off meself.

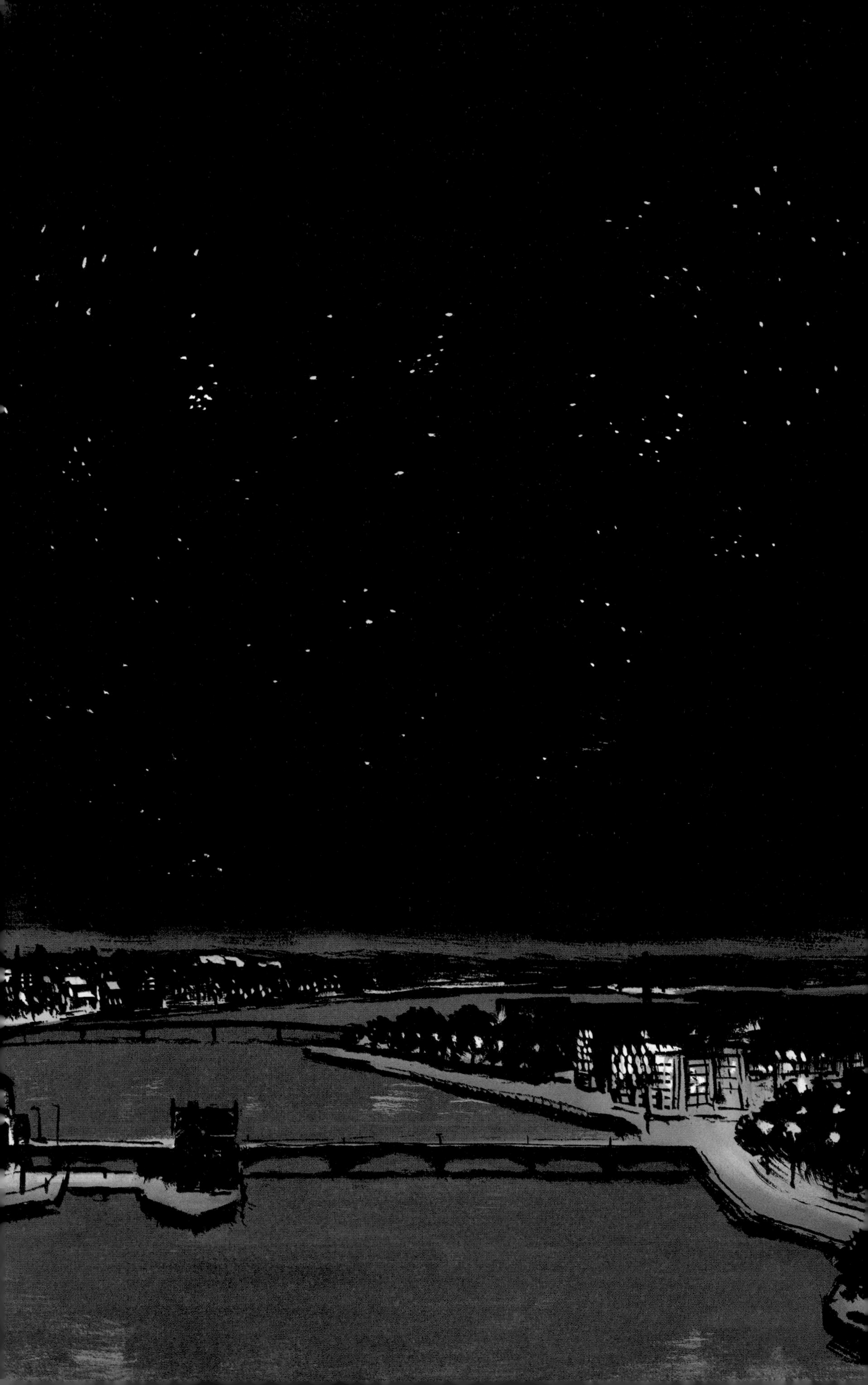

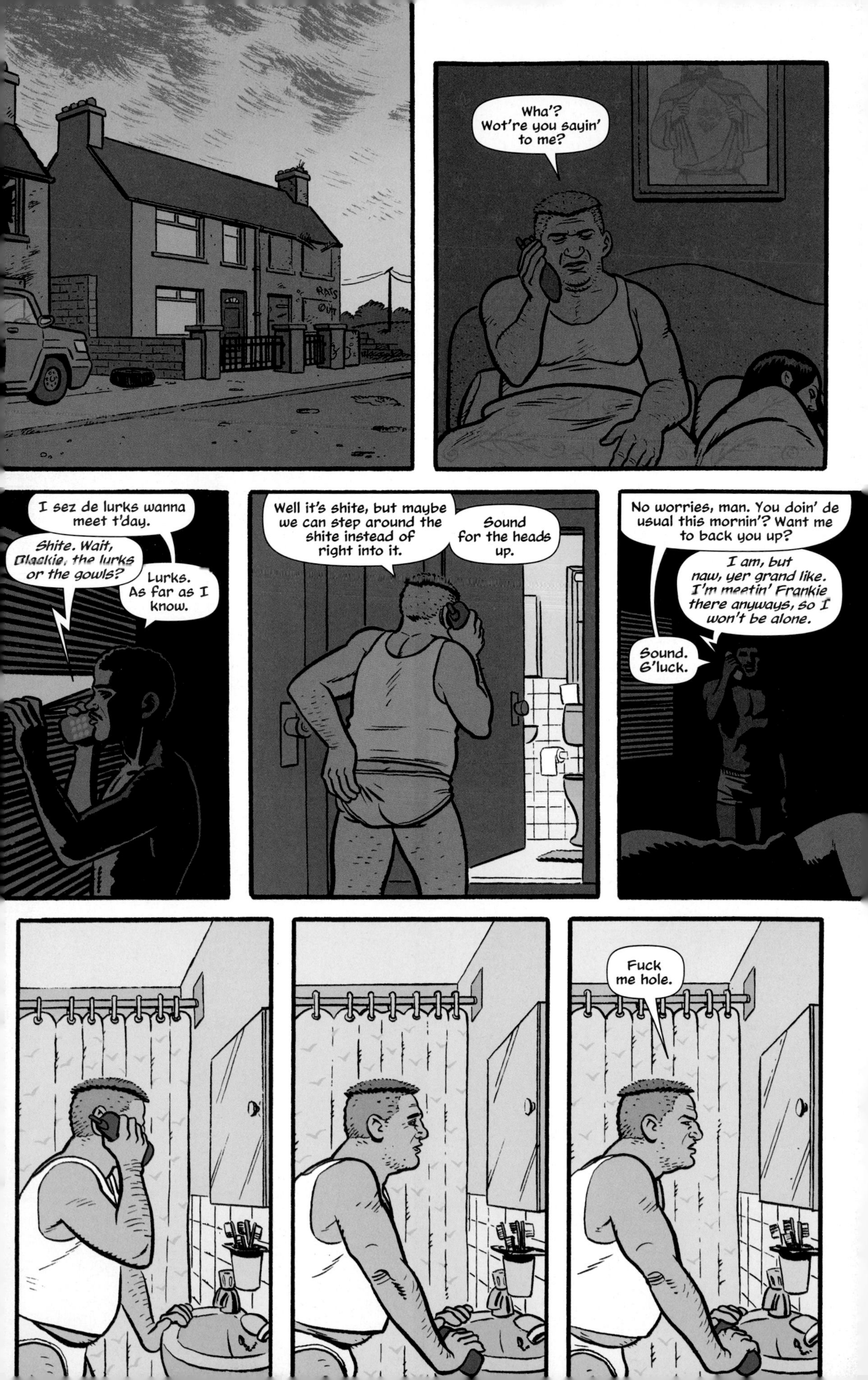

RATS OUT
Wha'? Wot're you sayin' to me?
I sez de lurks wanna meet t'day.
Shite. Wait, Blackie, the lurks or the gowls?
Lurks. As far as I know.
Well it's shite, but maybe we can step around the shite instead of right into it.
Sound for the heads up.
No worries, man. You doin' de usual this mornin'? Want me to back you up?
I am, but naw, yer grand like. I'm meetin' Frankie there anyways, so I won't be alone.
Sound. G'luck.
Fuck me hole.

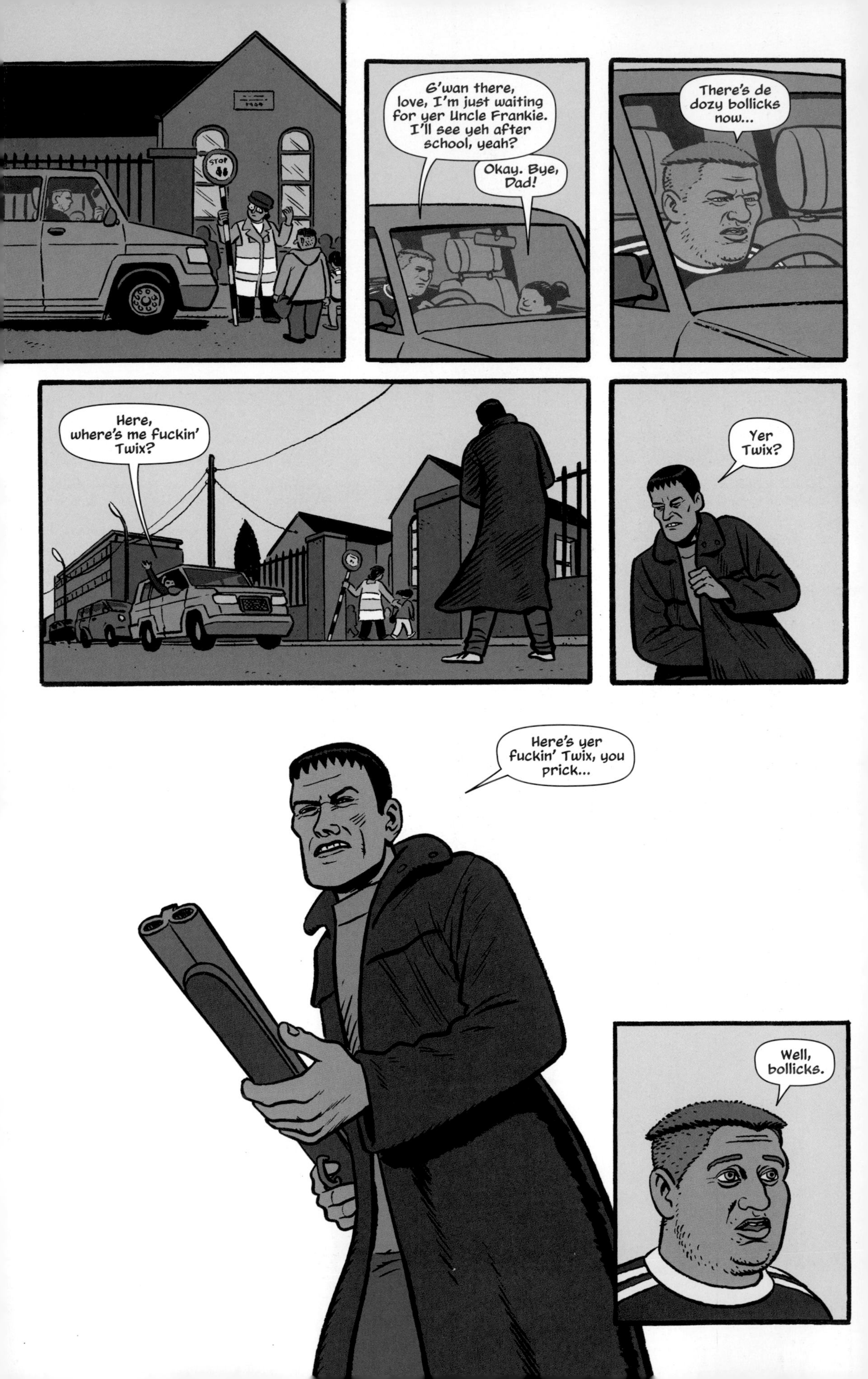
STOP
G'wan there, love, I'm just waiting for yer Uncle Frankie. I'll see yeh after school, yeah?
Okay. Bye, Dad!
There's de dozy bollicks now...
Here, where's me fuckin' Twix?
Yer Twix?
Here's yer fuckin' Twix, you prick...
Well, bollicks.

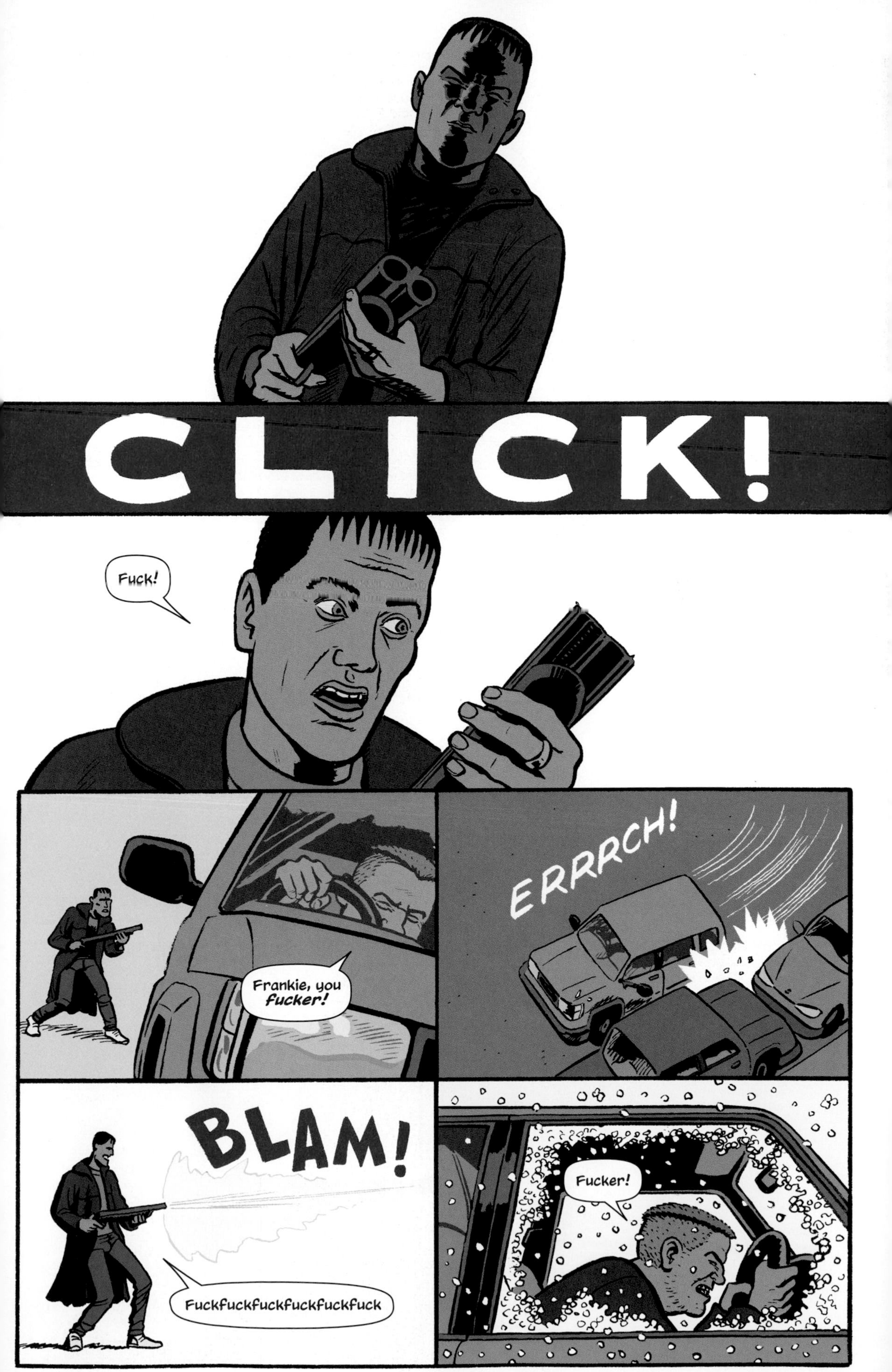
CLICK!
Fuck!
Frankie, you fucker!
ERRRCH!
BLAM!
Fuckfuckfuckfuckfuckfuck
Fucker!

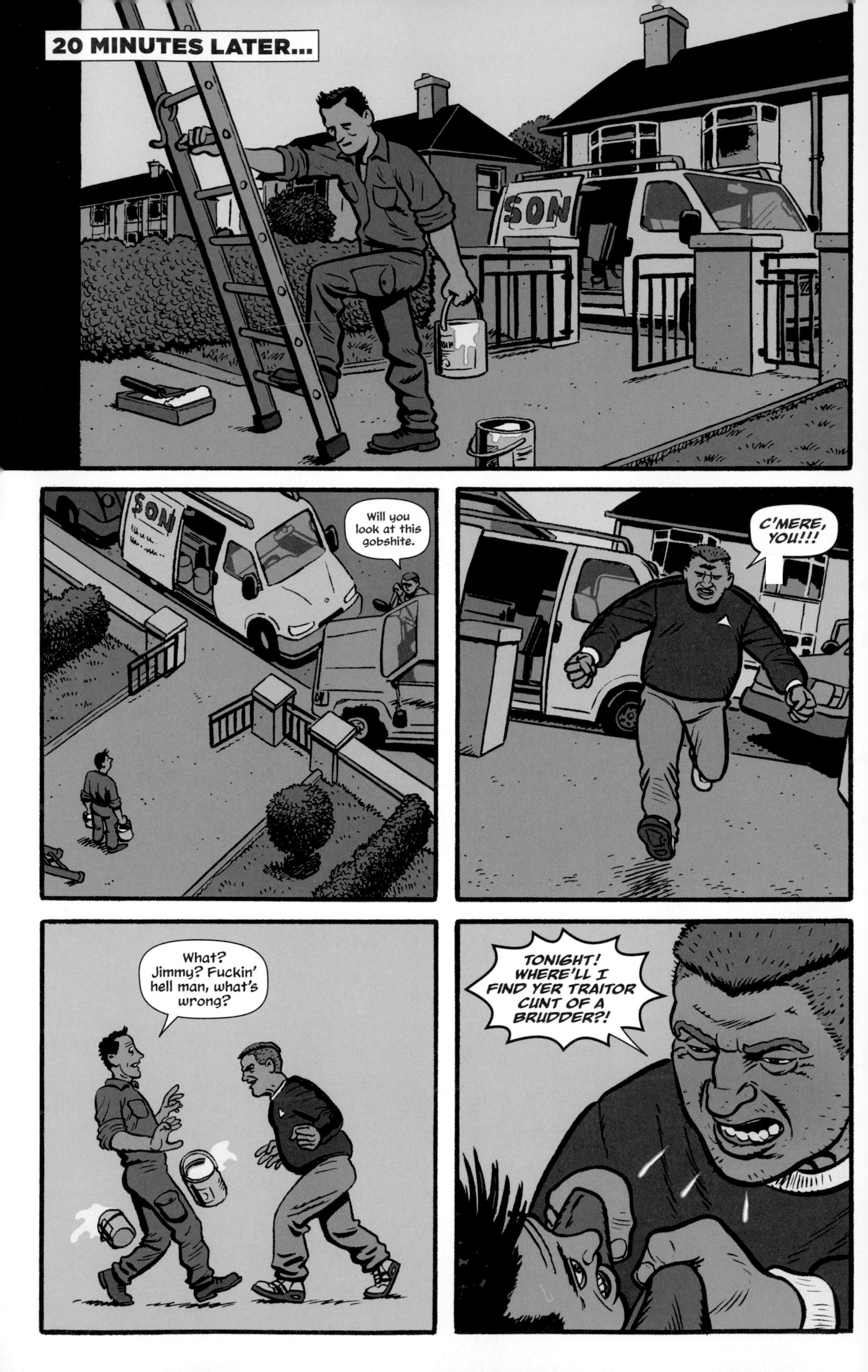
20 MINUTES LATER...
SON
SON
Will you look at this gobshite.
C'MERE, YOU!!!
What? Jimmy? Fuckin' hell man, what's wrong?
TONIGHT! WHERE'LL I FIND YER TRAITOR CUNT OF A BRUDDER?!

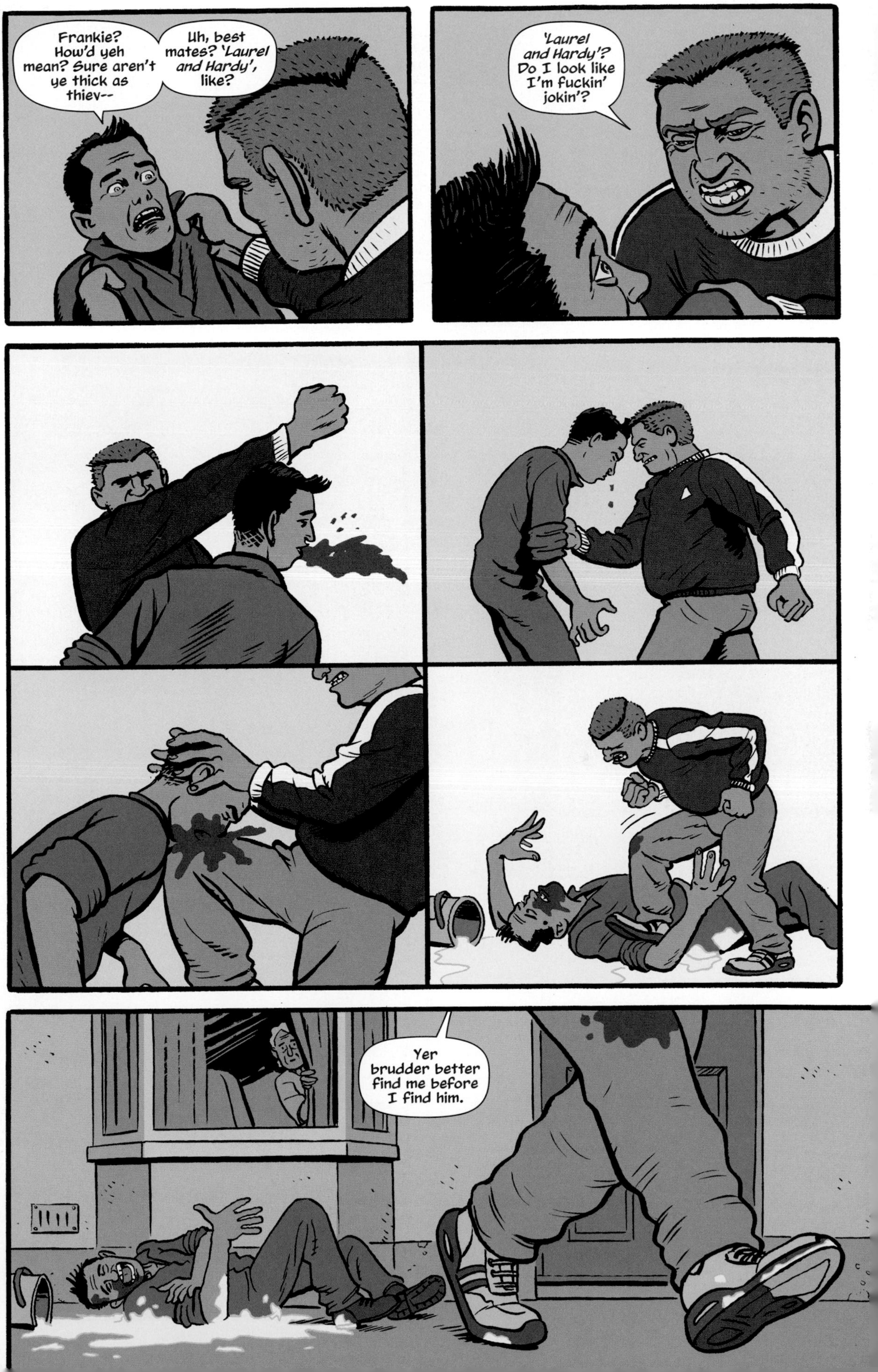
Frankie? How'd yeh mean? Sure aren't ye thick as thiev--
Uh, best mates? 'Laurel and Hardy', like?
'Laurel and Hardy'? Do I look like I'm fuckin' jokin'?
Yer brudder better find me before I find him.

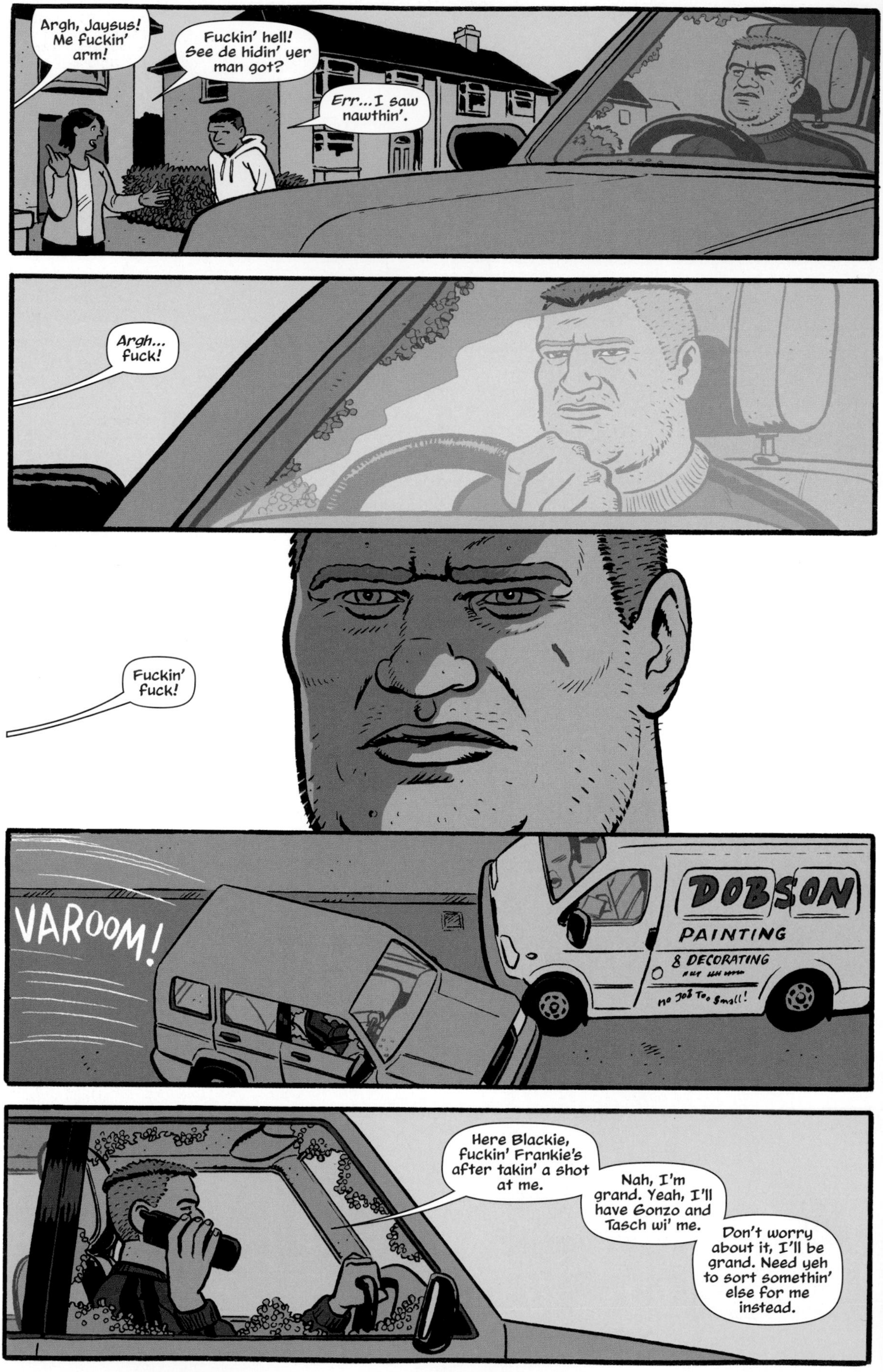
Argh, Jaysus! Me fuckin' arm!
Fuckin' hell! See de hidin' yer man got?
Err...I saw nawthin'.
Argh... fuck!
Fuckin' fuck!
VAROOM!
DOBSON PAINTING & DECORATING
NO JOB TOO SMALL!
Here Blackie, fuckin' Frankie's after takin' a shot at me.
Nah, I'm grand. Yeah, I'll have Gonzo and Tasch wi' me.
Don't worry about it, I'll be grand. Need yeh to sort somethin' else for me instead.

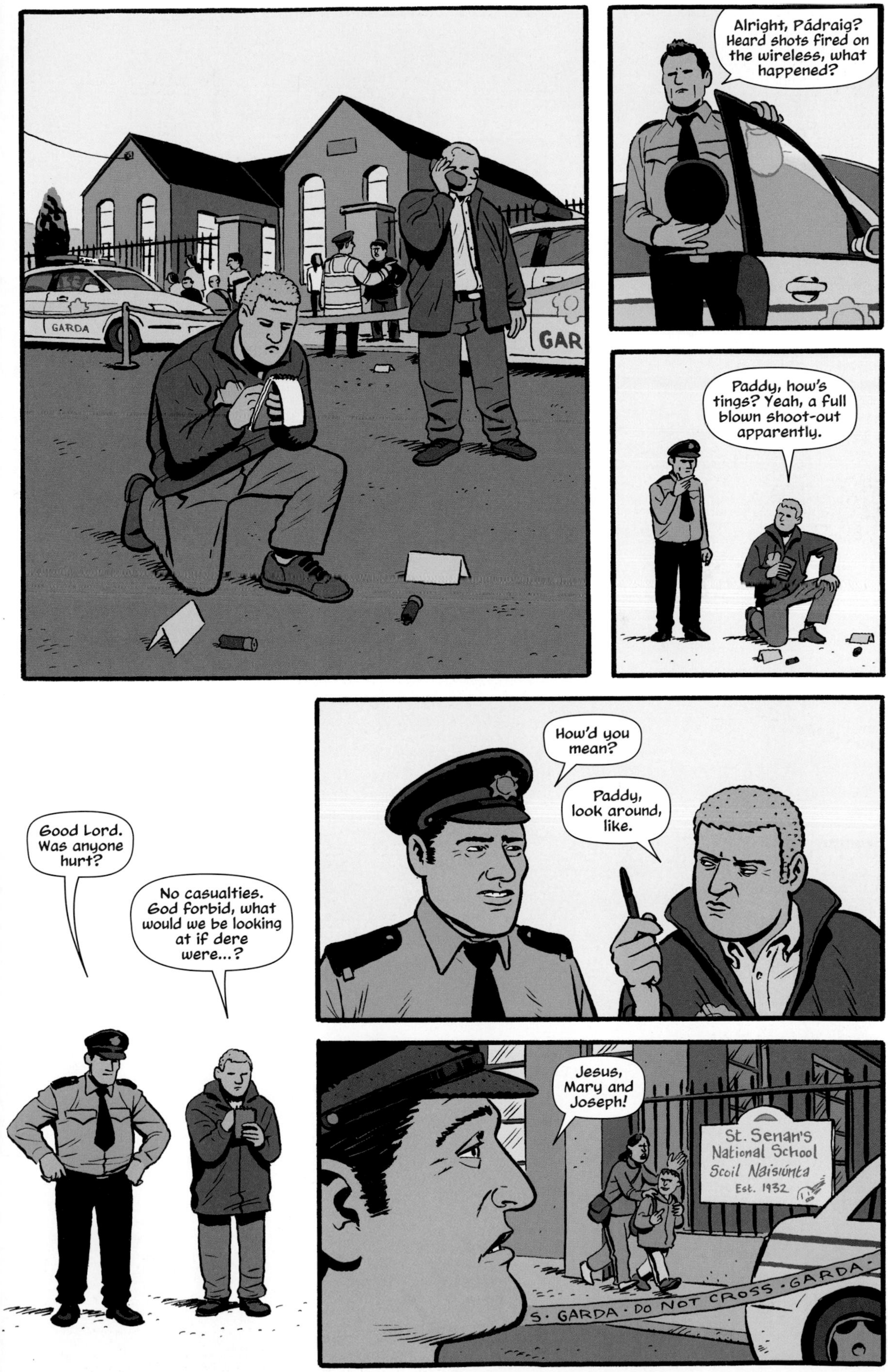
GARDA
GAR
Alright, Pádraig? Heard shots fired on the wireless, what happened?
Paddy, how's tings? Yeah, a full blown shoot-out apparently.
How'd you mean?
Paddy, look around, like.
Good Lord. Was anyone hurt?
No casualties. God forbid, what would we be looking at if dere were...?
Jesus, Mary and Joseph!
St. Senan's National School
Scoil Náisiúnta
Est. 1932
S · GARDA · DO NOT CROSS · GARDA

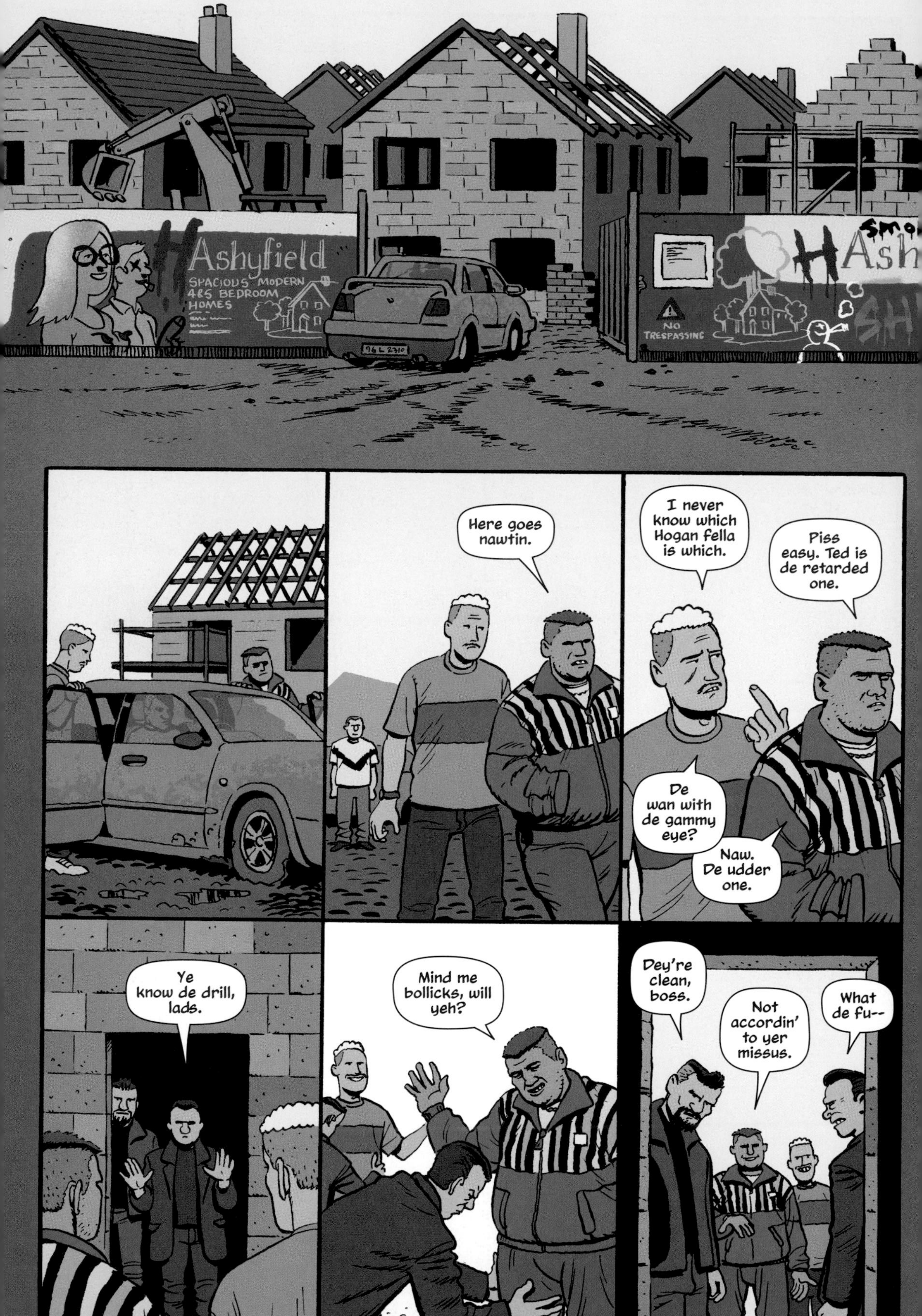

Ashyfield
SPACIOUS MODERN
4&5 BEDROOM
HOMES
NO TRESPASSING
Here goes nawtin.
I never know which Hogan fella is which.
Piss easy. Ted is de retarded one.
De wan with de gammy eye?
Naw. De udder one.
Ye know de drill, lads.
Mind me bollicks, will yeh?
Dey're clean, boss.
Not accordin' to yer missus.
What de fu--

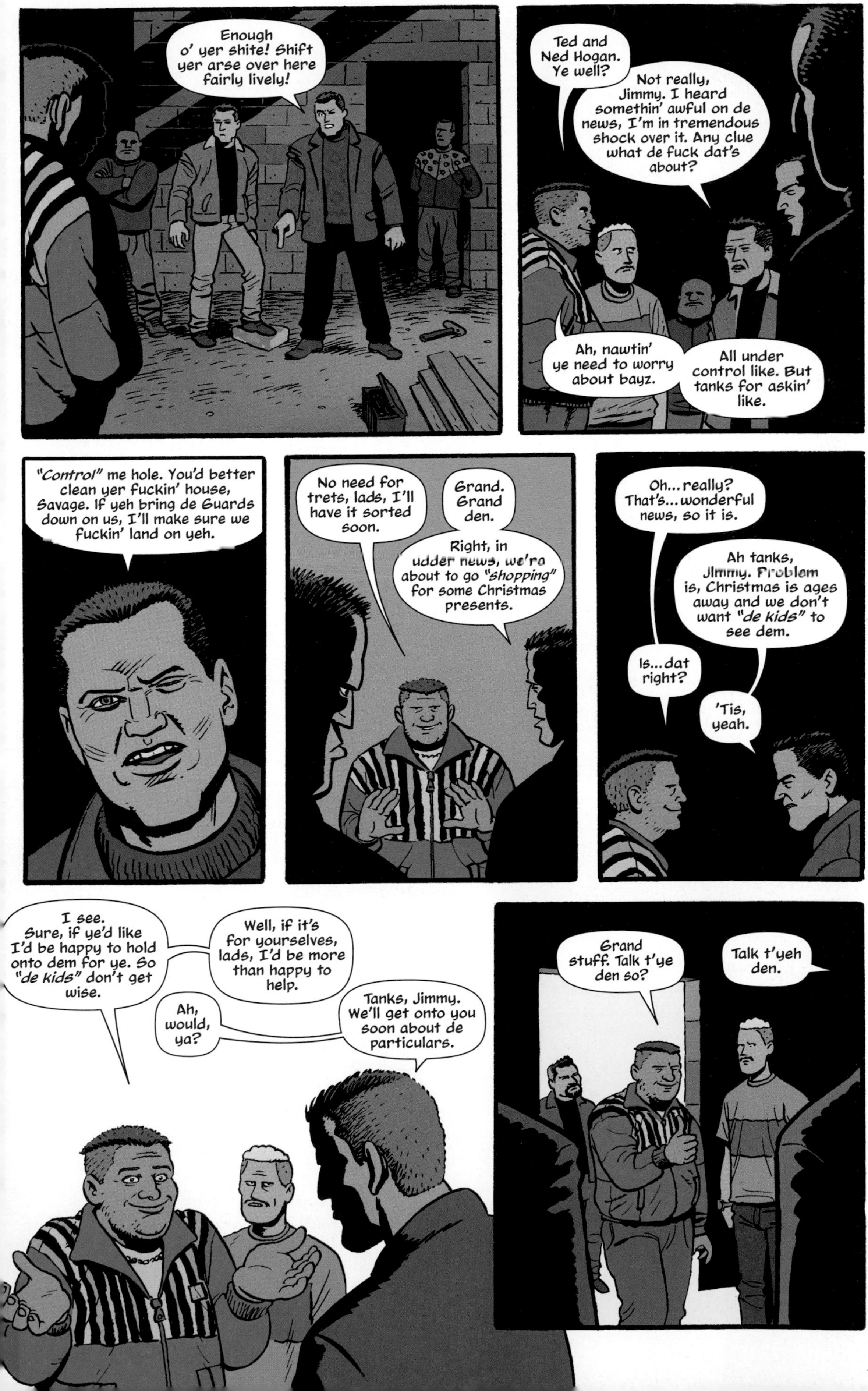
Enough o' yer shite! Shift yer arse over here fairly lively!
Ted and Ned Hogan. Ye well?
Not really, Jimmy. I heard somethin' awful on de news, I'm in tremendous shock over it. Any clue what de fuck dat's about?
Ah, nawtin' ye need to worry about bayz.
All under control like. But tanks for askin' like.
"Control" me hole. You'd better clean yer fuckin' house, Savage. If yeh bring de Guards down on us, I'll make sure we fuckin' land on yeh.
No need for trets, lads, I'll have it sorted soon.
Grand. Grand den.
Right, in udder news, we're about to go "shopping" for some Christmas presents.
Oh... really? That's... wonderful news, so it is.
Ah tanks, Jimmy. Problem is, Christmas is ages away and we don't want "de kids" to see dem.
Is... dat right?
'Tis, yeah.
I see. Sure, if ye'd like I'd be happy to hold onto dem for ye. So "de kids" don't get wise.
Well, if it's for yourselves, lads, I'd be more than happy to help.
Ah, would, ya?
Tanks, Jimmy. We'll get onto you soon about de particulars.
Grand stuff. Talk t'ye den so?
Talk t'yeh den.

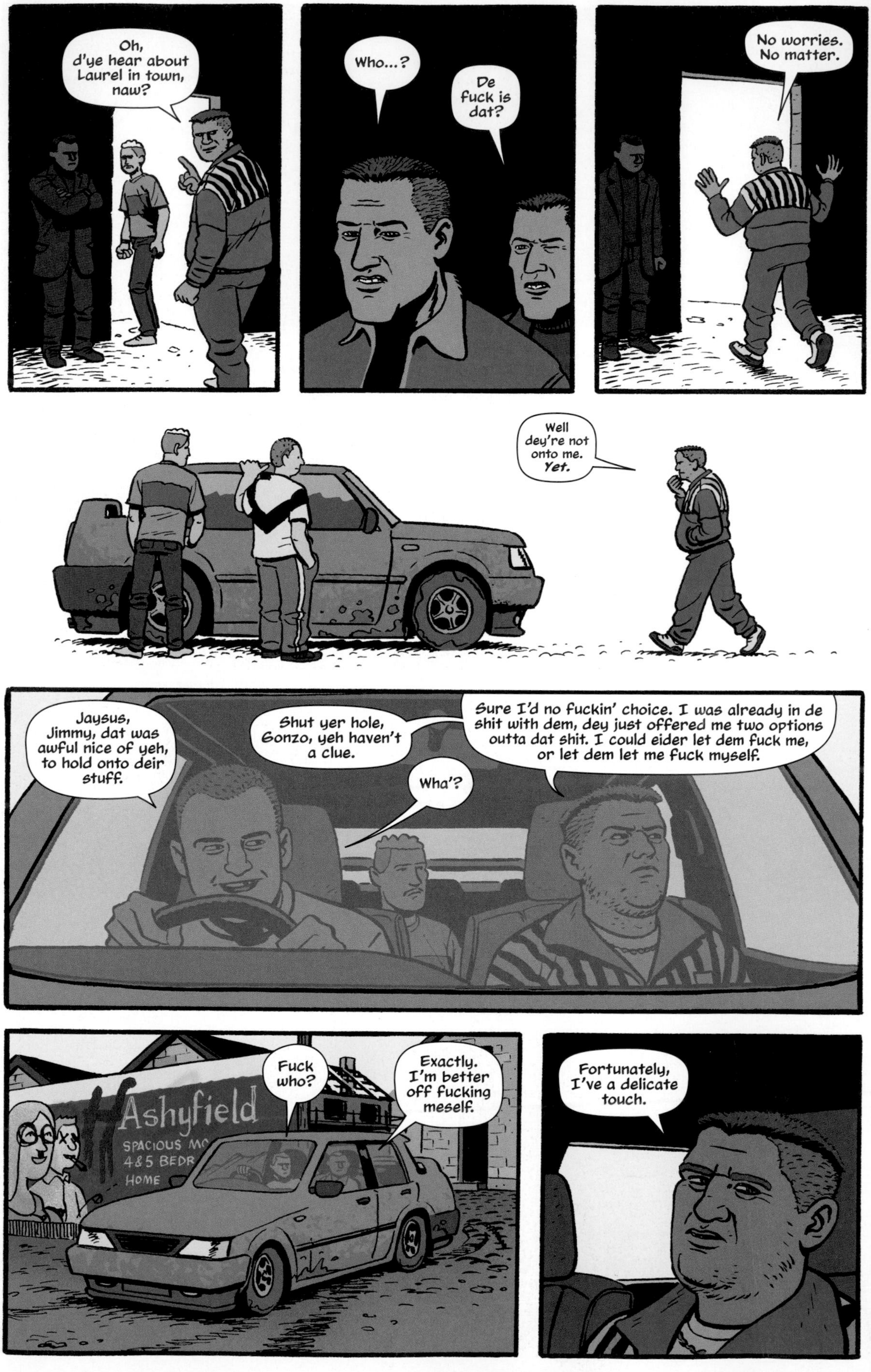
Oh, d'ye hear about Laurel in town, naw?
Who...?
De fuck is dat?
No worries. No matter.
Well dey're not onto me. *Yet.*
Jaysus, Jimmy, dat was awful nice of yeh, to hold onto deir stuff.
Shut yer hole, Gonzo, yeh haven't a clue.
Wha'?
Sure I'd no fuckin' choice. I was already in de shit with dem, dey just offered me two options outta dat shit. I could eider let dem fuck me, or let dem let me fuck myself.
Ashyfield
SPACIOUS MO
4&5 BEDR
HOME
Fuck who?
Exactly. I'm better off fucking meself.
Fortunately, I've a delicate touch.

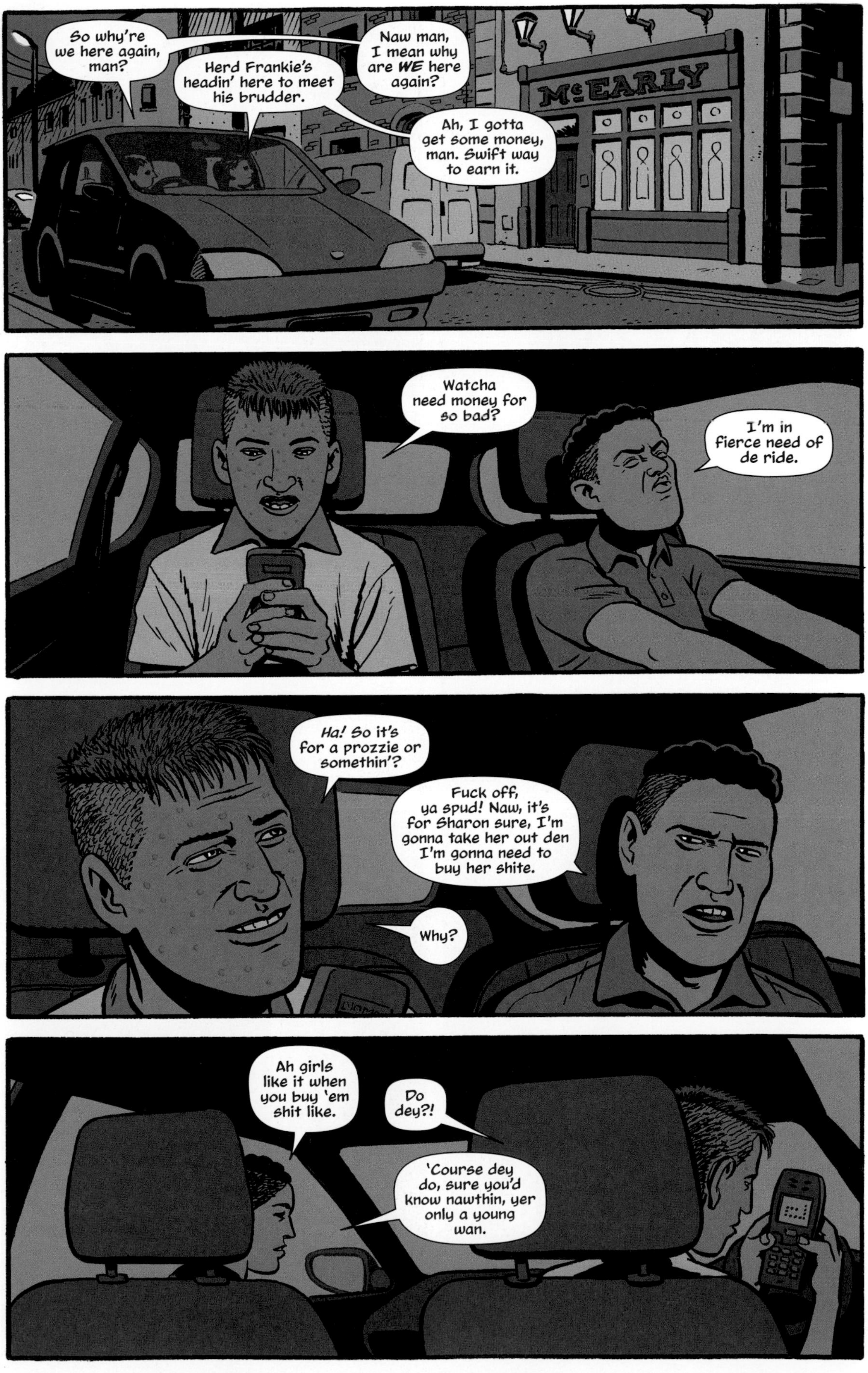
So why're we here again, man?
Herd Frankie's headin' here to meet his brudder.
Naw man, I mean why are WE here again?
Ah, I gotta get some money, man. Swift way to earn it.
McEARLY
Watcha need money for so bad?
I'm in fierce need of de ride.
Ha! So it's for a prozzie or somethin'?
Fuck off, ya spud! Naw, it's for Sharon sure, I'm gonna take her out den I'm gonna need to buy her shite.
Why?
Ah girls like it when you buy 'em shit like.
Do dey?!
'Course dey do, sure you'd know nawthin, yer only a young wan.

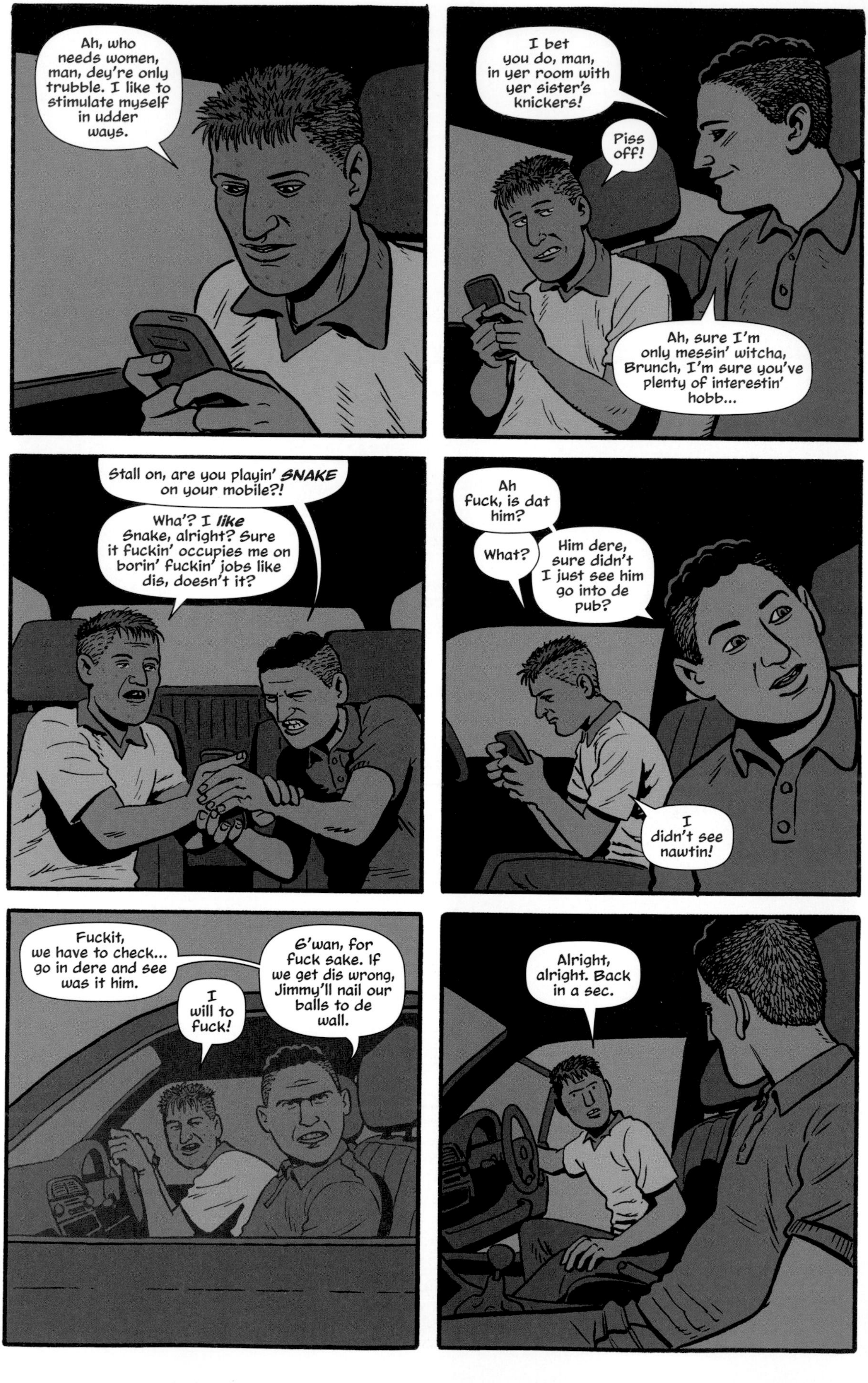
Ah, who needs women, man, dey're only trubble. I like to stimulate myself in udder ways.
I bet you do, man, in yer room with yer sister's knickers!
Piss off!
Ah, sure I'm only messin' witcha, Brunch, I'm sure you've plenty of interestin' hobb...
Stall on, are you playin' SNAKE on your mobile?!
Wha'? I like Snake, alright? Sure it fuckin' occupies me on borin' fuckin' jobs like dis, doesn't it?
Ah fuck, is dat him?
What?
Him dere, sure didn't I just see him go into de pub?
I didn't see nawtin!
Fuckit, we have to check... go in dere and see was it him.
I will to fuck!
G'wan, for fuck sake. If we get dis wrong, Jimmy'll nail our balls to de wall.
Alright, alright. Back in a sec.

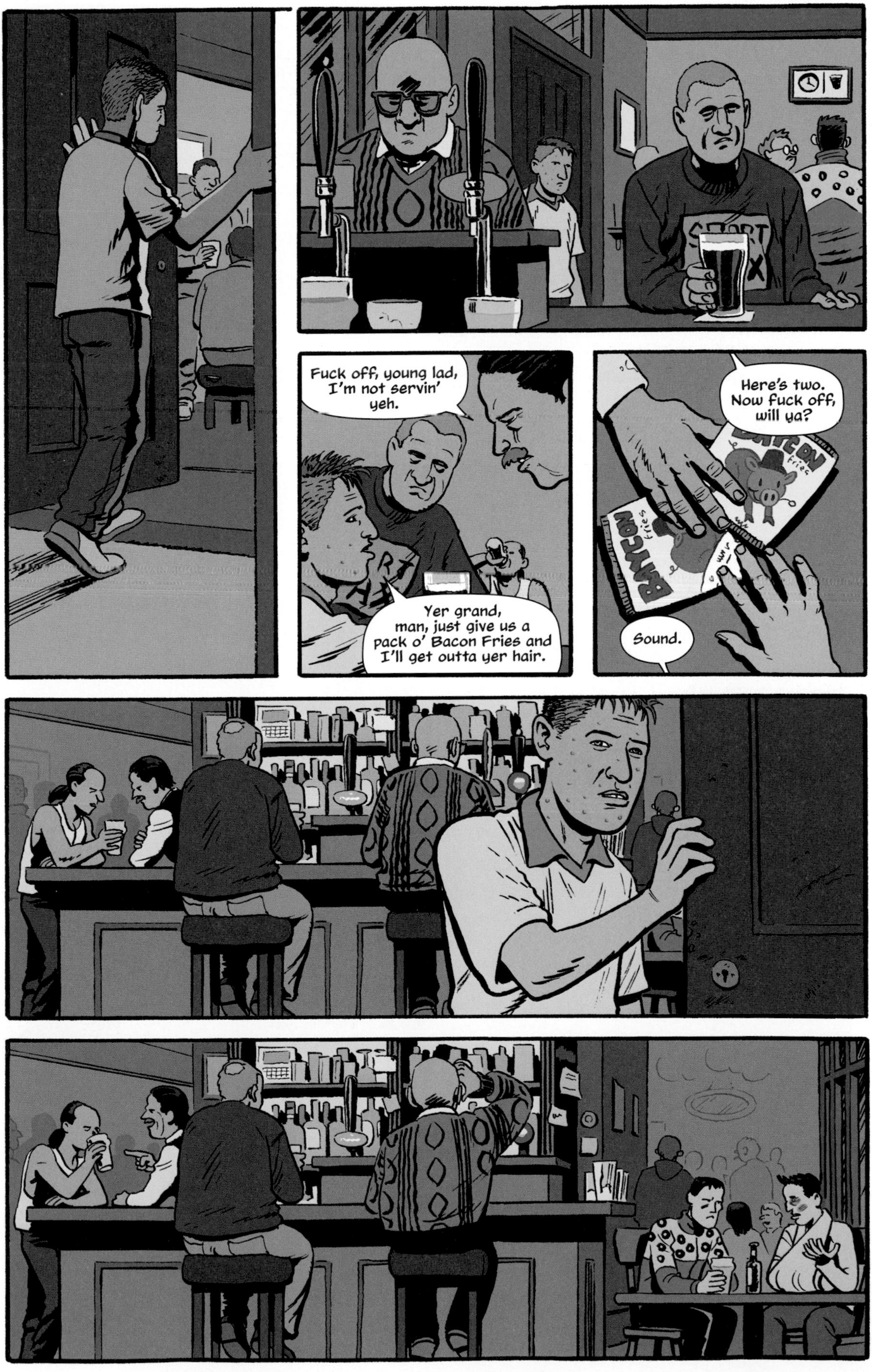

Fuck off, young lad, I'm not servin' yeh.
Yer grand, man, just give us a pack o' Bacon Fries and I'll get outta yer hair.
Here's two. Now fuck off, will ya?
Sound.

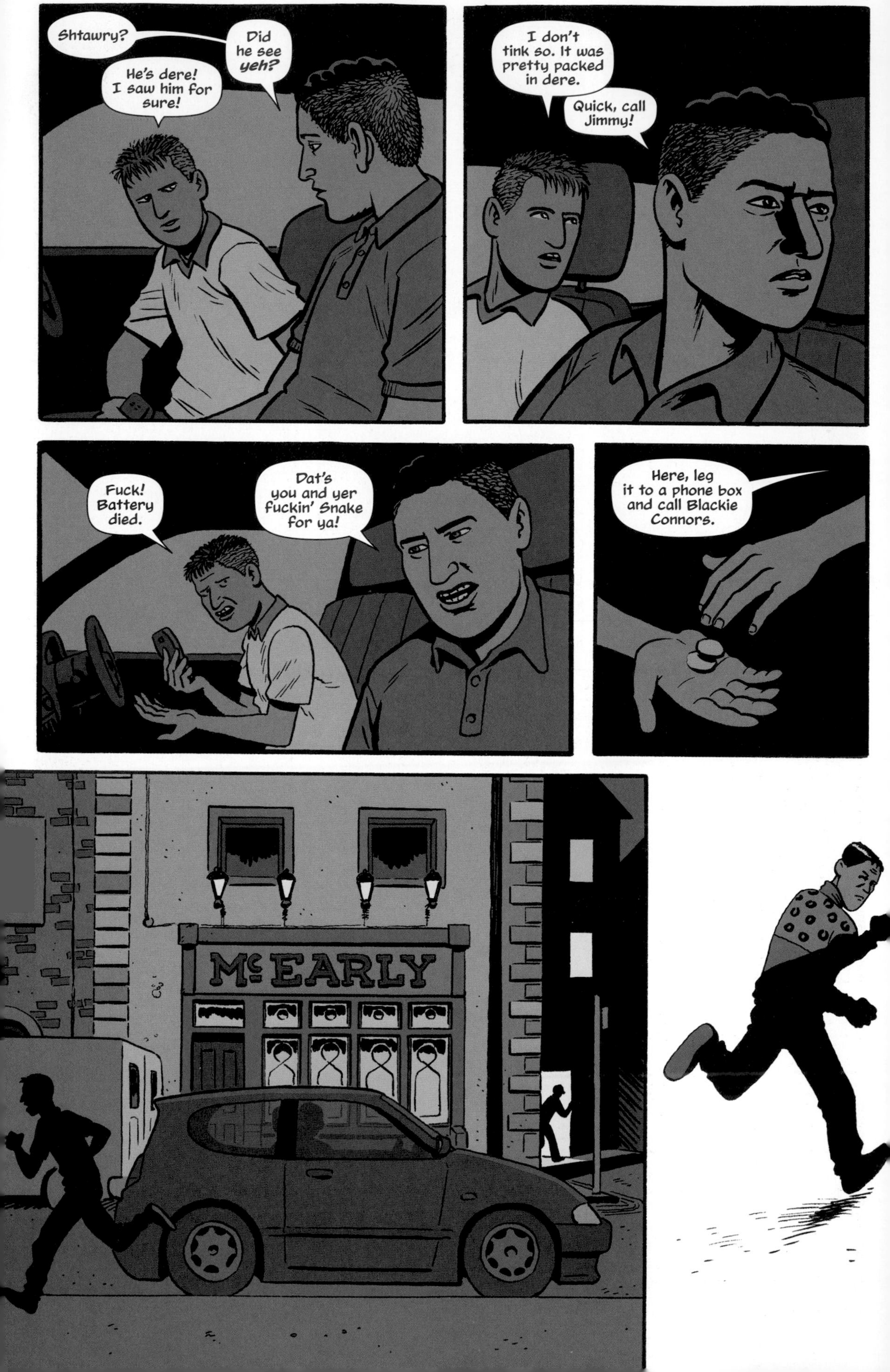
Shtawry?
Did he see yeh?
He's dere! I saw him for sure!
I don't tink so. It was pretty packed in dere.
Quick, call Jimmy!
Fuck! Battery died.
Dat's you and yer fuckin' Snake for ya!
Here, leg it to a phone box and call Blackie Connors.
McEARLY

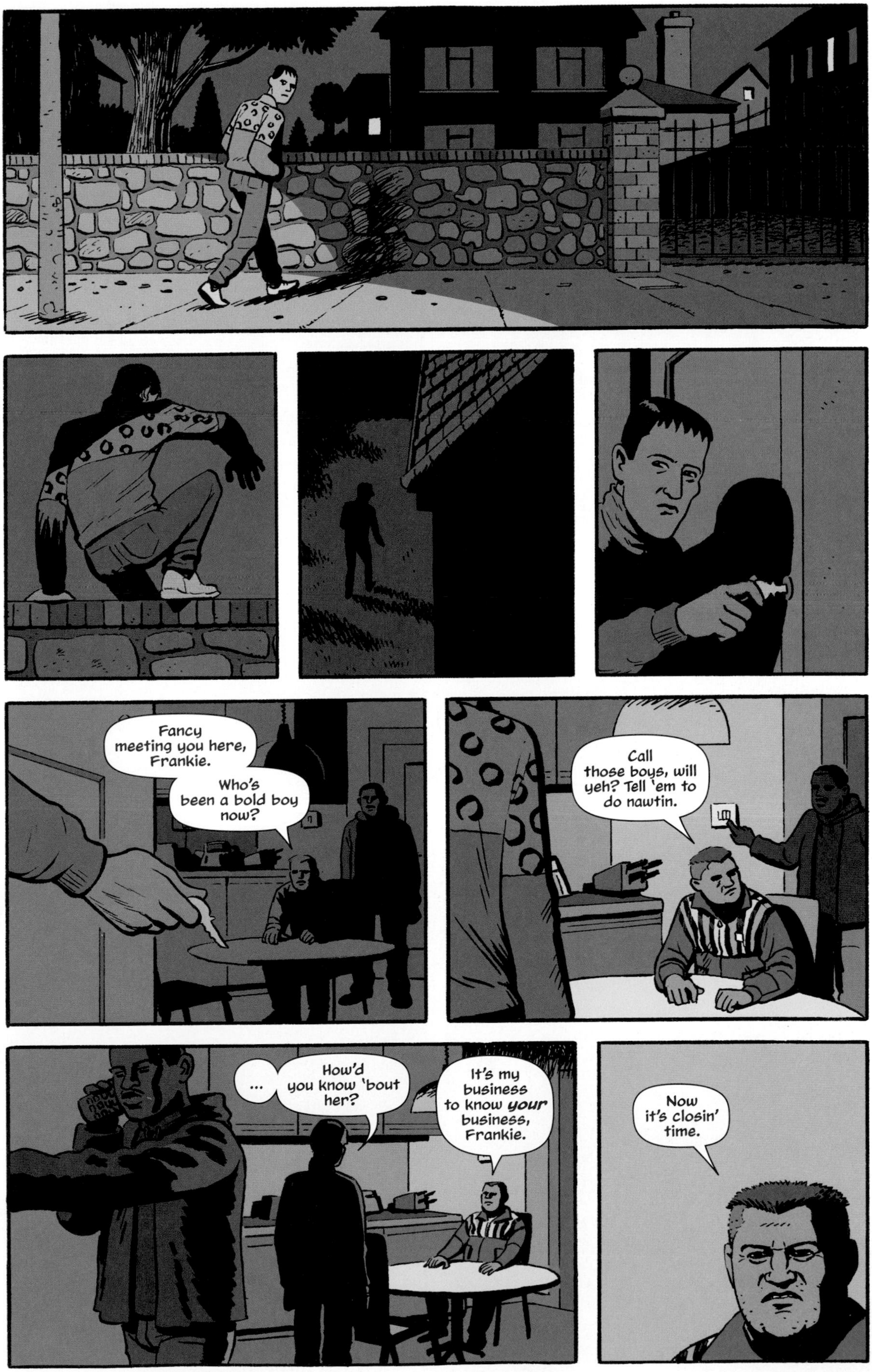
Fancy meeting you here, Frankie.
Who's been a bold boy now?
Call those boys, will yeh? Tell 'em to do nawtin.
...
How'd you know 'bout her?
It's my business to know *your* business, Frankie.
Now it's closin' time.

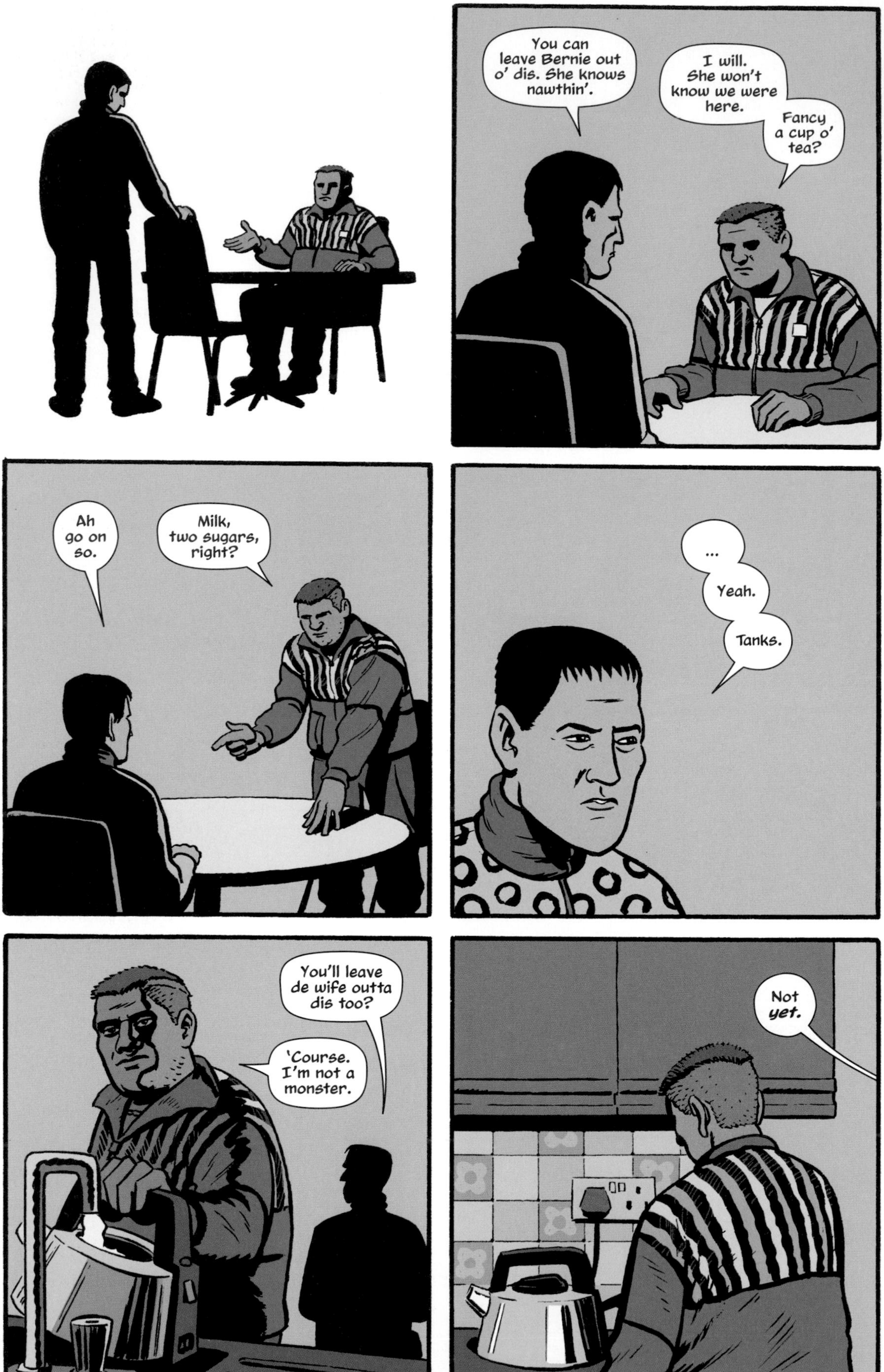

You can leave Bernie out o' dis. She knows nawthin'.
I will. She won't know we were here.
Fancy a cup o' tea?
Ah go on so.
Milk, two sugars, right?
...
Yeah.
Tanks.
You'll leave de wife outta dis too?
'Course. I'm not a monster.
Not *yet.*

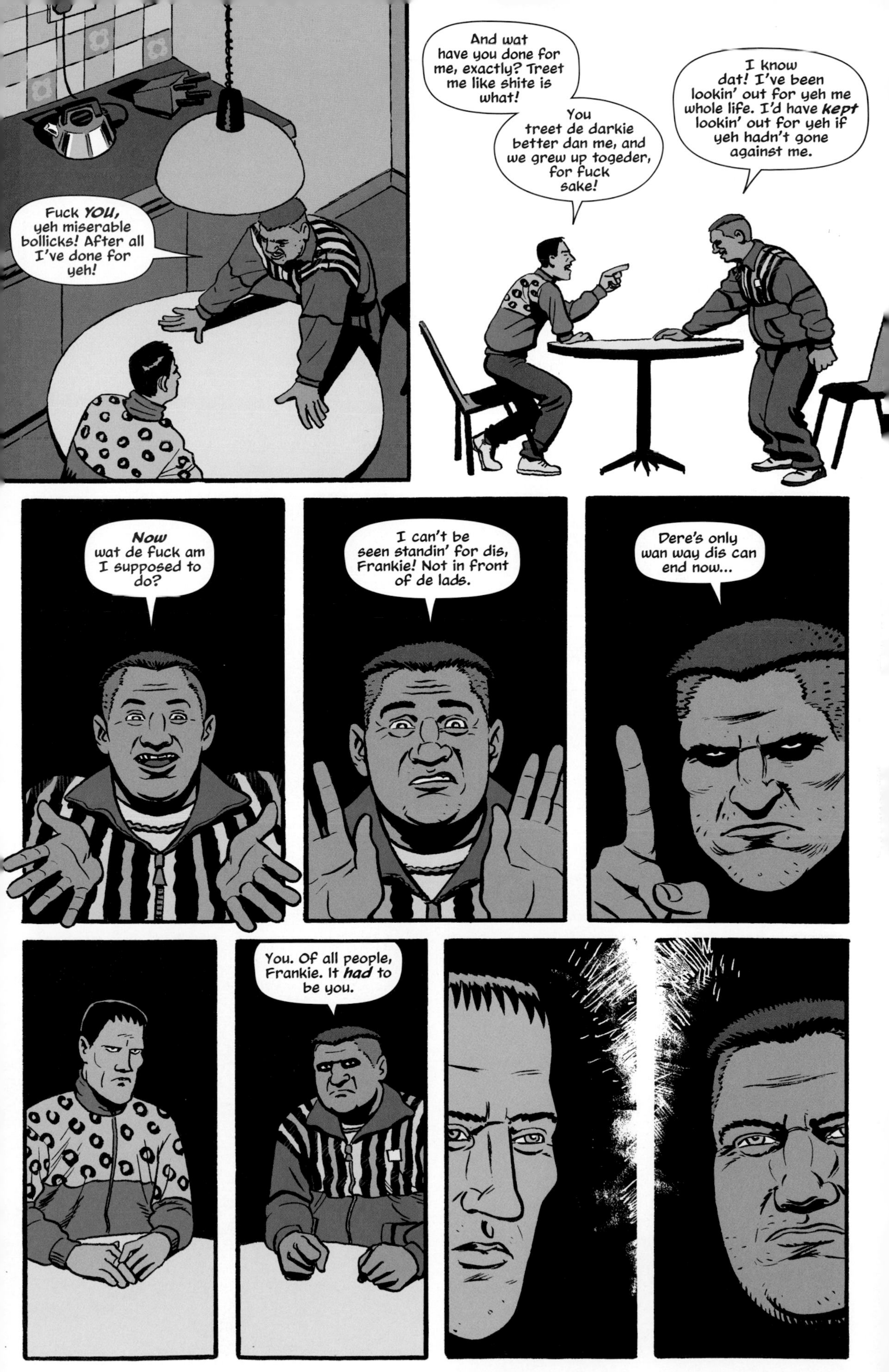

Fuck YOU, yeh miserable bollicks! After all I've done for yeh!
And wat have you done for me, exactly? Treet me like shite is what!
You treet de darkie better dan me, and we grew up togeder, for fuck sake!
I know dat! I've been lookin' out for yeh me whole life. I'd have kept lookin' out for yeh if yeh hadn't gone against me.
Now wat de fuck am I supposed to do?
I can't be seen standin' for dis, Frankie! Not in front of de lads.
Dere's only wan way dis can end now...
You. Of all people, Frankie. It had to be you.

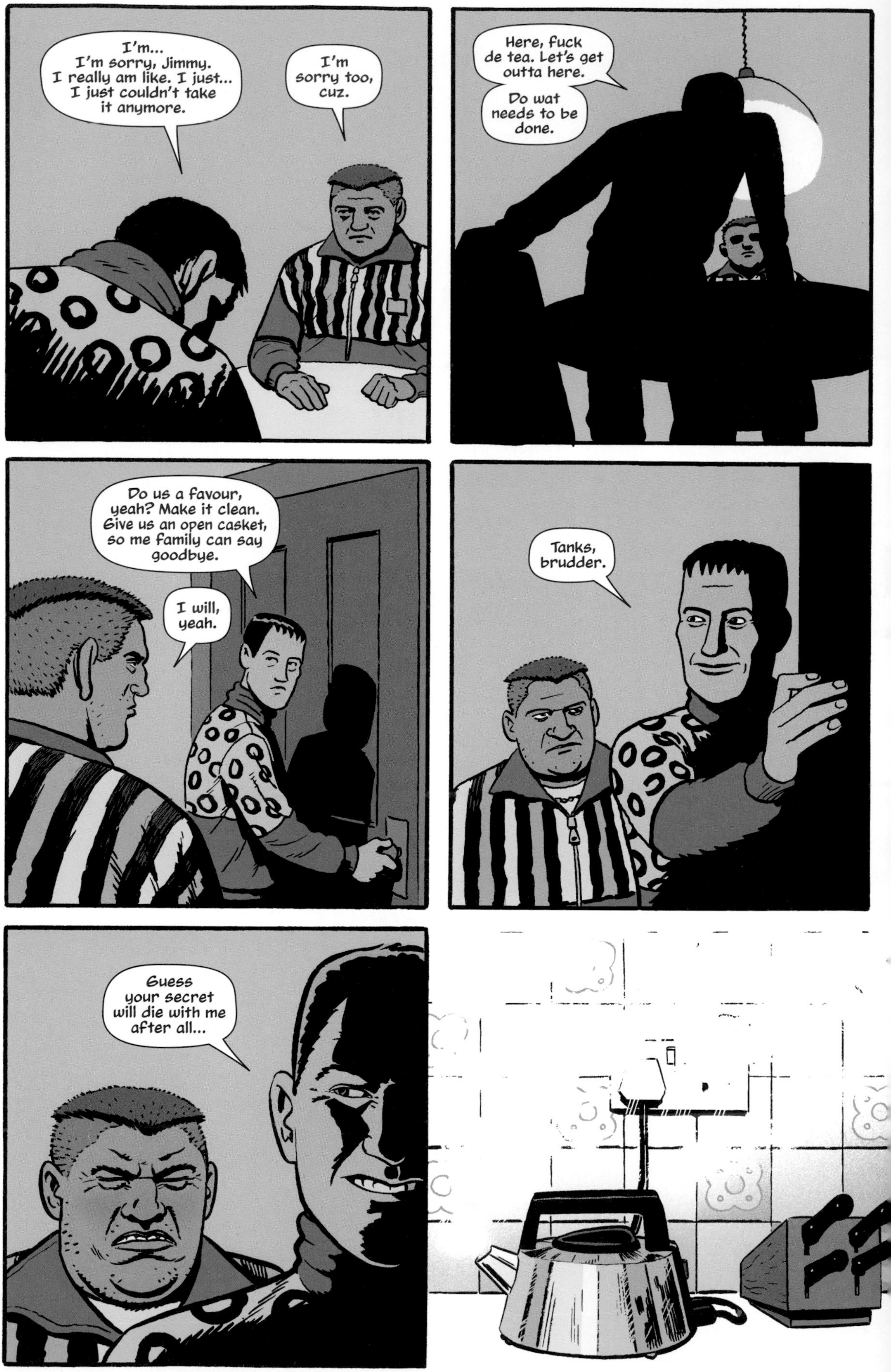
I'm... I'm sorry, Jimmy. I really am like. I just... I just couldn't take it anymore.
I'm sorry too, cuz.
Here, fuck de tea. Let's get outta here.
Do wat needs to be done.
Do us a favour, yeah? Make it clean. Give us an open casket, so me family can say goodbye.
I will, yeah.
Tanks, brudder.
Guess your secret will die with me after all...

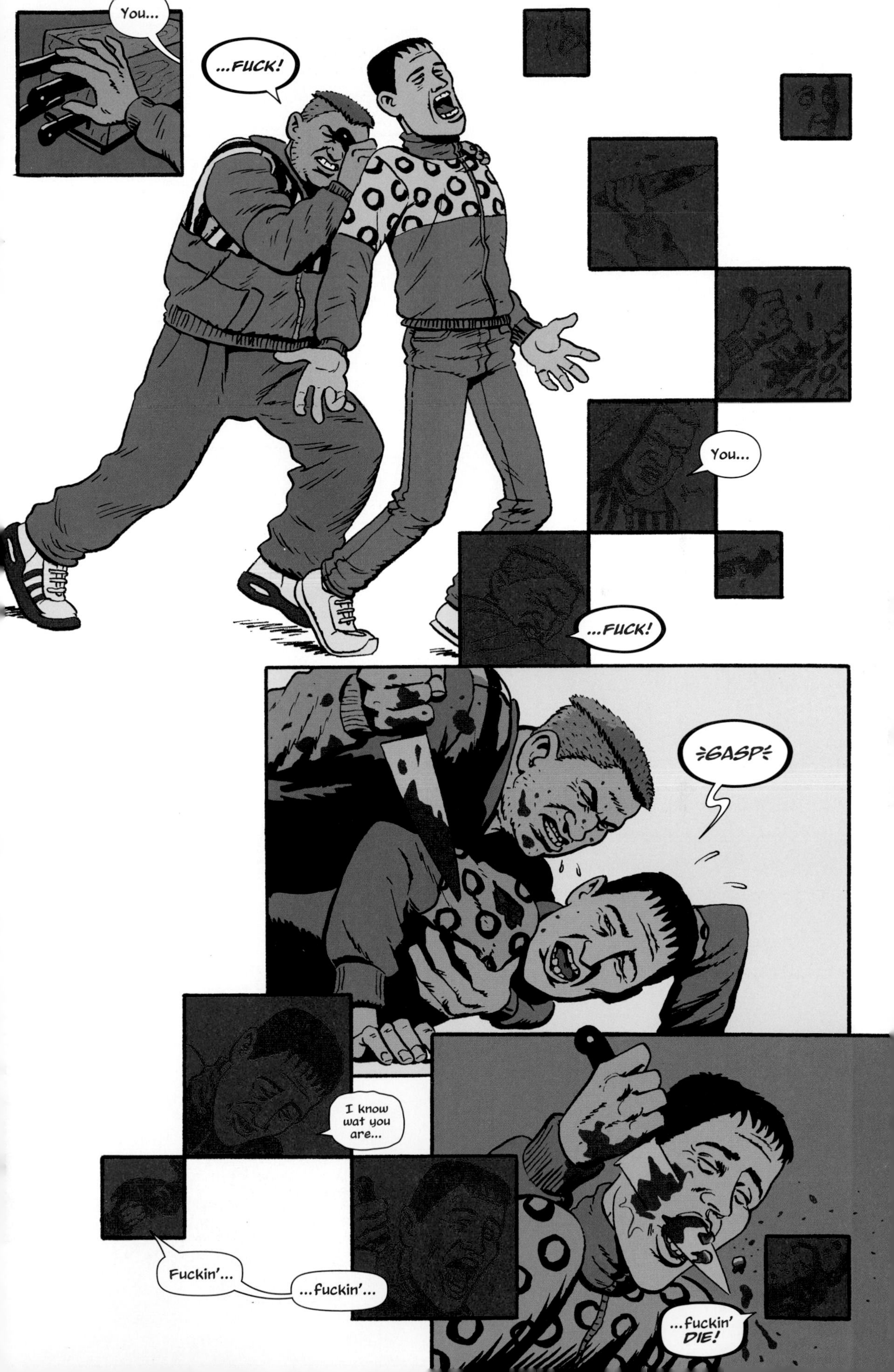
You...
...FUCK!
You...
...FUCK!
GASP
I know wat you are...
Fuckin'...
...fuckin'...
...fuckin' DIE!

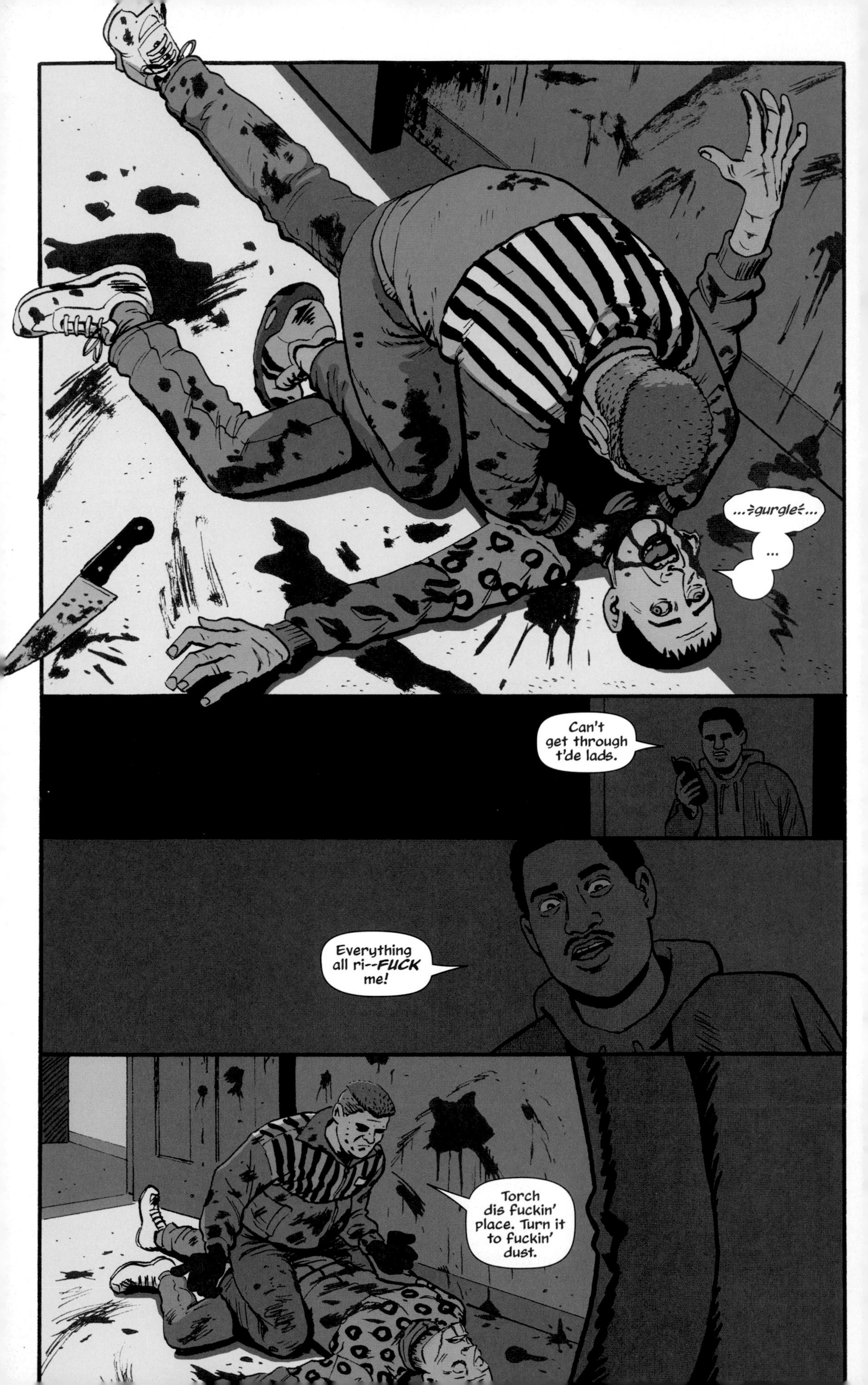

...gurgle...
...
Can't get through t'de lads.
Everything all ri--FUCK me!
Torch dis fuckin' place. Turn it to fuckin' dust.

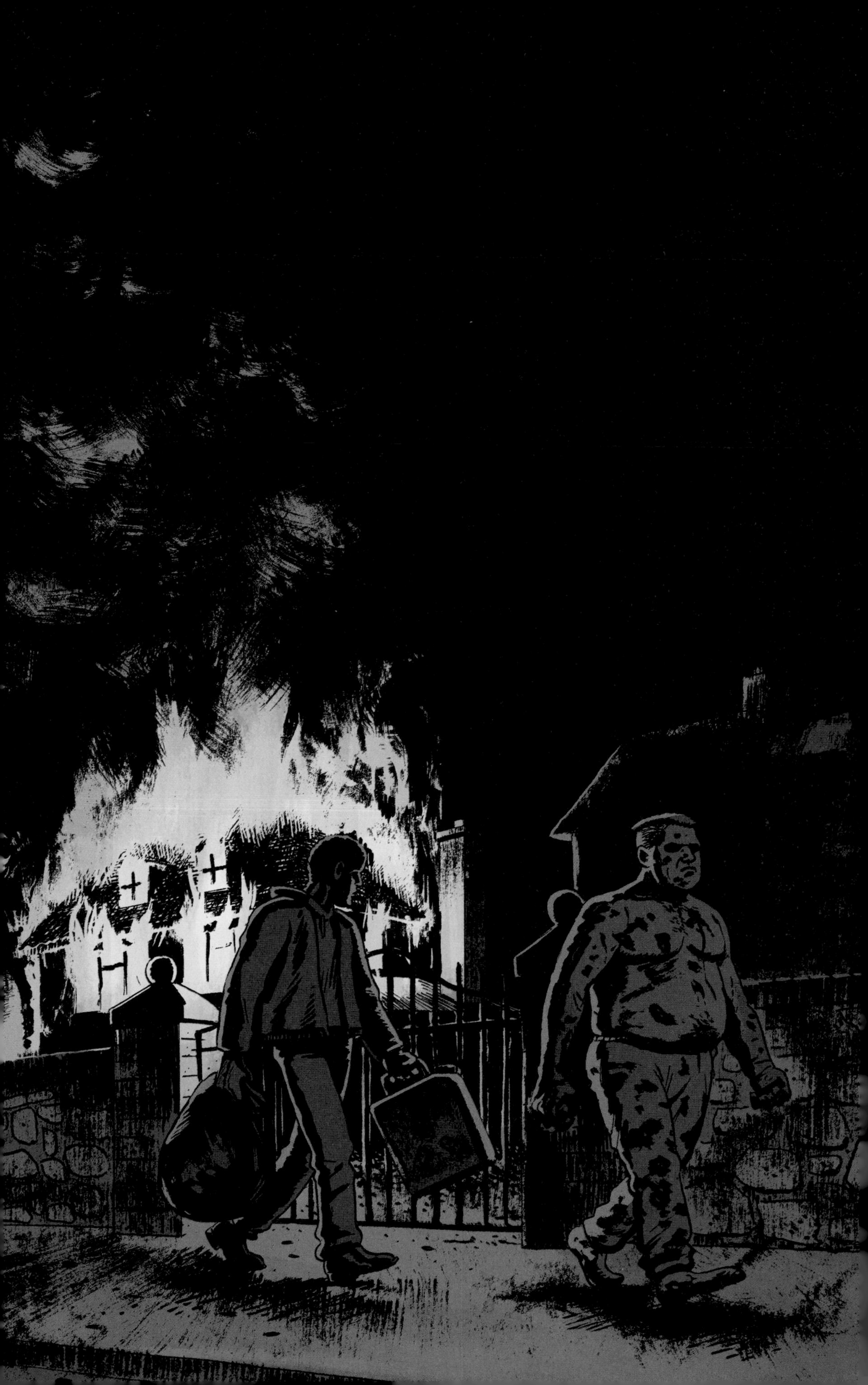

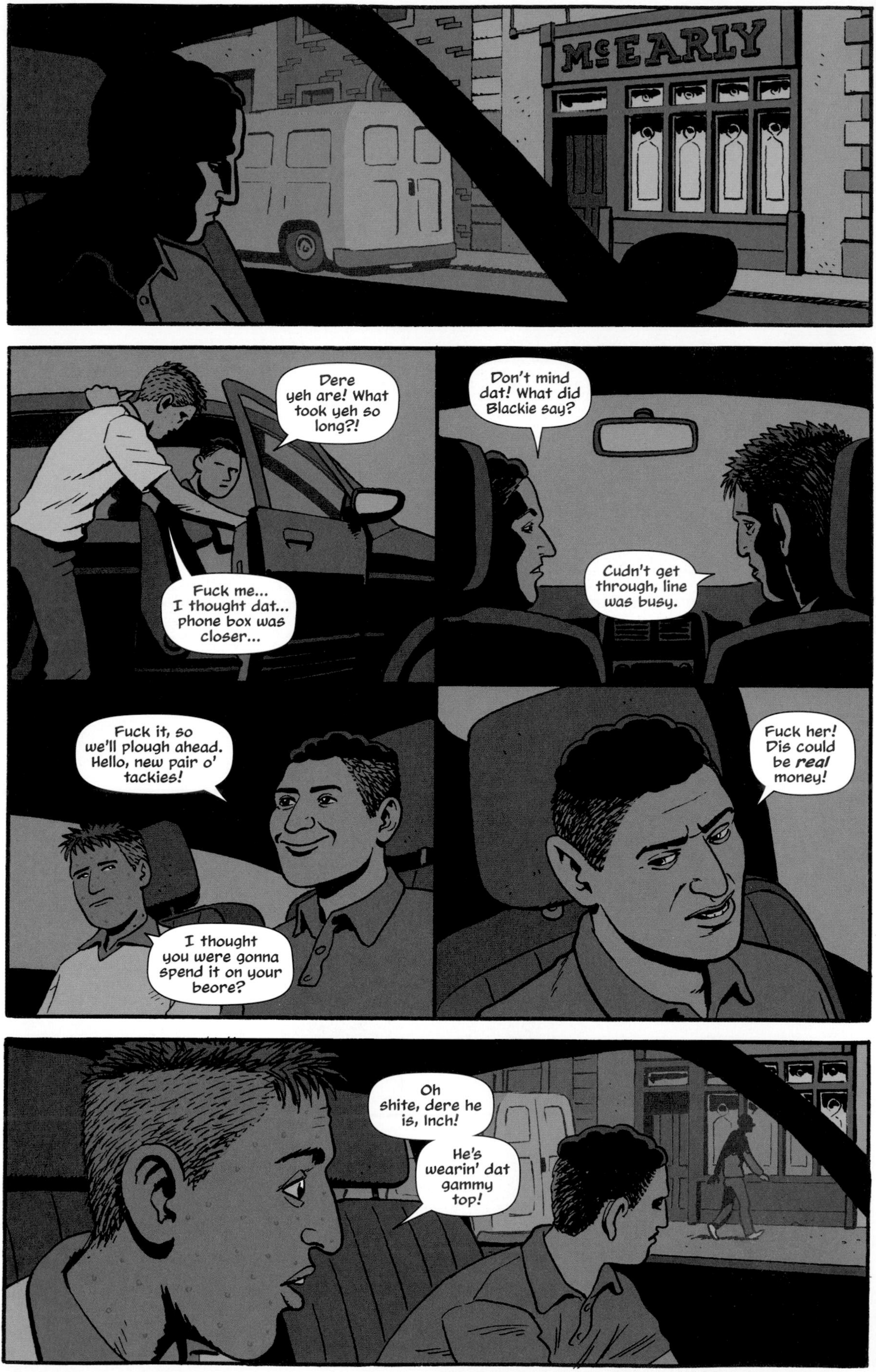
McEARLY
Dere yeh are! What took yeh so long?!
Fuck me... I thought dat... phone box was closer...
Don't mind dat! What did Blackie say?
Cudn't get through, line was busy.
Fuck it, so we'll plough ahead. Hello, new pair o' tackies!
I thought you were gonna spend it on your beore?
Fuck her! Dis could be *real* money!
Oh shite, dere he is, Inch!
He's wearin' dat gammy top!

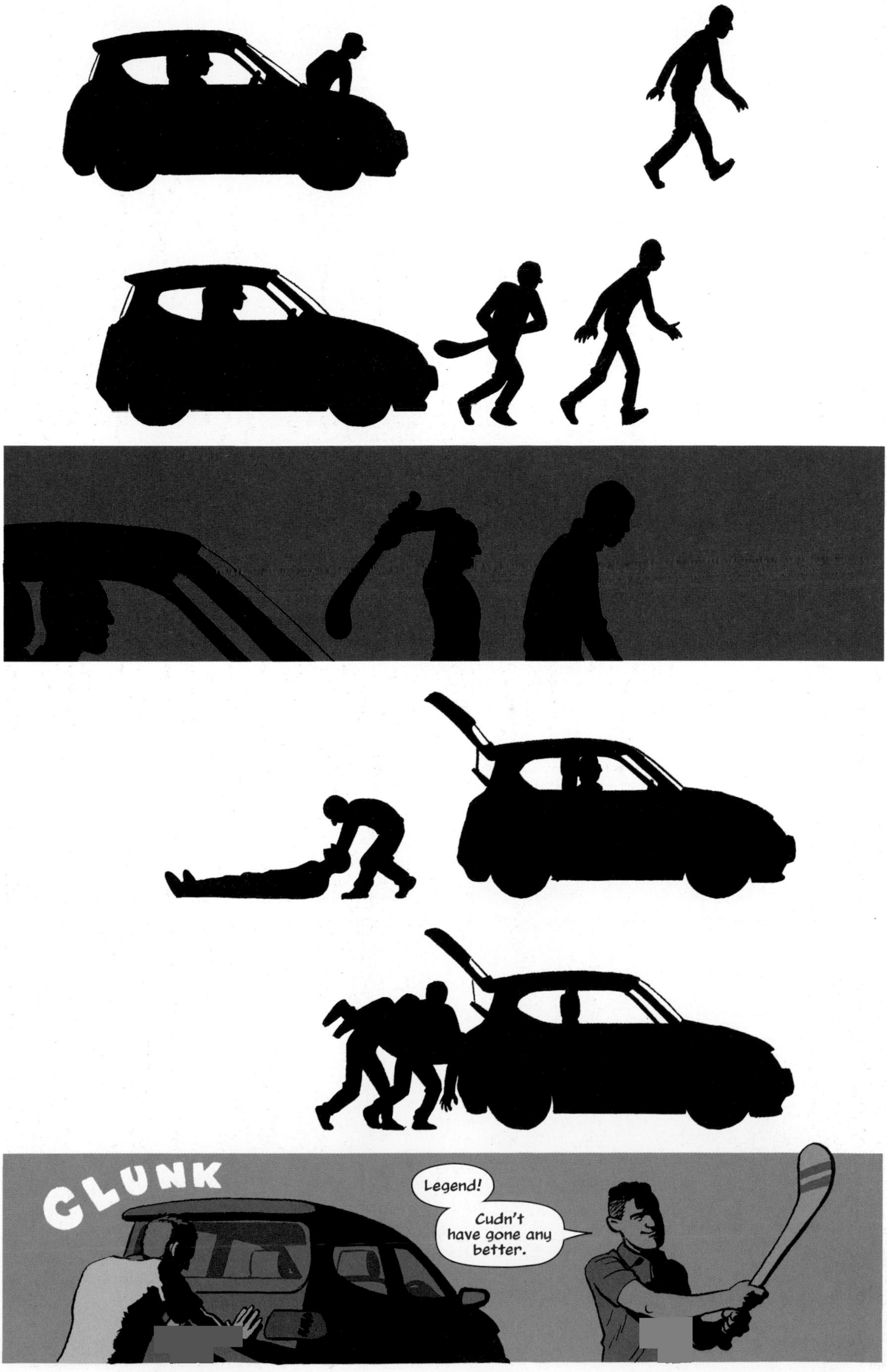
CLUNK
Legend!
Cudn't have gone any better.

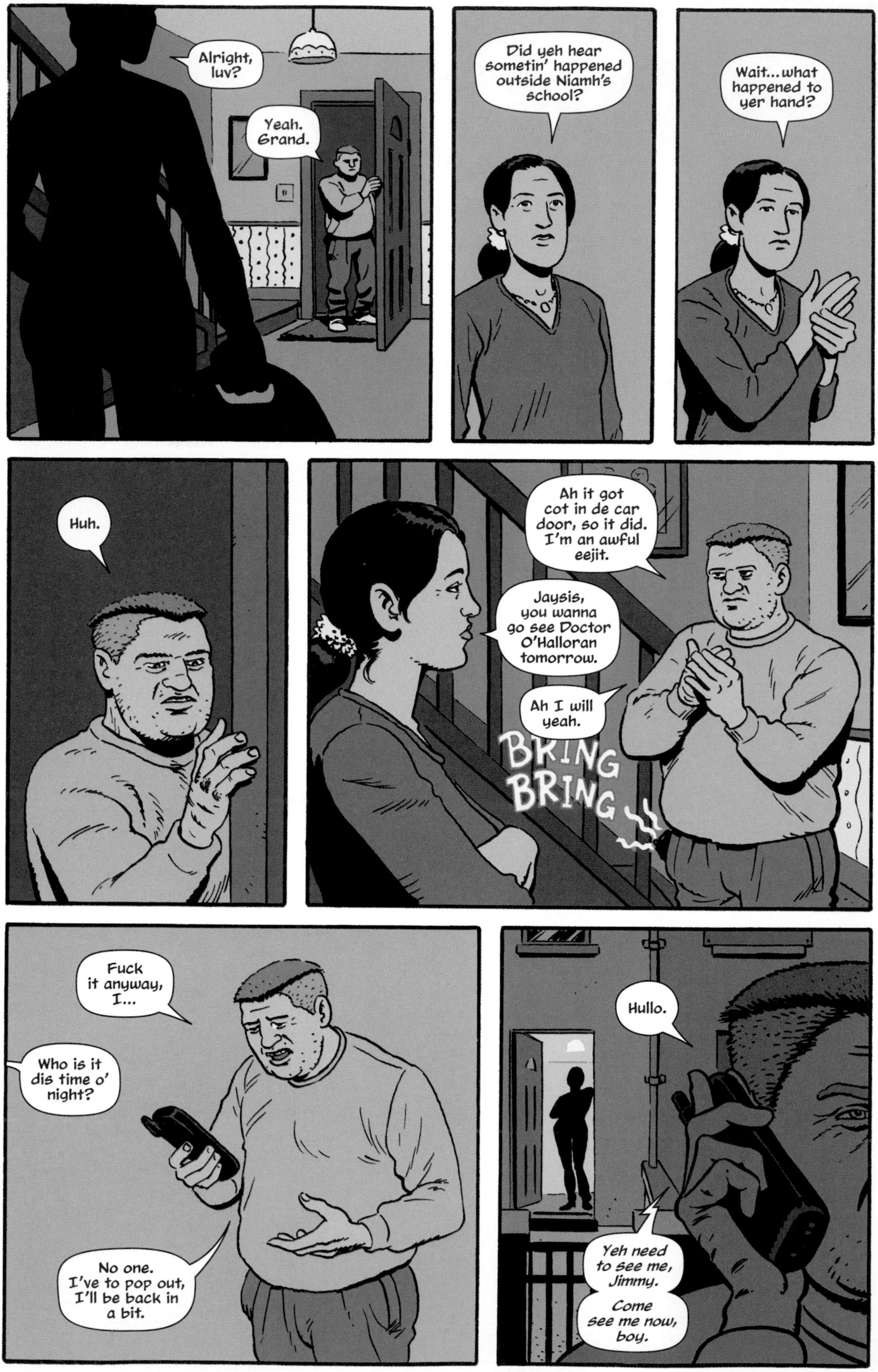
Alright, luv?
Yeah. Grand.
Did yeh hear sometin' happened outside Niamh's school?
Wait...what happened to yer hand?
Huh.
Ah it got cot in de car door, so it did. I'm an awful eejit.
Jaysis, you wanna go see Doctor O'Halloran tomorrow.
Ah I will yeah.
BRING BRING
Fuck it anyway, I...
Who is it dis time o' night?
No one. I've to pop out, I'll be back in a bit.
Hullo.
Yeh need to see me, Jimmy.
Come see me now, boy.

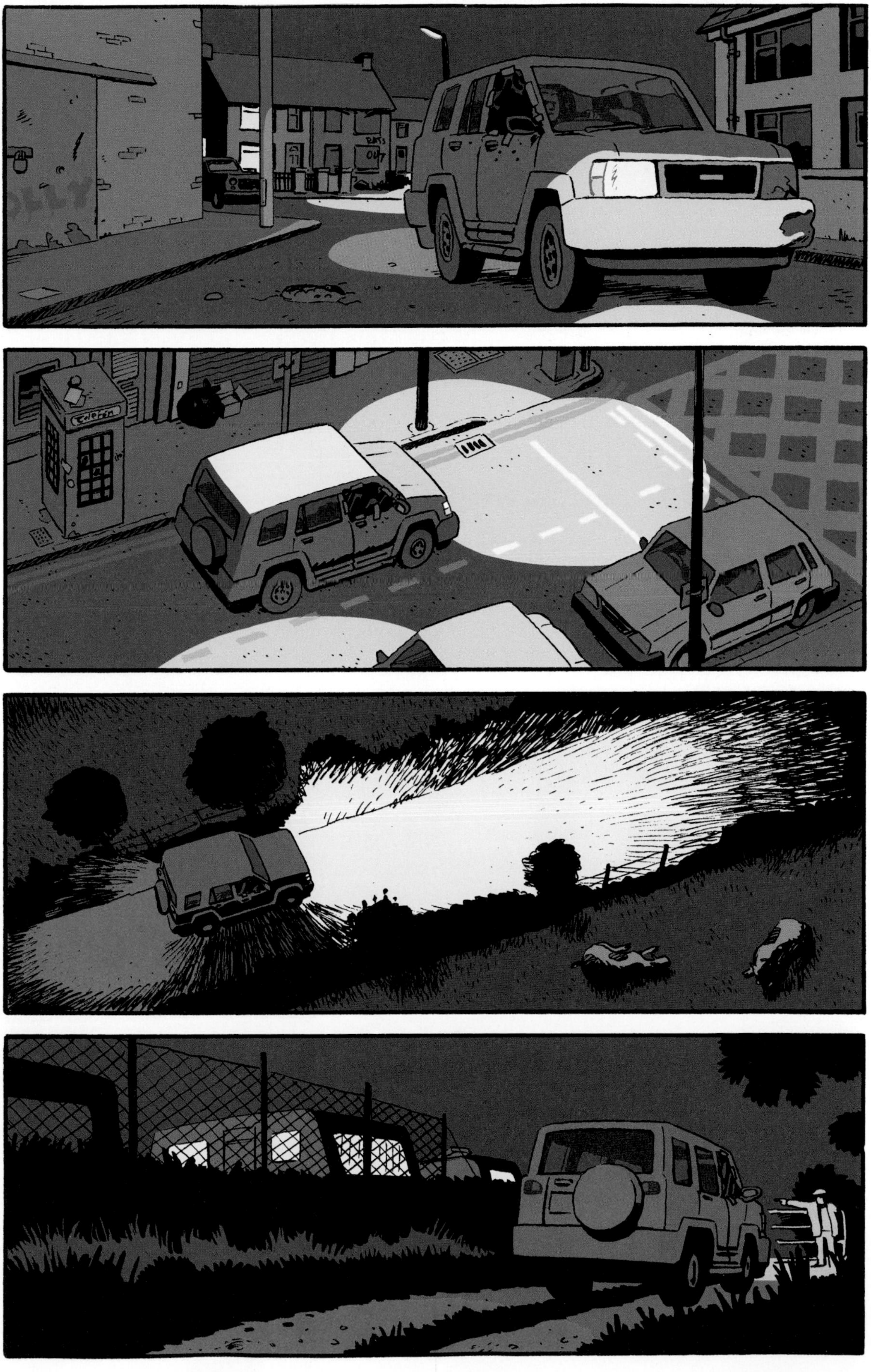
RATS
OUT

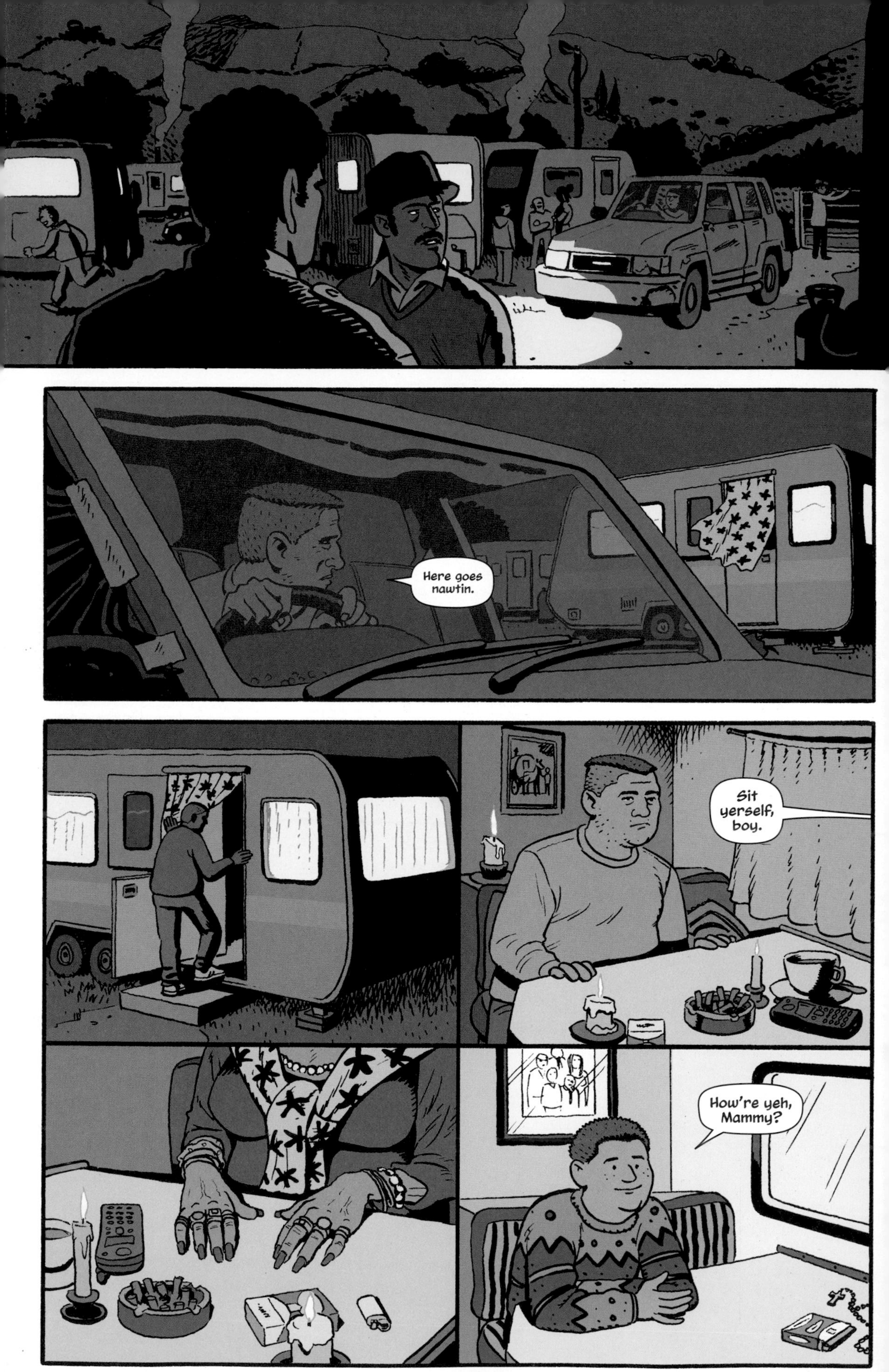
Here goes nawtin.
Sit yerself, boy.
How're yeh, Mammy?

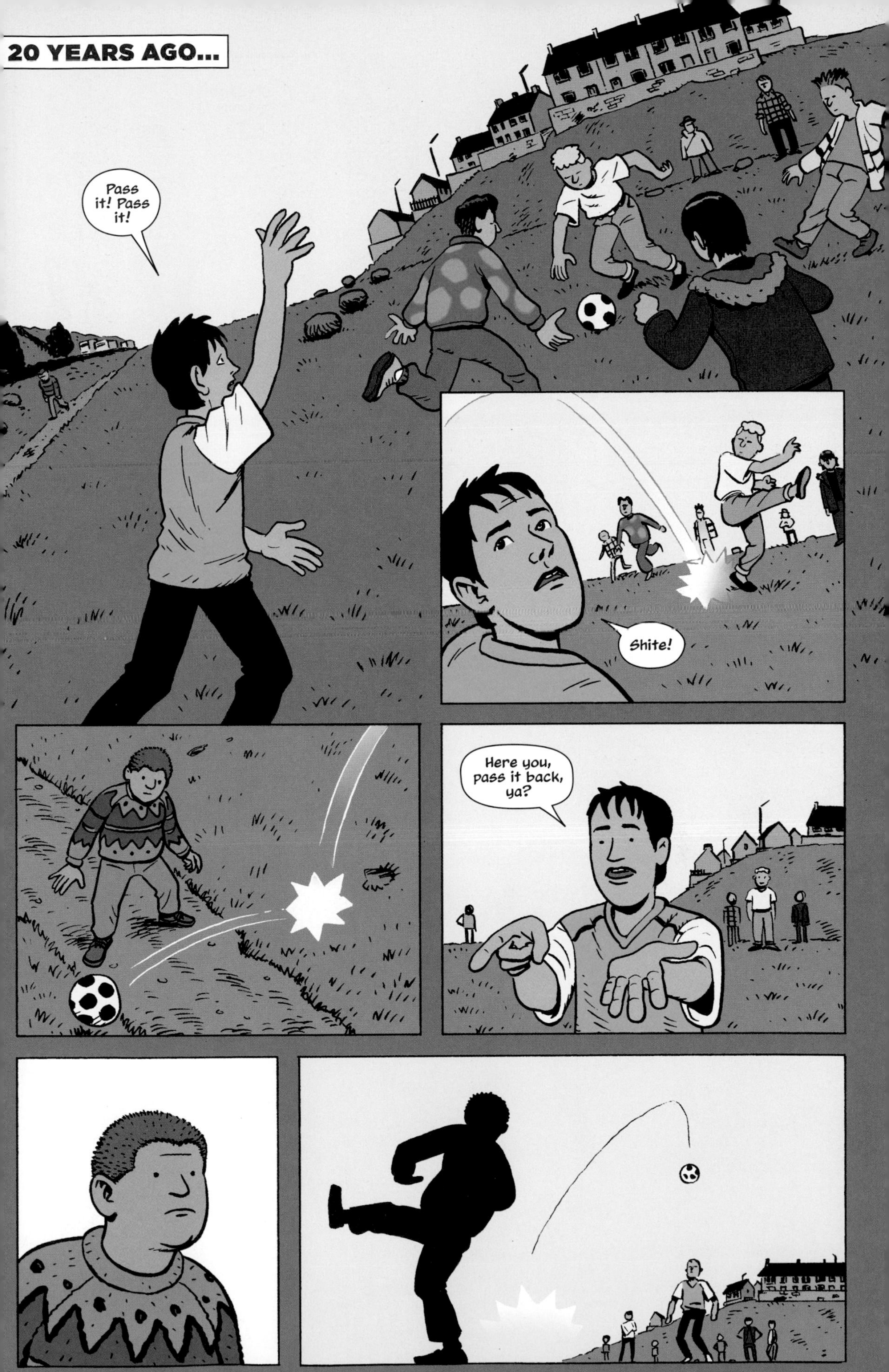
20 YEARS AGO...
Pass it! Pass it!
Shite!
Here you, pass it back, ya?

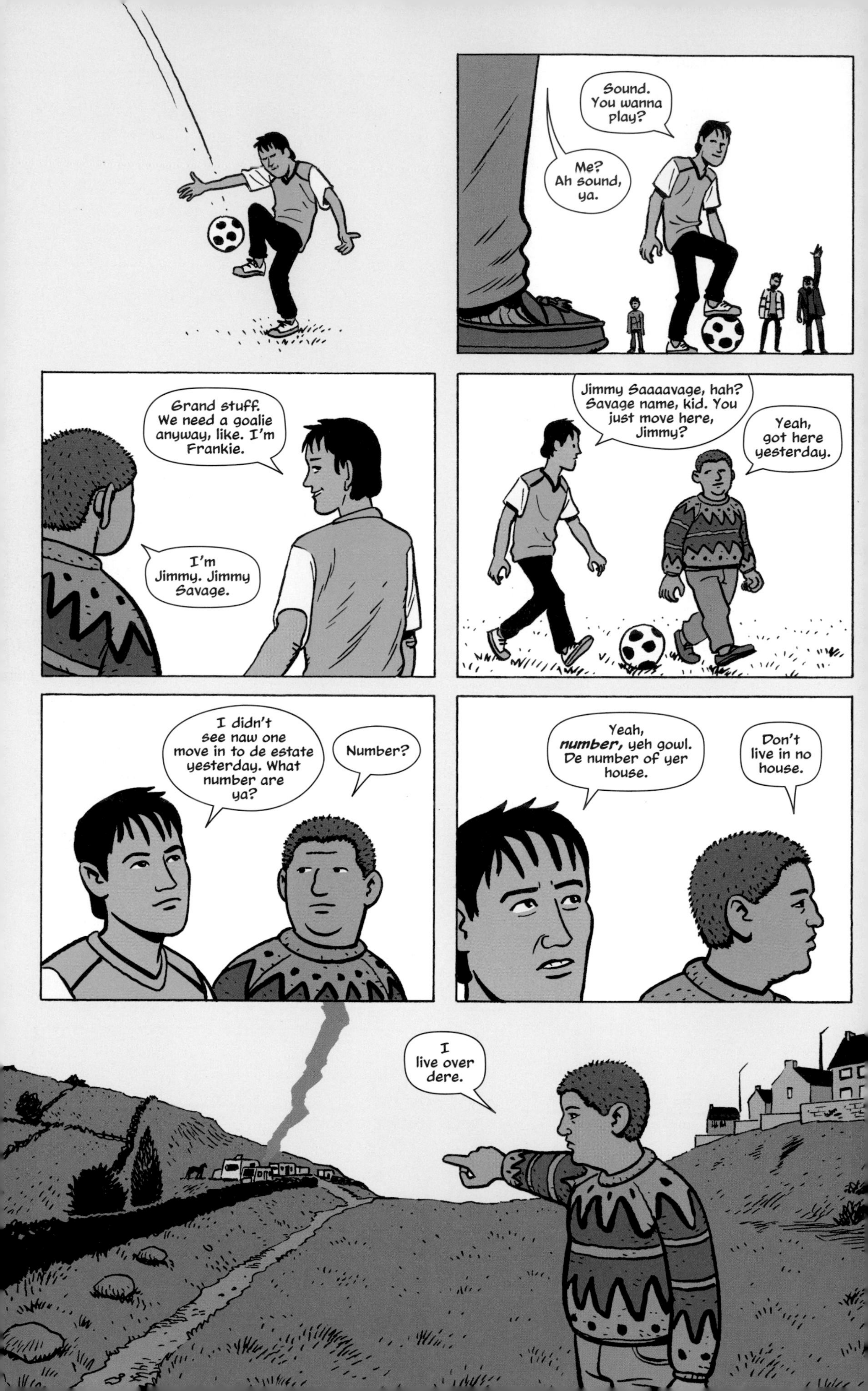
Sound. You wanna play?
Me? Ah sound, ya.
Grand stuff. We need a goalie anyway, like. I'm Frankie.
I'm Jimmy. Jimmy Savage.
Jimmy Saaaavage, hah? Savage name, kid. You just move here, Jimmy?
Yeah, got here yesterday.
I didn't see naw one move in to de estate yesterday. What number are ya?
Number?
Yeah, ***number,*** yeh gowl. De number of yer house.
Don't live in no house.
I live over dere.

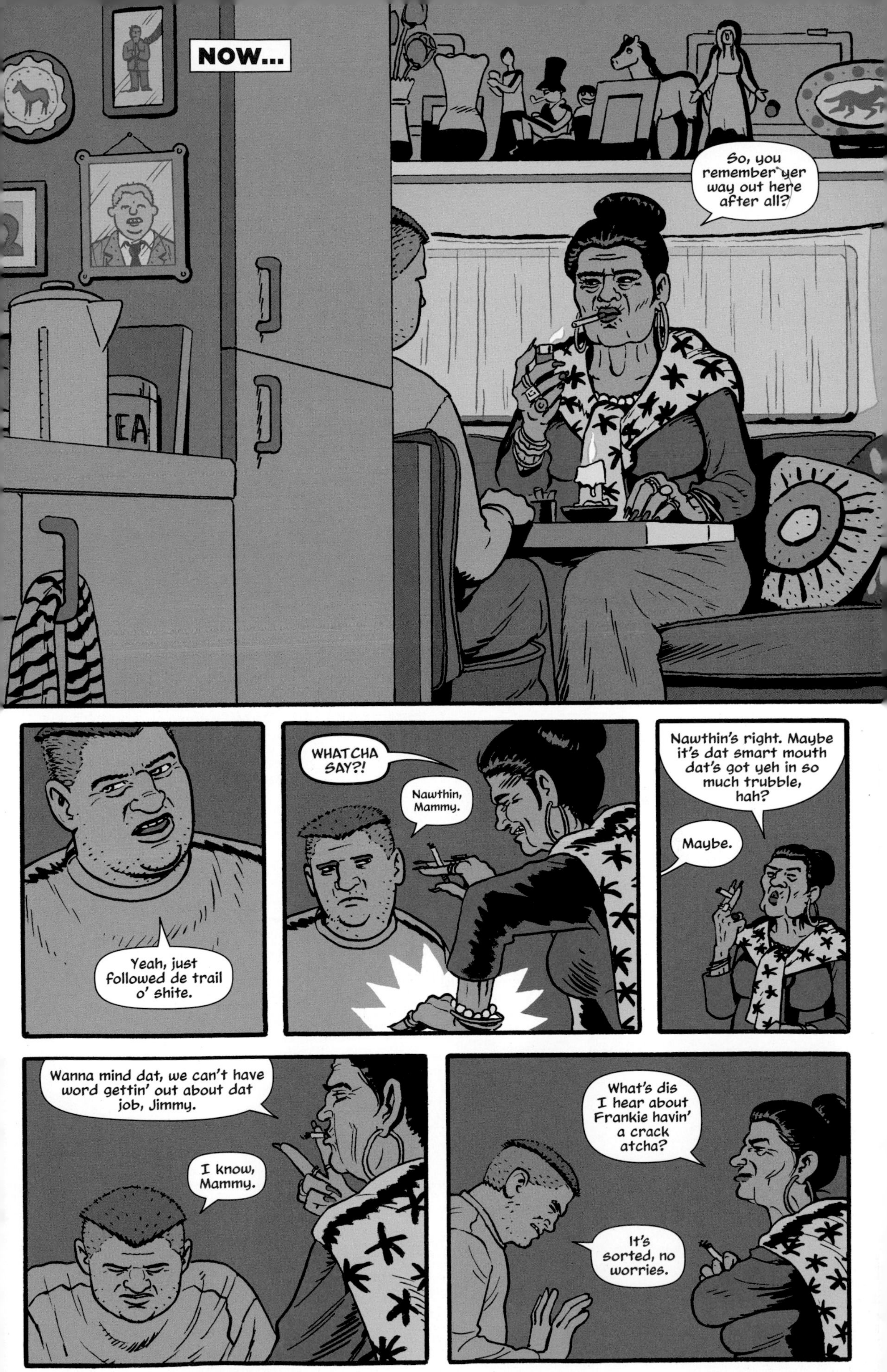
NOW...
So, you remember yer way out here after all?
Yeah, just followed de trail o' shite.
WHATCHA SAY?!
Nawthin, Mammy.
Nawthin's right. Maybe it's dat smart mouth dat's got yeh in so much trubble, hah?
Maybe.
Wanna mind dat, we can't have word gettin' out about dat job, Jimmy.
I know, Mammy.
What's dis I hear about Frankie havin' a crack atcha?
It's sorted, no worries.

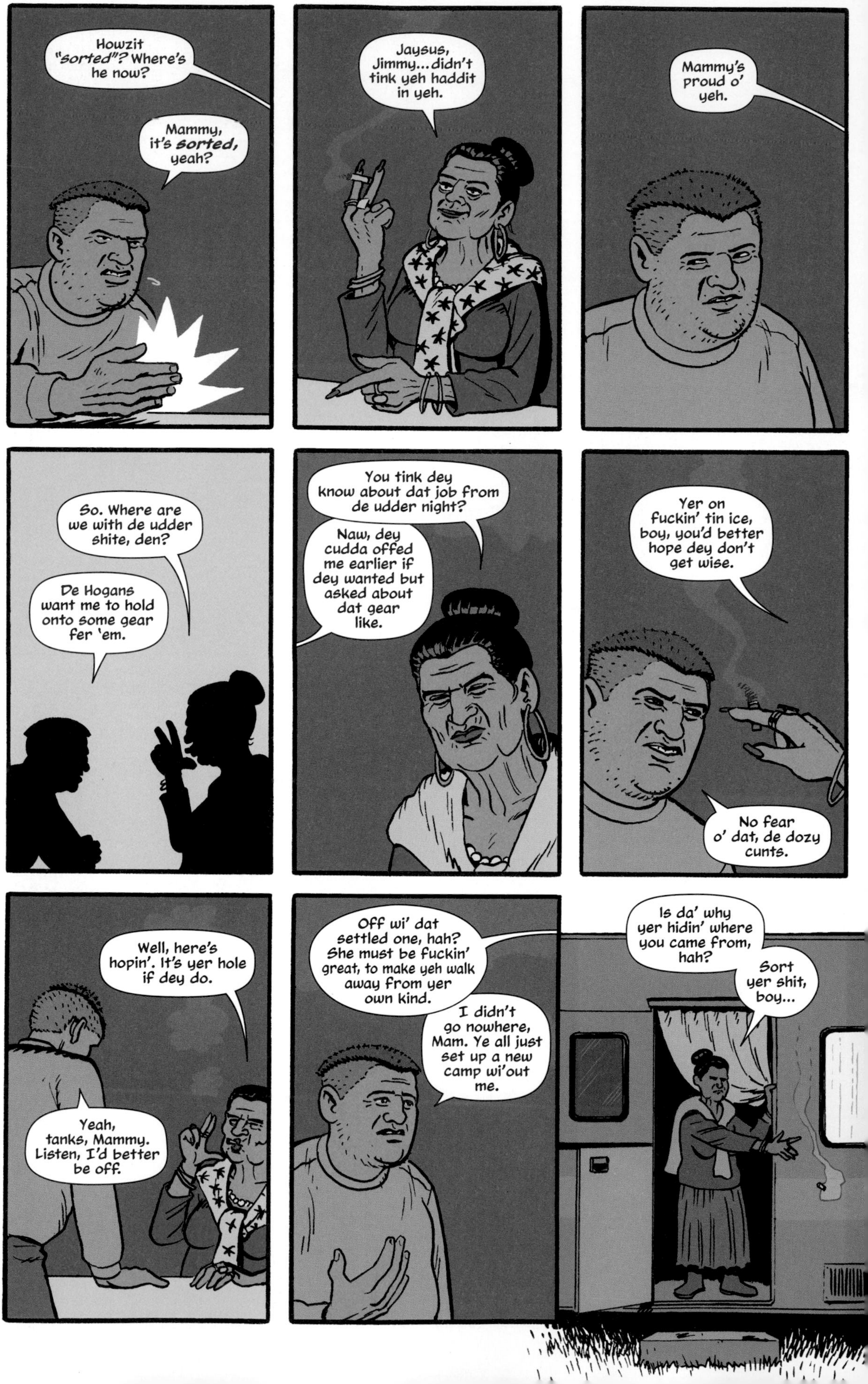

Howzit "sorted"? Where's he now?
Mammy, it's sorted, yeah?
Jaysus, Jimmy...didn't tink yeh haddit in yeh.
Mammy's proud o' yeh.
So. Where are we with de udder shite, den?
De Hogans want me to hold onto some gear fer 'em.
You tink dey know about dat job from de udder night?
Naw, dey cudda offed me earlier if dey wanted but asked about dat gear like.
Yer on fuckin' tin ice, boy, you'd better hope dey don't get wise.
No fear o' dat, de dozy cunts.
Well, here's hopin'. It's yer hole if dey do.
Yeah, tanks, Mammy. Listen, I'd better be off.
Off wi' dat settled one, hah? She must be fuckin' great, to make yeh walk away from yer own kind.
I didn't go nowhere, Mam. Ye all just set up a new camp wi'out me.
Is da' why yer hidin' where you came from, hah?
Sort yer shit, boy...

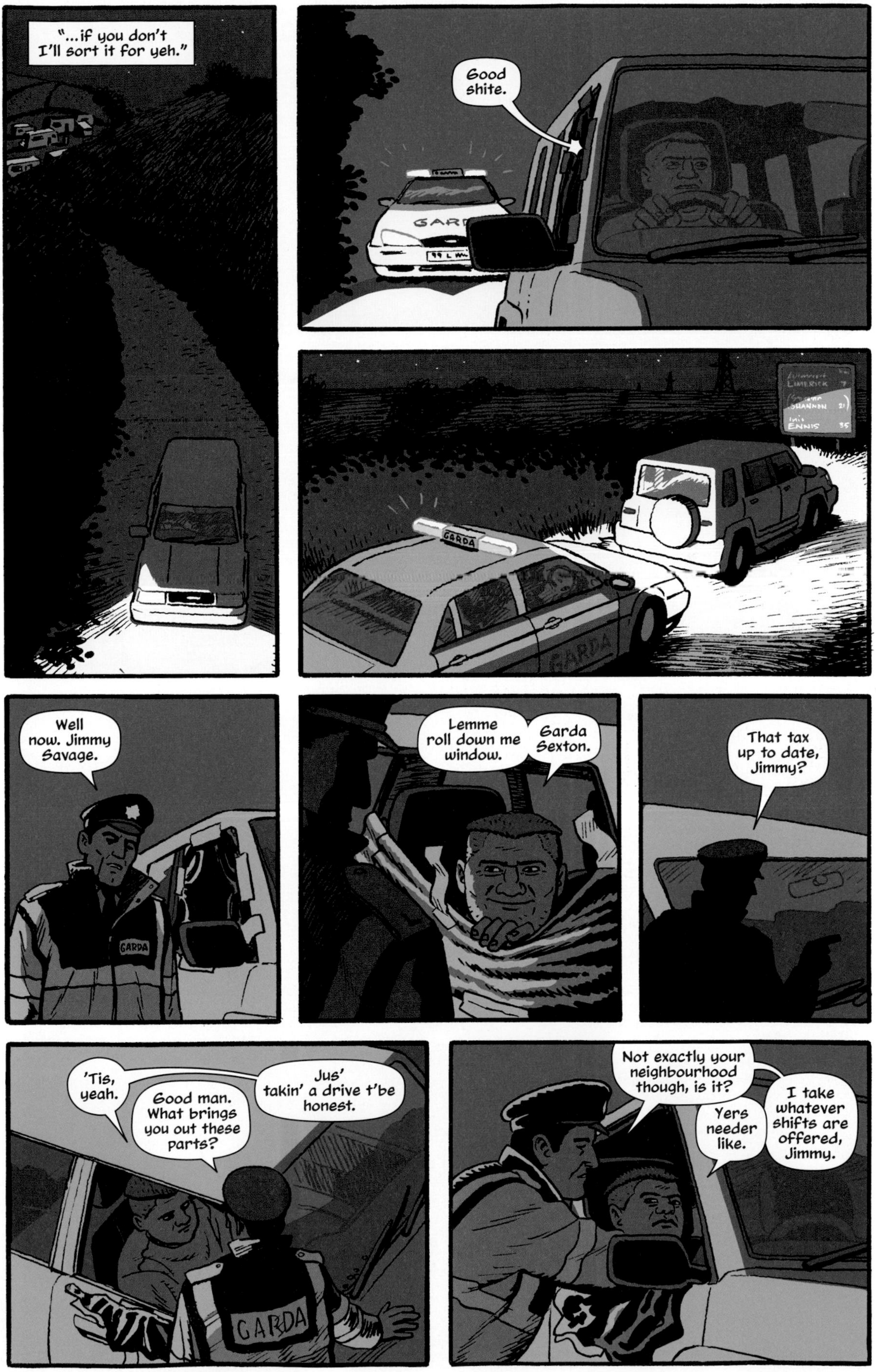
"...if you don't I'll sort it for yeh."
Good shite.
GARDA
GARDA
LIMERICK
SHANNON
ENNIS
GARDA
Well now. Jimmy Savage.
GARDA
Lemme roll down me window.
Garda Sexton.
That tax up to date, Jimmy?
'Tis, yeah.
Good man. What brings you out these parts?
Jus' takin' a drive t'be honest.
GARDA
Not exactly your neighbourhood though, is it?
Yers needer like.
I take whatever shifts are offered, Jimmy.

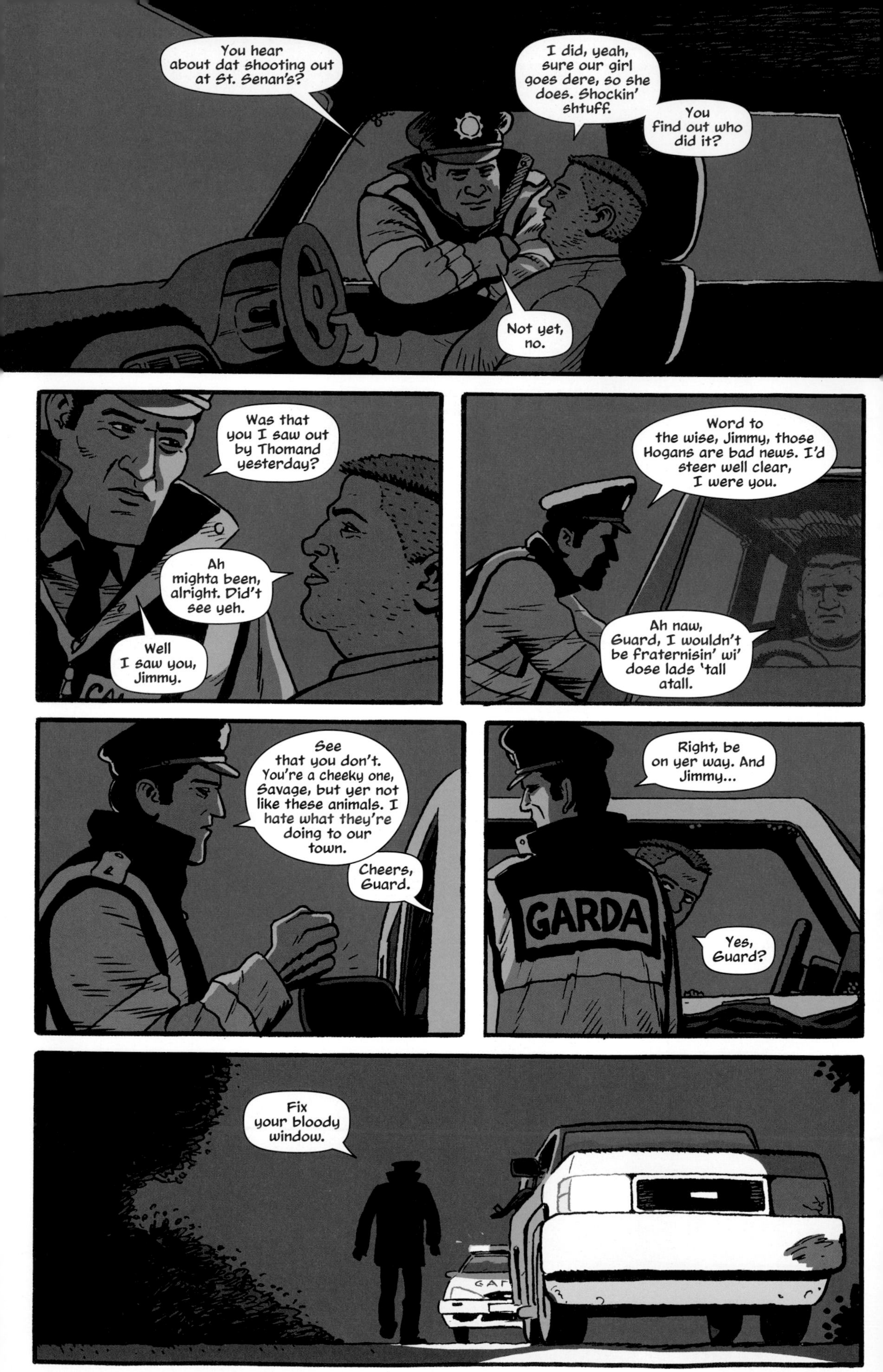
You hear about dat shooting out at St. Senan's?
I did, yeah, sure our girl goes dere, so she does. Shockin' shtuff.
You find out who did it?
Not yet, no.
Was that you I saw out by Thomand yesterday?
Ah mighta been, alright. Didn't see yeh.
Well I saw you, Jimmy.
Word to the wise, Jimmy, those Hogans are bad news. I'd steer well clear, I were you.
Ah naw, Guard, I wouldn't be fraternisin' wi' dose lads 'tall atall.
See that you don't. You're a cheeky one, Savage, but yer not like these animals. I hate what they're doing to our town.
Cheers, Guard.
Right, be on yer way. And Jimmy...
GARDA
Yes, Guard?
Fix your bloody window.

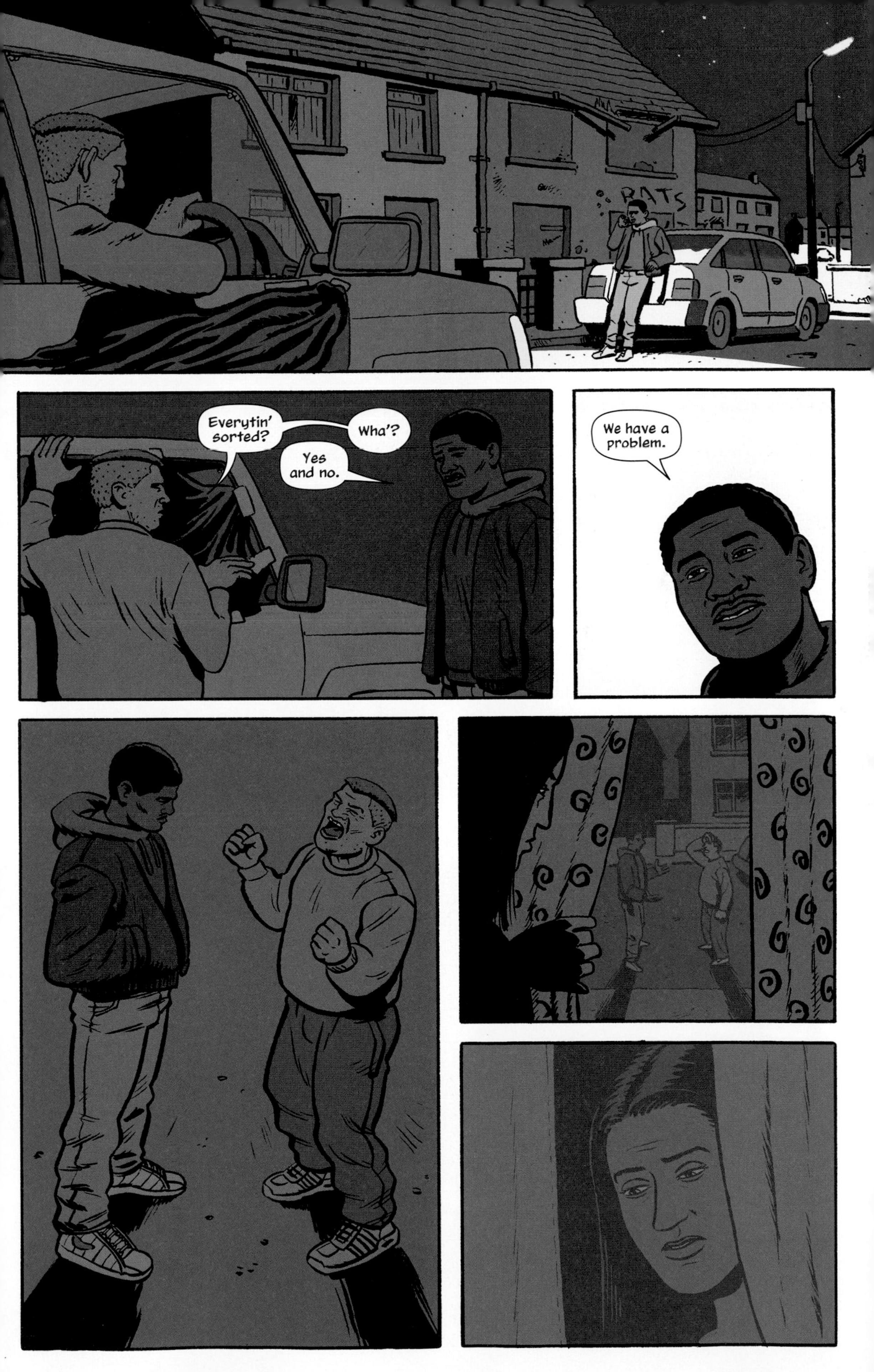
RATS
Everytin' sorted?
Wha'?
Yes and no.
We have a problem.

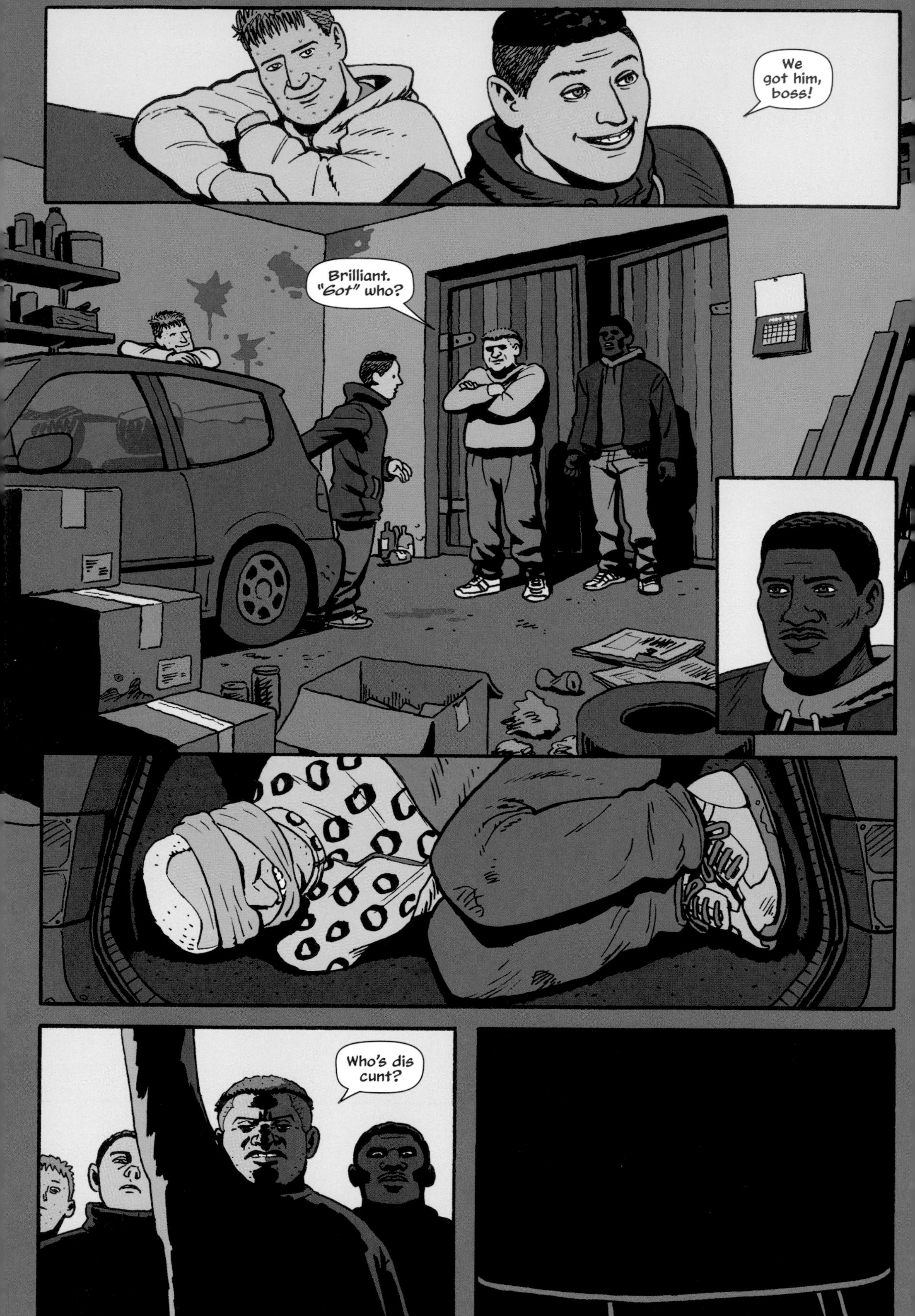
We got him, boss!
Brilliant. "Got" who?
Who's dis cunt?

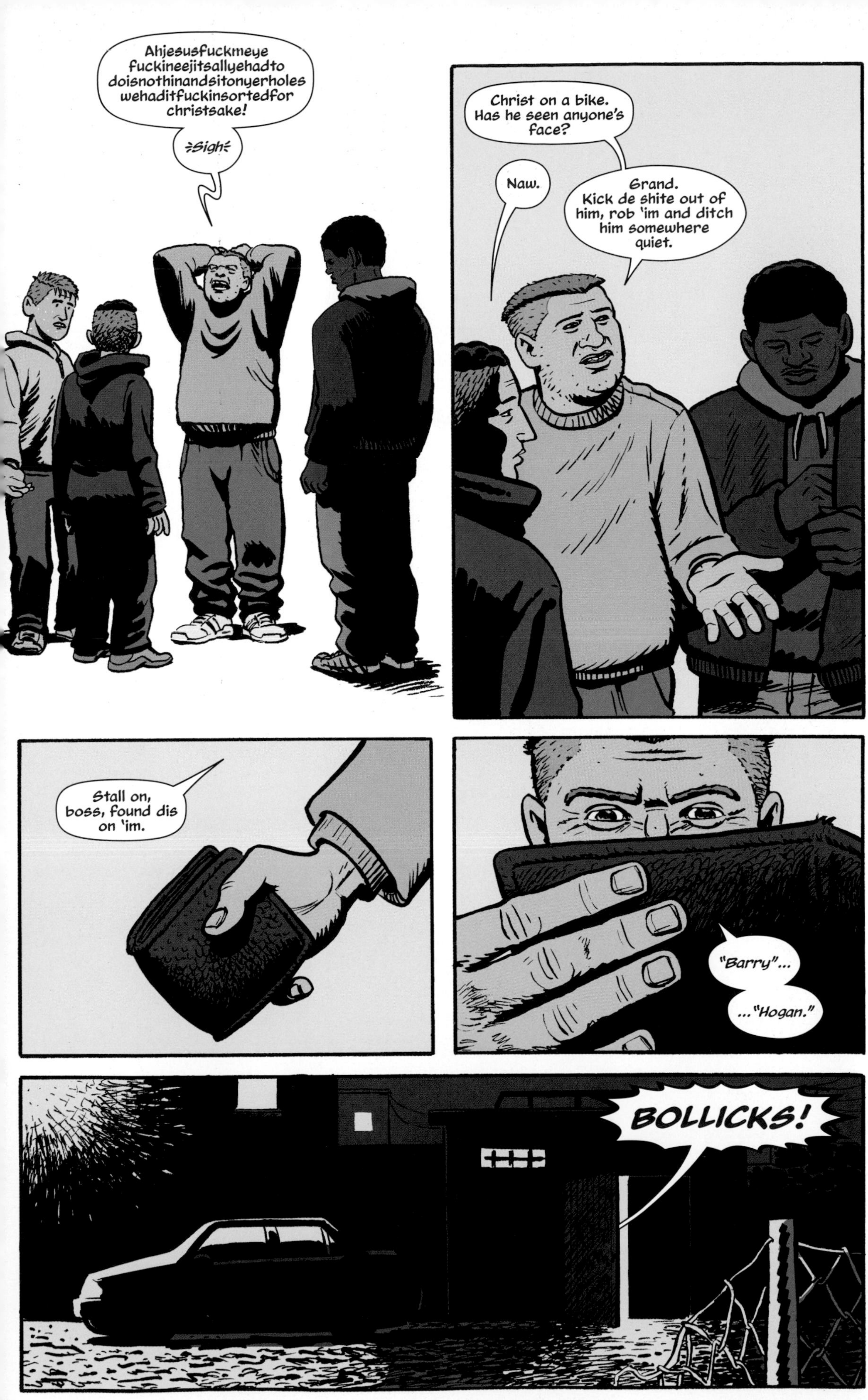
Ahjesusfuckmeye fuckineejitsallyehadto doisnothinandsitonyerholes wehaditfuckinsortedfor christsake!
Sigh
Christ on a bike. Has he seen anyone's face?
Naw.
Grand. Kick de shite out of him, rob 'im and ditch him somewhere quiet.
Stall on, boss, found dis on 'im.
"Barry"...
..."Hogan."
BOLLICKS!

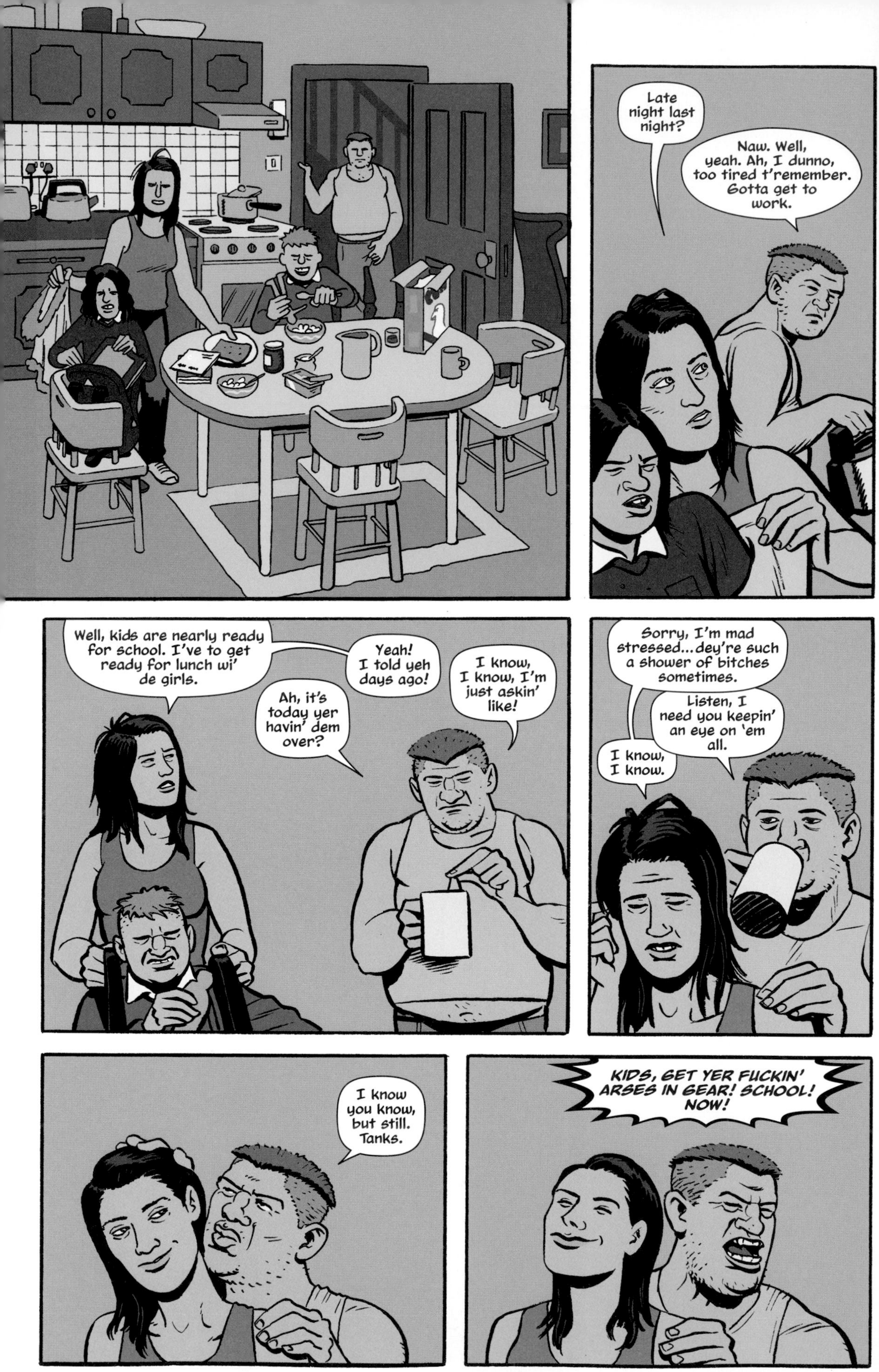
Late night last night?
Naw. Well, yeah. Ah, I dunno, too tired t'remember. Gotta get to work.
Well, kids are nearly ready for school. I've to get ready for lunch wi' de girls.
Ah, it's today yer havin' dem over?
Yeah! I told yeh days ago!
I know, I know, I'm just askin' like!
Sorry, I'm mad stressed...dey're such a shower of bitches sometimes.
I know, I know.
Listen, I need you keepin' an eye on 'em all.
I know you know, but still. Tanks.
KIDS, GET YER FUCKIN' ARSES IN GEAR! SCHOOL! NOW!

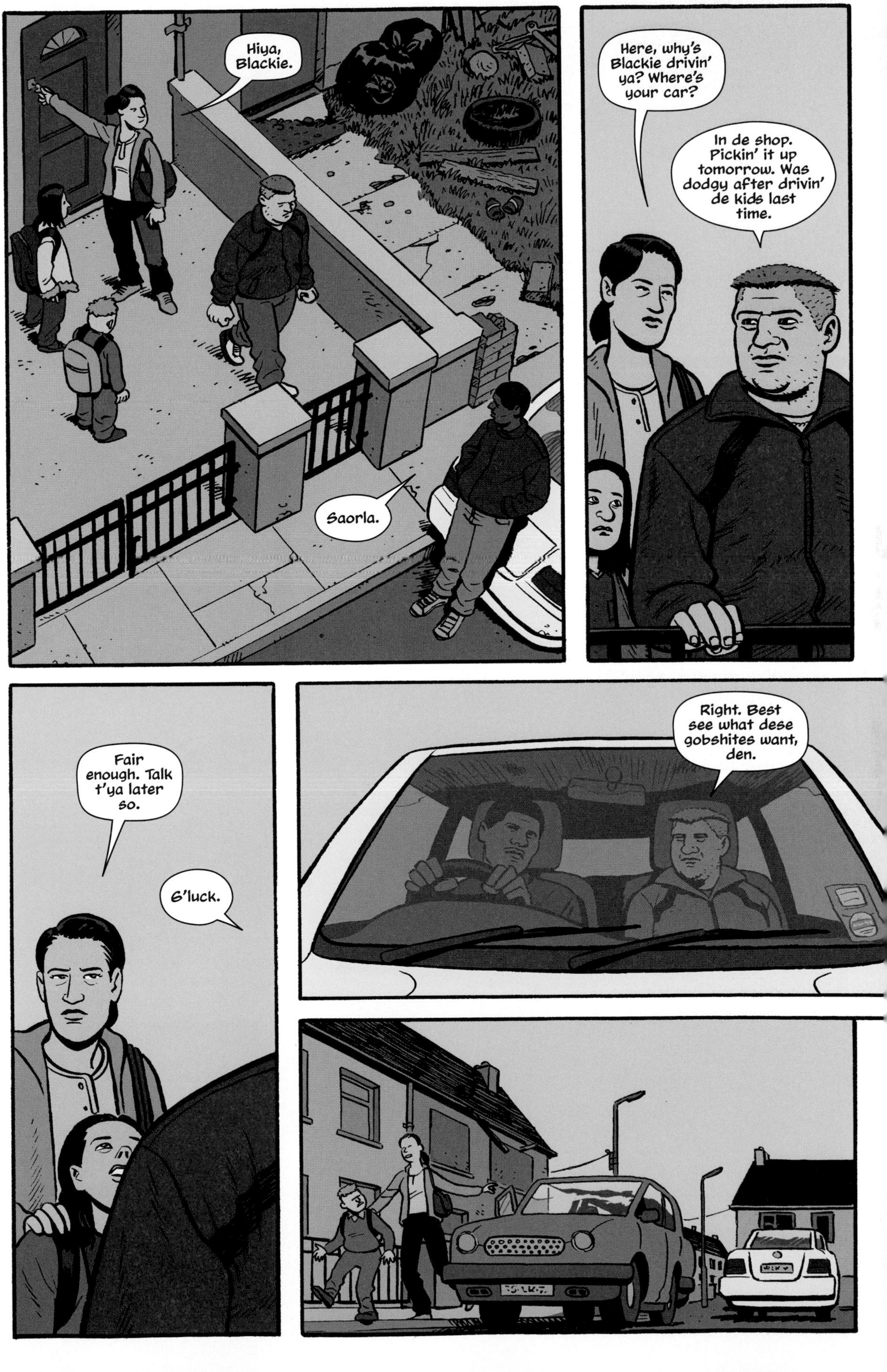
Hiya, Blackie.
Saorla.
Here, why's Blackie drivin' ya? Where's your car?
In de shop. Pickin' it up tomorrow. Was dodgy after drivin' de kids last time.
Fair enough. Talk t'ya later so.
G'luck.
Right. Best see what dese gobshites want, den.

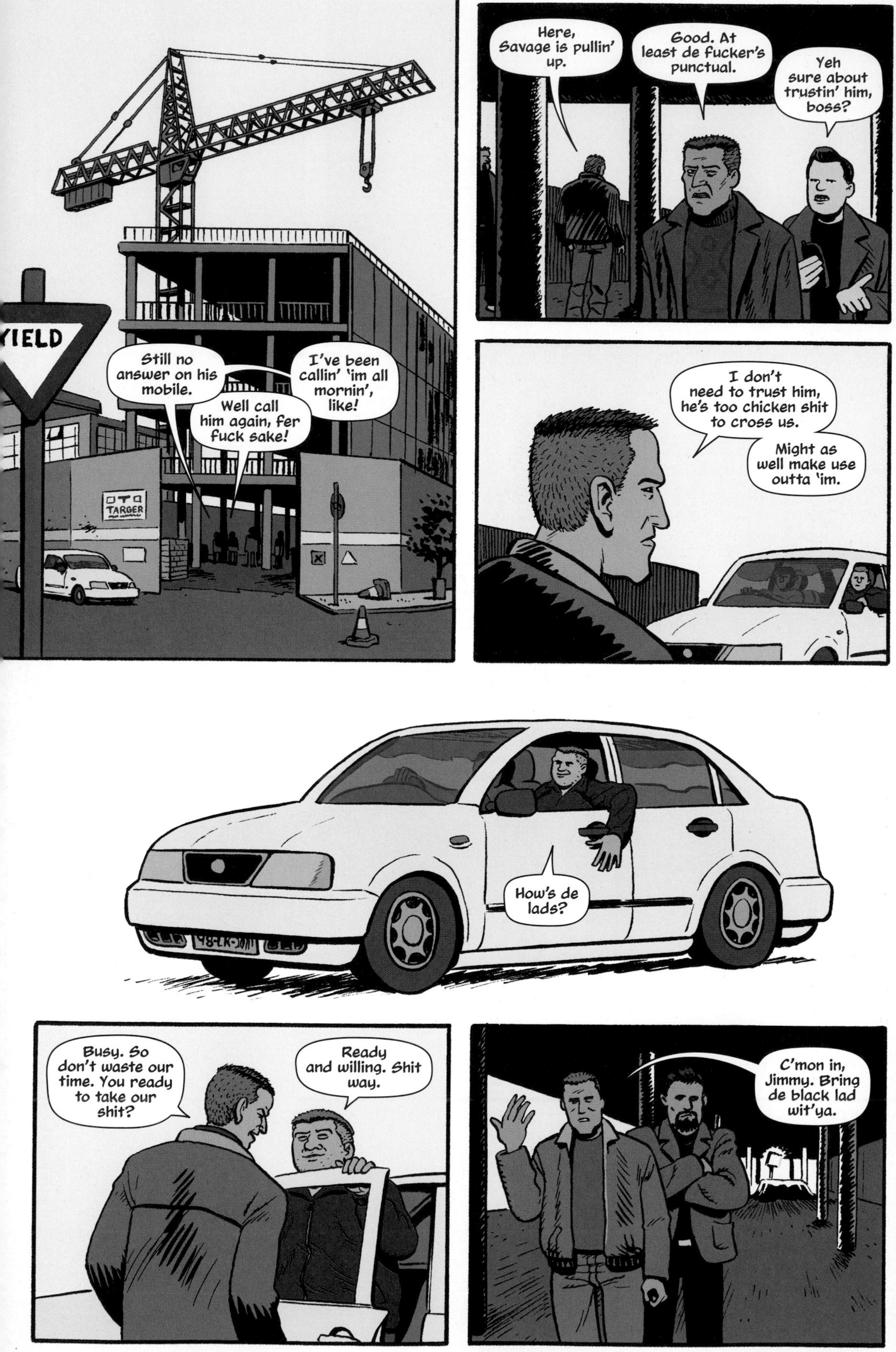
YIELD
Still no answer on his mobile.
I've been callin' 'im all mornin', like!
Well call him again, fer fuck sake!
TARGER
Here, Savage is pullin' up.
Good. At least de fucker's punctual.
Yeh sure about trustin' him, boss?
I don't need to trust him, he's too chicken shit to cross us.
Might as well make use outta 'im.
How's de lads?
Busy. So don't waste our time. You ready to take our shit?
Ready and willing. Shit way.
C'mon in, Jimmy. Bring de black lad wit'ya.

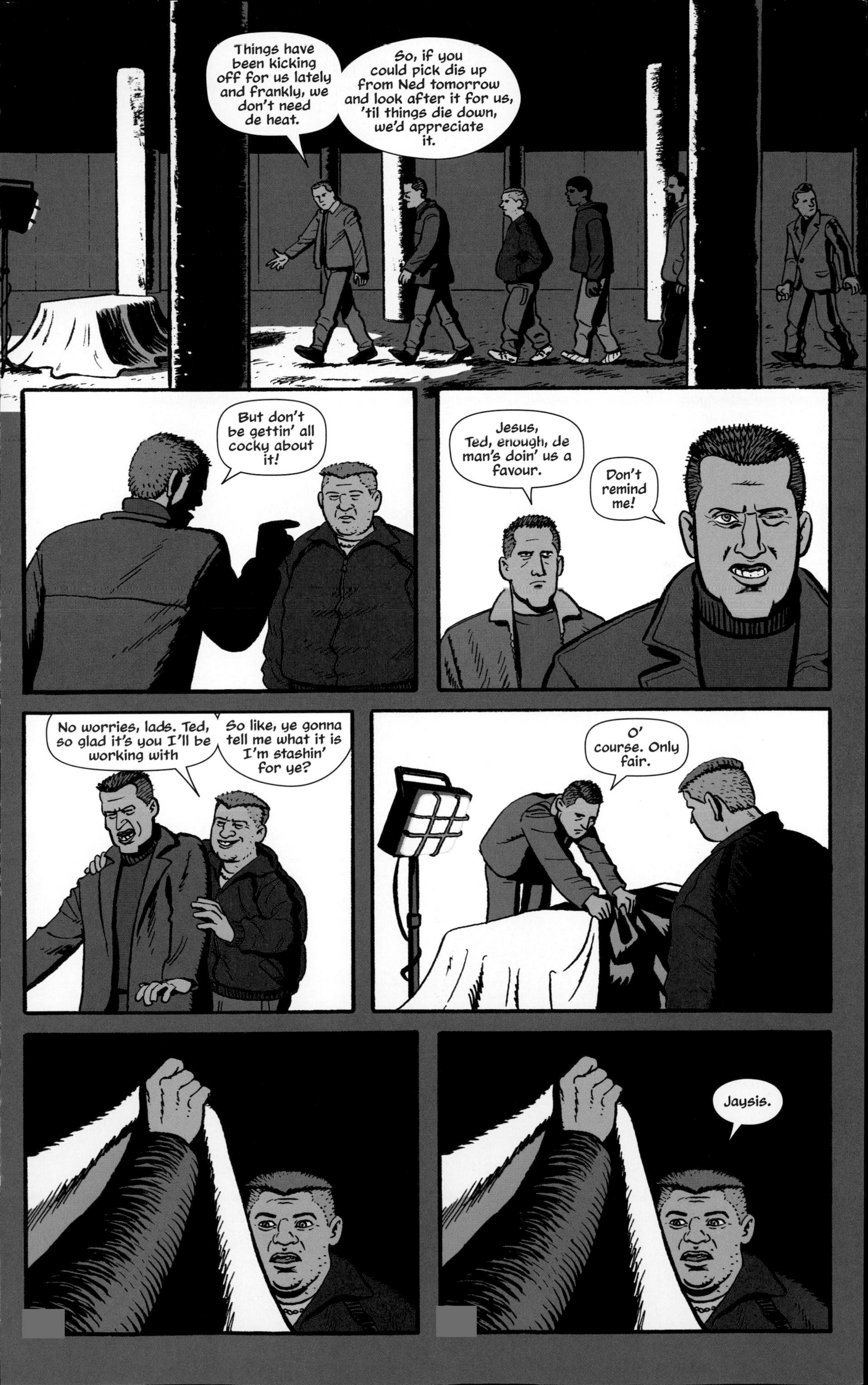
Things have been kicking off for us lately and frankly, we don't need de heat.
So, if you could pick dis up from Ned tomorrow and look after it for us, 'til things die down, we'd appreciate it.
But don't be gettin' all cocky about it!
Jesus, Ted, enough, de man's doin' us a favour.
Don't remind me!
No worries, lads. Ted, so glad it's you I'll be working with
So like, ye gonna tell me what it is I'm stashin' for ye?
O' course. Only fair.
Jaysis.

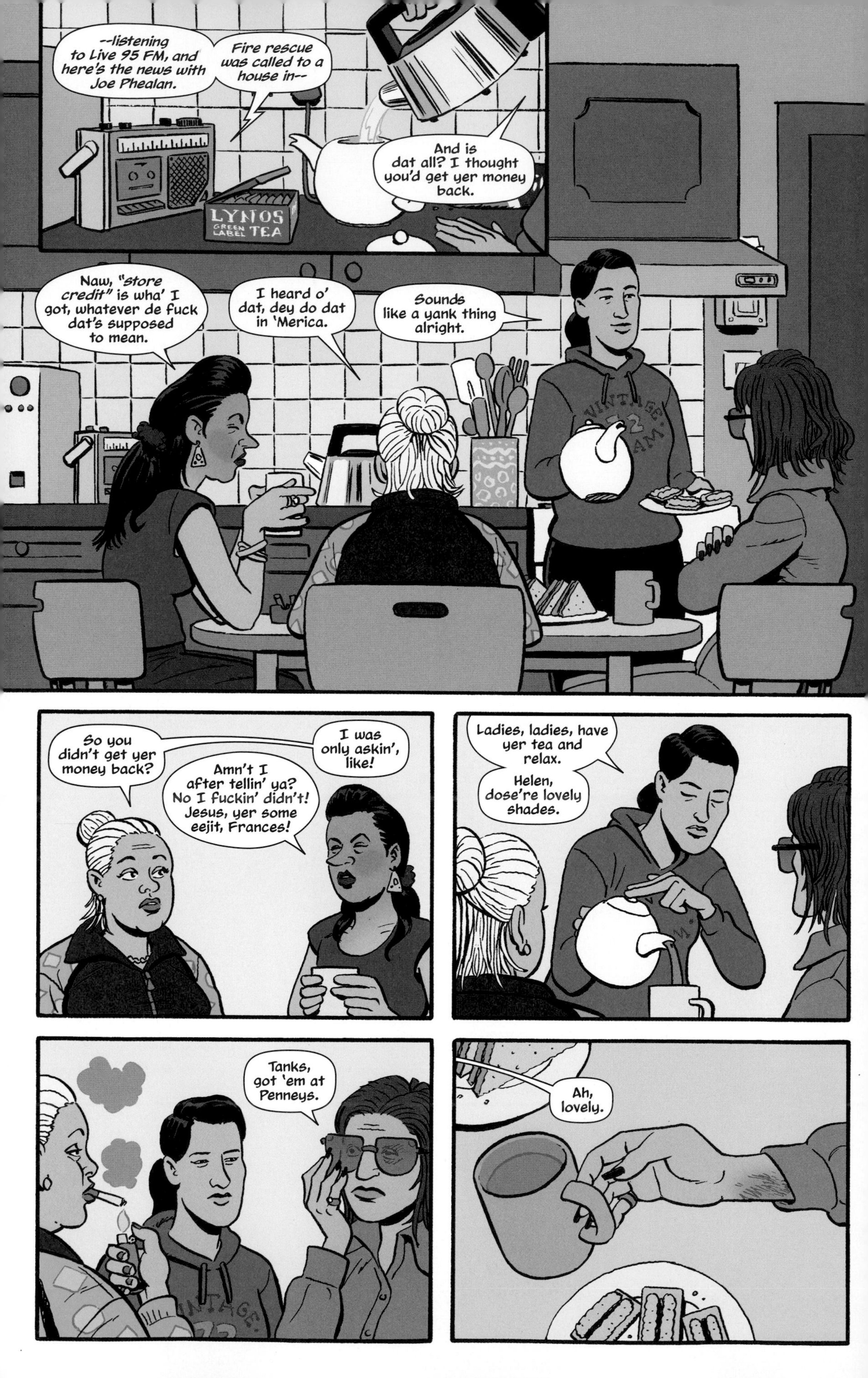
--listening to Live 95 FM, and here's the news with Joe Phealan.
Fire rescue was called to a house in--
LYNOS GREEN LABEL TEA
And is dat all? I thought you'd get yer money back.
Naw, "store credit" is wha' I got, whatever de fuck dat's supposed to mean.
I heard o' dat, dey do dat in 'Merica.
Sounds like a yank thing alright.
So you didn't get yer money back?
I was only askin', like!
Amn't I after tellin' ya? No I fuckin' didn't! Jesus, yer some eejit, Frances!
Ladies, ladies, have yer tea and relax.
Helen, dose're lovely shades.
Tanks, got 'em at Penneys.
Ah, lovely.

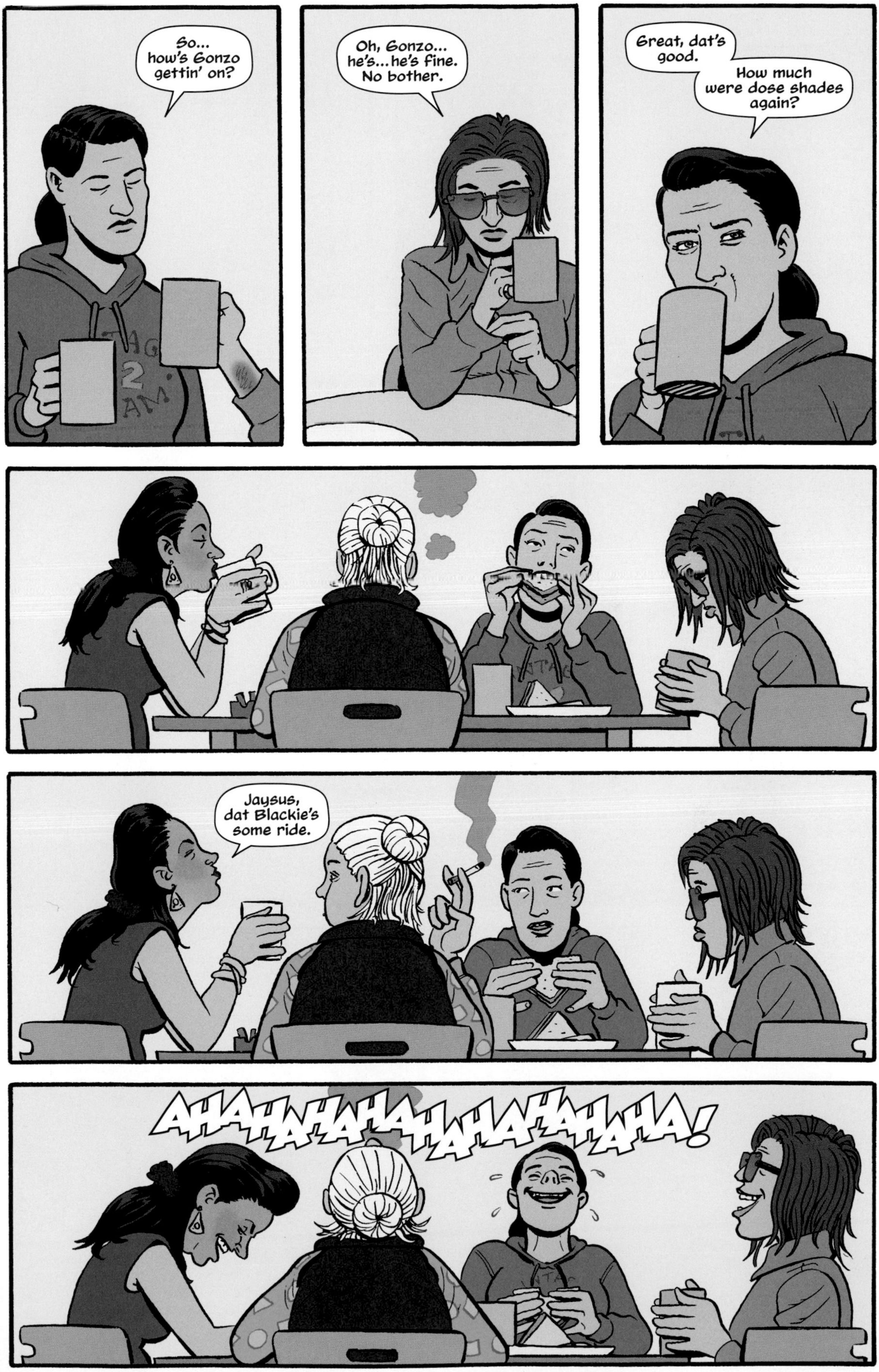
So... how's Gonzo gettin' on?
Oh, Gonzo... he's... he's fine. No bother.
Great, dat's good.
How much were dose shades again?
Jaysus, dat Blackie's some ride.
AHAHAHAHAHAHAHAHAHAHA!

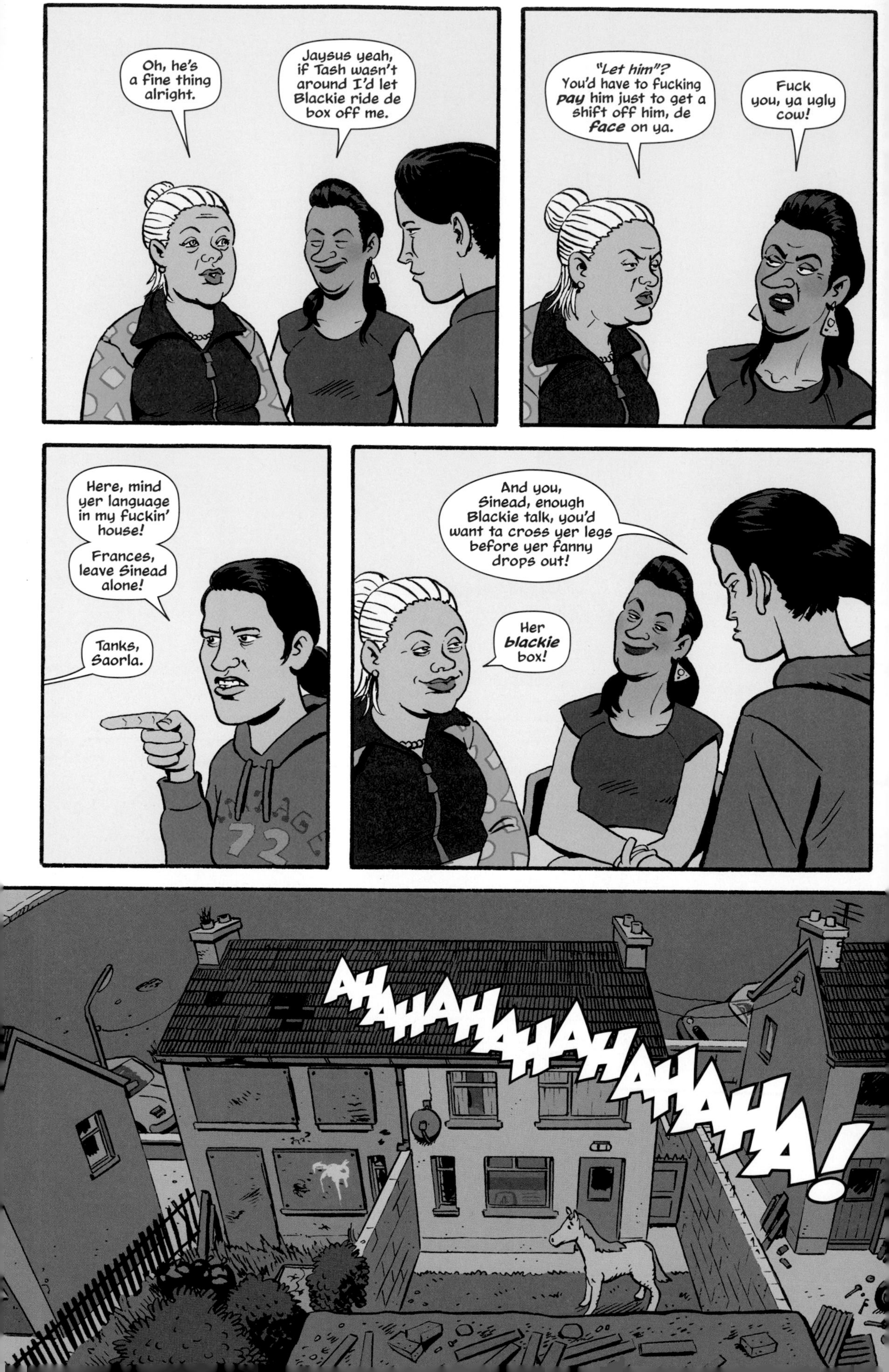
Oh, he's a fine thing alright.
Jaysus yeah, if Tash wasn't around I'd let Blackie ride de box off me.
"Let him"? You'd have to fucking pay him just to get a shift off him, de face on ya.
Fuck you, ya ugly cow!
Here, mind yer language in my fuckin' house!
Frances, leave Sinead alone!
Tanks, Saorla.
And you, Sinead, enough Blackie talk, you'd want ta cross yer legs before yer fanny drops out!
Her blackie box!
AHAHAHAHAHAHAHAHA!

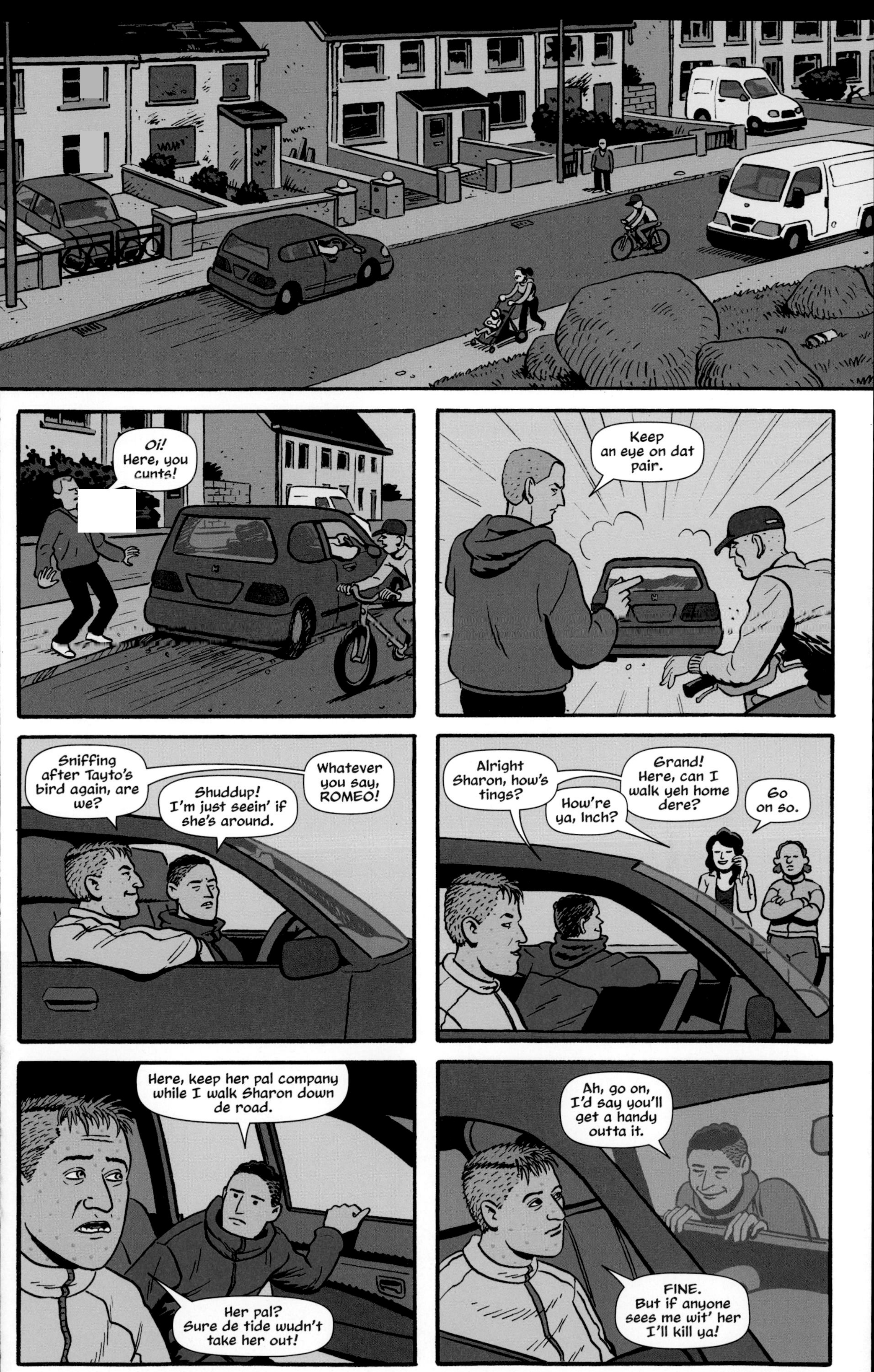
Oi! Here, you cunts!
Keep an eye on dat pair.
Sniffing after Tayto's bird again, are we?
Shuddup! I'm just seein' if she's around.
Whatever you say, ROMEO!
Alright Sharon, how's tings?
How're ya, Inch?
Grand! Here, can I walk yeh home dere?
Go on so.
Here, keep her pal company while I walk Sharon down de road.
Her pal? Sure de tide wudn't take her out!
Ah, go on, I'd say you'll get a handy outta it.
FINE. But if anyone sees me wit' her I'll kill ya!

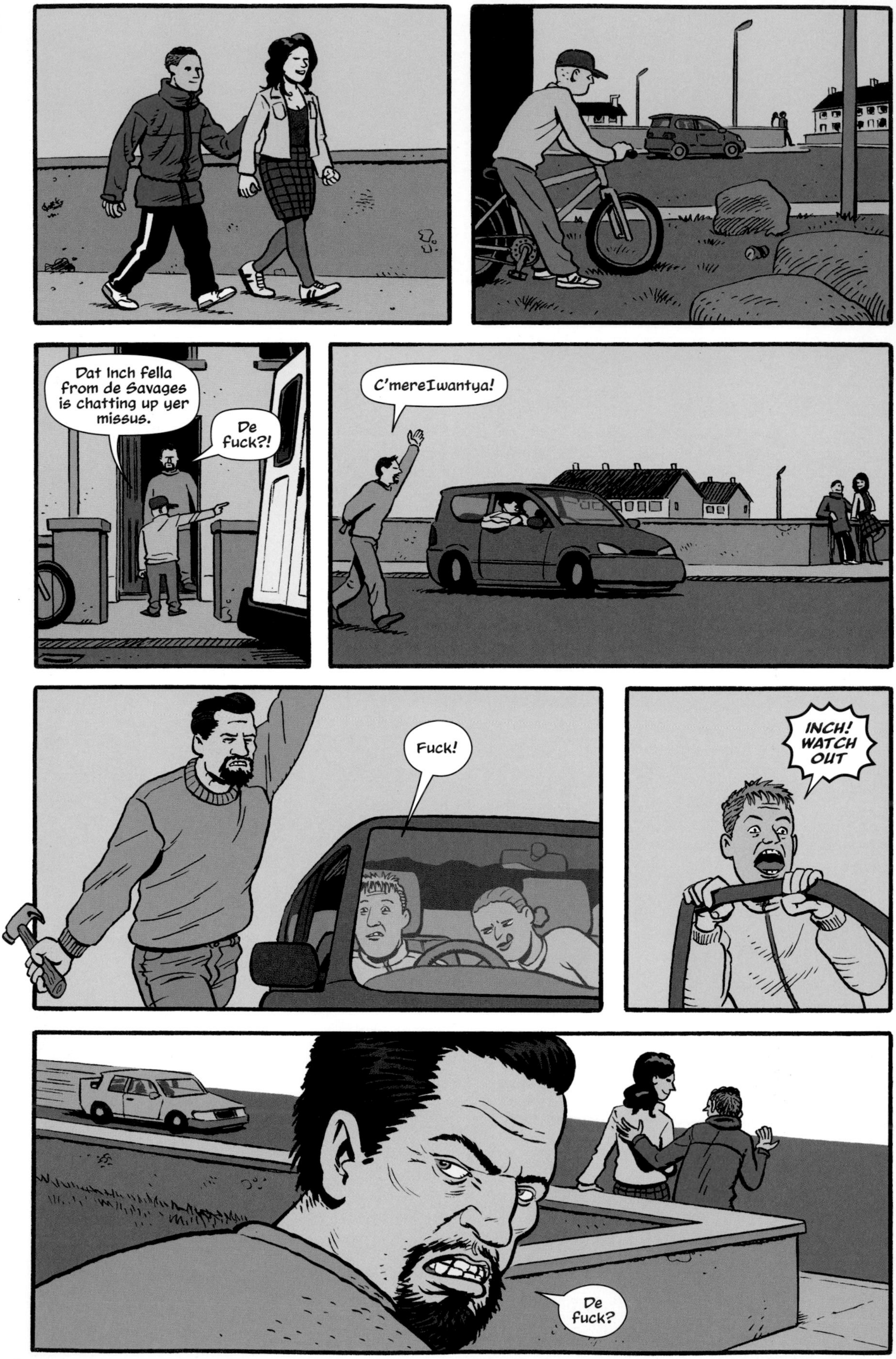
Dat Inch fella from de Savages is chatting up yer missus.
De fuck?!
C'mereIwantya!
Fuck!
INCH! WATCH OUT
De fuck?

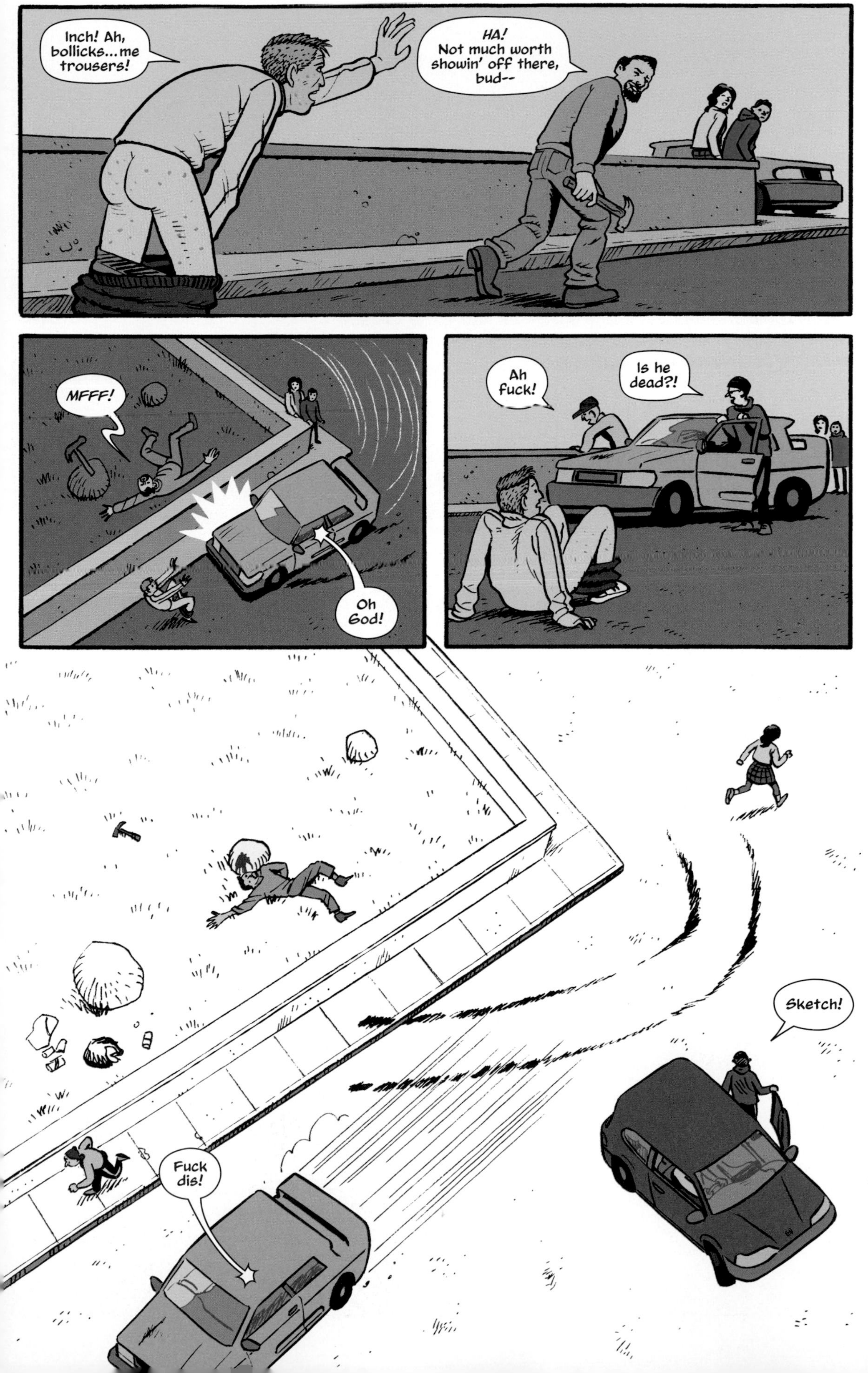
Inch! Ah, bollicks...me trousers!
HA! Not much worth showin' off there, bud--
MFFF!
Oh God!
Ah fuck!
Is he dead?!
Sketch!
Fuck dis!

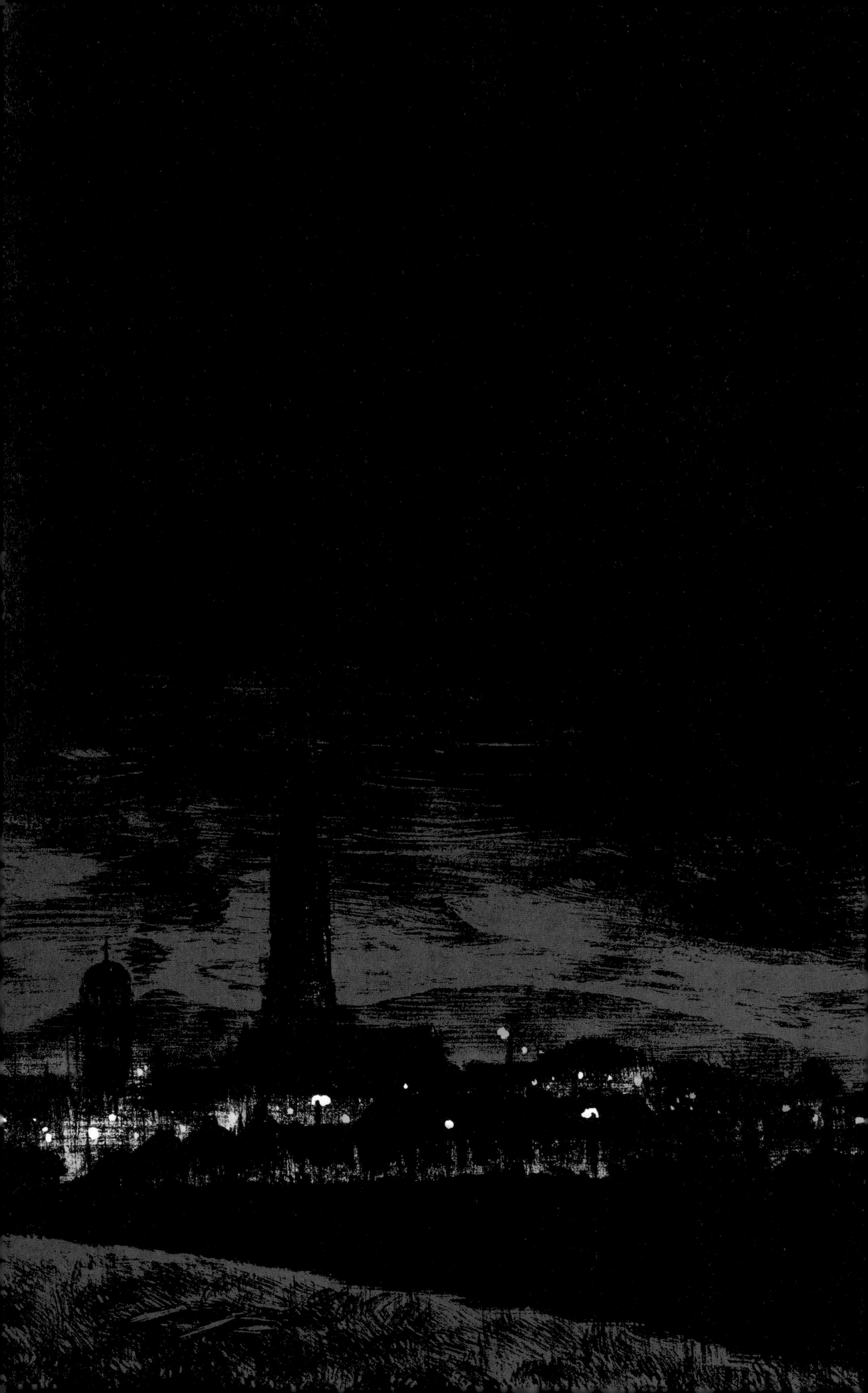

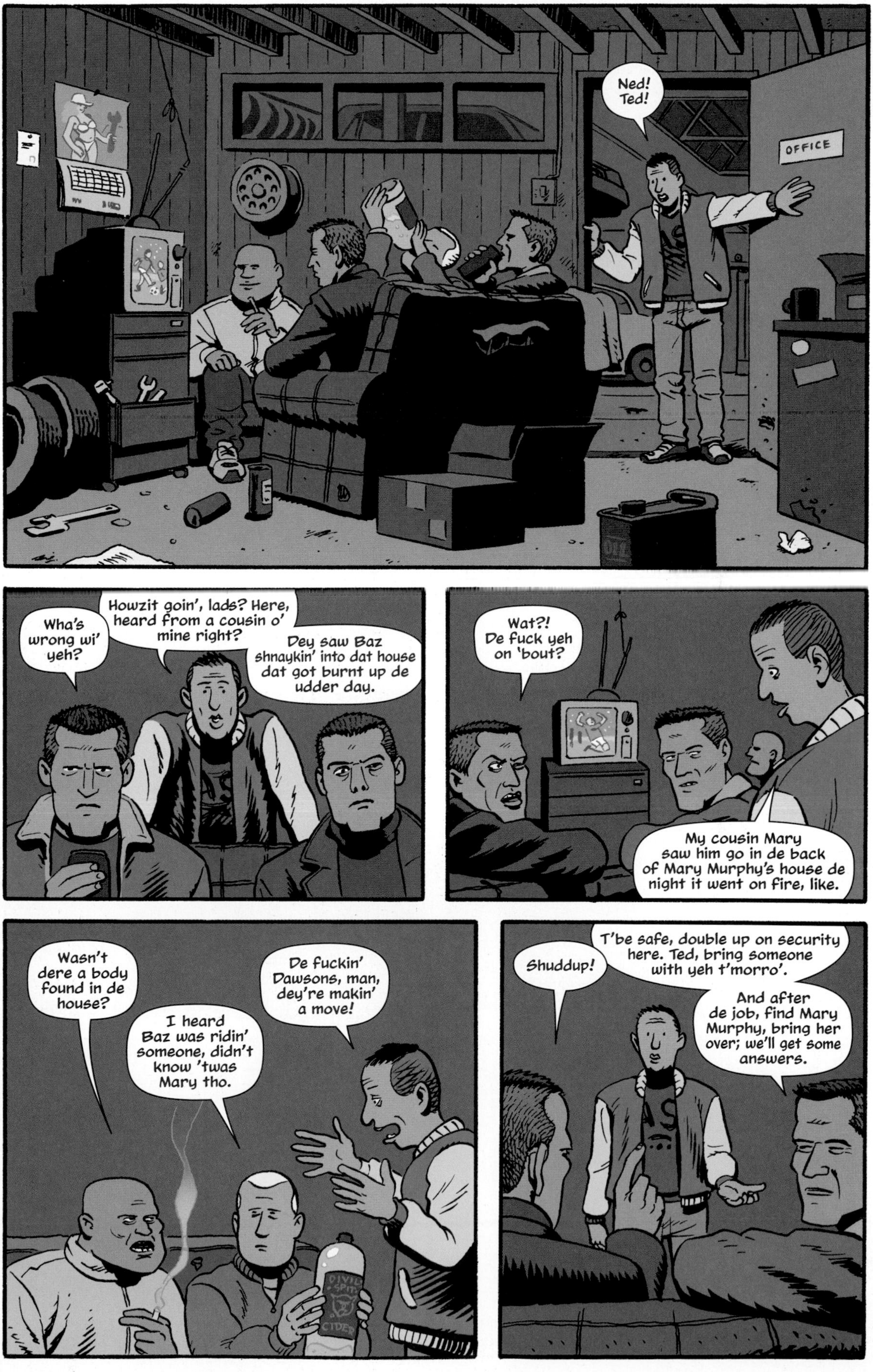
Ned!
Ted!
OFFICE
Wha's wrong wi' yeh?
Howzit goin', lads? Here, heard from a cousin o' mine right?
Dey saw Baz shnaykin' into dat house dat got burnt up de udder day.
Wat?! De fuck yeh on 'bout?
My cousin Mary saw him go in de back of Mary Murphy's house de night it went on fire, like.
Wasn't dere a body found in de house?
I heard Baz was ridin' someone, didn't know 'twas Mary tho.
De fuckin' Dawsons, man, dey're makin' a move!
CIDER
Shuddup!
T'be safe, double up on security here. Ted, bring someone with yeh t'morro'.
And after de job, find Mary Murphy, bring her over; we'll get some answers.

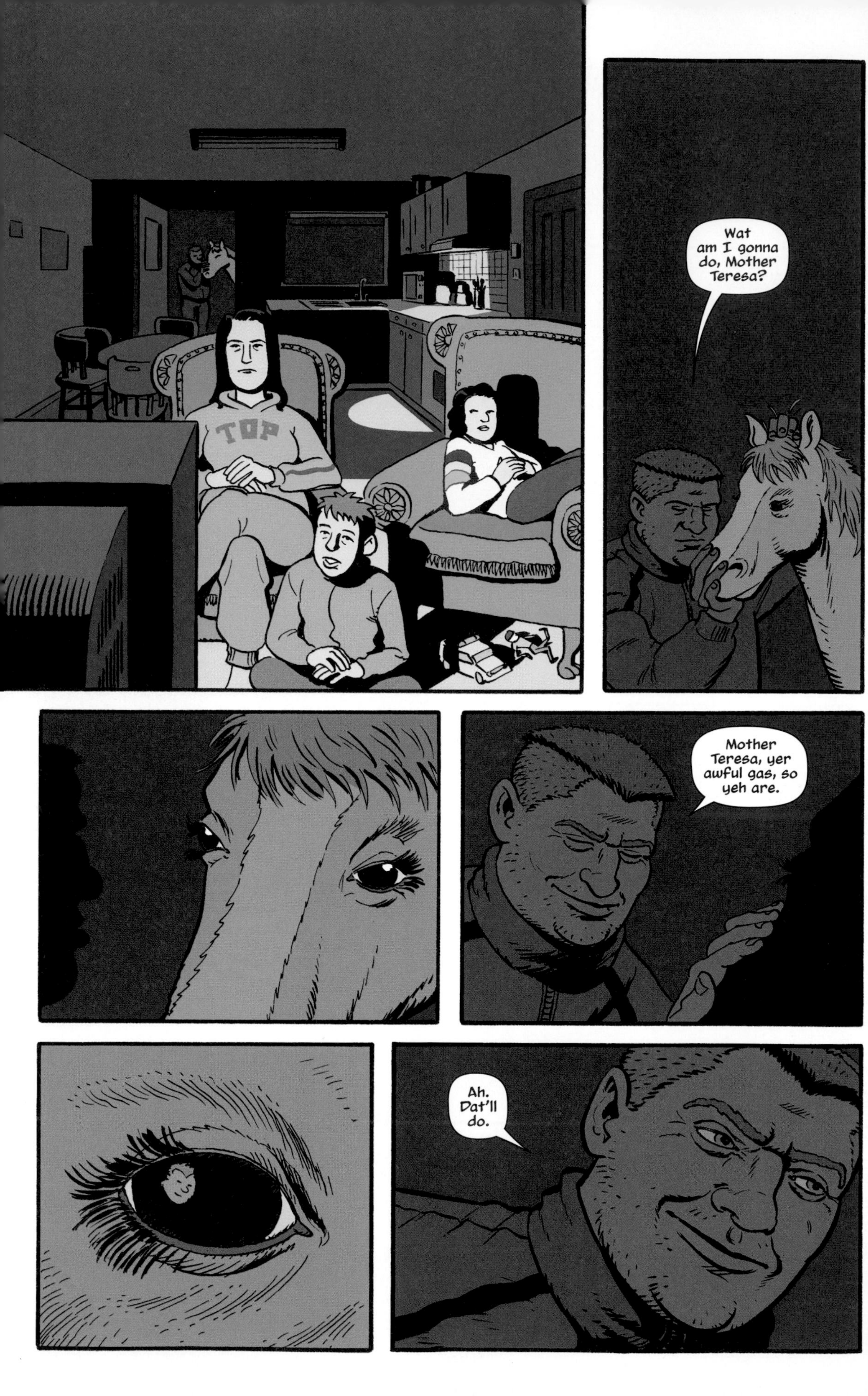
Wat am I gonna do, Mother Teresa?
Mother Teresa, yer awful gas, so yeh are.
Ah. Dat'll do.

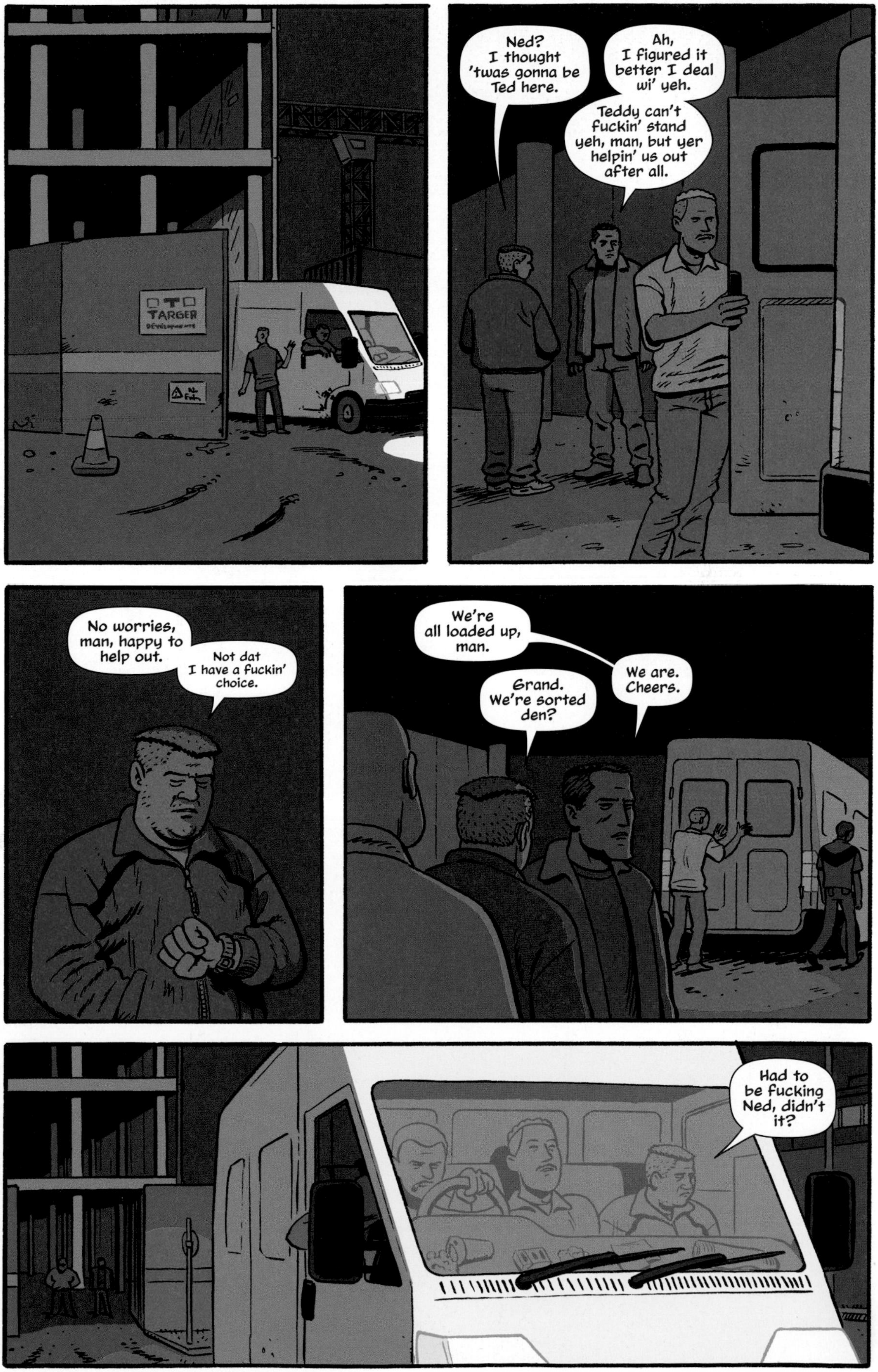
TARGER DÉVELOPPEMENTS
Ned? I thought 'twas gonna be Ted here.
Ah, I figured it better I deal wi' yeh.
Teddy can't fuckin' stand yeh, man, but yer helpin' us out after all.
No worries, man, happy to help out.
Not dat I have a fuckin' choice.
We're all loaded up, man.
We are. Cheers.
Grand. We're sorted den?
Had to be fucking Ned, didn't it?

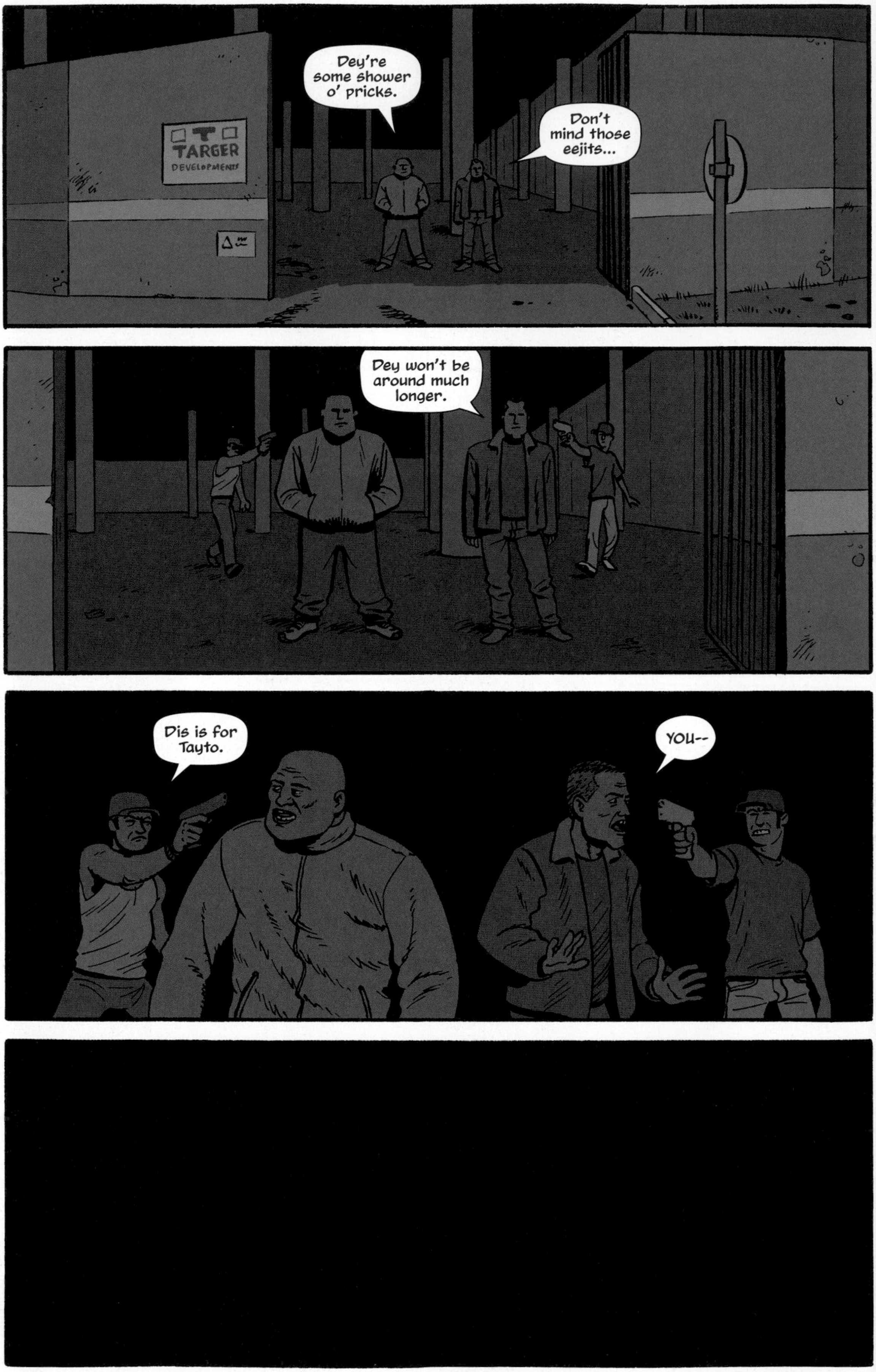
TARGER DEVELOPMENTS
Dey're some shower o' pricks.
Don't mind those eejits...
Dey won't be around much longer.
Dis is for Tayto.
YOU--

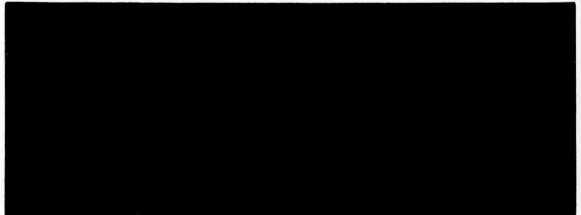

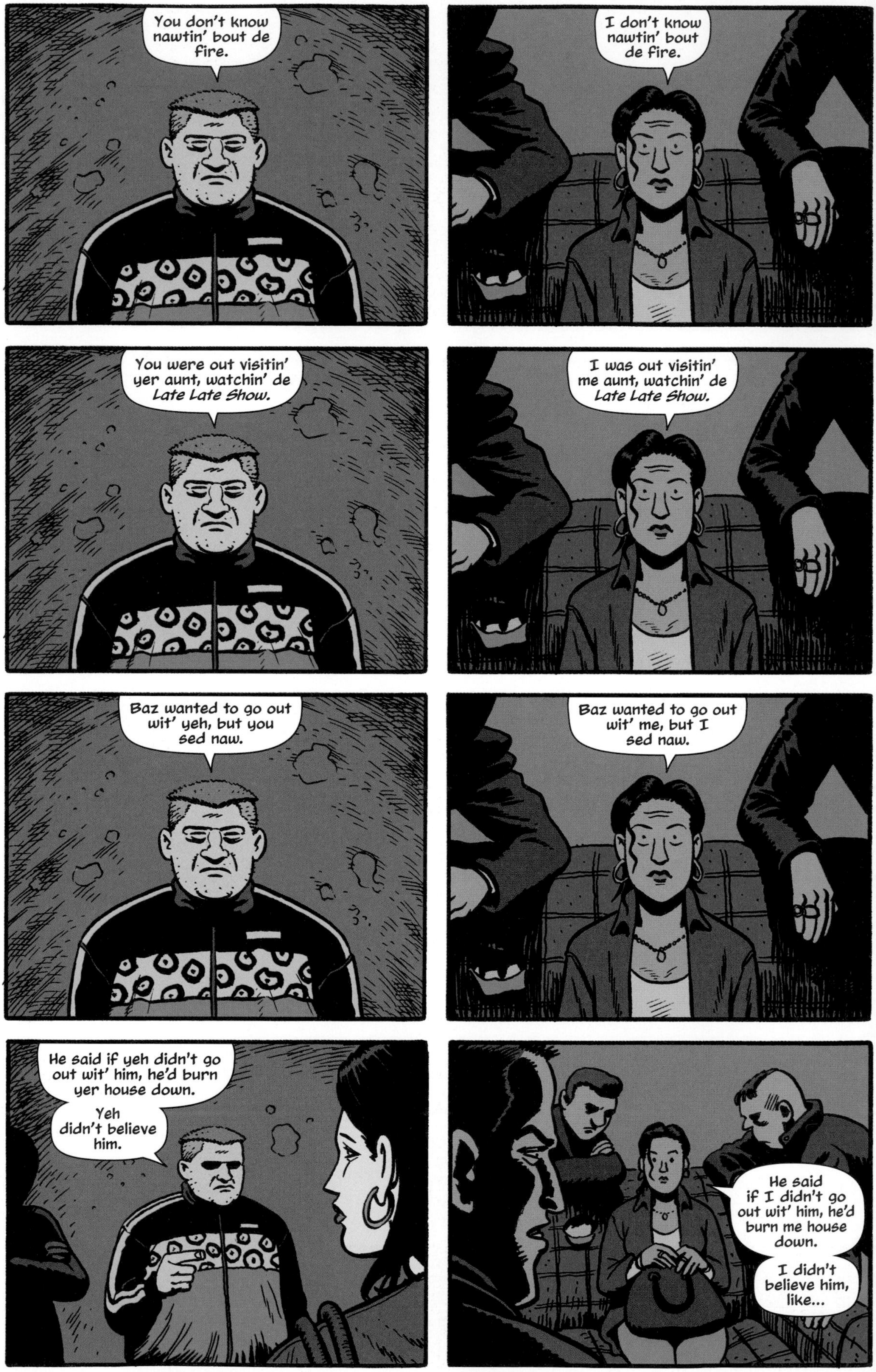
You don't know nawtin' bout de fire.
I don't know nawtin' bout de fire.
You were out visitin' yer aunt, watchin' de *Late Late Show.*
I was out visitin' me aunt, watchin' de *Late Late Show.*
Baz wanted to go out wit' yeh, but you sed naw.
Baz wanted to go out wit' me, but I sed naw.
He said if yeh didn't go out wit' him, he'd burn yer house down.
Yeh didn't believe him.
He said if I didn't go out wit' him, he'd burn me house down.
I didn't believe him, like...

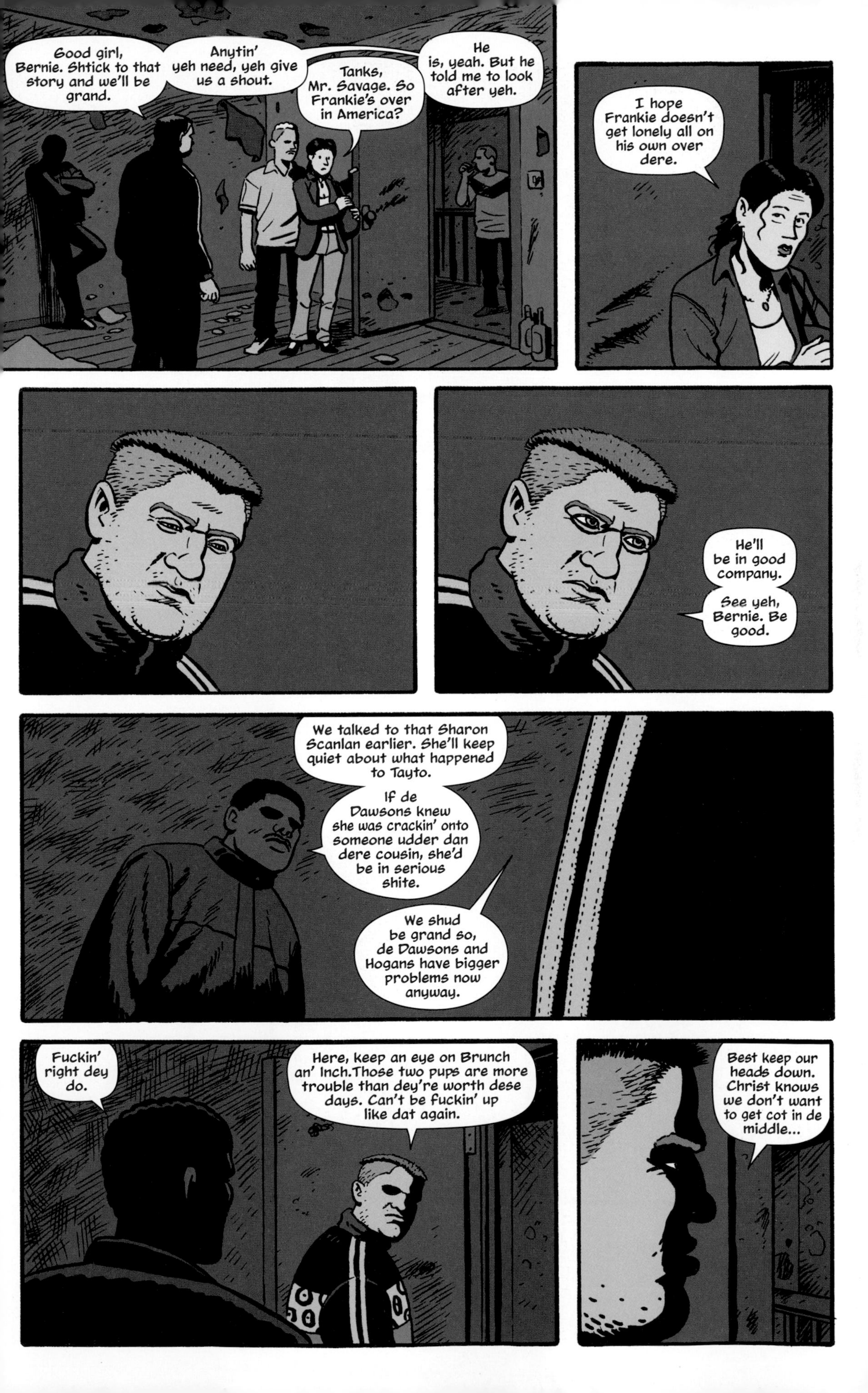

Good girl, Bernie. Shtick to that story and we'll be grand.
Anytin' yeh need, yeh give us a shout.
Tanks, Mr. Savage. So Frankie's over in America?
He is, yeah. But he told me to look after yeh.
I hope Frankie doesn't get lonely all on his own over dere.
He'll be in good company.
See yeh, Bernie. Be good.
We talked to that Sharon Scanlan earlier. She'll keep quiet about what happened to Tayto.
If de Dawsons knew she was crackin' onto someone udder dan dere cousin, she'd be in serious shite.
We shud be grand so, de Dawsons and Hogans have bigger problems now anyway.
Fuckin' right dey do.
Here, keep an eye on Brunch an' Inch.Those two pups are more trouble than dey're worth dese days. Can't be fuckin' up like dat again.
Best keep our heads down. Christ knows we don't want to get cot in de middle...

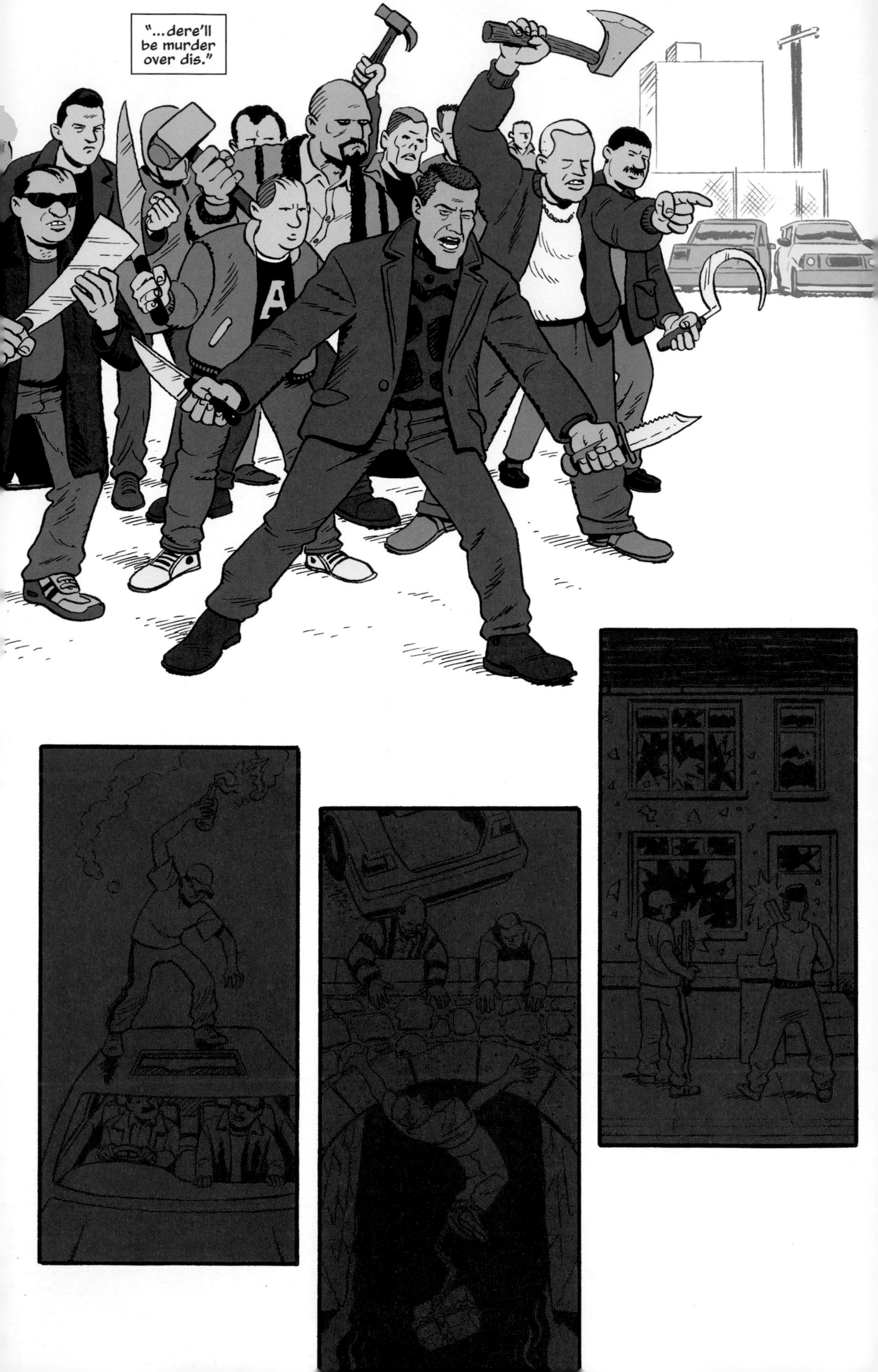
"...dere'll be murder over dis."

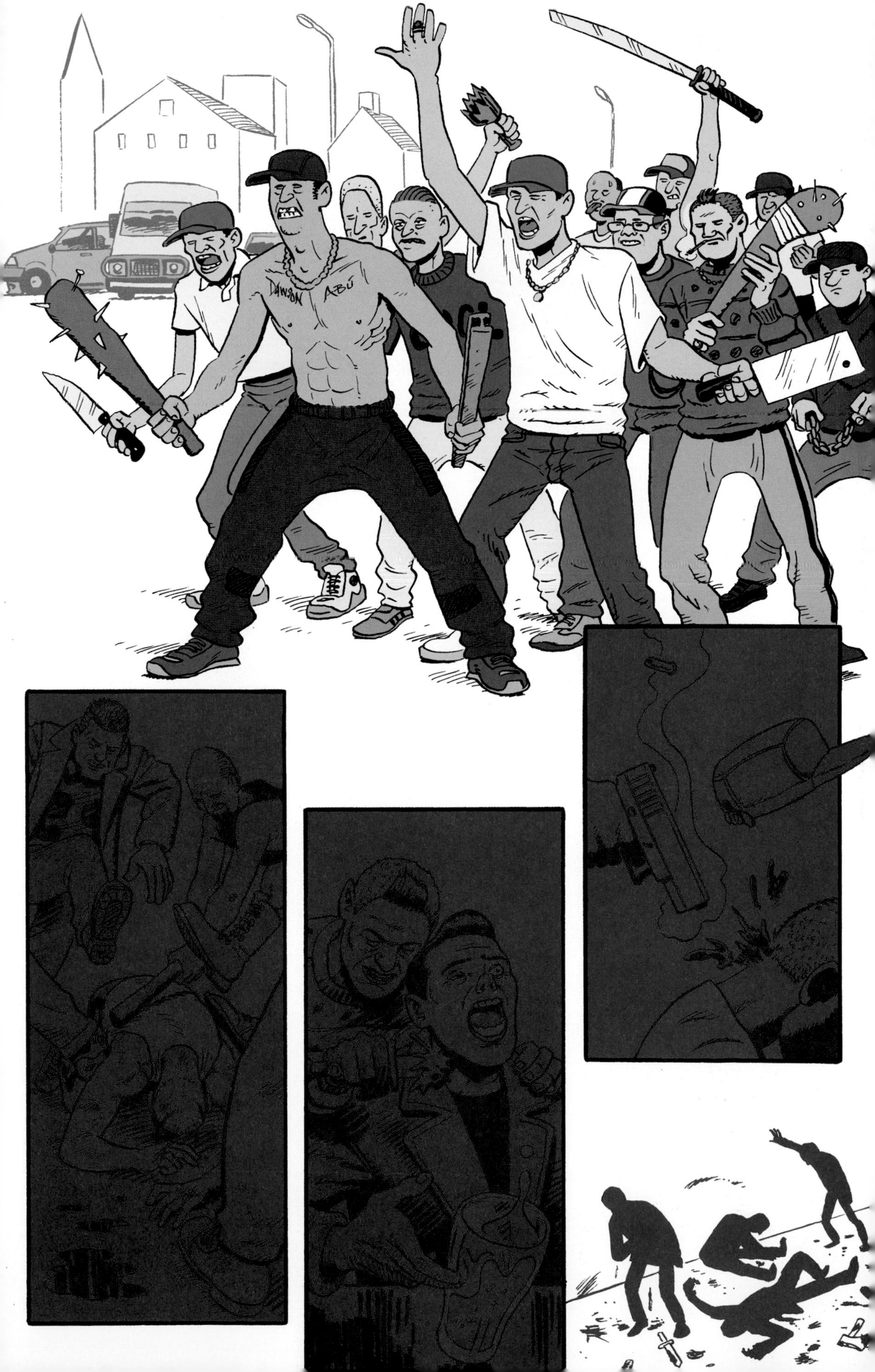
DAWSON
ABÚ

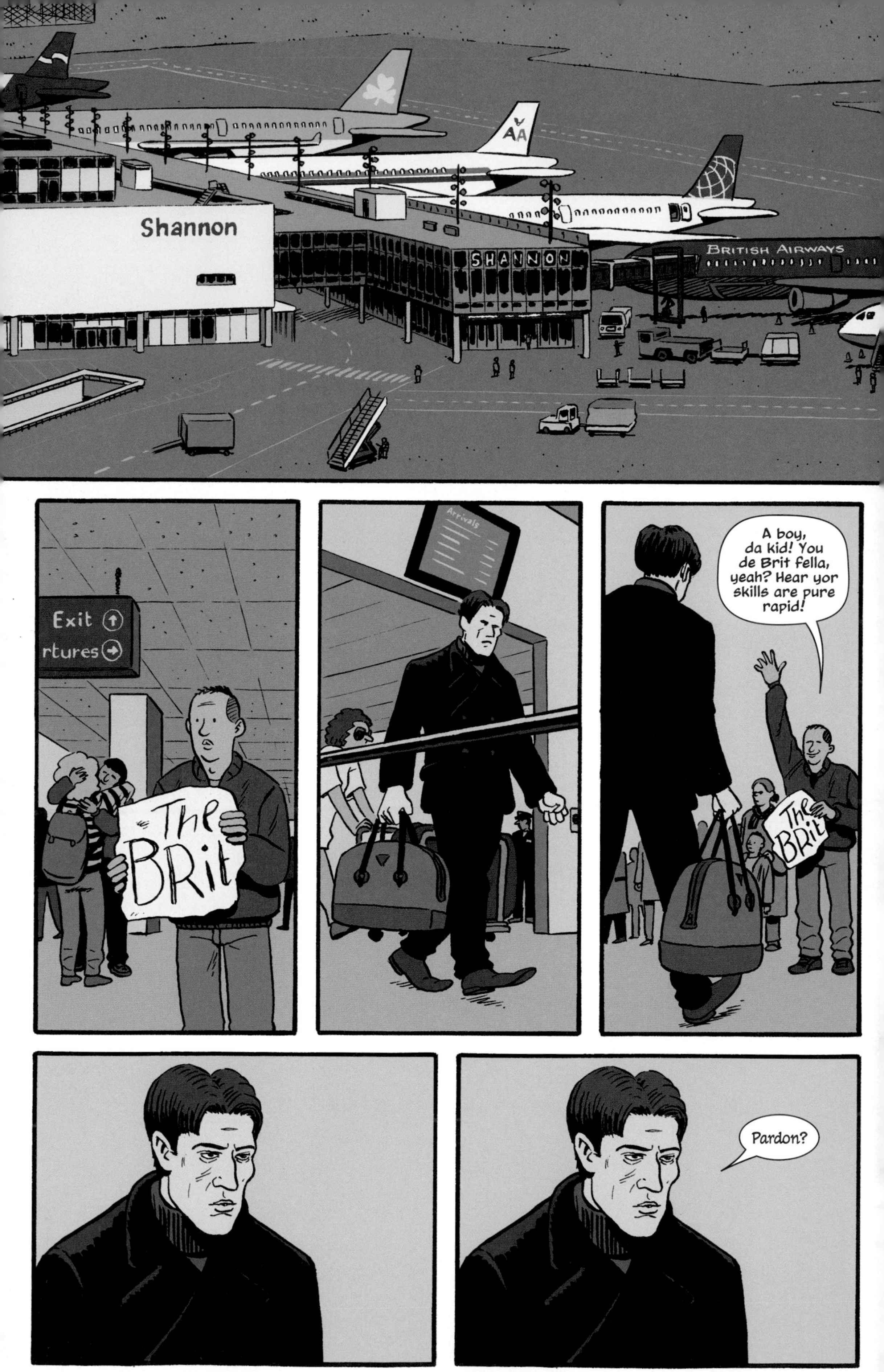
Shannon
SHANNON
BRITISH AIRWAYS
Exit
rtures
The Brit
Arrivals
A boy, da kid! You de Brit fella, yeah? Hear yor skills are pure rapid!
The Brit
Pardon?

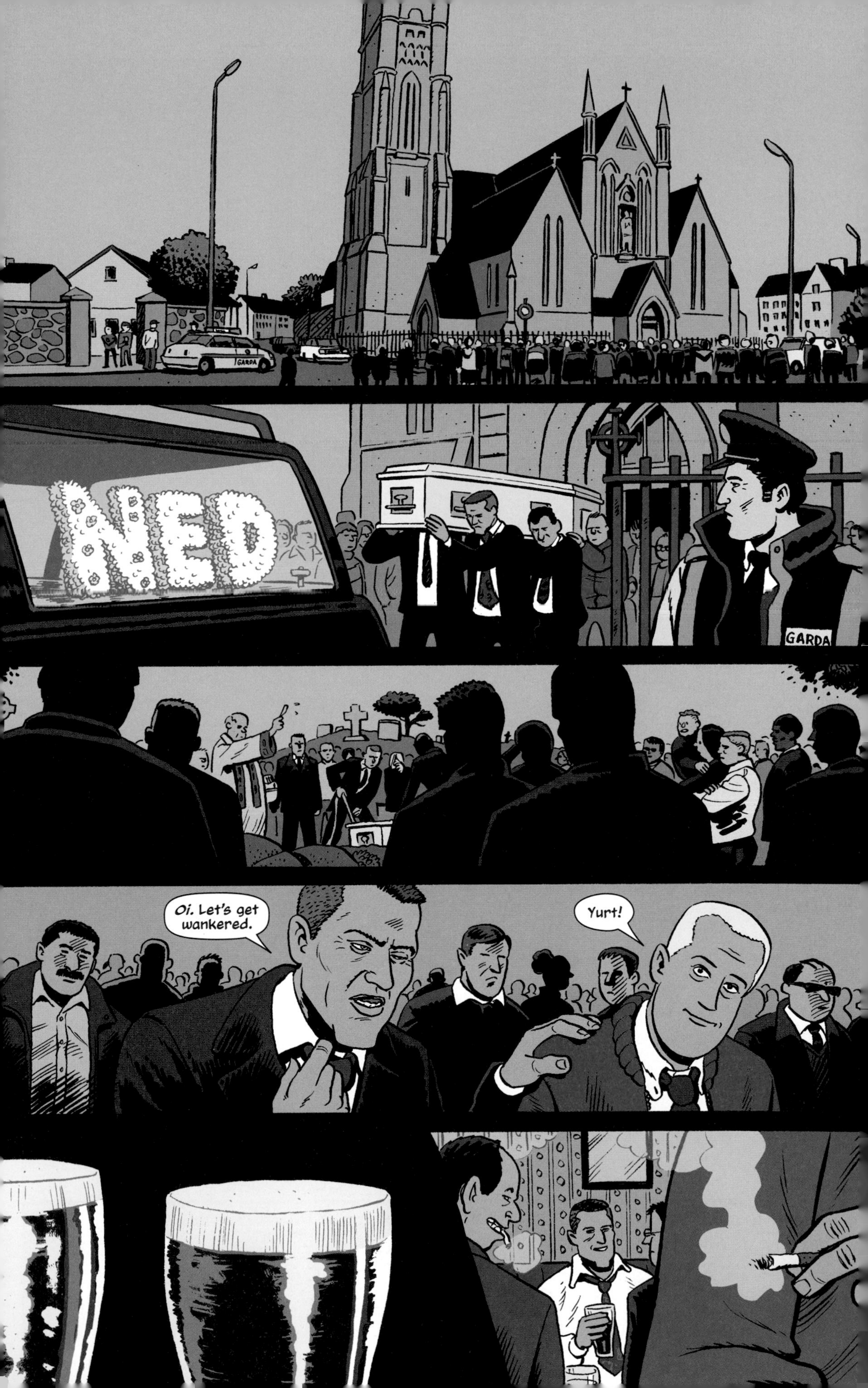
GARDA
NED
GARDA
Oi. Let's get wankered.
Yurt!

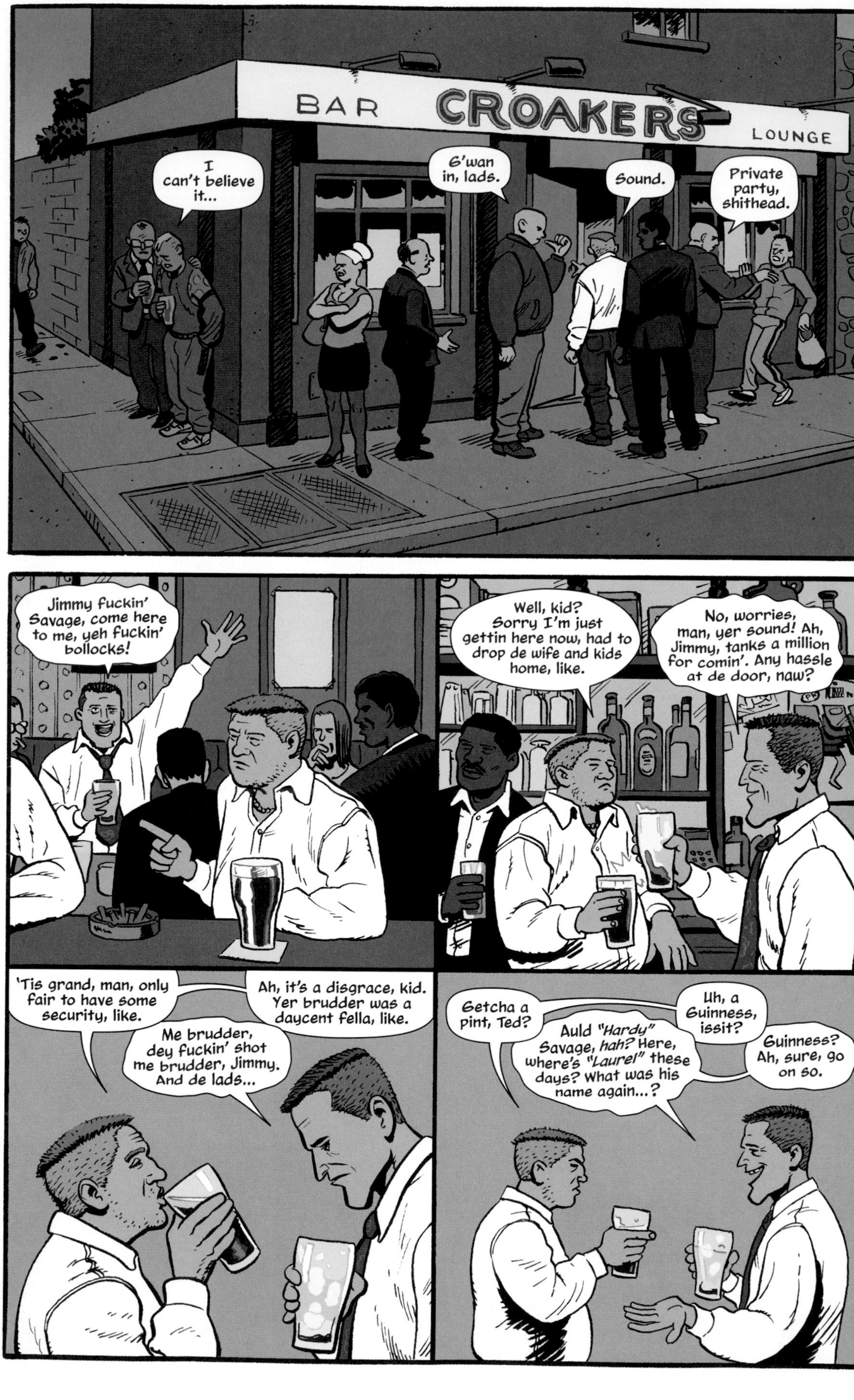
BAR
CROAKERS
LOUNGE
I can't believe it...
G'wan in, lads.
Sound.
Private party, shithead.
Jimmy fuckin' Savage, come here to me, yeh fuckin' bollocks!
Well, kid? Sorry I'm just gettin here now, had to drop de wife and kids home, like.
No, worries, man, yer sound! Ah, Jimmy, tanks a million for comin'. Any hassle at de door, naw?
'Tis grand, man, only fair to have some security, like.
Ah, it's a disgrace, kid. Yer brudder was a daycent fella, like.
Me brudder, dey fuckin' shot me brudder, Jimmy. And de lads...
Getcha a pint, Ted?
Uh, a Guinness, issit?
Auld *"Hardy"* Savage, *hah?* Here, where's *"Laurel"* these days? What was his name again...?
Guinness? Ah, sure, go on so.

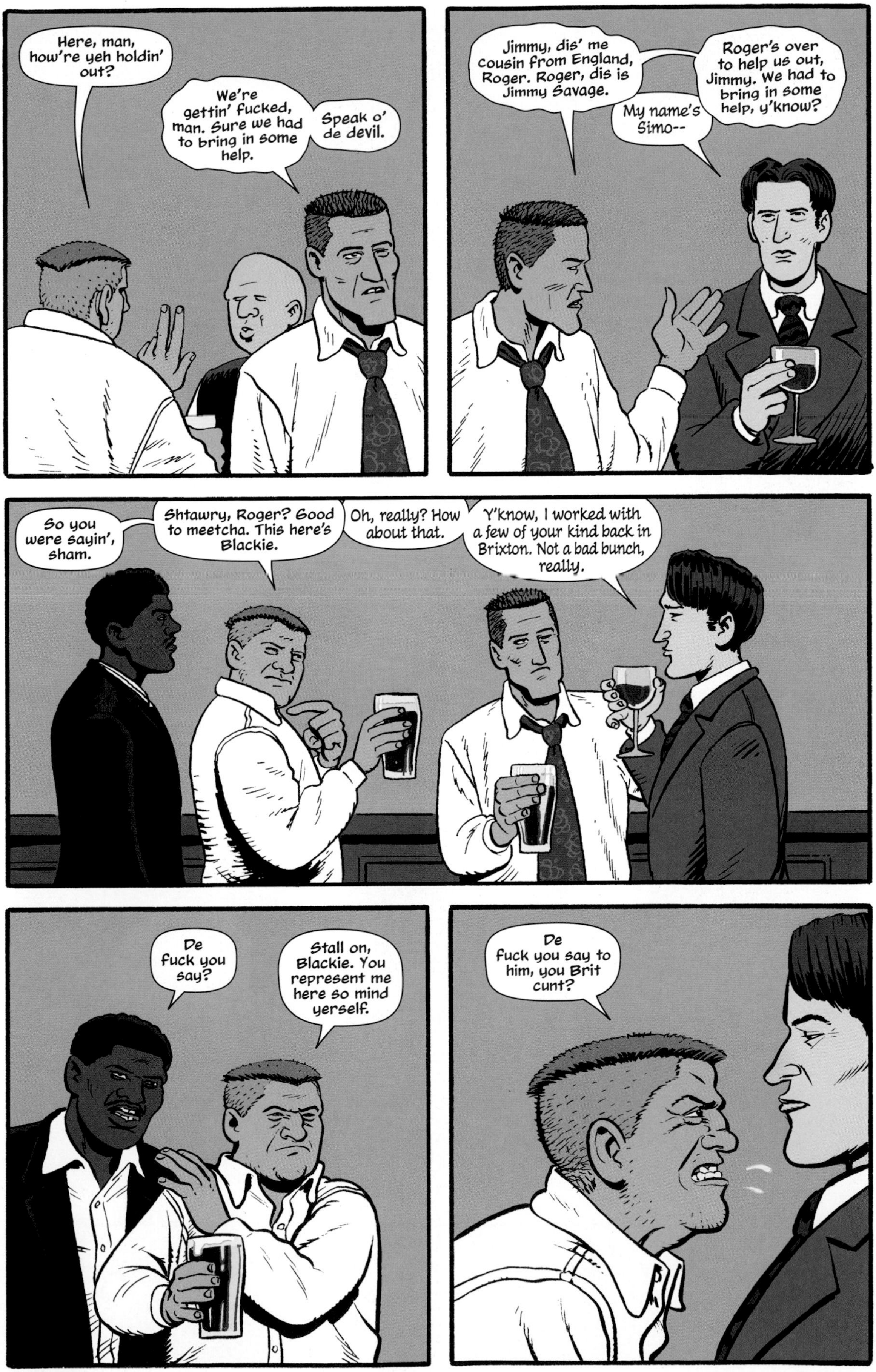
Here, man, how're yeh holdin' out?
We're gettin' fucked, man. Sure we had to bring in some help.
Speak o' de devil.
Jimmy, dis' me cousin from England, Roger. Roger, dis is Jimmy Savage.
My name's Simo--
Roger's over to help us out, Jimmy. We had to bring in some help, y'know?
So you were sayin', sham.
Shtawry, Roger? Good to meetcha. This here's Blackie.
Oh, really? How about that.
Y'know, I worked with a few of your kind back in Brixton. Not a bad bunch, really.
De fuck you say?
Stall on, Blackie. You represent me here so mind yerself.
De fuck you say to him, you Brit cunt?

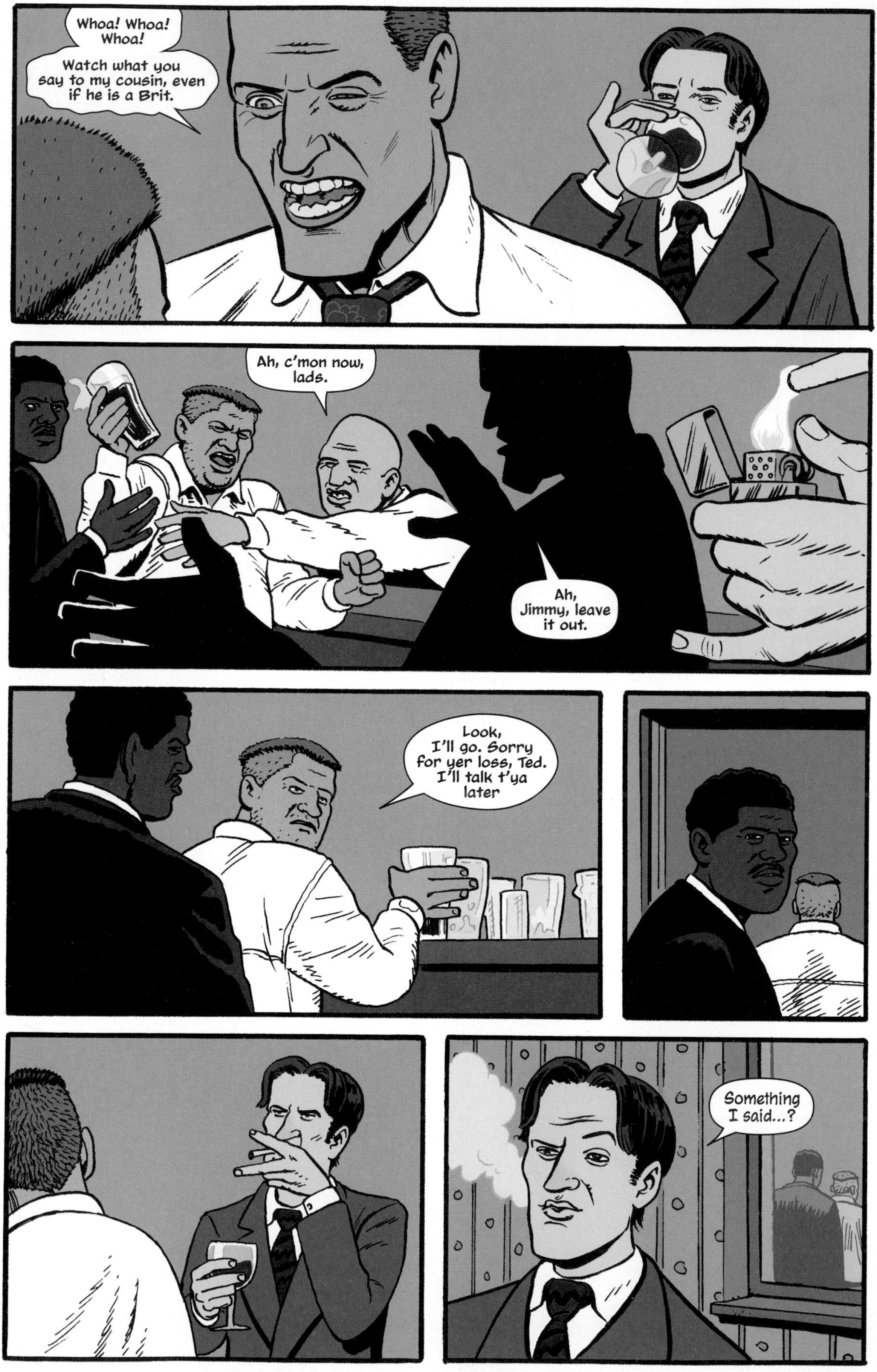

Whoa! Whoa! Whoa!
Watch what you say to my cousin, even if he is a Brit.
Ah, c'mon now, lads.
Ah, Jimmy, leave it out.
Look, I'll go. Sorry for yer loss, Ted. I'll talk t'ya later
Something I said...?

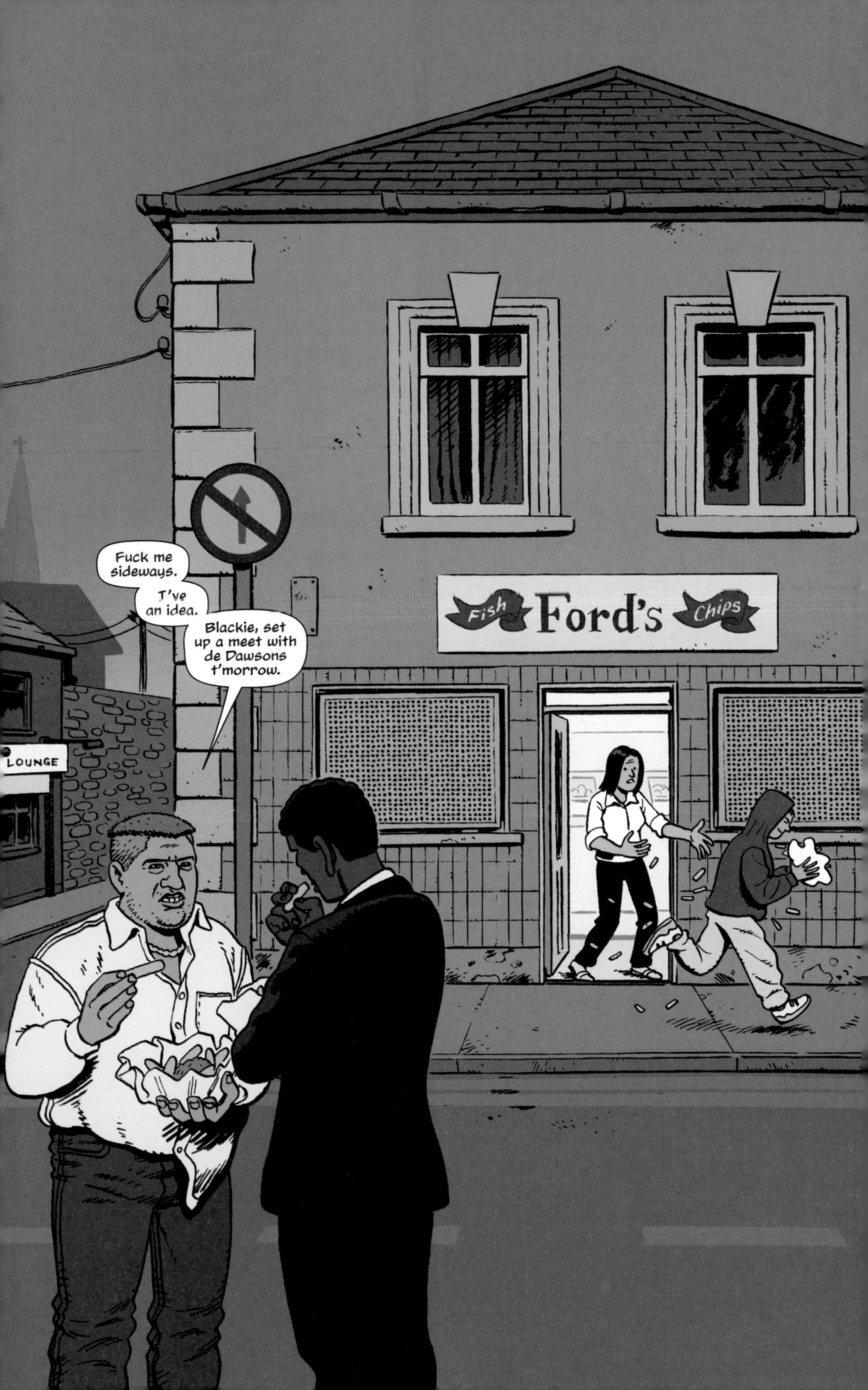
Fuck me sideways.
I've an idea.
Blackie, set up a meet with de Dawsons t'morrow.
Fish Ford's Chips
LOUNGE

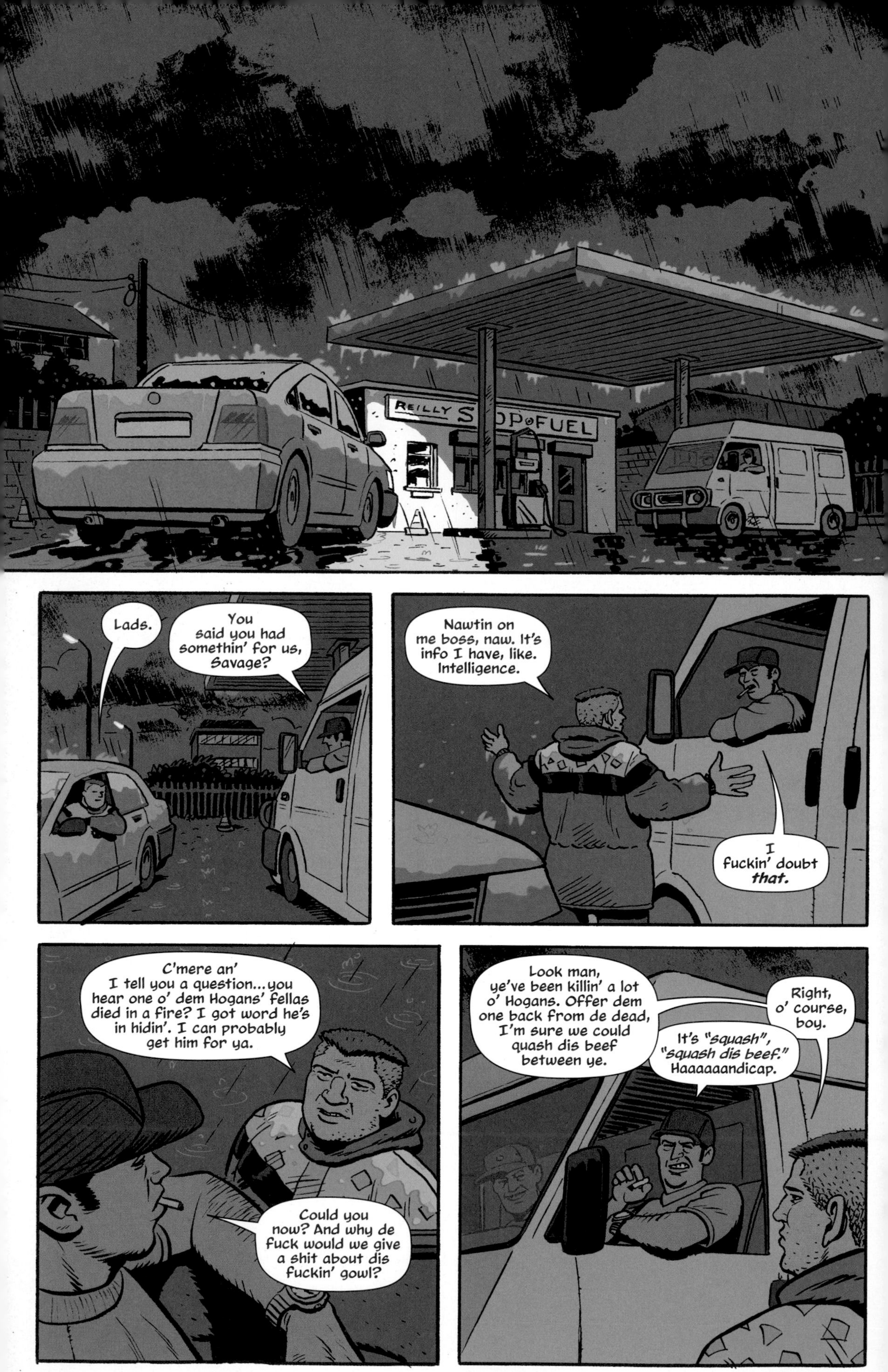
REILLY SHOP FUEL
Lads.
You said you had somethin' for us, Savage?
Nawtin on me boss, naw. It's info I have, like. Intelligence.
I fuckin' doubt *that.*
C'mere an' I tell you a question... you hear one o' dem Hogans' fellas died in a fire? I got word he's in hidin'. I can probably get him for ya.
Could you now? And why de fuck would we give a shit about dis fuckin' gowl?
Look man, ye've been killin' a lot o' Hogans. Offer dem one back from de dead, I'm sure we could quash dis beef between ye.
It's "*squash*", "*squash dis beef.*" Haaaaaandicap.
Right, o' course, boy.

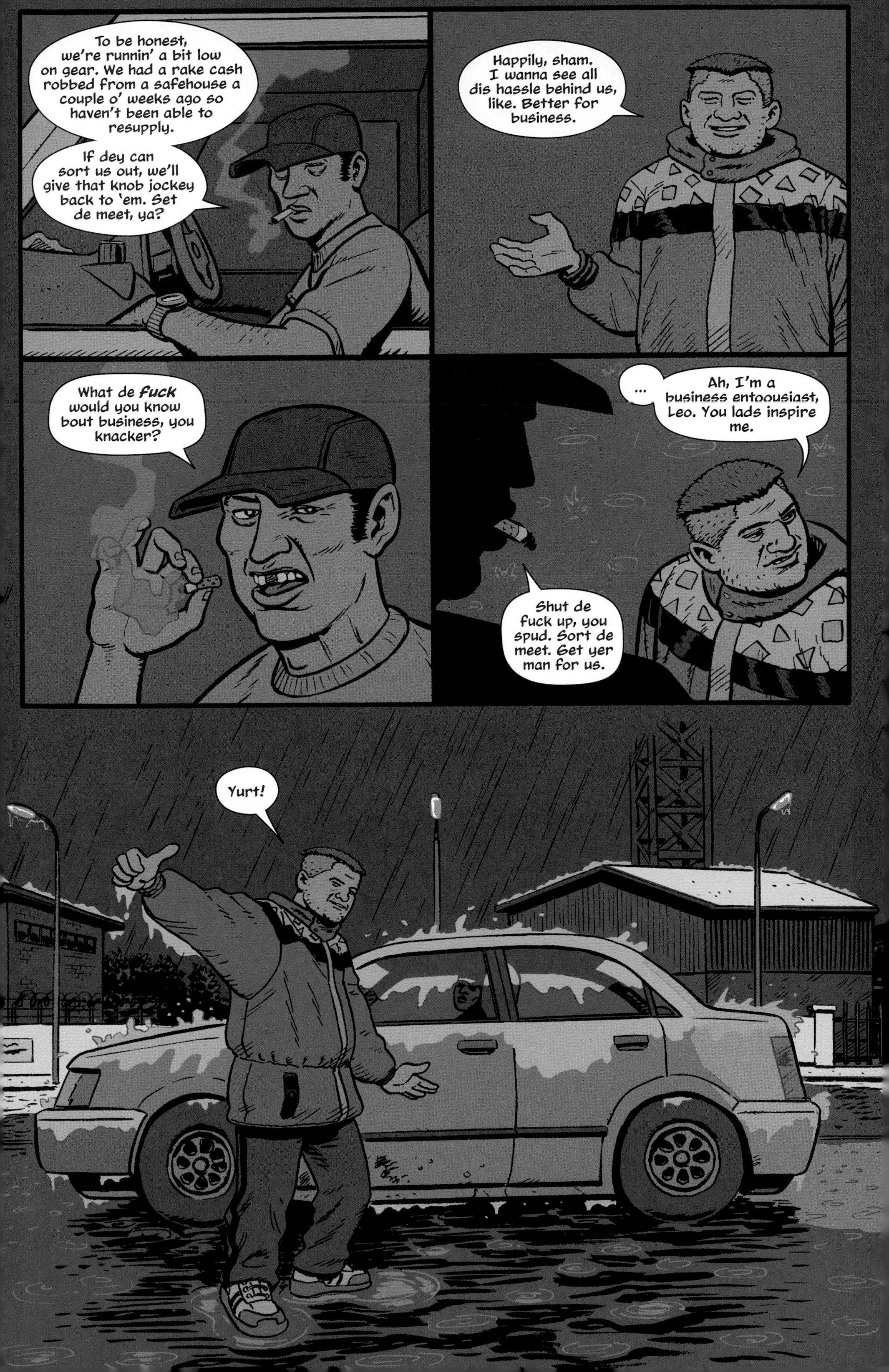
To be honest, we're runnin' a bit low on gear. We had a rake cash robbed from a safehouse a couple o' weeks ago so haven't been able to resupply.
If dey can sort us out, we'll give that knob jockey back to 'em. Set de meet, ya?
Happily, sham. I wanna see all dis hassle behind us, like. Better for business.
What de *fuck* would you know bout business, you knacker?
...
Ah, I'm a business entoousiast, Leo. You lads inspire me.
Shut de fuck up, you spud. Sort de meet. Get yer man for us.
Yurt!

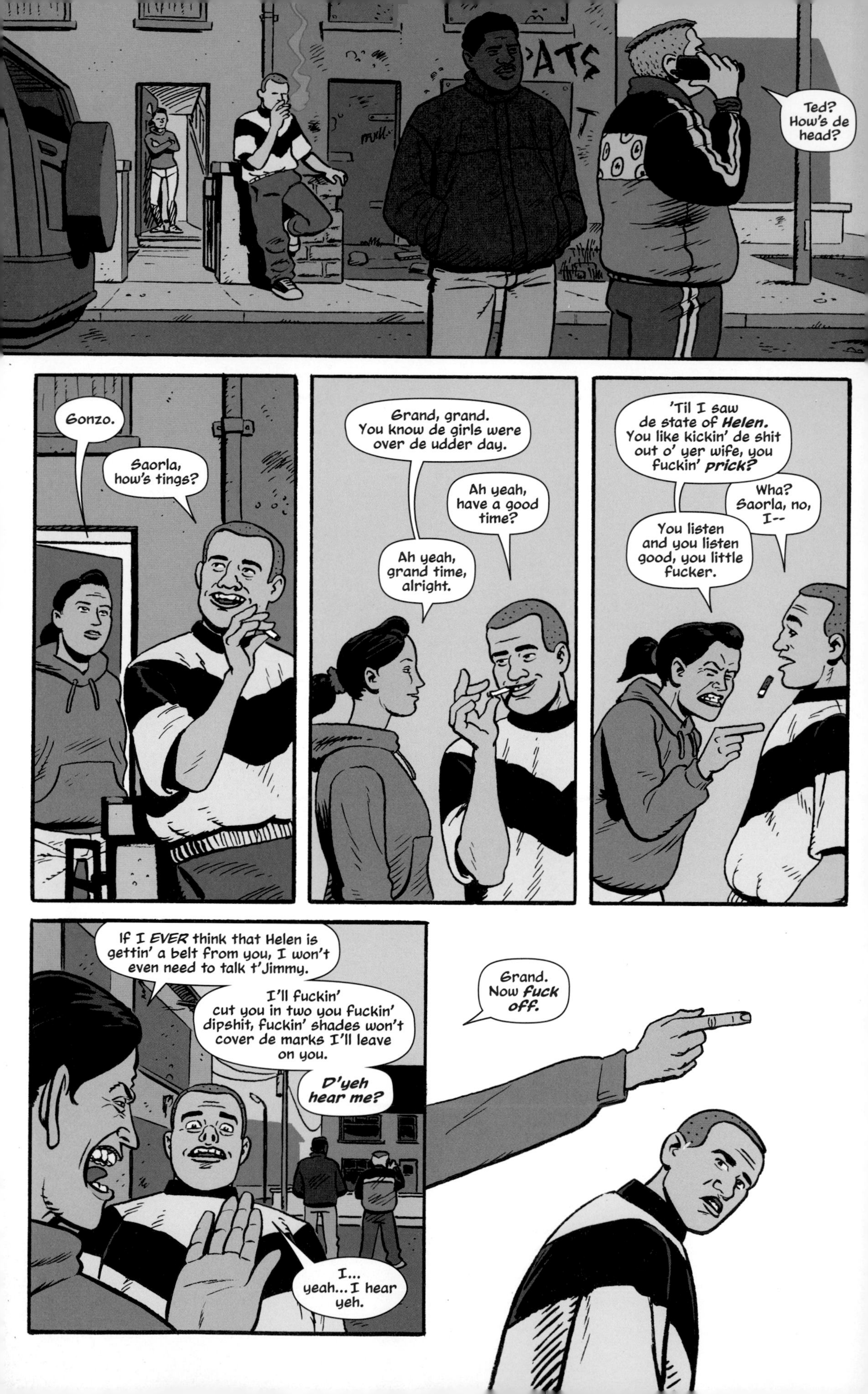

Ted? How's de head?
Gonzo.
Saorla, how's tings?
Grand, grand. You know de girls were over de udder day.
Ah yeah, have a good time?
Ah yeah, grand time, alright.
'Til I saw de state of Helen. You like kickin' de shit out o' yer wife, you fuckin' prick?
Wha? Saorla, no, I--
You listen and you listen good, you little fucker.
If I EVER think that Helen is gettin' a belt from you, I won't even need to talk t'Jimmy.
I'll fuckin' cut you in two you fuckin' dipshit, fuckin' shades won't cover de marks I'll leave on you.
D'yeh hear me?
I... yeah... I hear yeh.
Grand. Now fuck off.

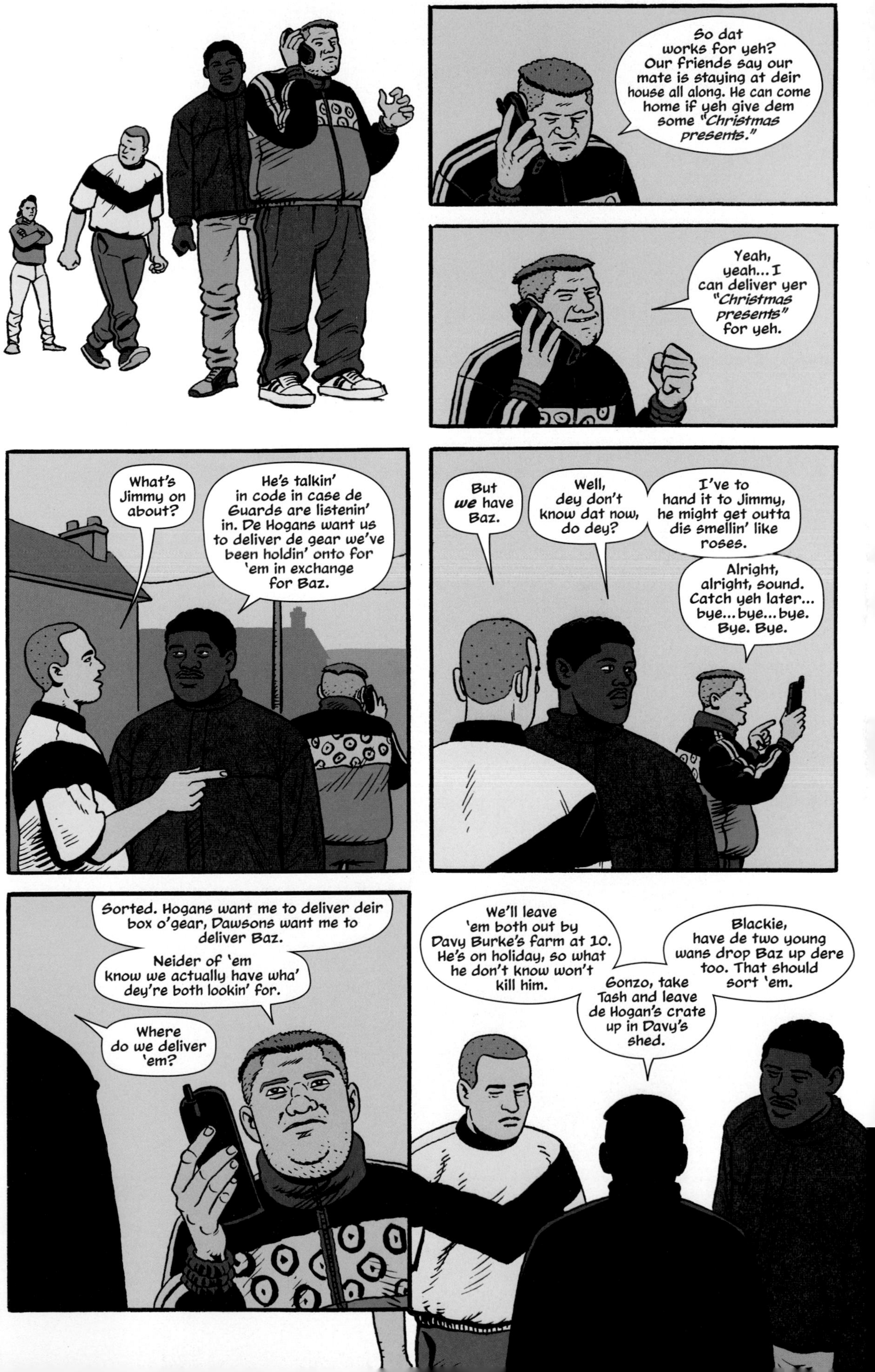
So dat works for yeh? Our friends say our mate is staying at deir house all along. He can come home if yeh give dem some "Christmas presents."
Yeah, yeah... I can deliver yer "Christmas presents" for yeh.
What's Jimmy on about?
He's talkin' in code in case de Guards are listenin' in. De Hogans want us to deliver de gear we've been holdin' onto for 'em in exchange for Baz.
But we have Baz.
Well, dey don't know dat now, do dey?
I've to hand it to Jimmy, he might get outta dis smellin' like roses.
Alright, alright, sound. Catch yeh later... bye... bye... bye. Bye. Bye.
Sorted. Hogans want me to deliver deir box o'gear, Dawsons want me to deliver Baz.
Neider of 'em know we actually have wha' dey're both lookin' for.
Where do we deliver 'em?
We'll leave 'em both out by Davy Burke's farm at 10. He's on holiday, so what he don't know won't kill him.
Gonzo, take Tash and leave de Hogan's crate up in Davy's shed.
Blackie, have de two young wans drop Baz up dere too. That should sort 'em.

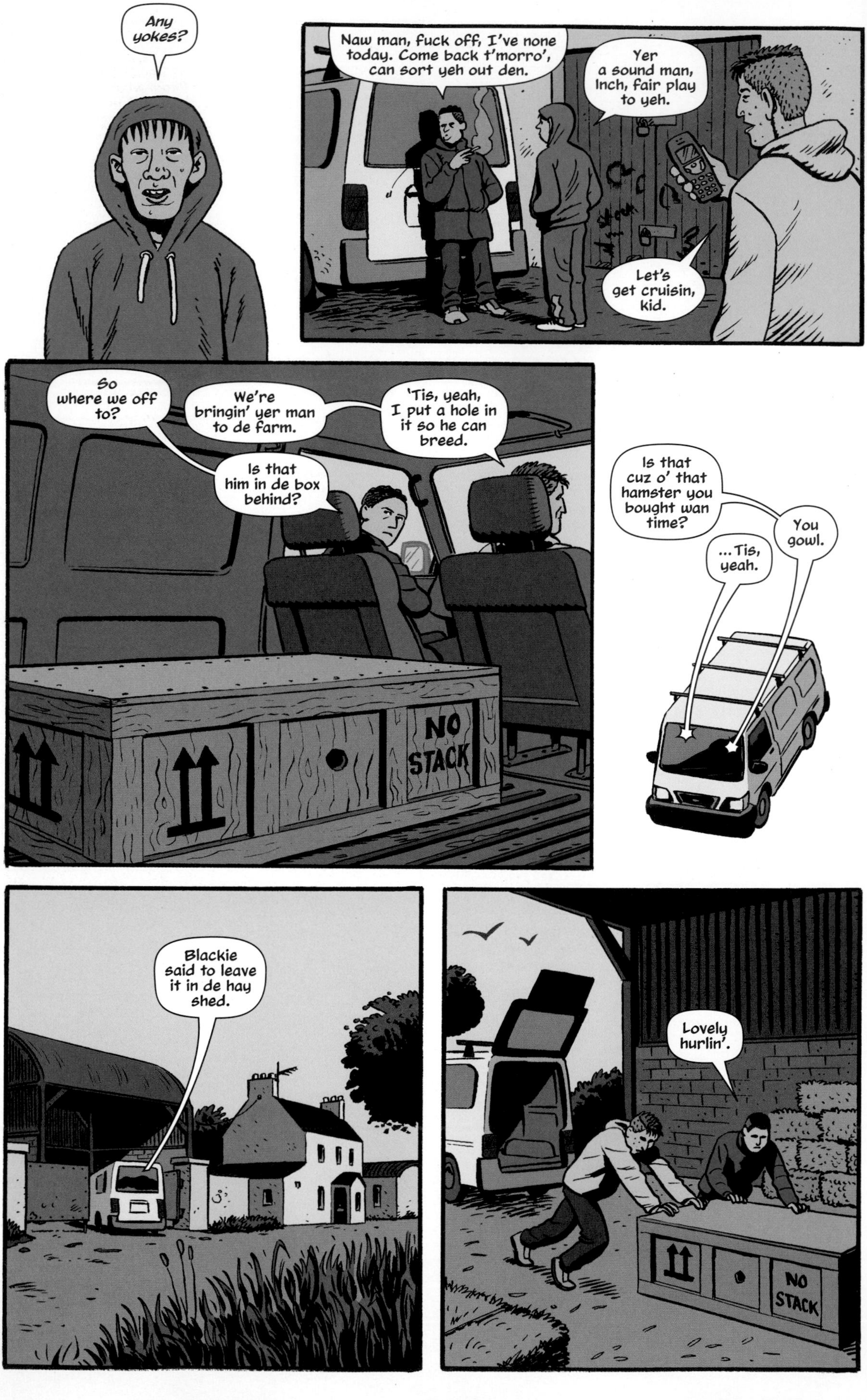
Any yokes?
Naw man, fuck off, I've none today. Come back t'morro', can sort yeh out den.
Yer a sound man, Inch, fair play to yeh.
Let's get cruisin, kid.
So where we off to?
We're bringin' yer man to de farm.
Is that him in de box behind?
'Tis, yeah, I put a hole in it so he can breed.
Is that cuz o' that hamster you bought wan time?
...Tis, yeah.
You gowl.
NO STACK
Blackie said to leave it in de hay shed.
Lovely hurlin'.
NO STACK

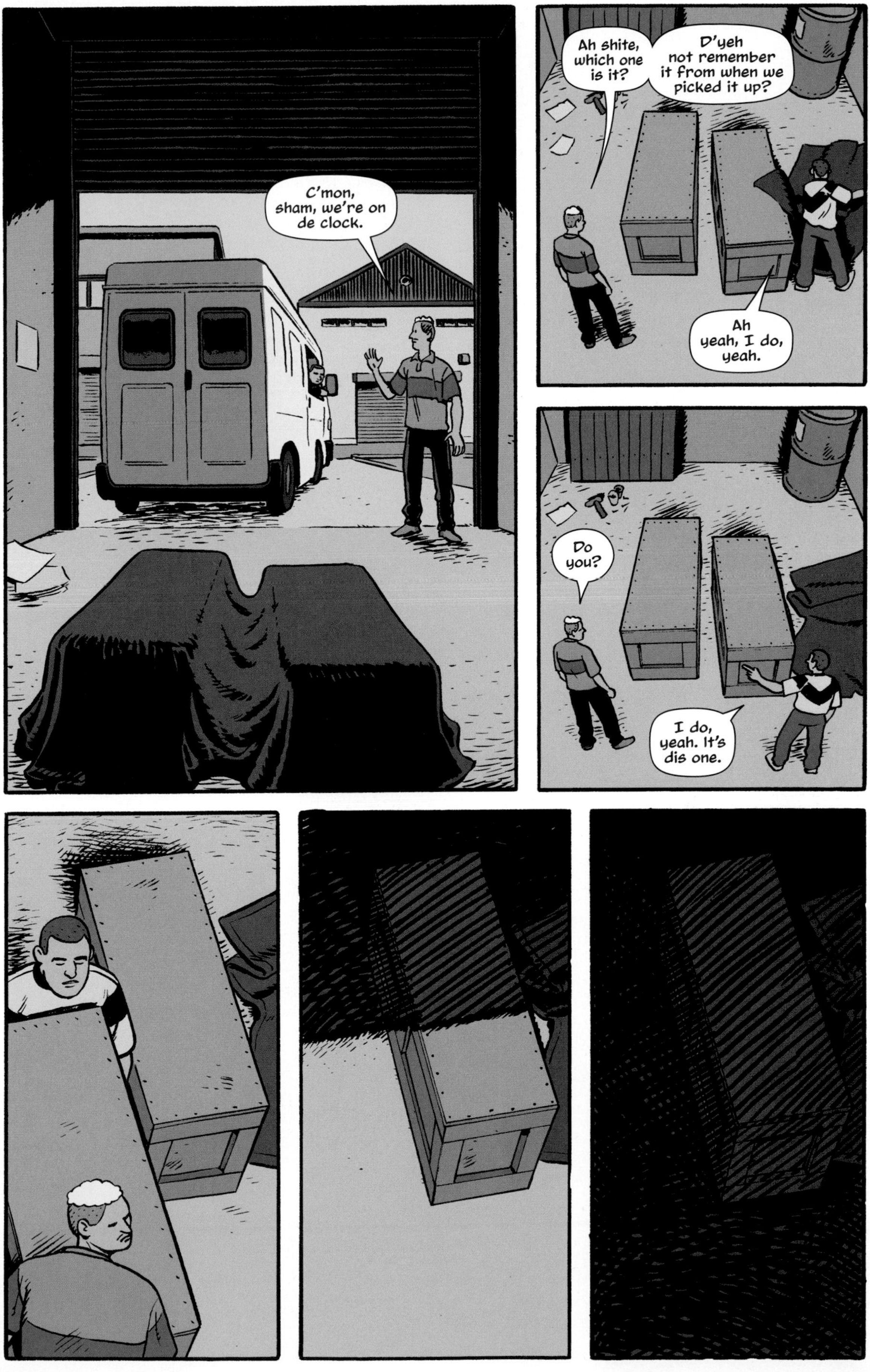
C'mon, sham, we're on de clock.
Ah shite, which one is it?
D'yeh not remember it from when we picked it up?
Ah yeah, I do, yeah.
Do you?
I do, yeah. It's dis one.

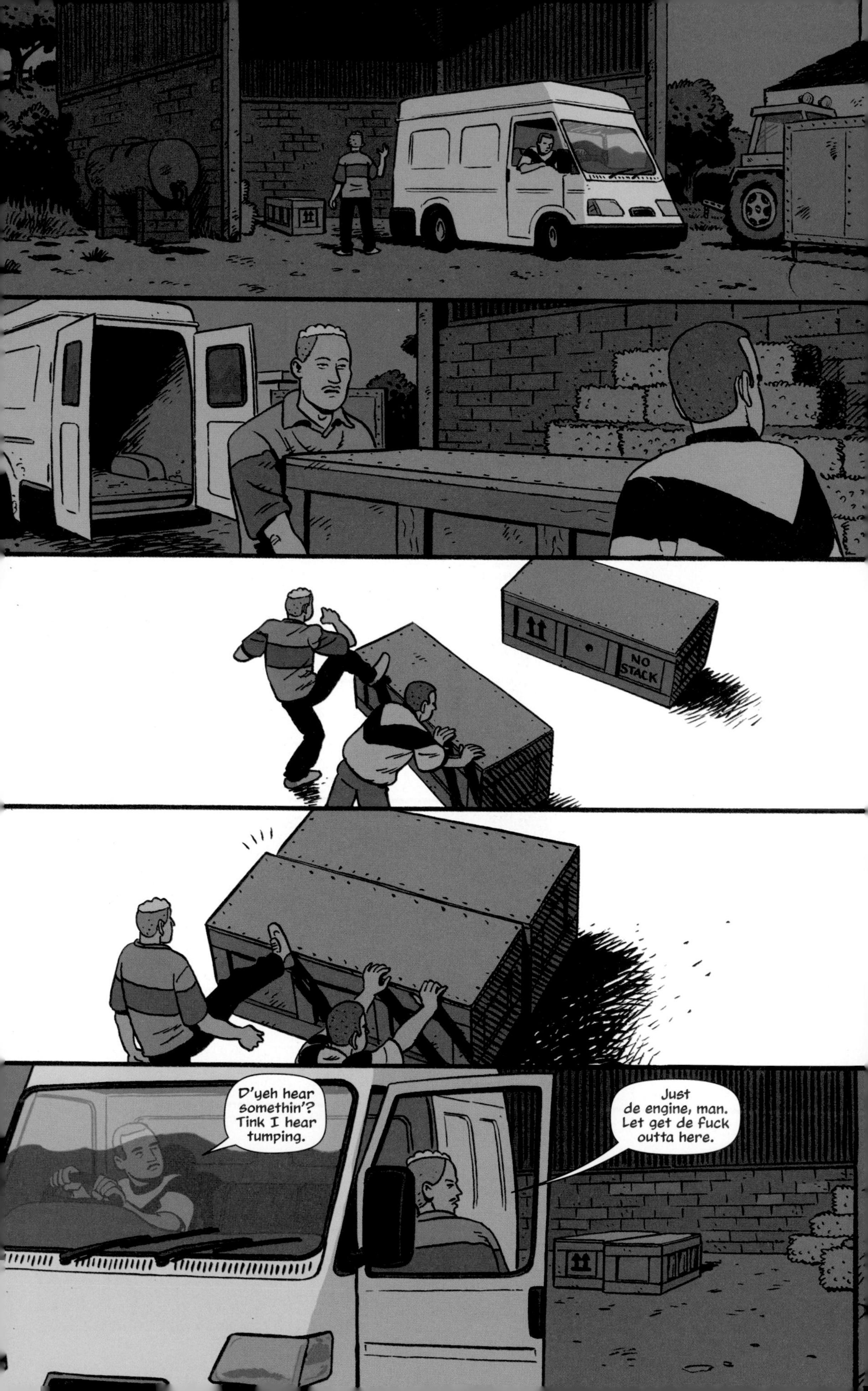
NO STACK
D'yeh hear somethin'? Tink I hear tumping.
Just de engine, man. Let get de fuck outta here.

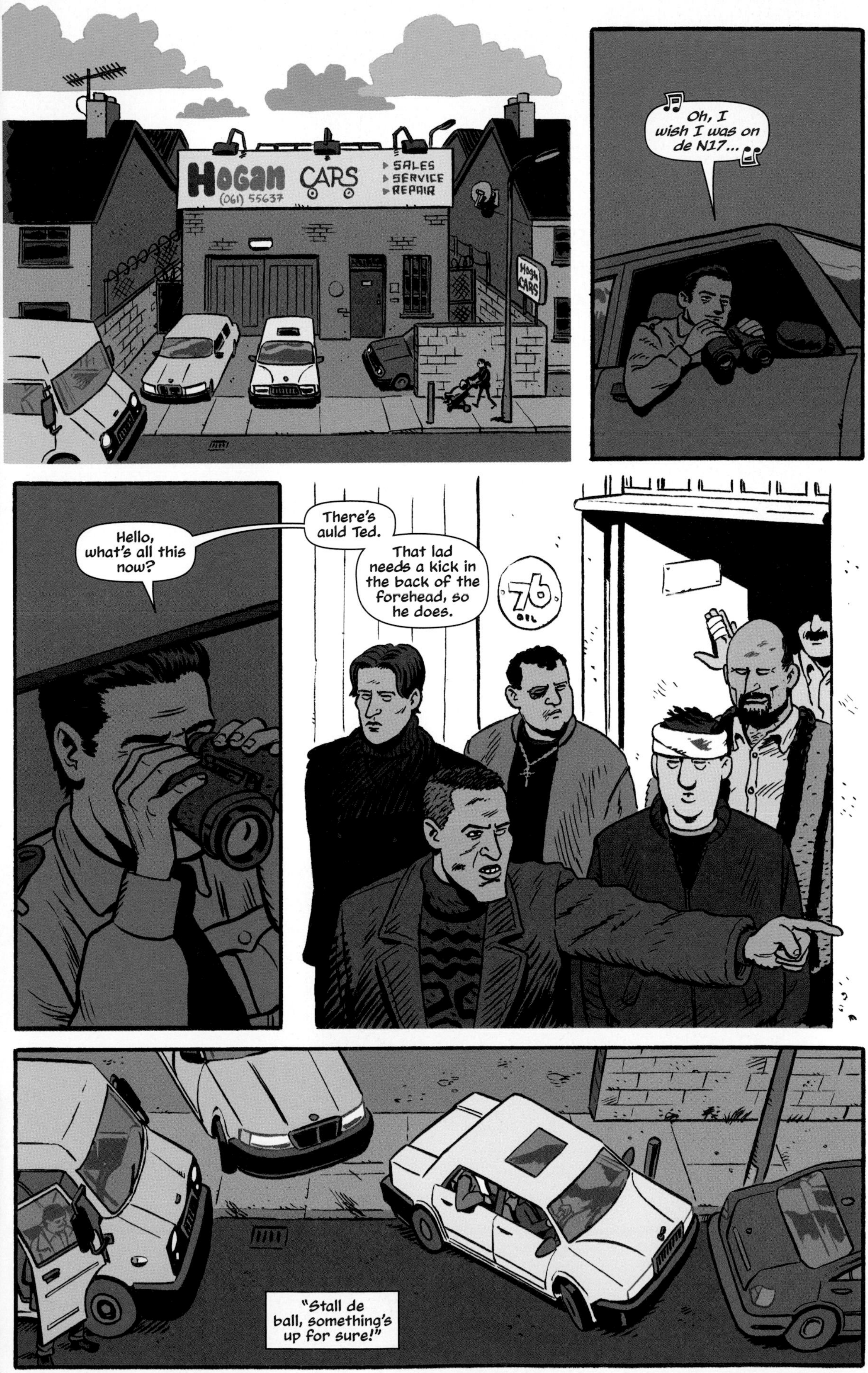
Hogan CARS
(061) 55637
SALES
SERVICE
REPAIR
Hogan CARS
Oh, I wish I was on de N17...
Hello, what's all this now?
There's auld Ted.
That lad needs a kick in the back of the forehead, so he does.
76
"Stall de ball, something's up for sure!"

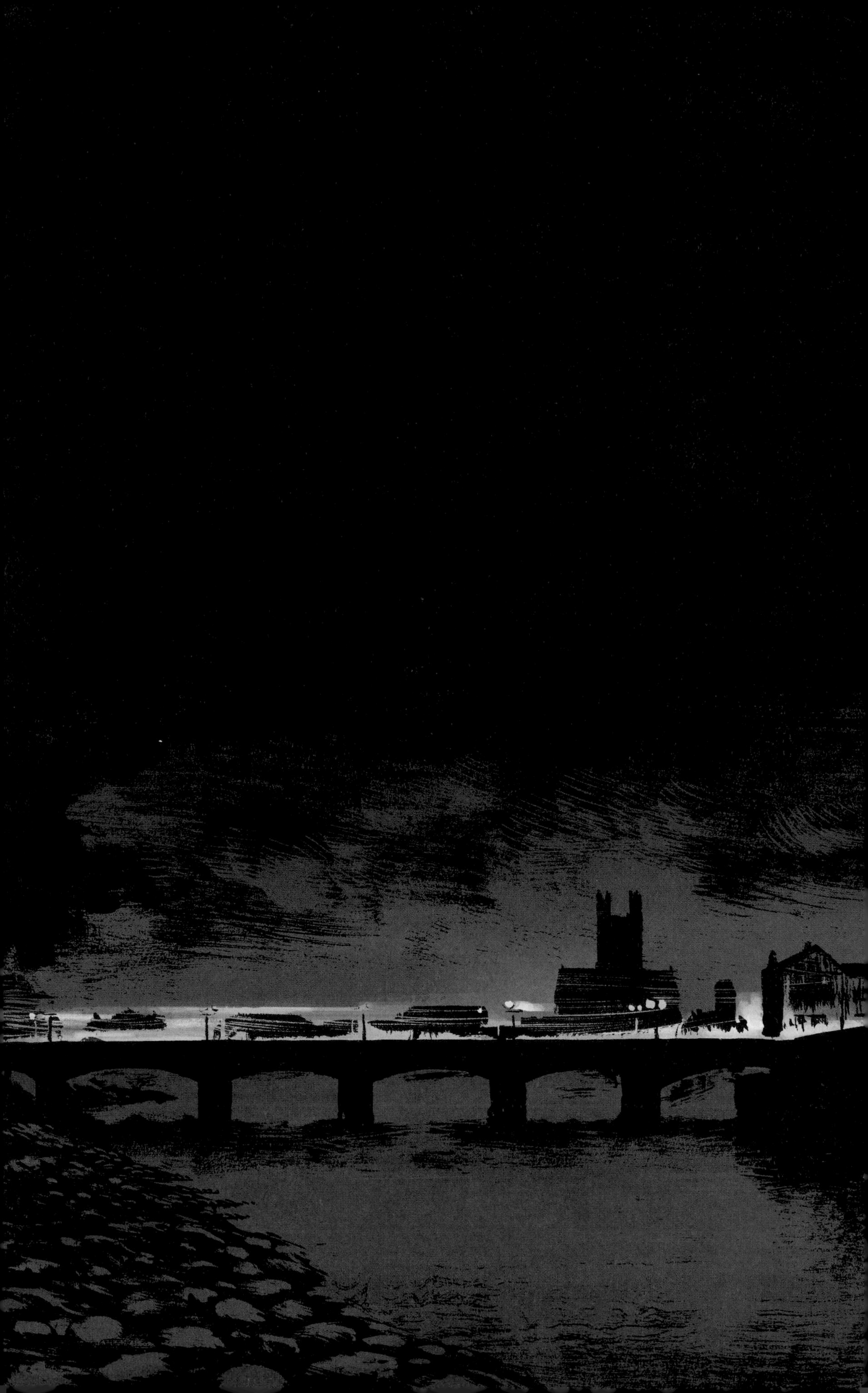

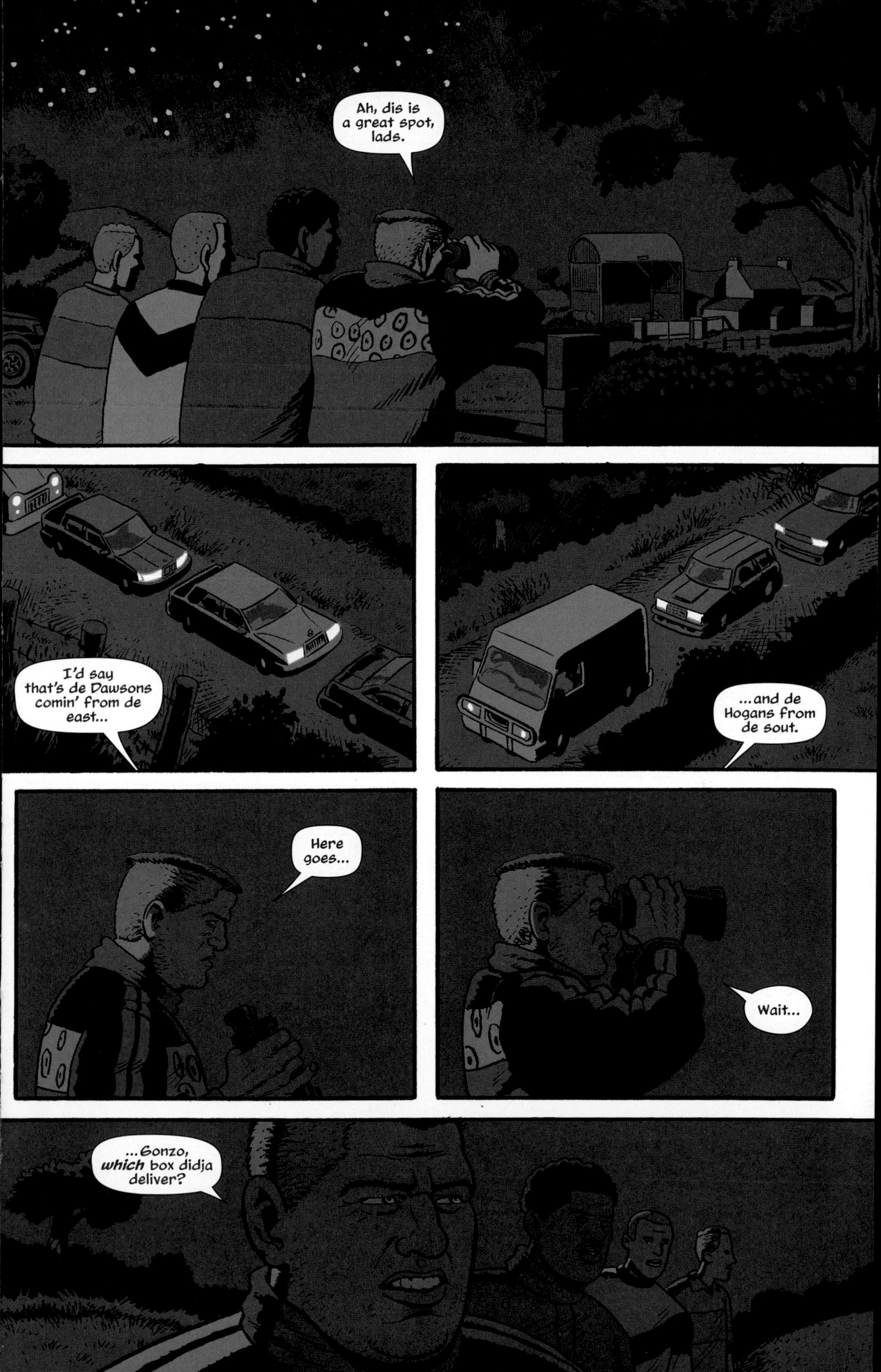
Ah, dis is a great spot, lads.
I'd say that's de Dawsons comin' from de east...
...and de Hogans from de sout.
Here goes...
Wait...
...Gonzo, *which* box didja deliver?

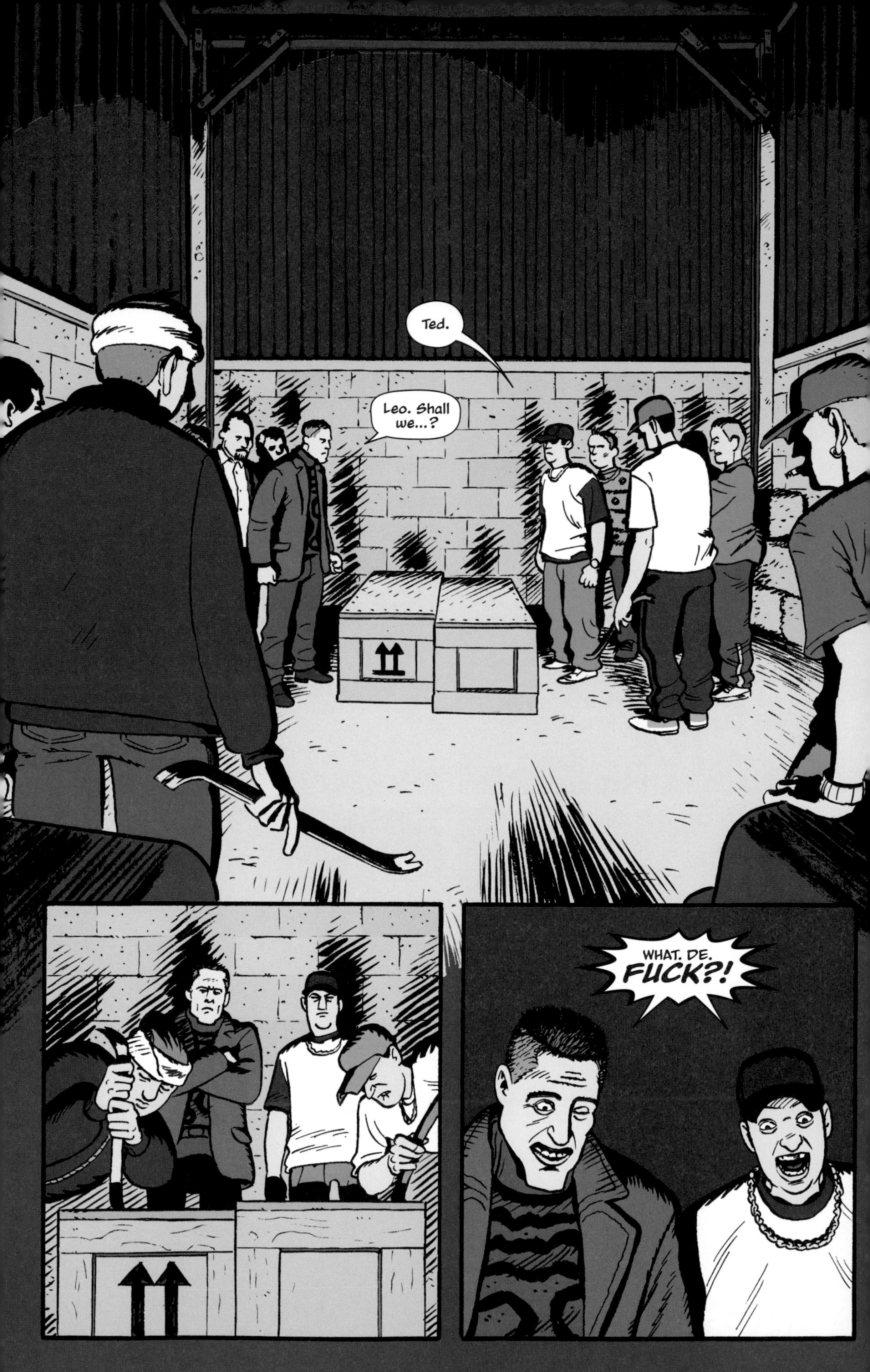
Ted.
Leo. Shall we...?
WHAT. DE. FUCK?!

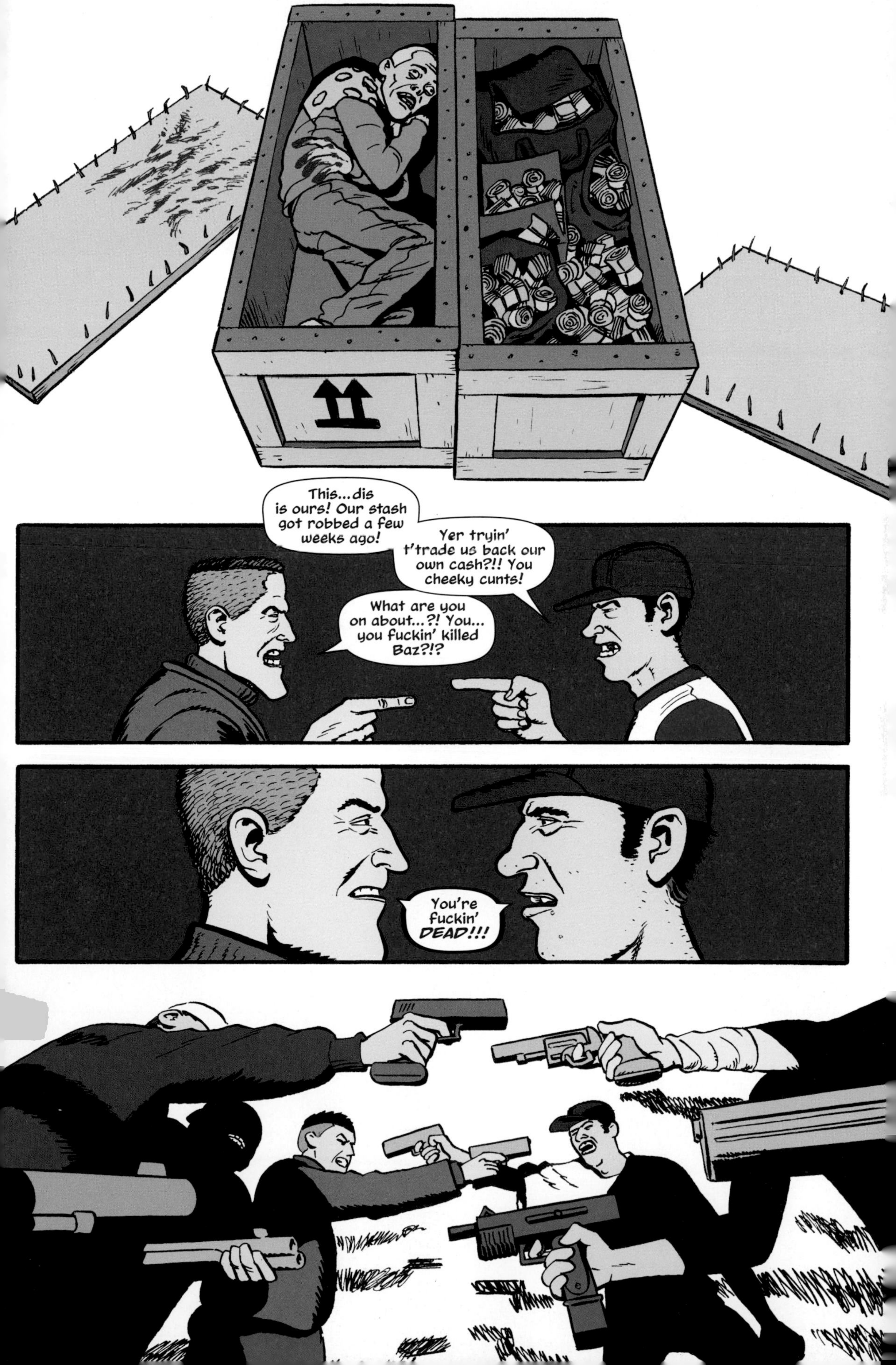
This...dis is ours! Our stash got robbed a few weeks ago!
Yer tryin' t'trade us back our own cash?!! You cheeky cunts!
What are you on about...?! You... you fuckin' killed Baz?!?
You're fuckin' DEAD!!!

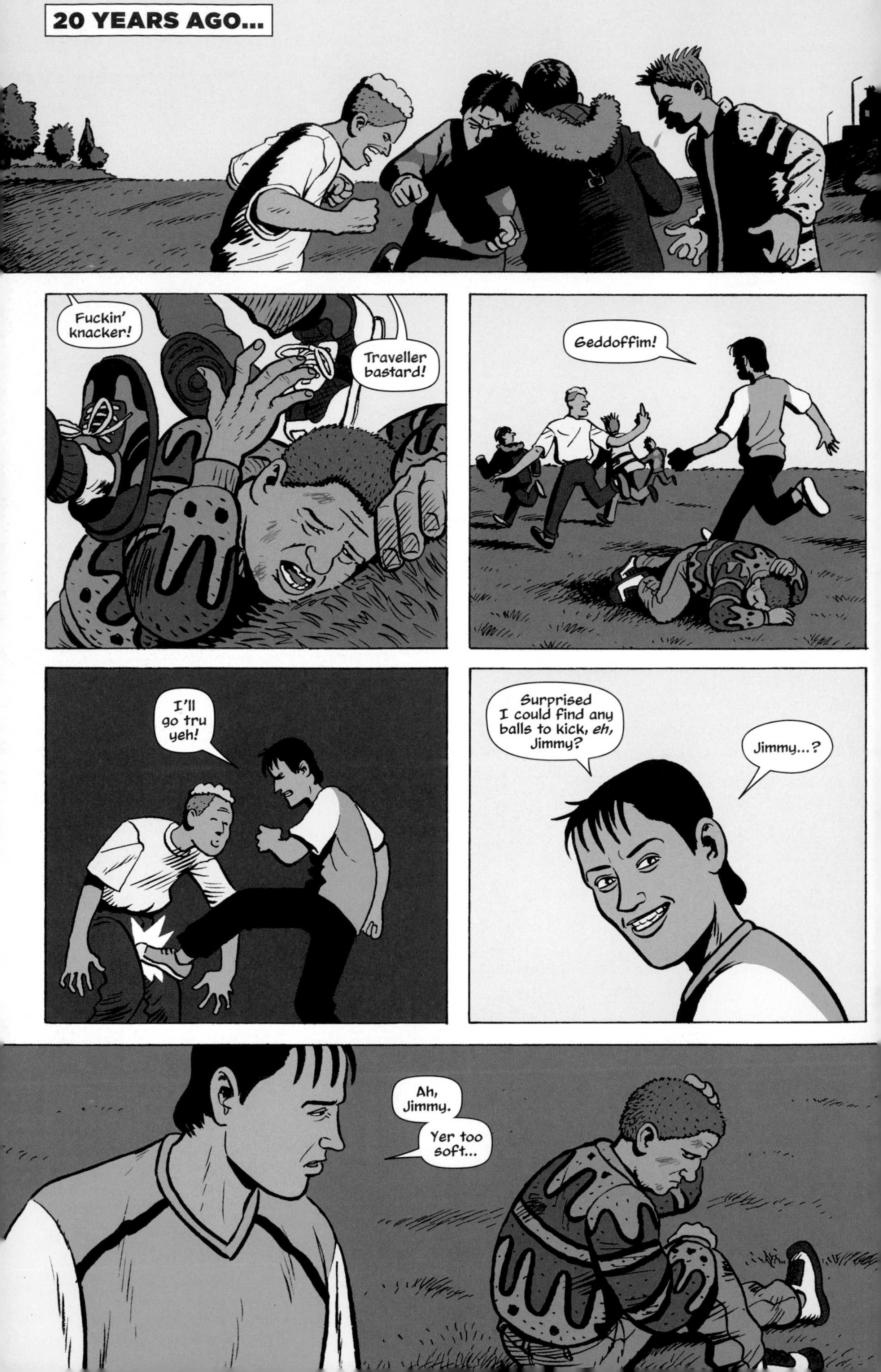
20 YEARS AGO...
Fuckin' knacker!
Traveller bastard!
Geddoffim!
I'll go tru yeh!
Surprised I could find any balls to kick, eh, Jimmy?
Jimmy...?
Ah, Jimmy.
Yer too soft...

"...yeh gotta be more hard."

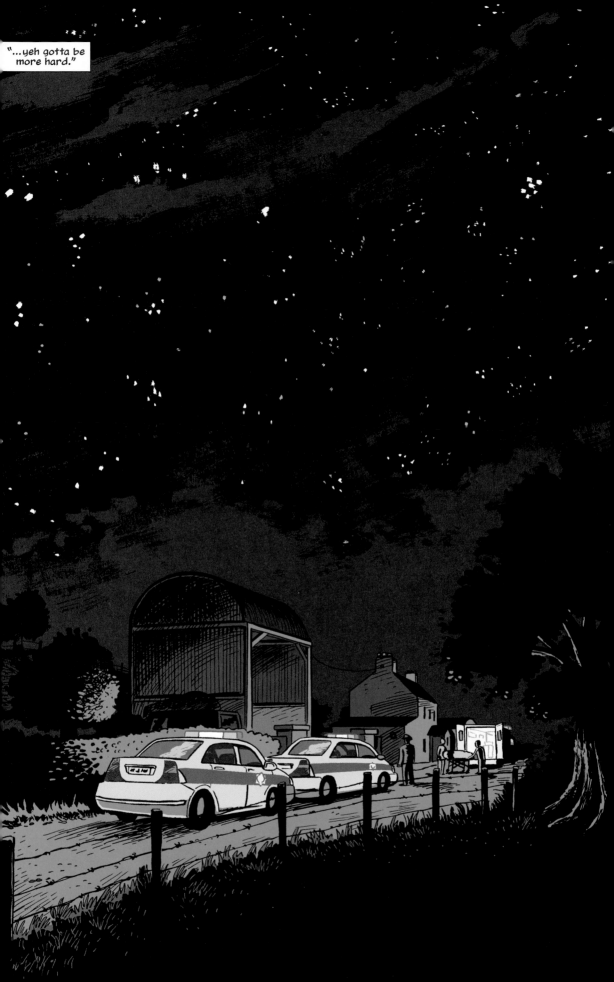

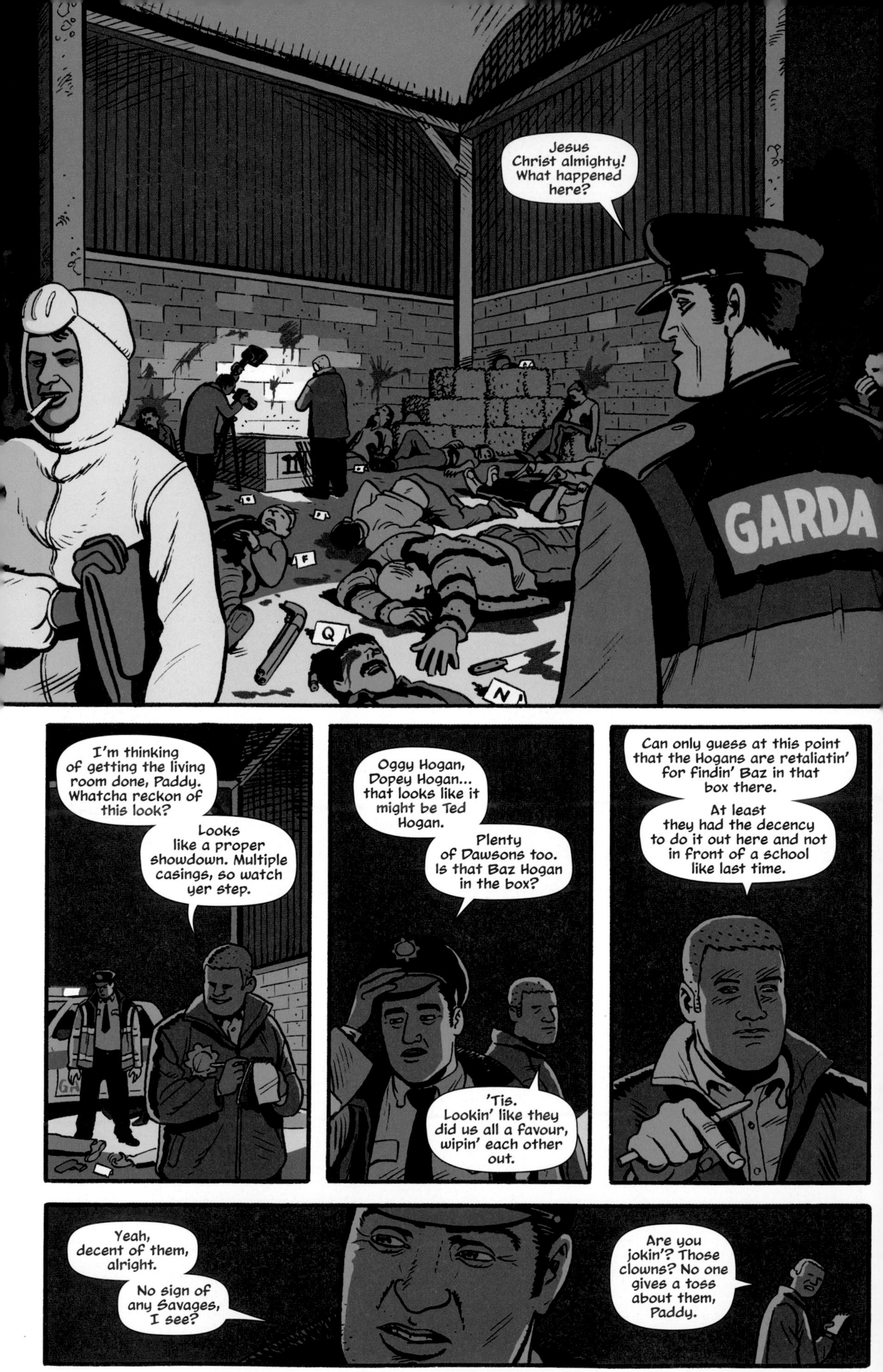
Jesus Christ almighty! What happened here?
GARDA
I'm thinking of getting the living room done, Paddy. Whatcha reckon of this look?
Looks like a proper showdown. Multiple casings, so watch yer step.
Oggy Hogan, Dopey Hogan... that looks like it might be Ted Hogan.
Plenty of Dawsons too. Is that Baz Hogan in the box?
'Tis. Lookin' like they did us all a favour, wipin' each other out.
Can only guess at this point that the Hogans are retaliatin' for findin' Baz in that box there.
At least they had the decency to do it out here and not in front of a school like last time.
Yeah, decent of them, alright.
No sign of any Savages, I see?
Are you jokin'? Those clowns? No one gives a toss about them, Paddy.

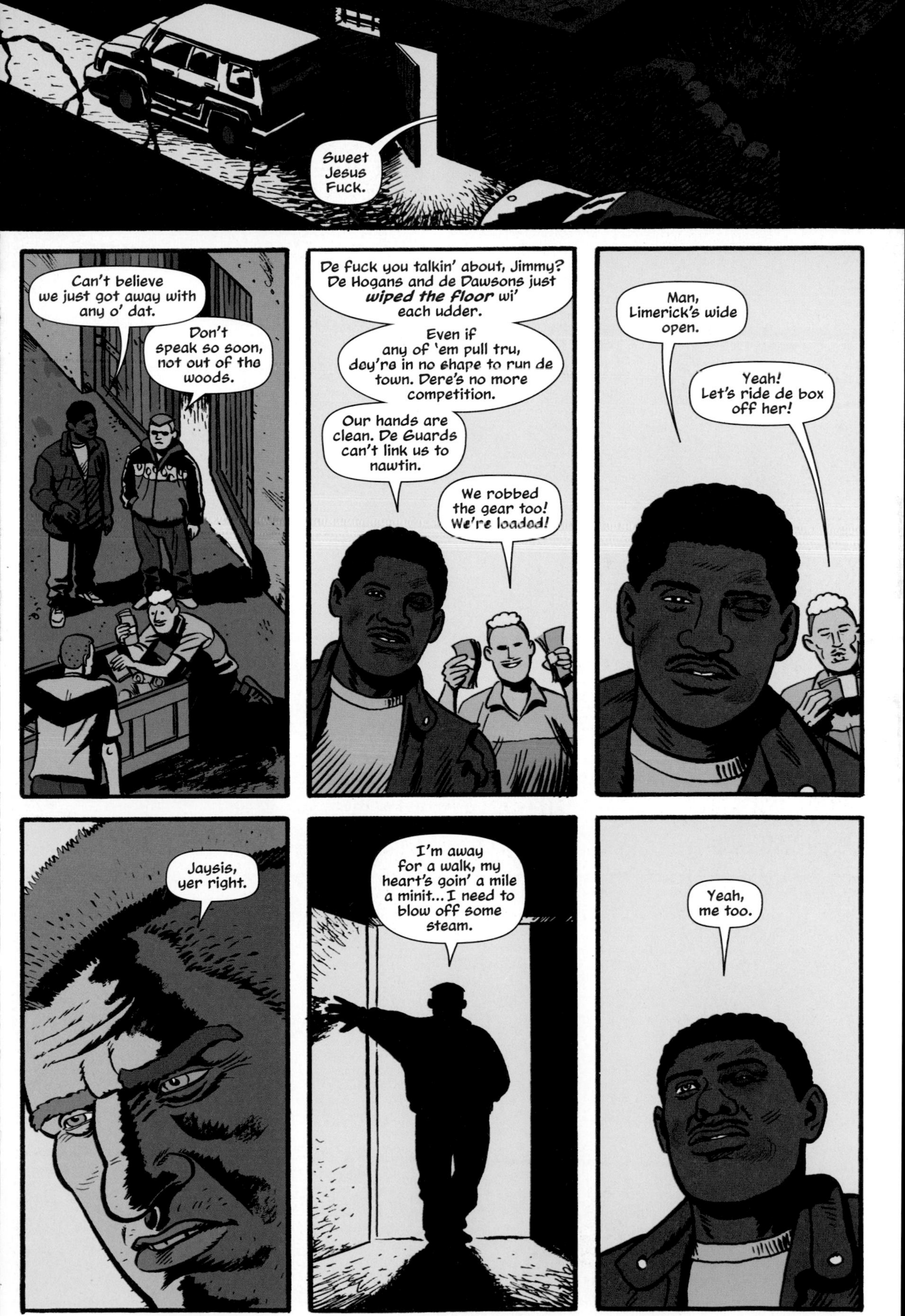
Sweet Jesus Fuck.
Can't believe we just got away with any o' dat.
Don't speak so soon, not out of the woods.
De fuck you talkin' about, Jimmy? De Hogans and de Dawsons just *wiped the floor* wi' each udder.
Even if any of 'em pull tru, dey're in no shape to run de town. Dere's no more competition.
Our hands are clean. De Guards can't link us to nawtin.
We robbed the gear too! We're loaded!
Man, Limerick's wide open.
Yeah! Let's ride de box off her!
Jaysis, yer right.
I'm away for a walk, my heart's goin' a mile a minit... I need to blow off some steam.
Yeah, me too.

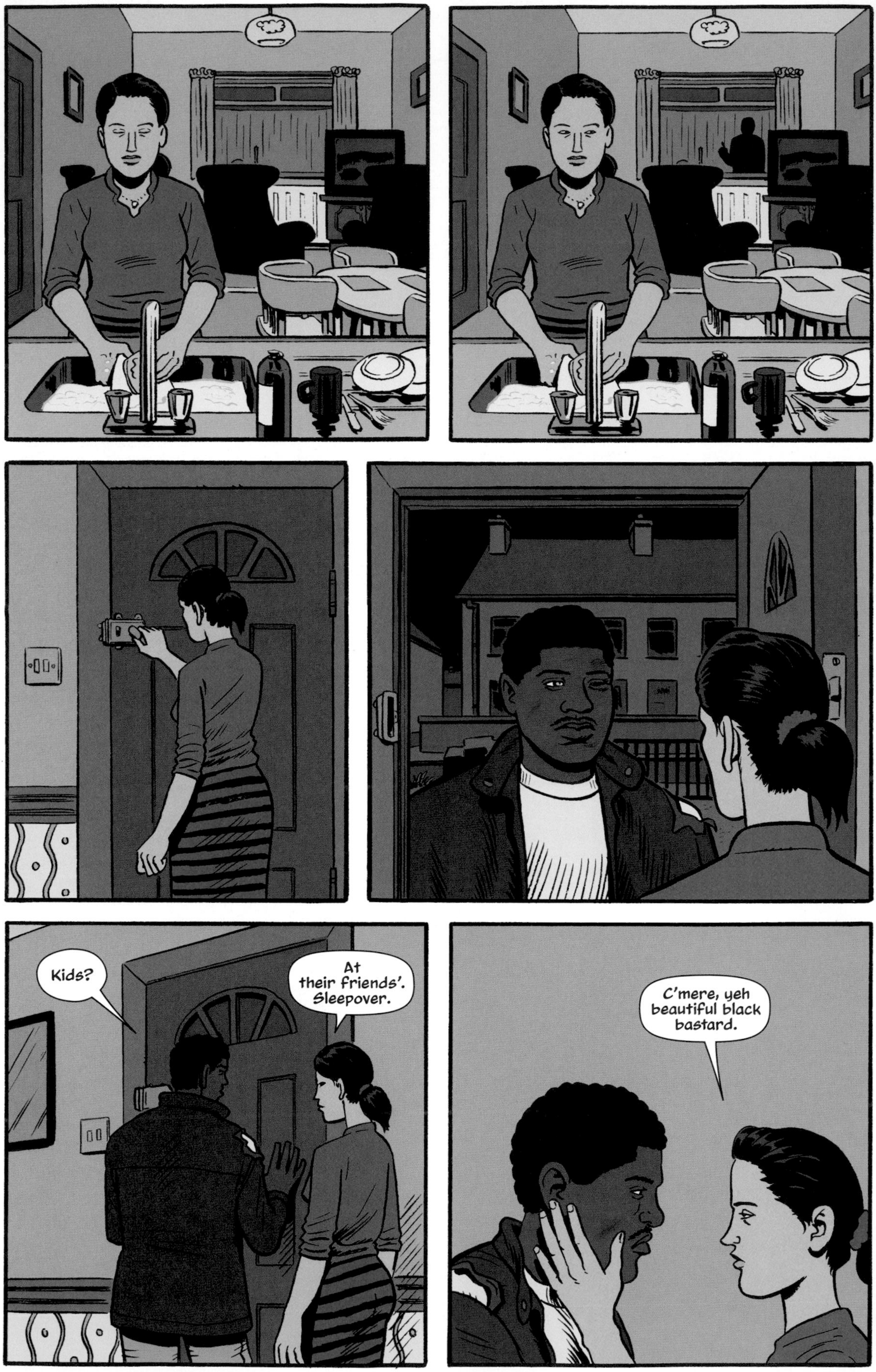
Kids?
At their friends'. Sleepover.
C'mere, yeh beautiful black bastard.

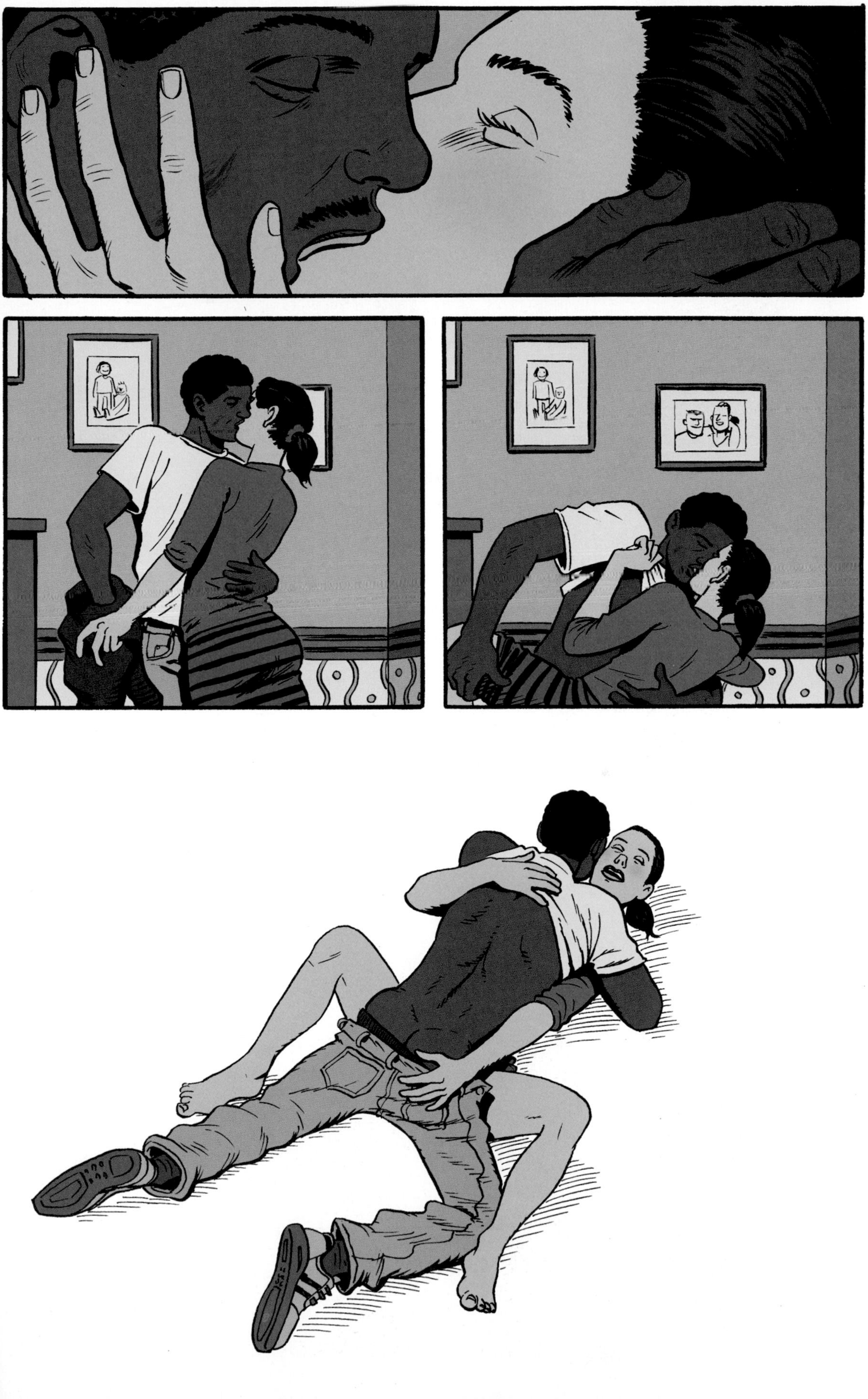

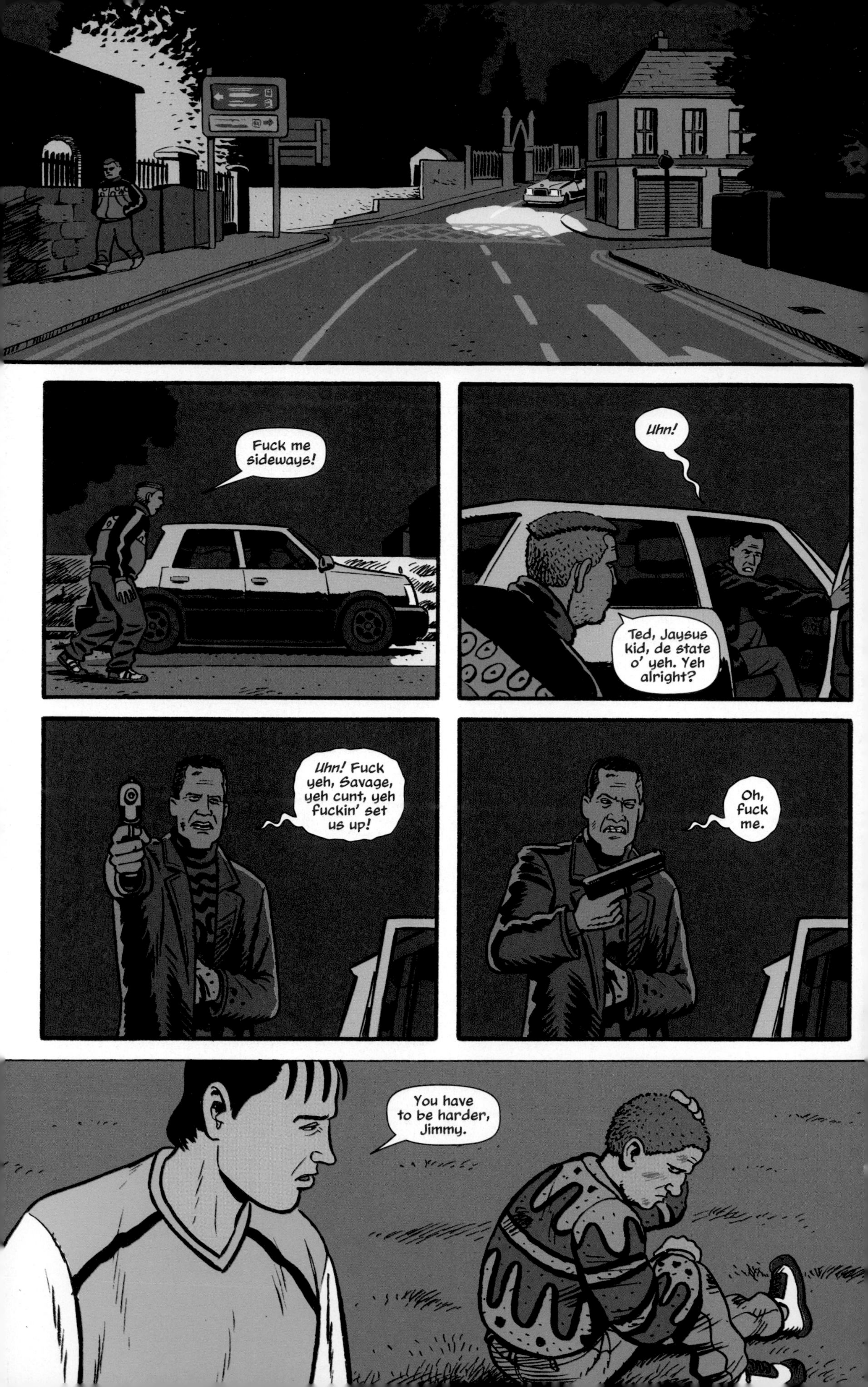
Fuck me sideways!
Uhn!
Ted, Jaysus kid, de state o' yeh. Yeh alright?
Uhn! Fuck yeh, Savage, yeh cunt, yeh fuckin' set us up!
Oh, fuck me.
You have to be harder, Jimmy.

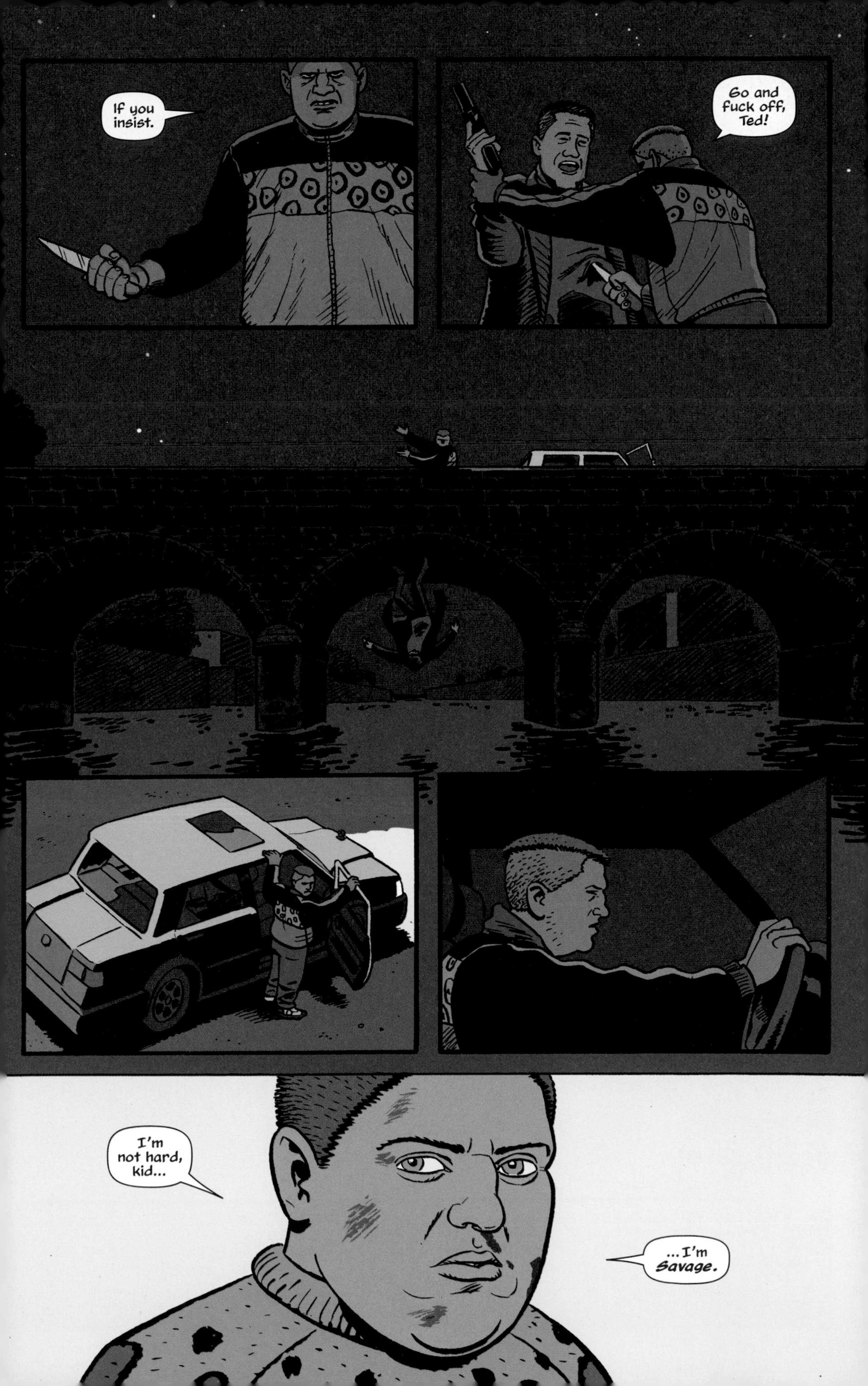
If you insist.
Go and fuck off, Ted!
I'm not hard, kid...
...I'm *Savage*.

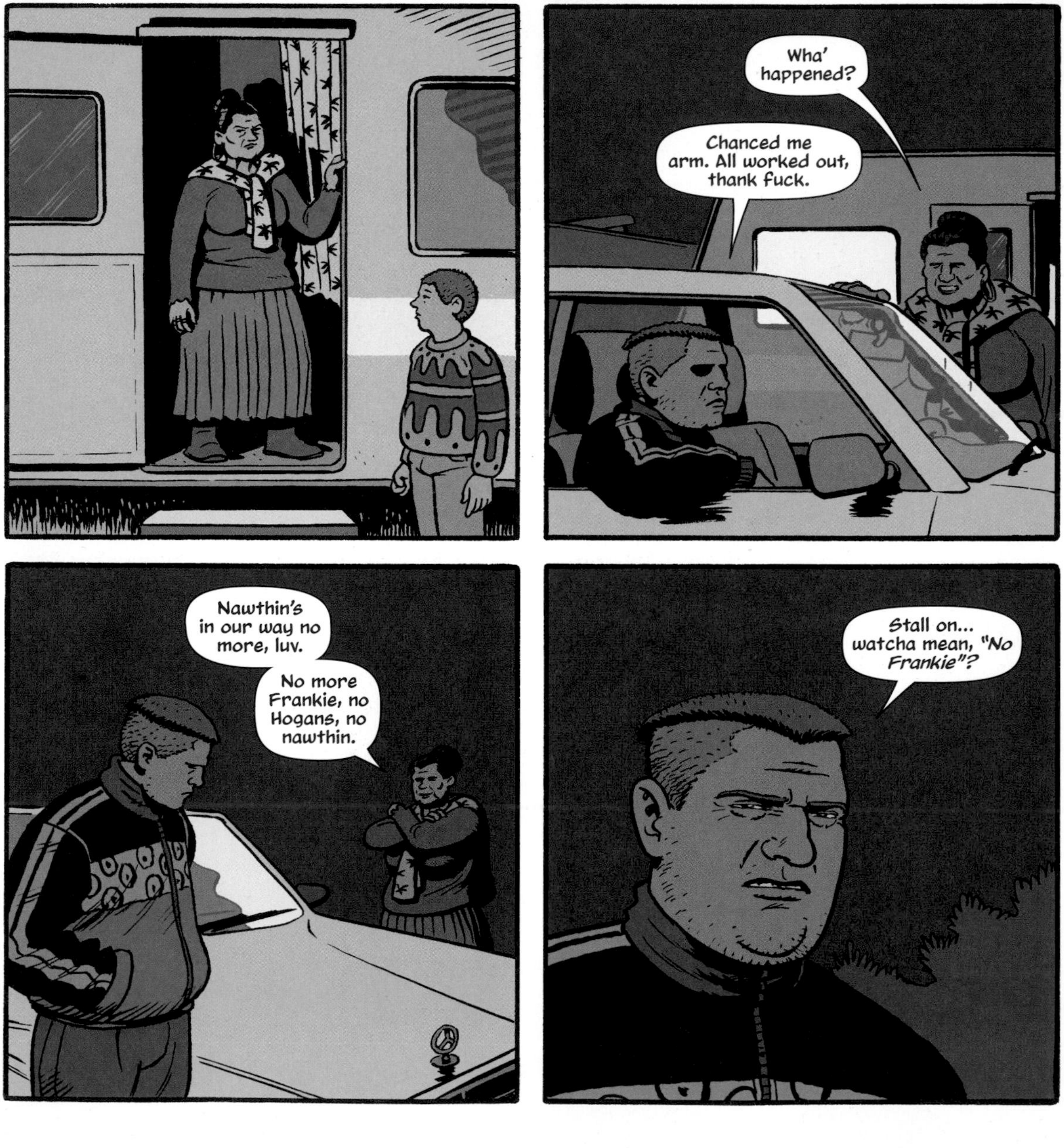
Wha' happened?
Chanced me arm. All worked out, thank fuck.
Nawthin's in our way no more, luv.
No more Frankie, no Hogans, no nawthin.
Stall on... watcha mean, "No Frankie"?

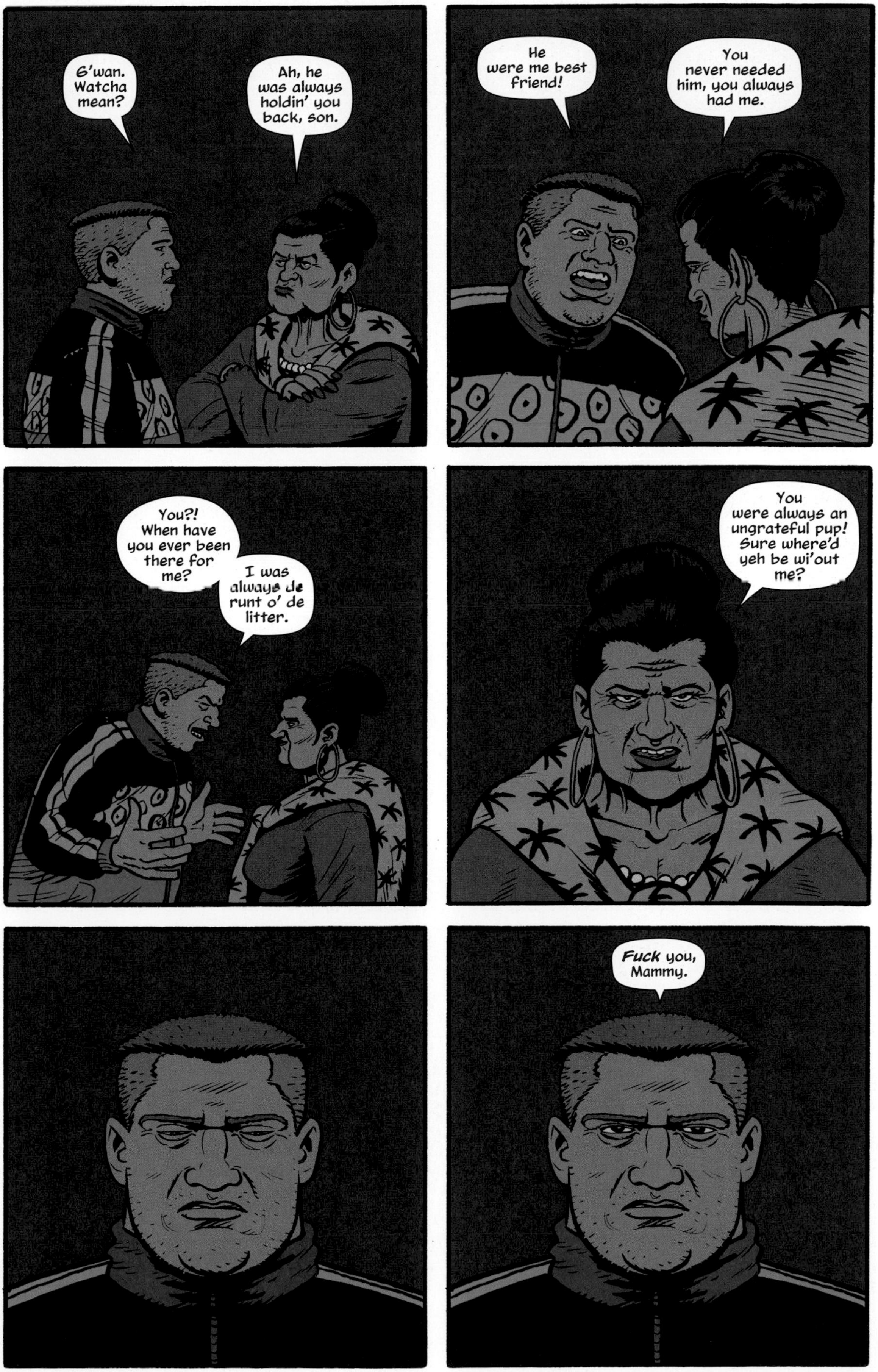
G'wan. Watcha mean?
Ah, he was always holdin' you back, son.
He were me best friend!
You never needed him, you always had me.
You?! When have you ever been there for me?
I was always de runt o' de litter.
You were always an ungrateful pup! Sure where'd yeh be wi'out me?
Fuck you, Mammy.

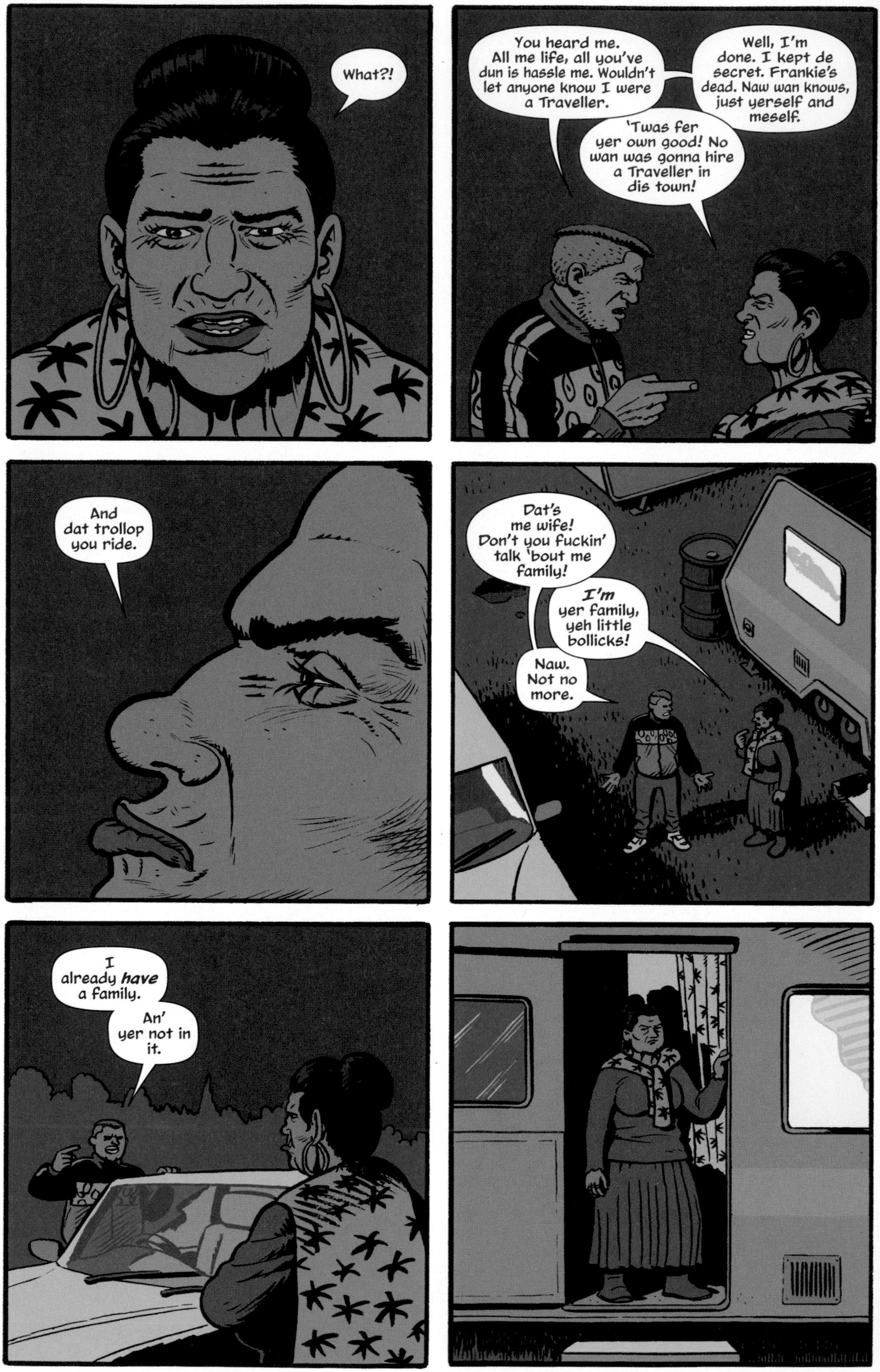
What?!
You heard me. All me life, all you've dun is hassle me. Wouldn't let anyone know I were a Traveller.
'Twas fer yer own good! No wan was gonna hire a Traveller in dis town!
Well, I'm done. I kept de secret. Frankie's dead. Naw wan knows, just yerself and meself.
And dat trollop you ride.
Dat's me wife! Don't you fuckin' talk 'bout me family!
I'm yer family, yeh little bollicks!
Naw. Not no more.
I already have a family.
An' yer not in it.

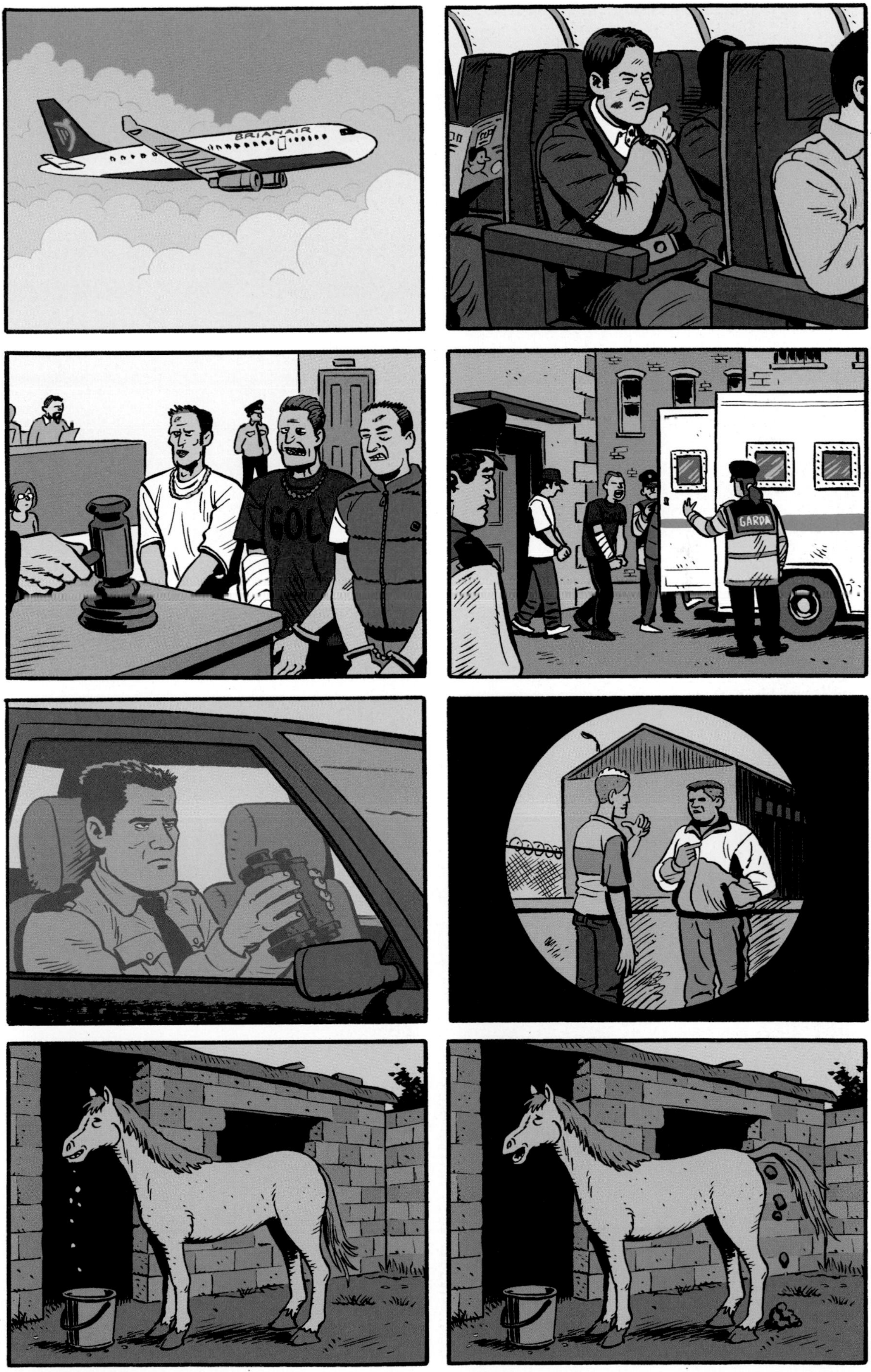
BRIANAIR
GARDA

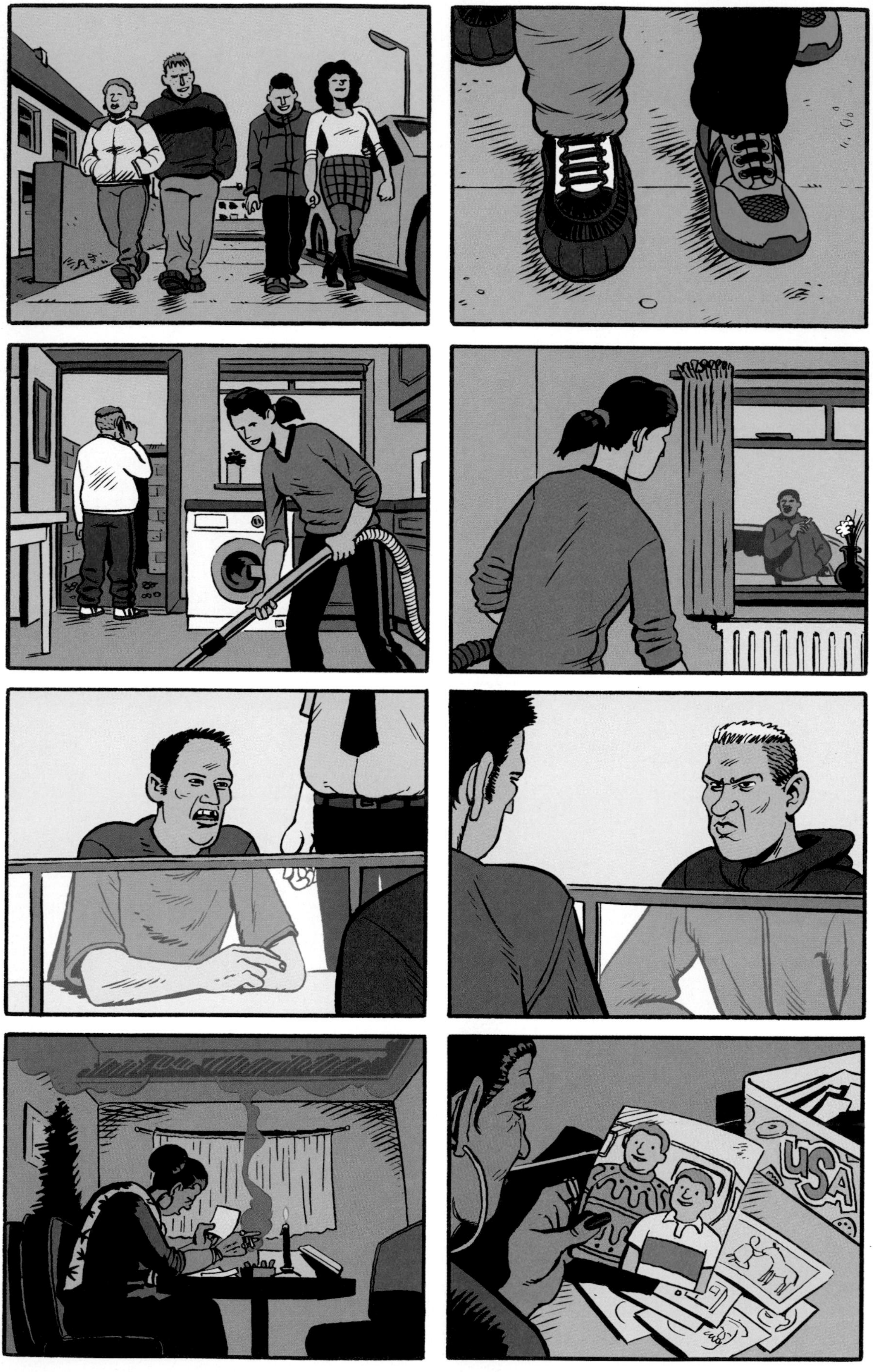
USA

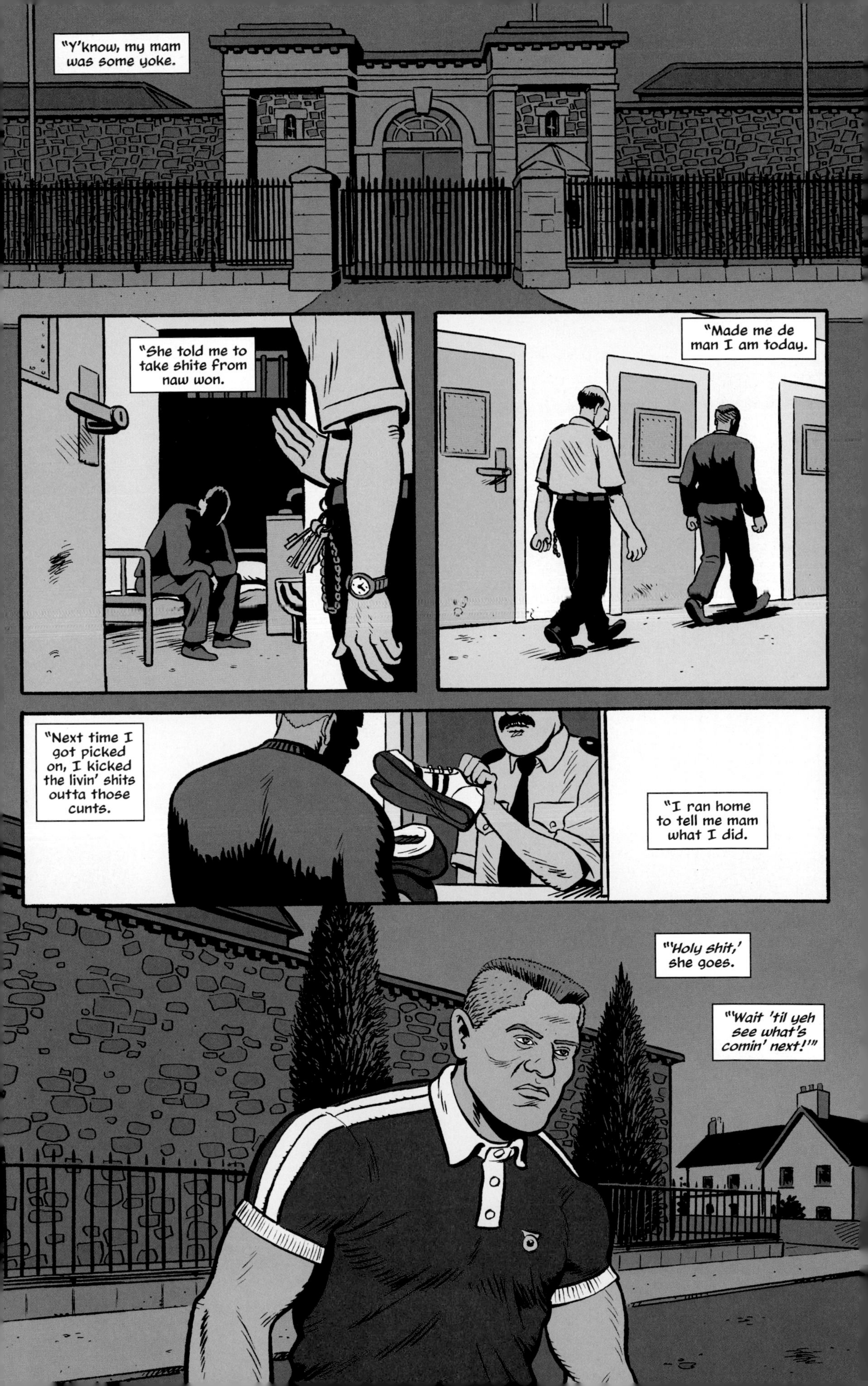
"Y'know, my mam was some yoke.
"She told me to take shite from naw won.
"Made me de man I am today.
"Next time I got picked on, I kicked the livin' shits outta those cunts.
"I ran home to tell me mam what I did.
"'Holy shit,' she goes.
"'Wait 'til yeh see what's comin' next!'"

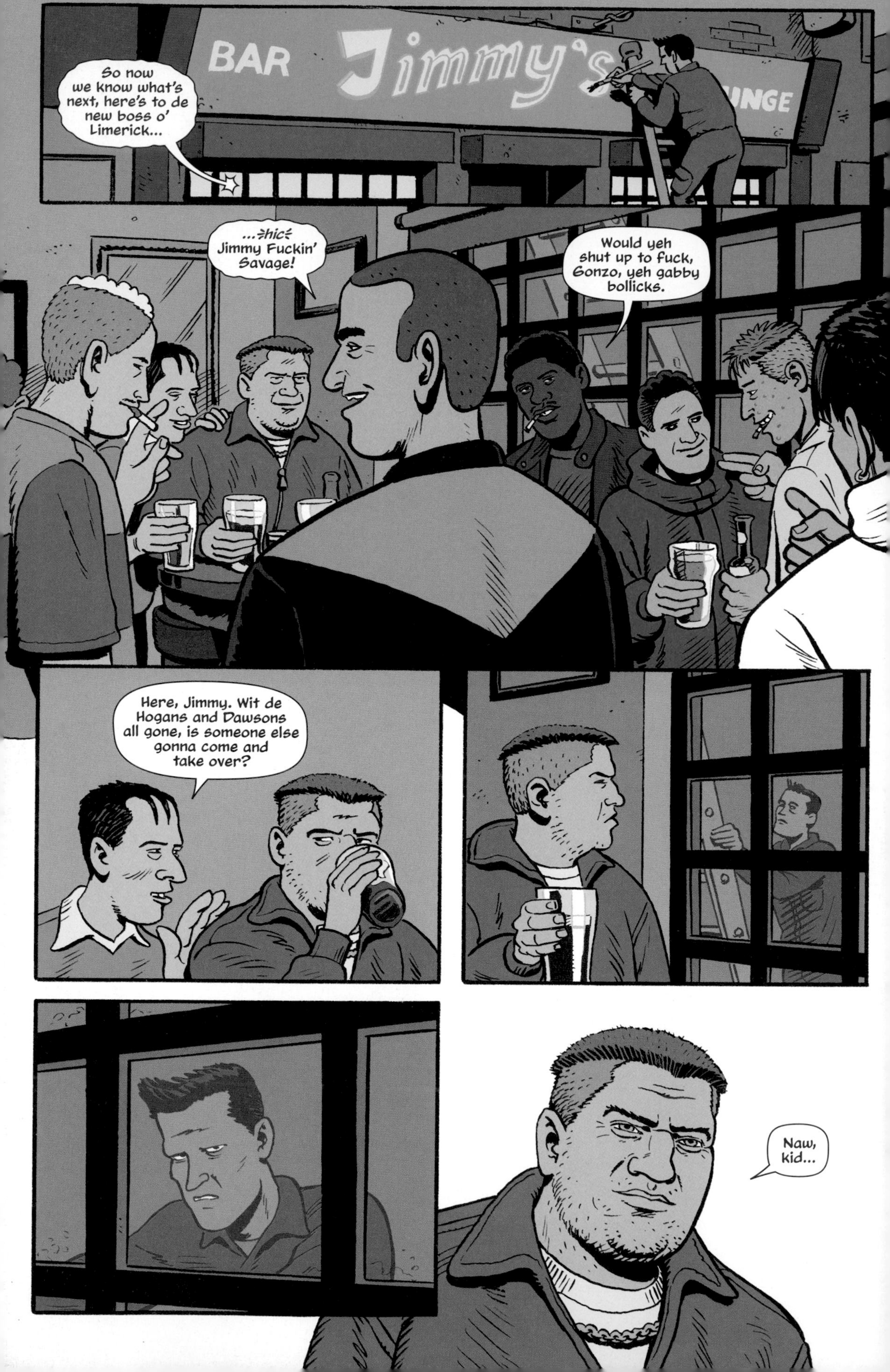
BAR Jimmy's LOUNGE
So now we know what's next, here's to de new boss o' Limerick...
...hic Jimmy Fuckin' Savage!
Would yeh shut up to fuck, Gonzo, yeh gabby bollicks.
Here, Jimmy. Wit de Hogans and Dawsons all gone, is someone else gonna come and take over?
Naw, kid...

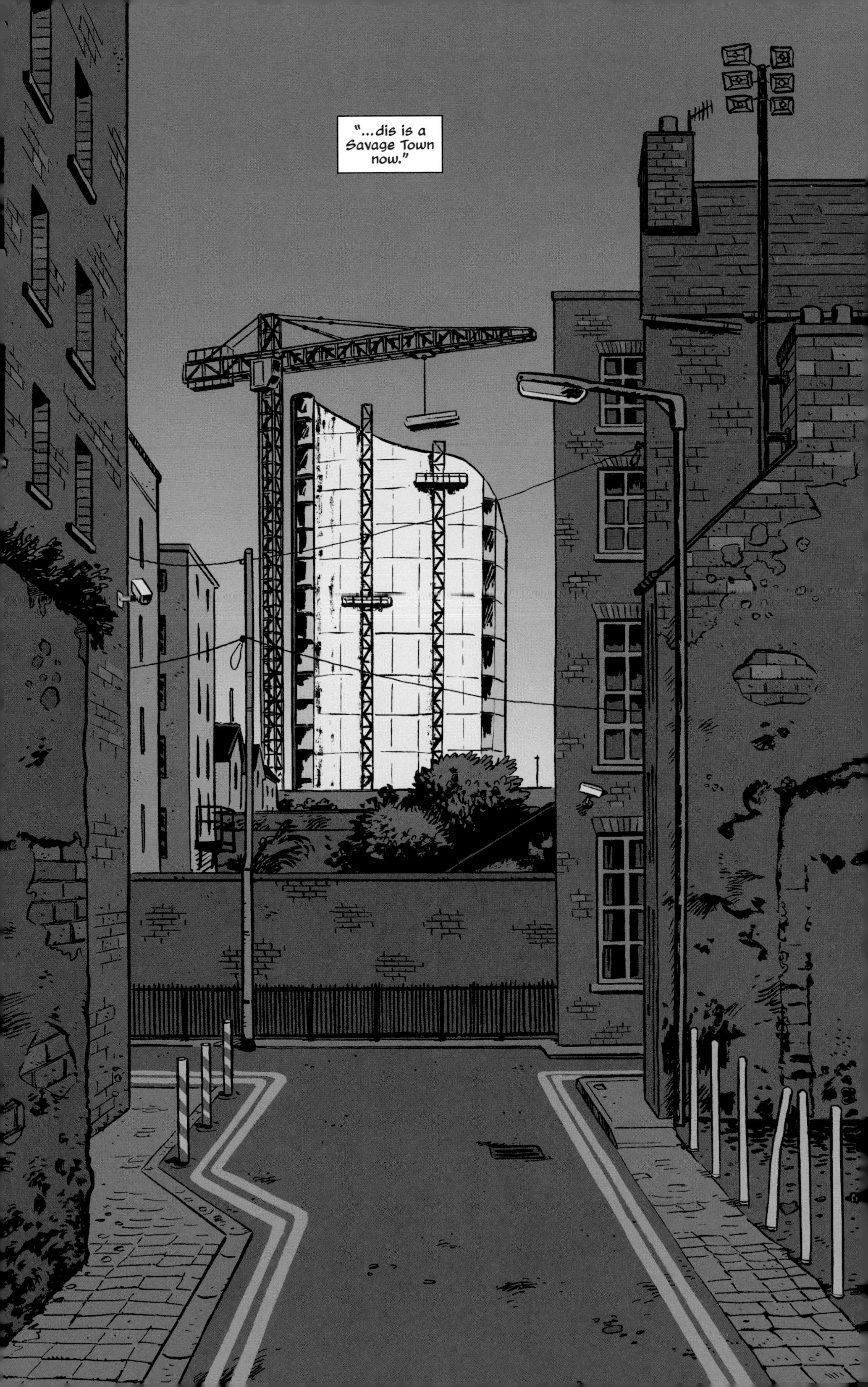
"...dis is a Savage Town now."

BONUS CRAIC

Jaysus... dat was some shockin' stuff, weren't it? Yer man endin' up in de box? Blackie and Saorla muckin' into each udder? Savage stuff, sham. At least evertin' werked out in de end. Except for Frankie... and de Hogans... and de Dawsons. Fuck it, sure at least the horse is alright!

Anyway, as a treet, here's a rake of sketches, layouts, preparational pages, cover ideas, design concepts by Emma, etc. Mad stuff, like. Sure feck it, you can just look at dis bit and ignore all that boring shite you just read, you fool. State o' yeh, like.

G'luck.

LAYOUTS
CHAPTER 1

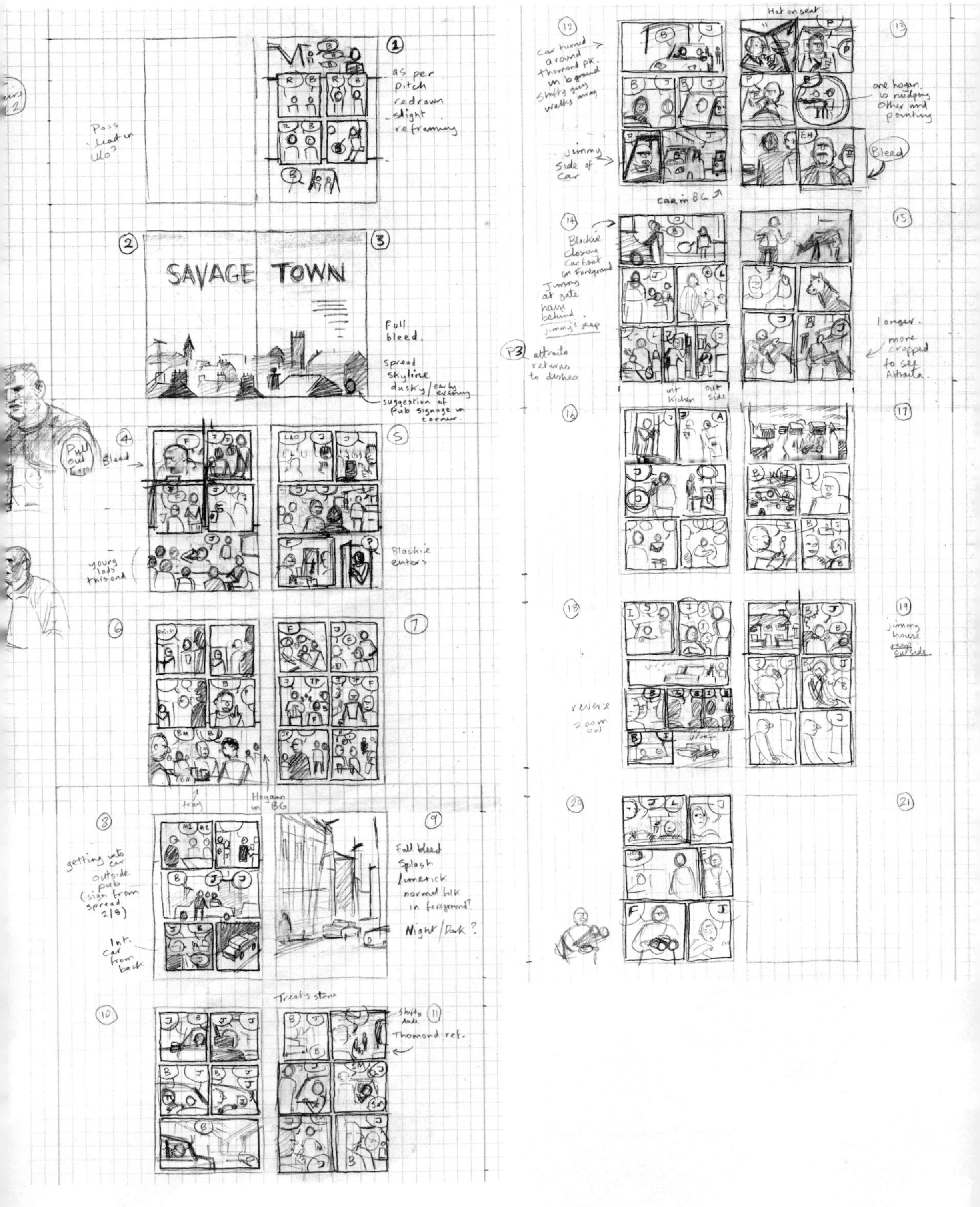

as per pitch redrawn slight reframing
SAVAGE TOWN
Full bleed.
Spread skyline dusky/early evening
suggestion of Pub signage in corner.
Blackie enters
Full bleed Splash Limerick normal folk in foreground?
Night/Dark?
getting into car outside pub (sign from spread 2/3)
Int. car from back
Thomond ref.
Hat on seat
one hogan is nudging other and pointing
Bleed
longer. more cropped to see Attracta.
attracta returns to dishes
int kitchen
out side
reverse zoom out

DRAWN BY **PHILIP BARRETT**

LAYOUTS
CHAPTER 2

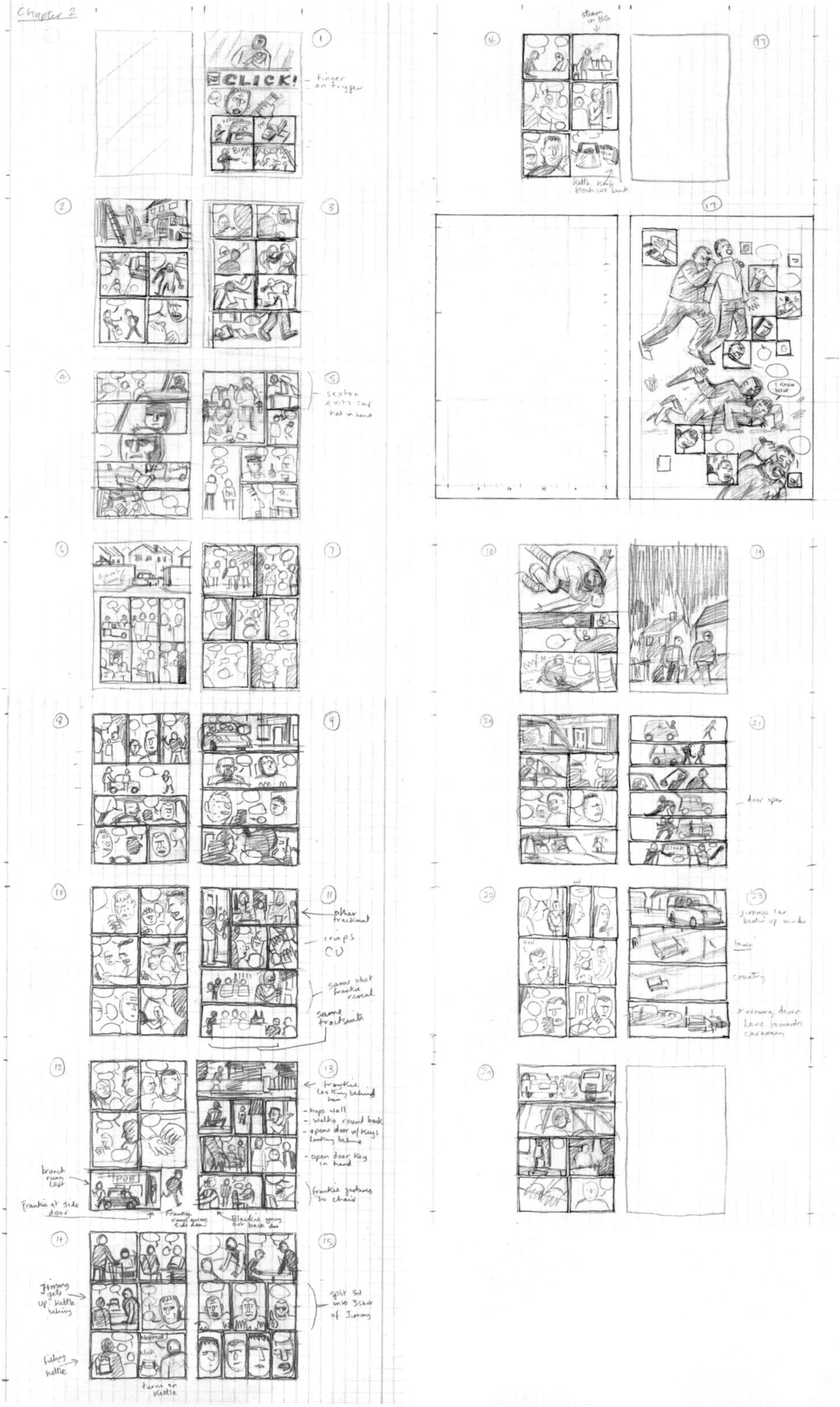

Chapter 2
CLICK!
finger on trigger
steam in BG
sexton exits car hat in hand
I KNOW WHAT
door open
other tracksuit
crisps CU
same shot frankie reveal
same tracksuits
Jimmys car backs up
frankie looking behind him
open door key in hand
frankie gestures to chair
Frankie at side door
split 3rd into 3shot of Jimmy
filling kettle
turns on kettle

DRAWN BY **PHILIP BARRETT**

LAYOUTS
CHAPTER 3

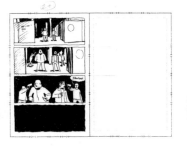

DRAWN BY **PHILIP BARRETT**

LAYOUTS
CHAPTER 4

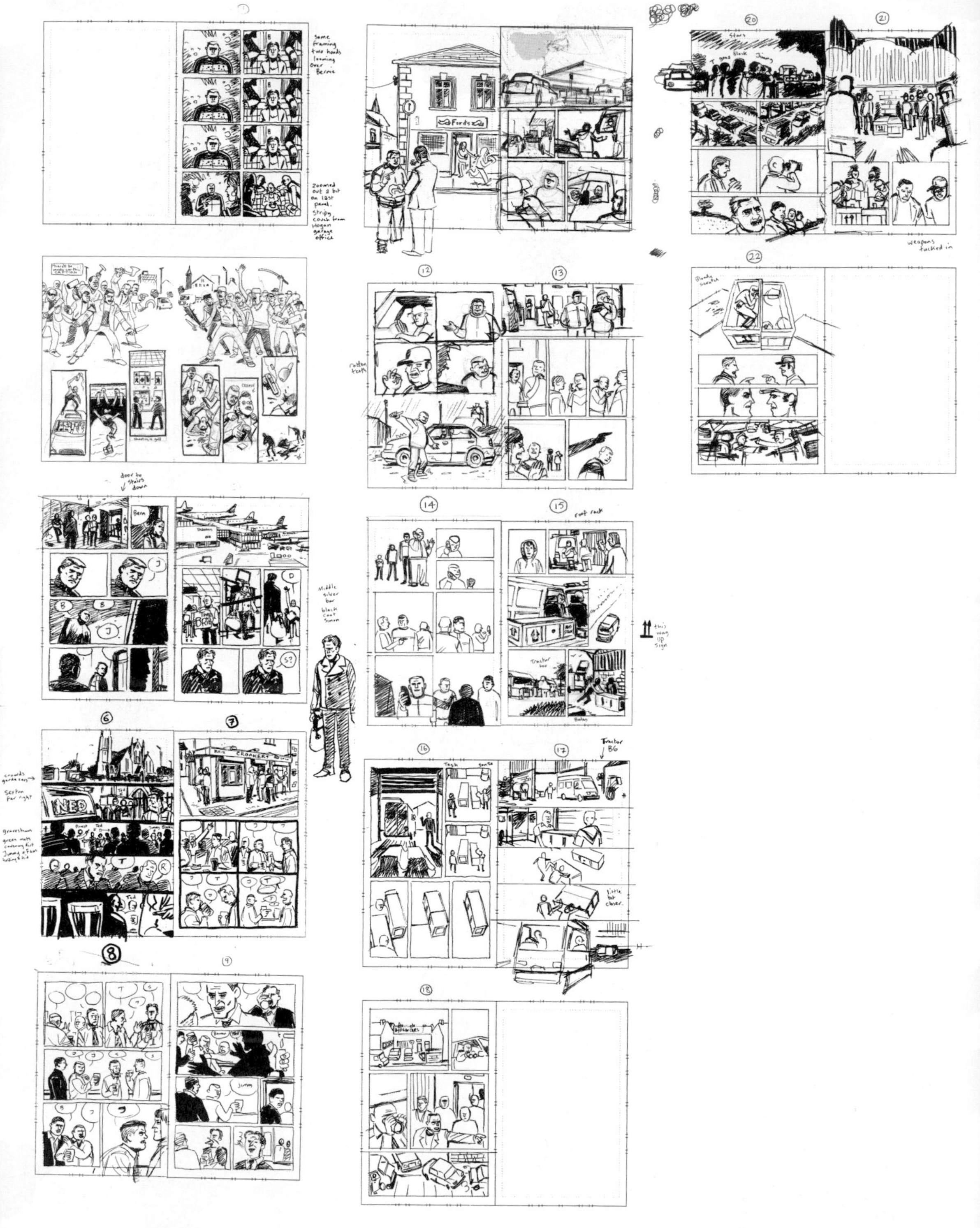

door to stairs down
rotten teeth
roof rack
this way up sign
Middle silver bar black coat Simon
Tractor B6
little bit closer
weapons tucked in

DRAWN BY **PHILIP BARRETT**

LAYOUTS
CHAPTER 5

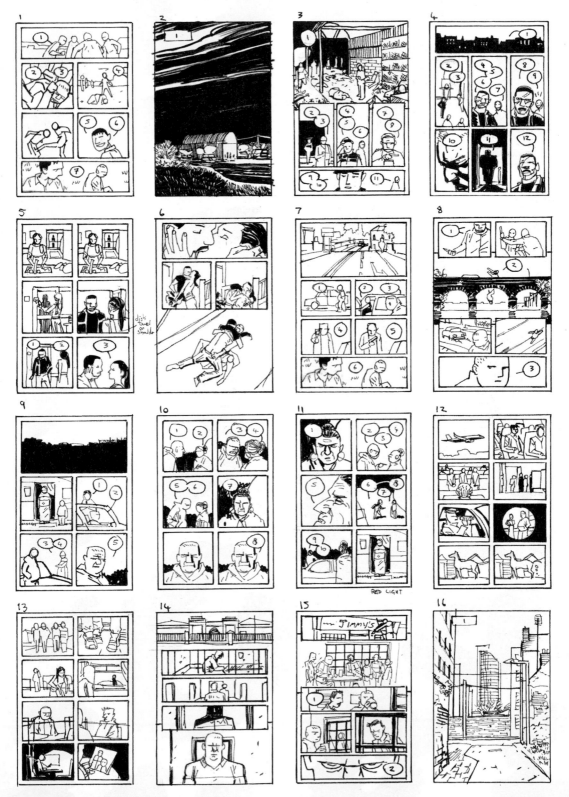

DRAWN BY **DECLAN SHALVEY**

CHARACTER SKETCHES

DRAWN BY **PHILIP BARRETT**

JIMMY

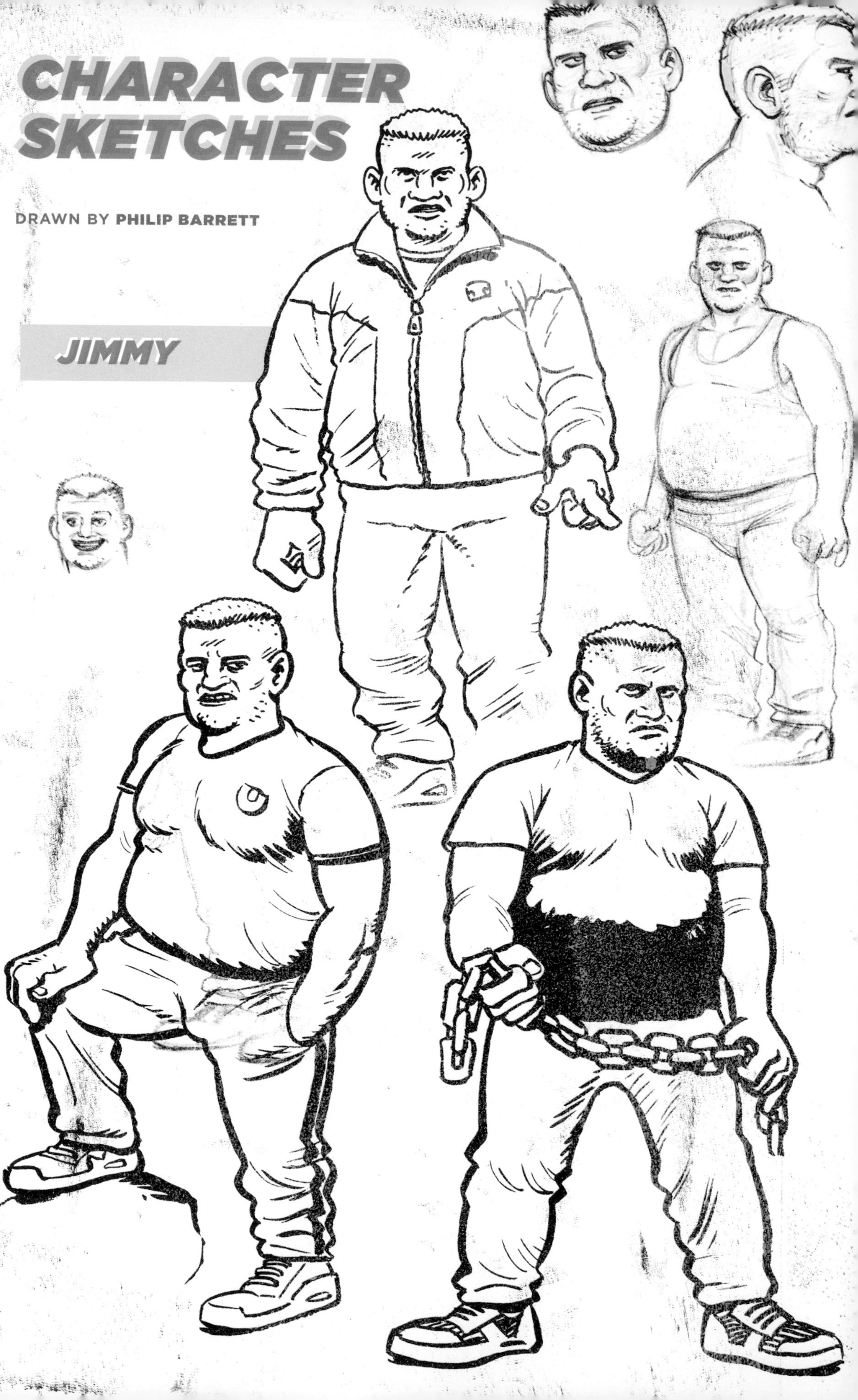

FRANKIE

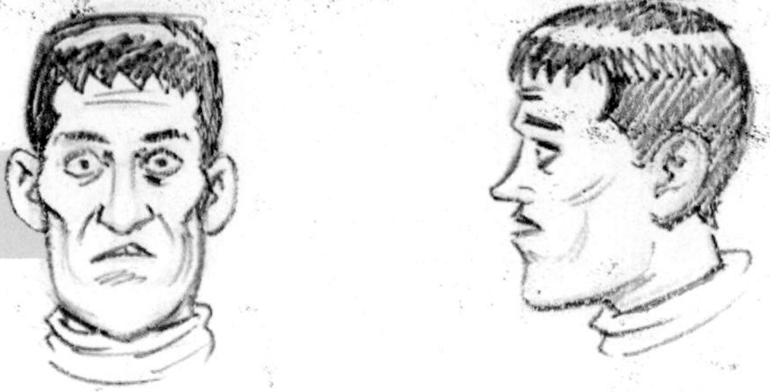

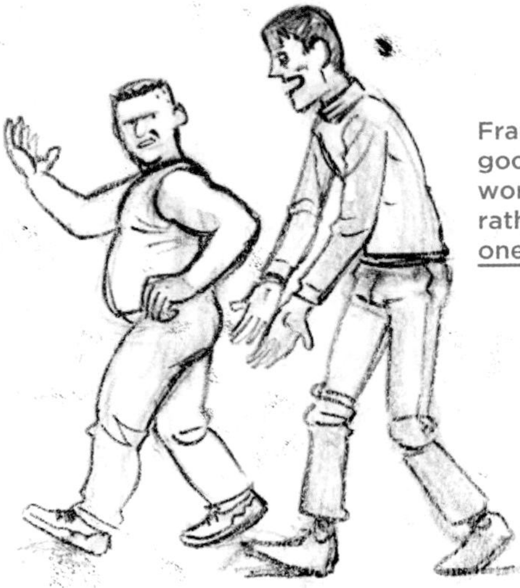

Frankie - tall, gangly and goofy. Maybe a neurotic worried expression mostly rather than a tough guy one.

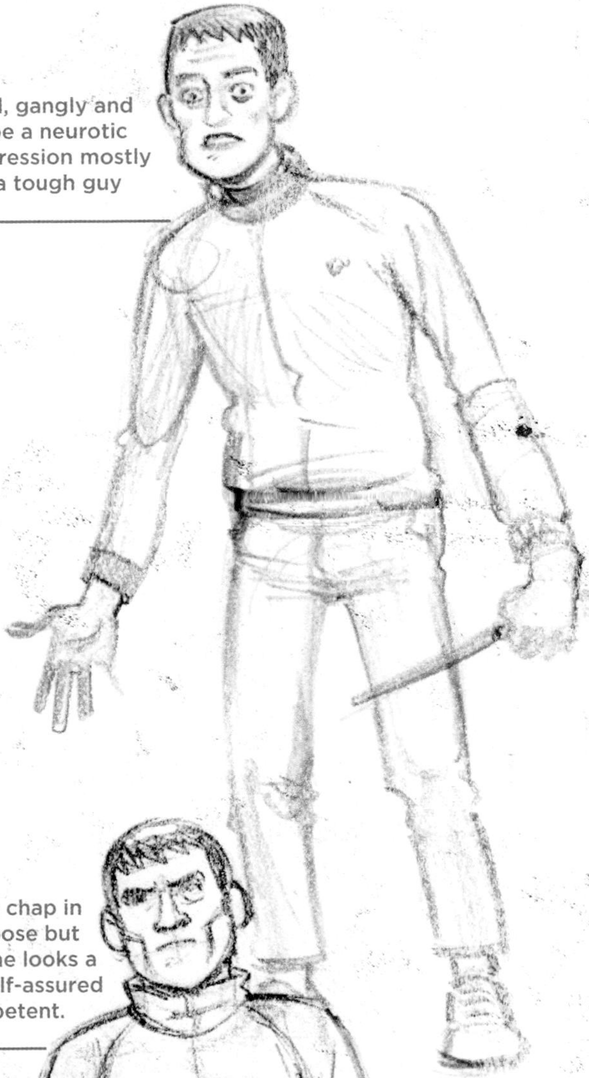

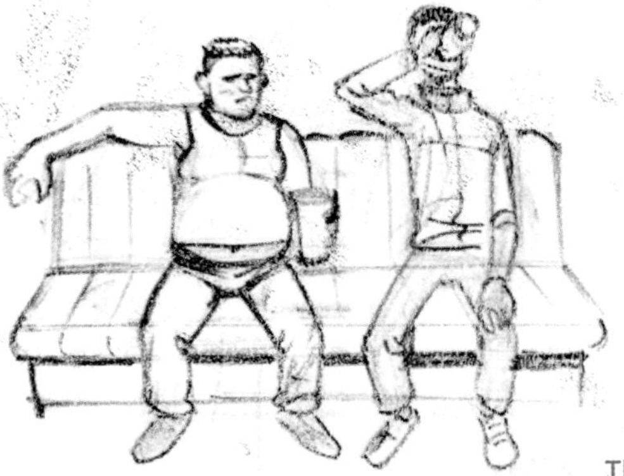

The same chap in another pose but perhaps he looks a bit too self-assured and competent.

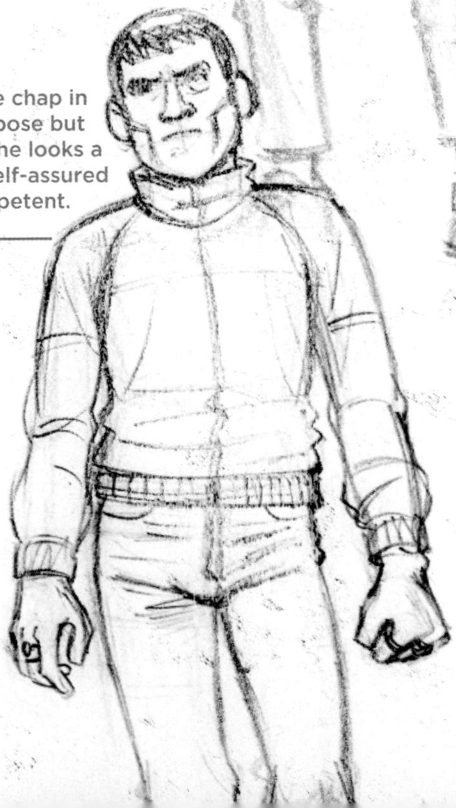

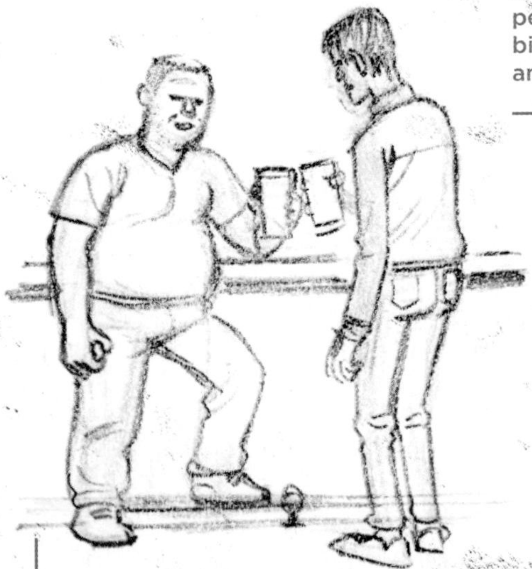

The body shapes work better as a 'double act'.

CHARACTER SKETCHES

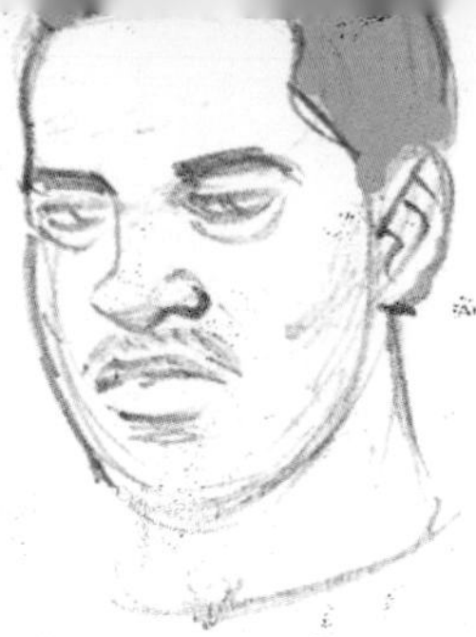

DRAWN BY **PHILIP BARRETT**

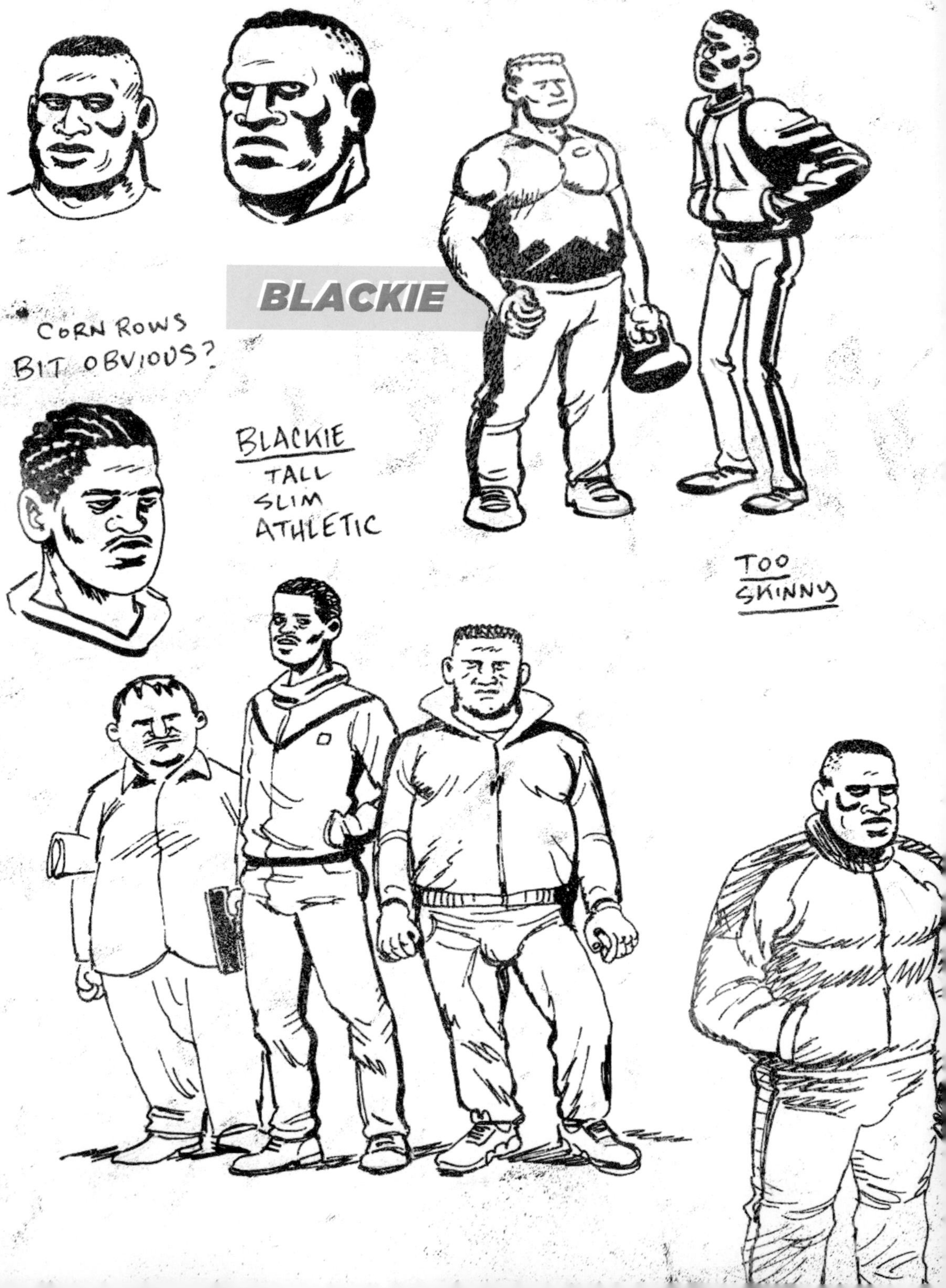
BLACKIE
CORN ROWS BIT OBVIOUS?
BLACKIE
TALL
SLIM
ATHLETIC
TOO SKINNY

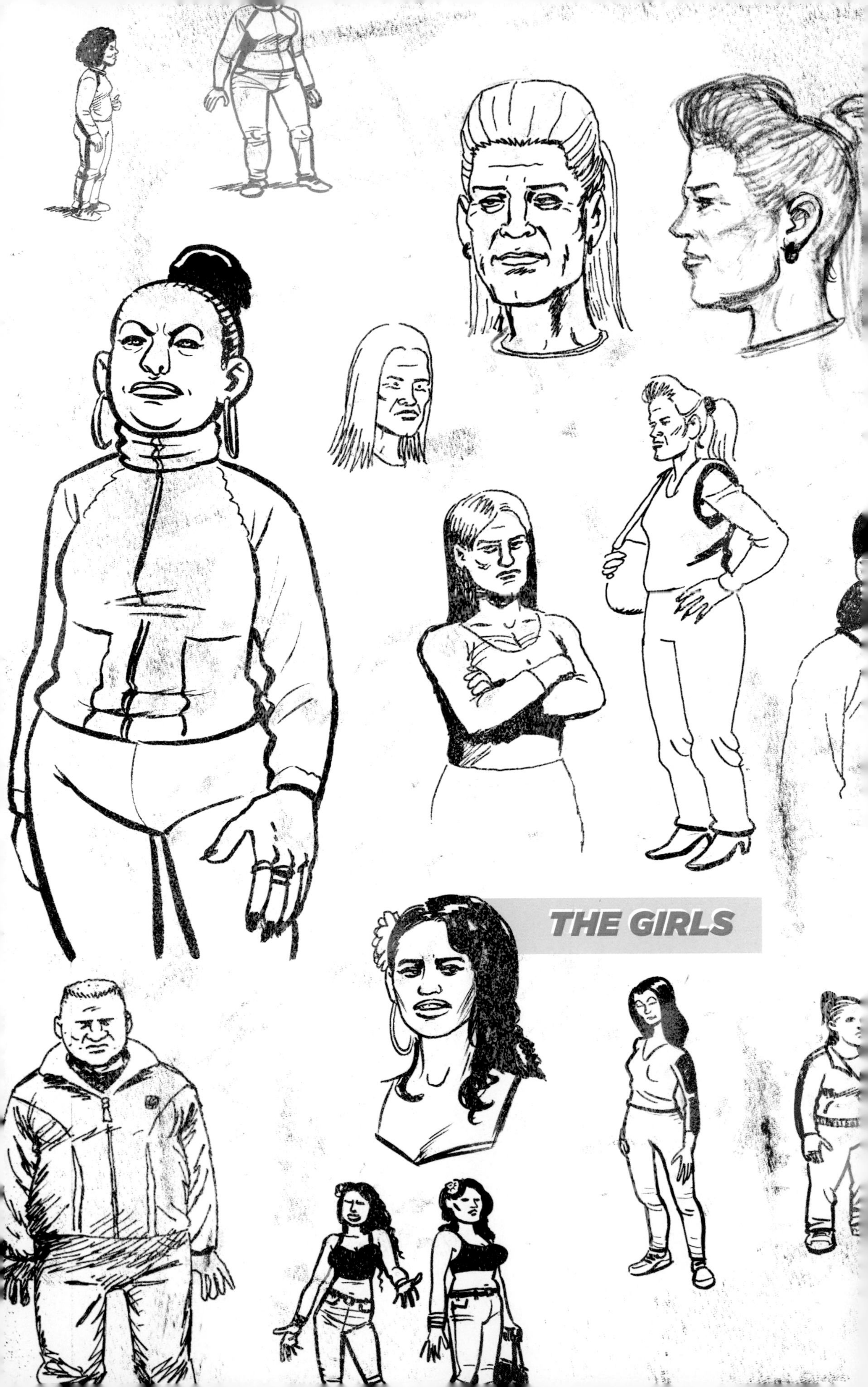

THE GIRLS

CHARACTER SKETCHES

DRAWN BY **PHILIP BARRETT**

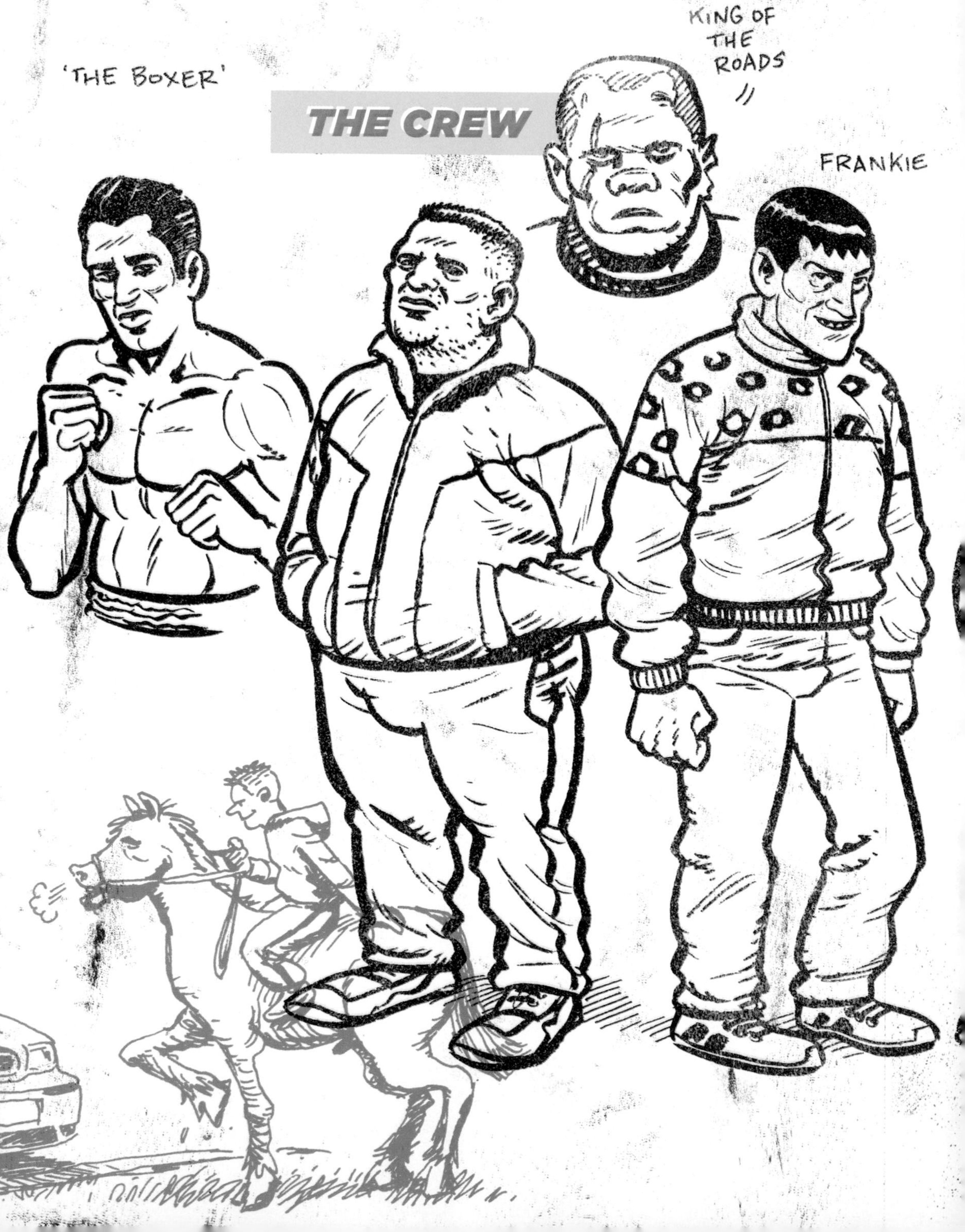

'THE BOXER'
THE CREW
KING OF THE ROADS
FRANKIE

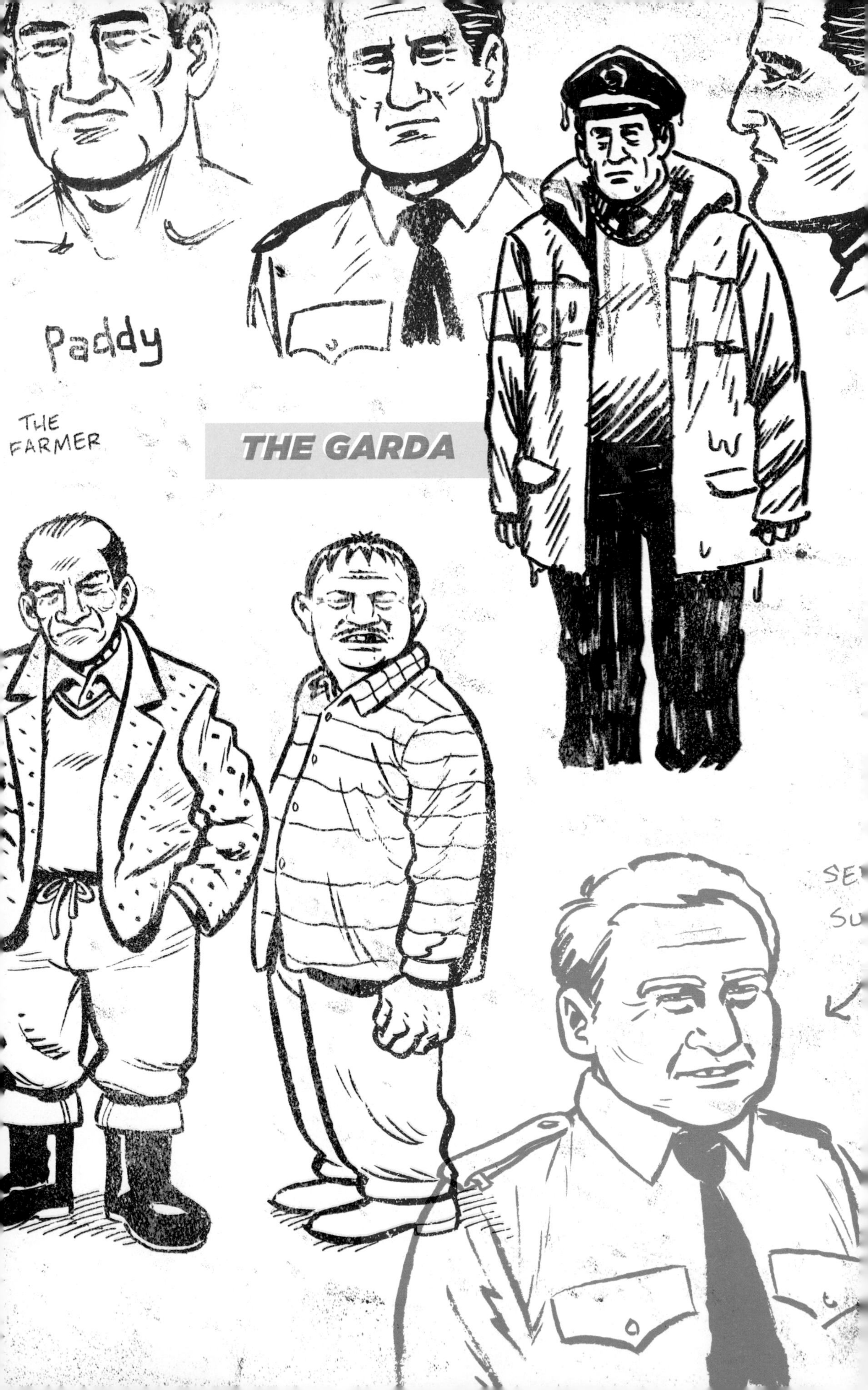
Paddy
THE FARMER
THE GARDA

SPOTS

DRAWN BY **PHILIP BARRETT**

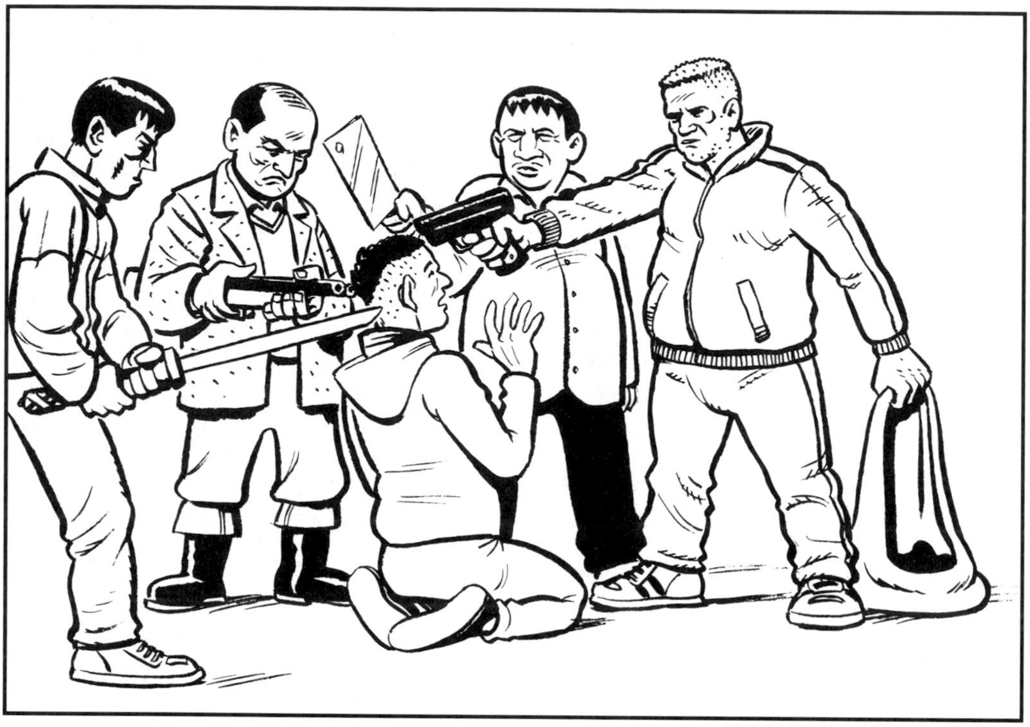

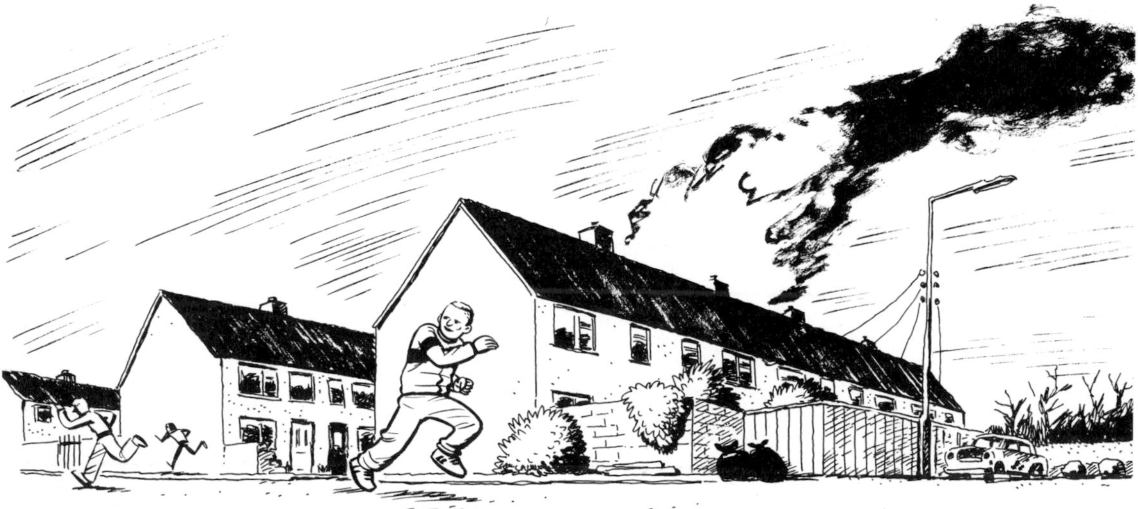

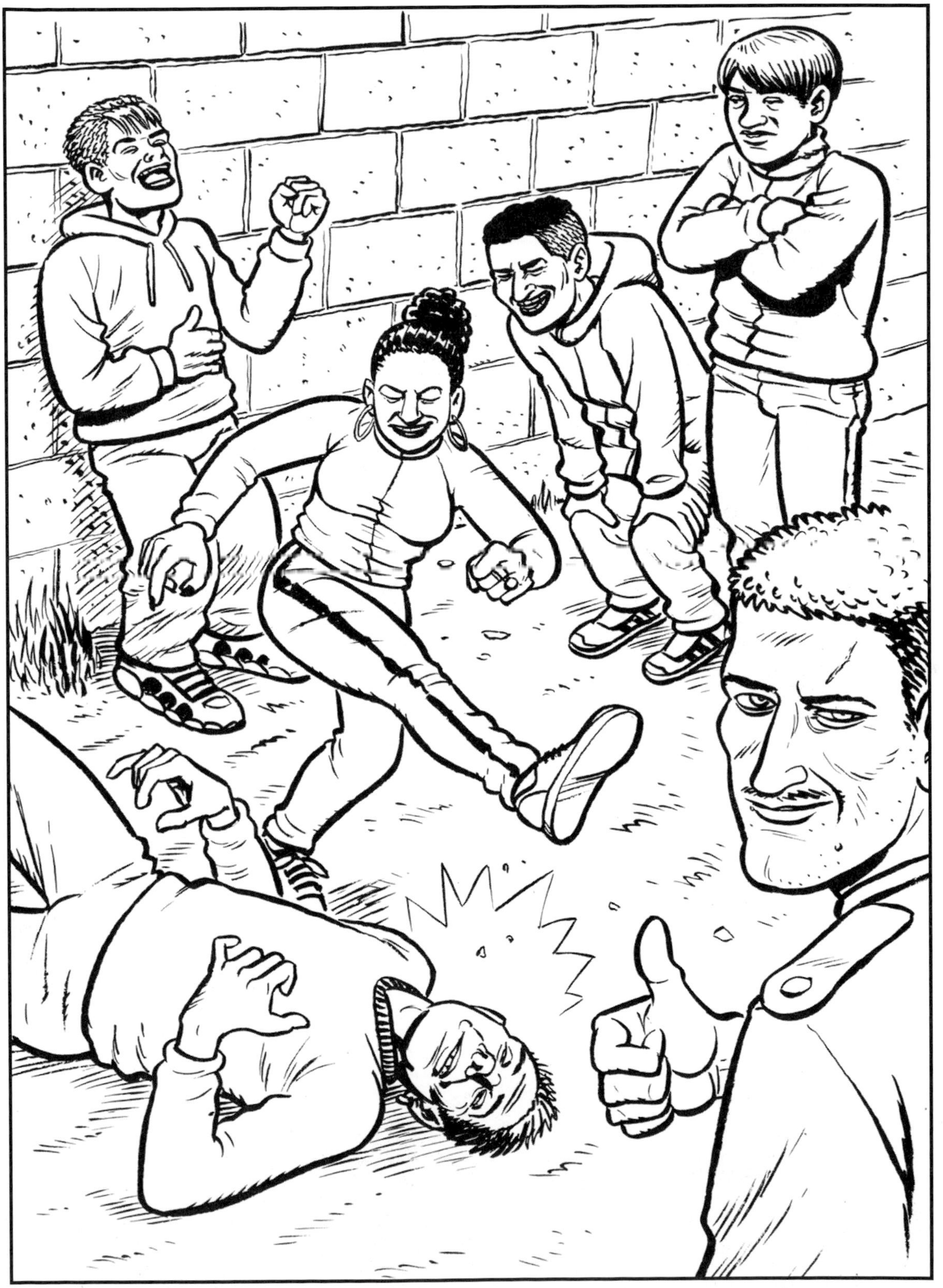

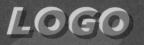

LOGO

DESIGNED BY **EMMA PRICE**

SAVAGE TOWN
SAVAGE TOWN
SAVAG€ TOWN
SAVAGE TOWN

Early Sketches

The initial sketches explored a range of themes; from the idea of the 'Celtic Tiger' - referring to the rapid economic growth of the Irish economy in the 1990s and early 21st century - to something that looked like a sports brand and wouldn't feel out of place on a tracksuit or sweatpants.

SAVAGE TOWN
SAVAGE TOWN
SAVAGE TOWN

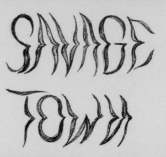

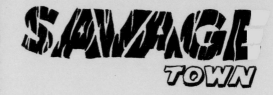

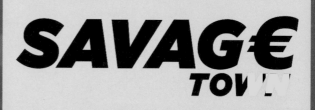

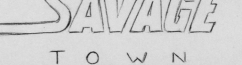

Developed Ideas

For the next stage Emma adapted both the sports brand and the Celtic Tiger ideas, refining the sketches into digital vector files and looking more closely at the shapes, colour and texture.

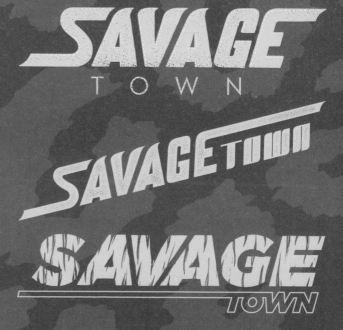

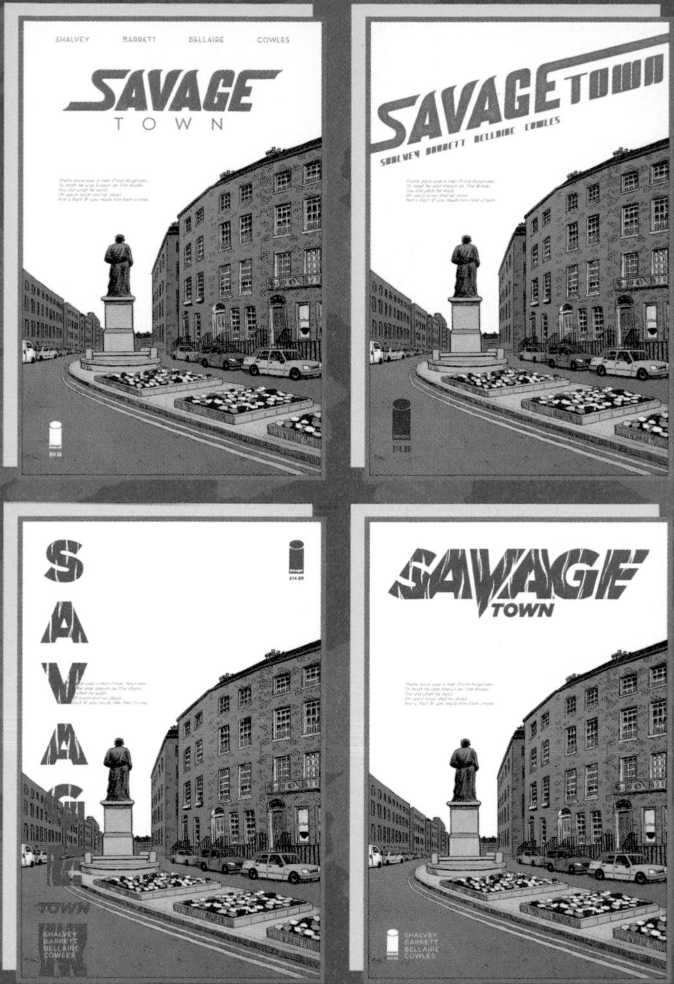
SHALVEY BARRETT BELLAIRE COWLES
SAVAGE TOWN
SAVAGE TOWN
SHALVEY BARRETT BELLAIRE COWLES
SAVAGE TOWN
SHALVEY BARRETT BELLAIRE COWLES
SAVAGE TOWN
SHALVEY BARRETT BELLAIRE COWLES

Cover Mock-ups

The logos were put onto an early cover idea, drawn by Philip, and Emma looked at some layout options for the final cover. Seeing the general design of the book starting to take shape helped us pick a logo style that was going to work for the book.

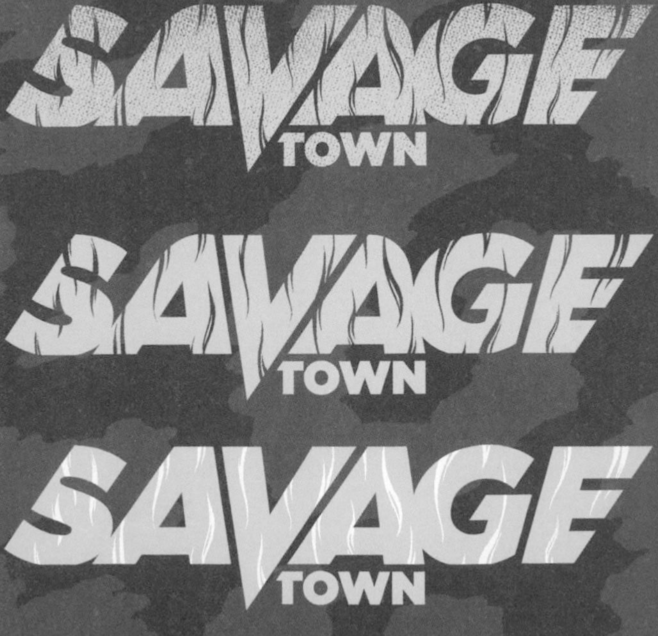
SAVAGE TOWN
SAVAGE TOWN
SAVAGE TOWN

Near-Finished Alternatives

We agreed the Celtic Tiger style was the way forward with its sharp edges and tiger stripes. Like the word, 'Savage', the tiger element has layered meaning, tying in not only with the Irish economy but the physical savagery of the beast and the brutality of the story being told.

COVERS

DRAWN BY **PHILIP BARRETT**

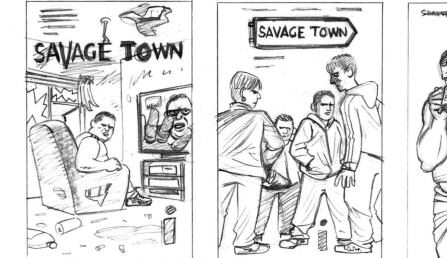

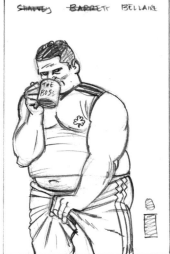

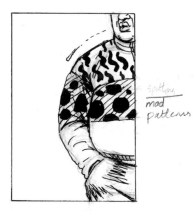

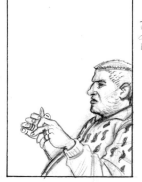

SAVAGE TOWN
NEW!

SAVAGE TOWN

BARRETT BELLAIRE
THE BOSS

spitting
mad
patterns

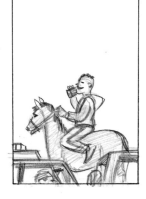

Jimmy
contemplative.
Bullet?

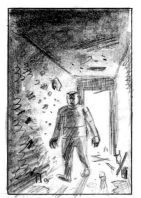

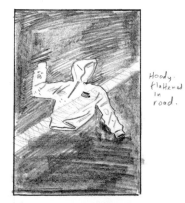

Hoody:
flattened
in
road.

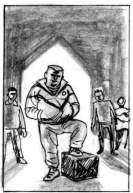

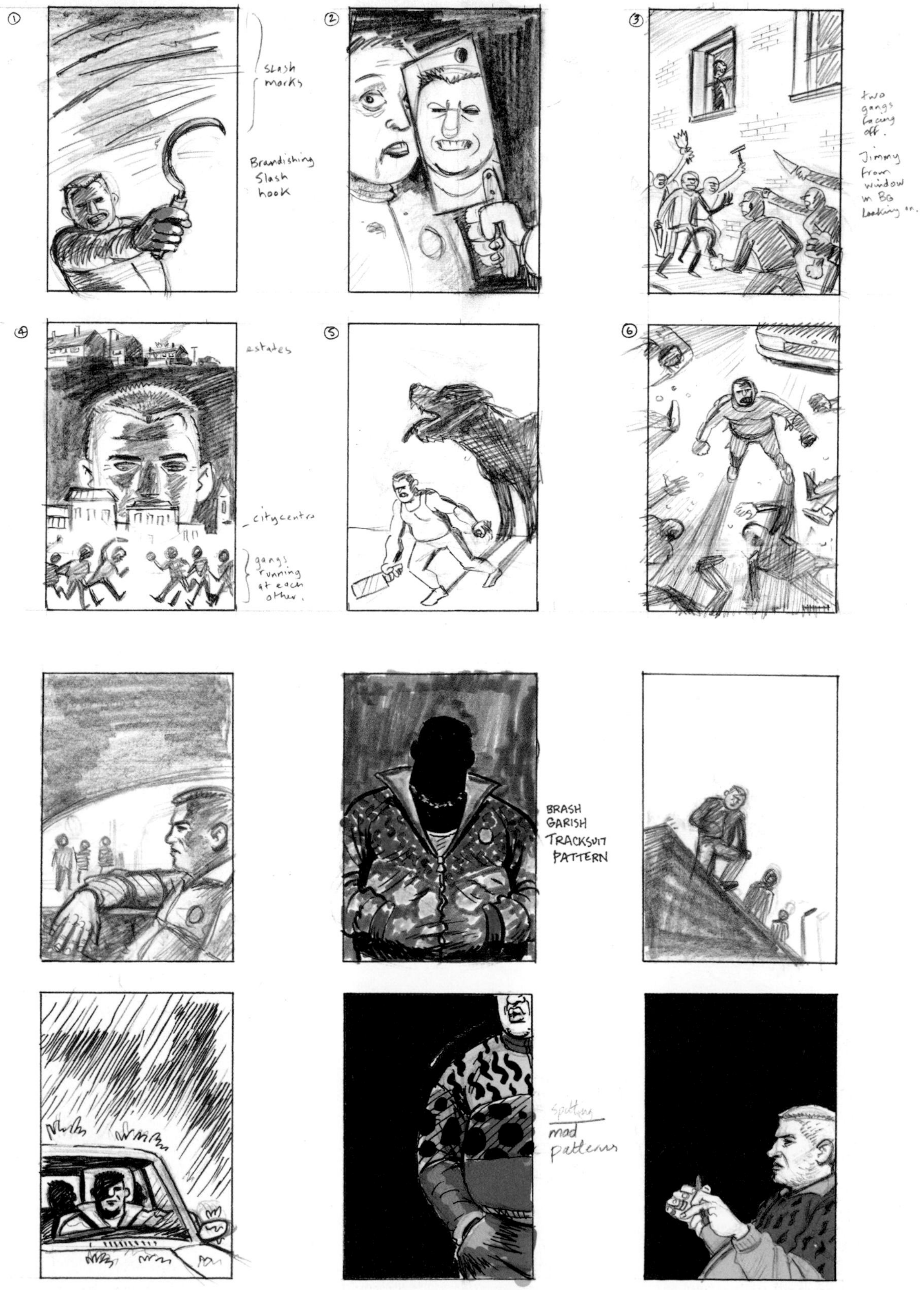
1
slash marks
Brandishing Slash hook
2
3
two gangs facing off.
Jimmy from window in BG looking on.
4
estates
city centre
gangs running at each other.
5
6
BRASH GARISH TRACKSUIT PATTERN
spitting
mad patterns

PITCH CONCEPTS

DRAWN BY **PHILIP BARRETT**

INKS

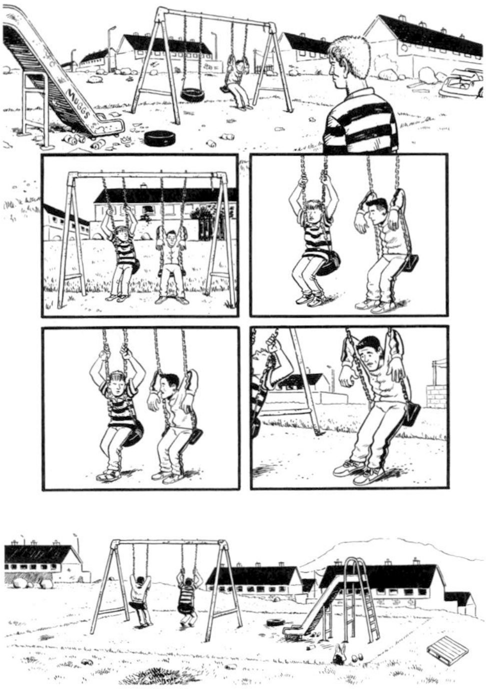
MUGGS

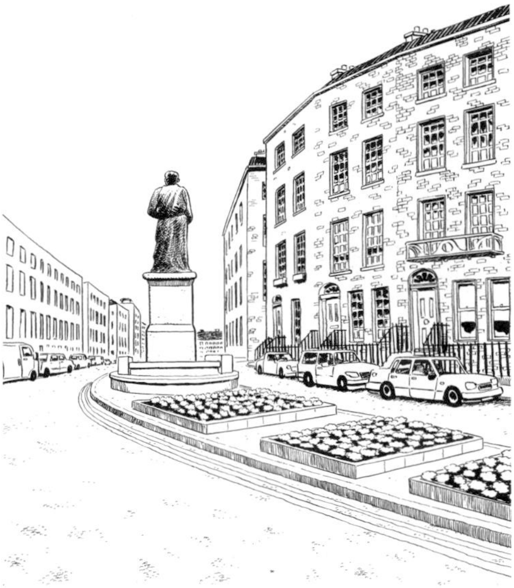

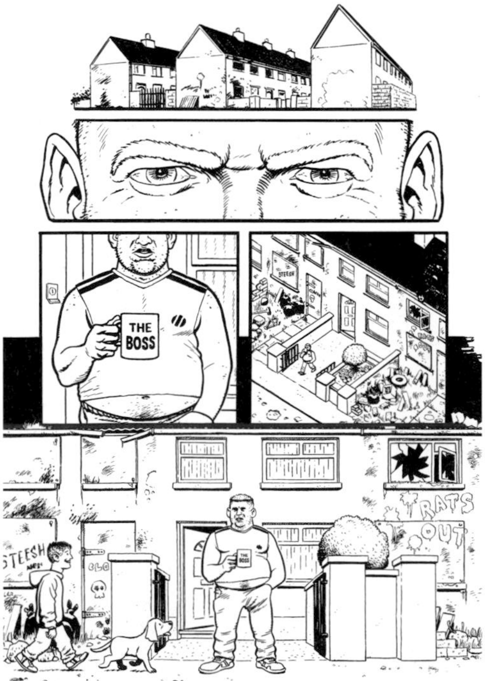
THE BOSS
STEESH
RATS OUT

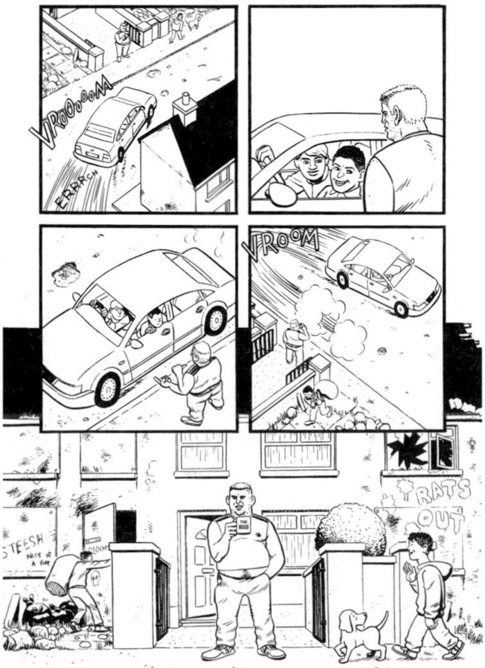
VROOOooOM
ERRRCH
VROOM
STEESH
RATS OUT

COLOURS

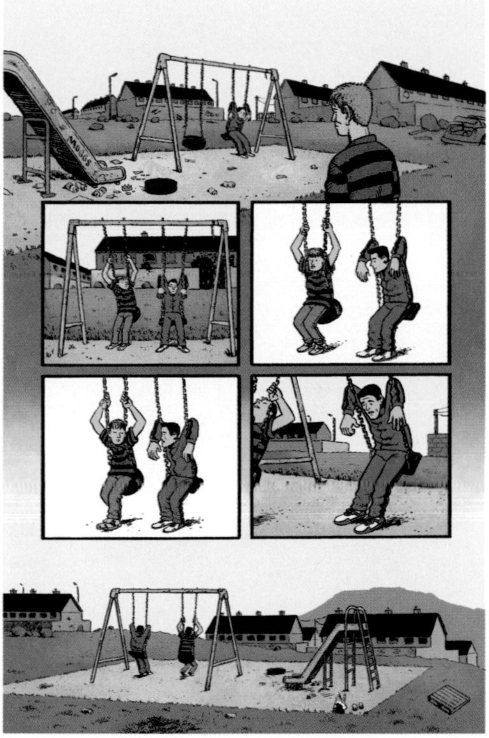

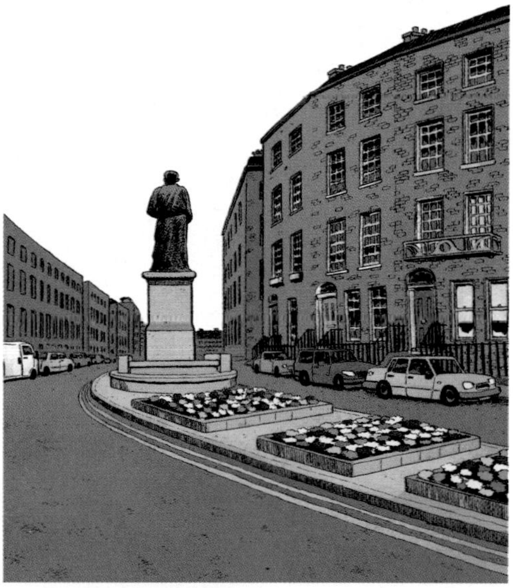

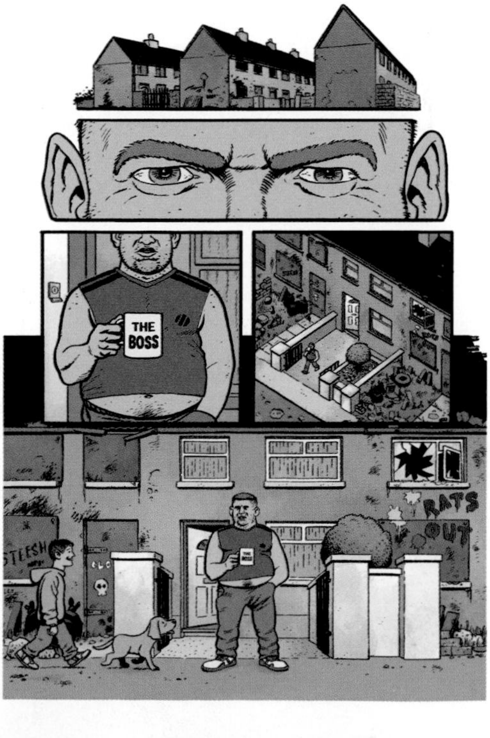
THE BOSS
STEESH
RATS
OUT

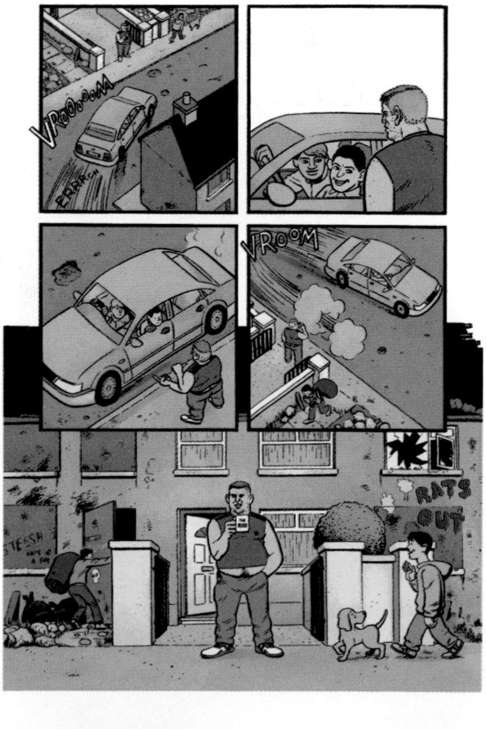
VROOM
STEESH
RATS
OUT

IMAGE+ COVER

DRAWN BY **PHILIP BARRETT**

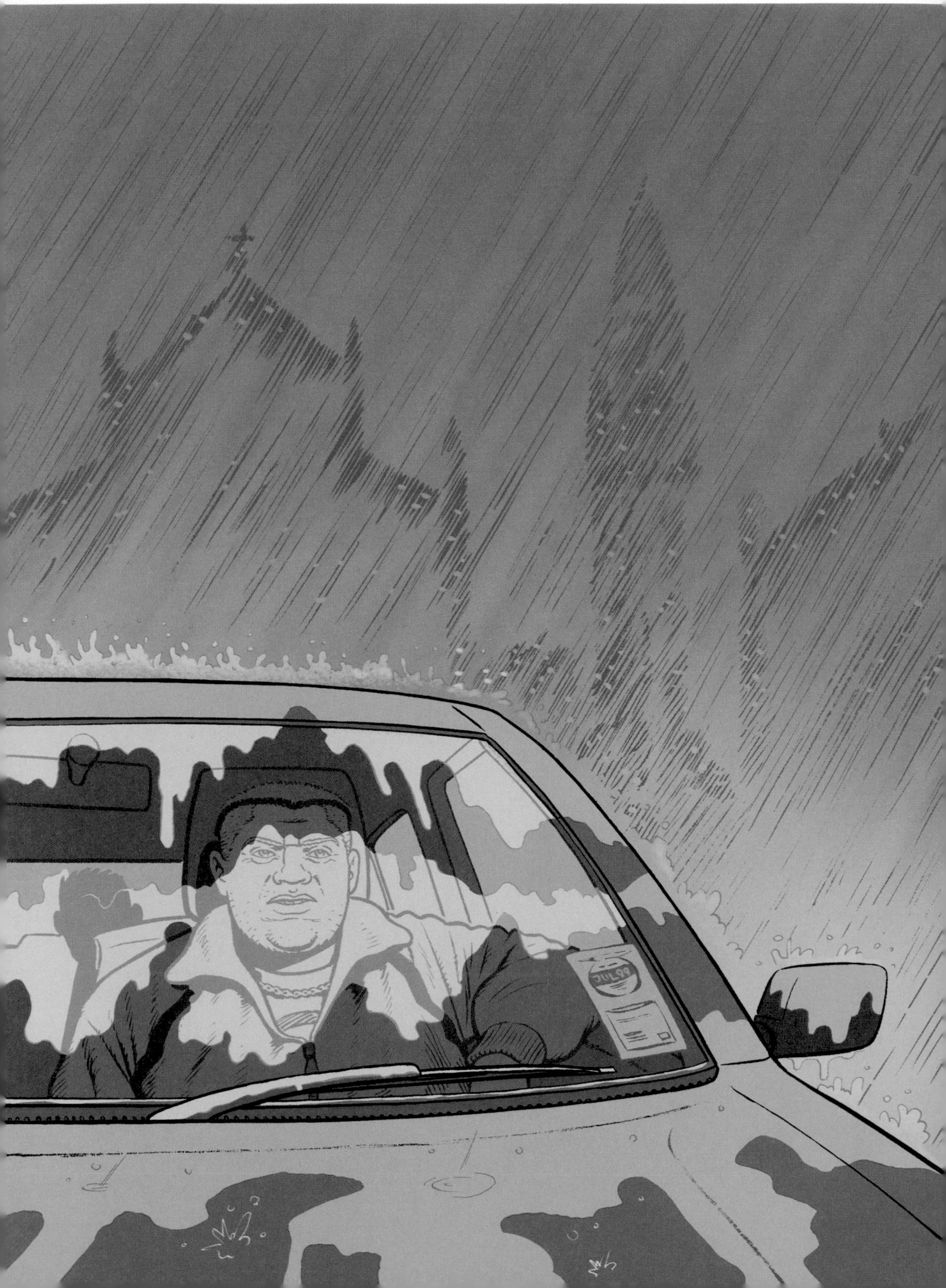

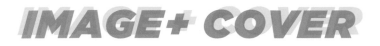

LOCATION TEST

DRAWN BY **PHILIP BARRETT**

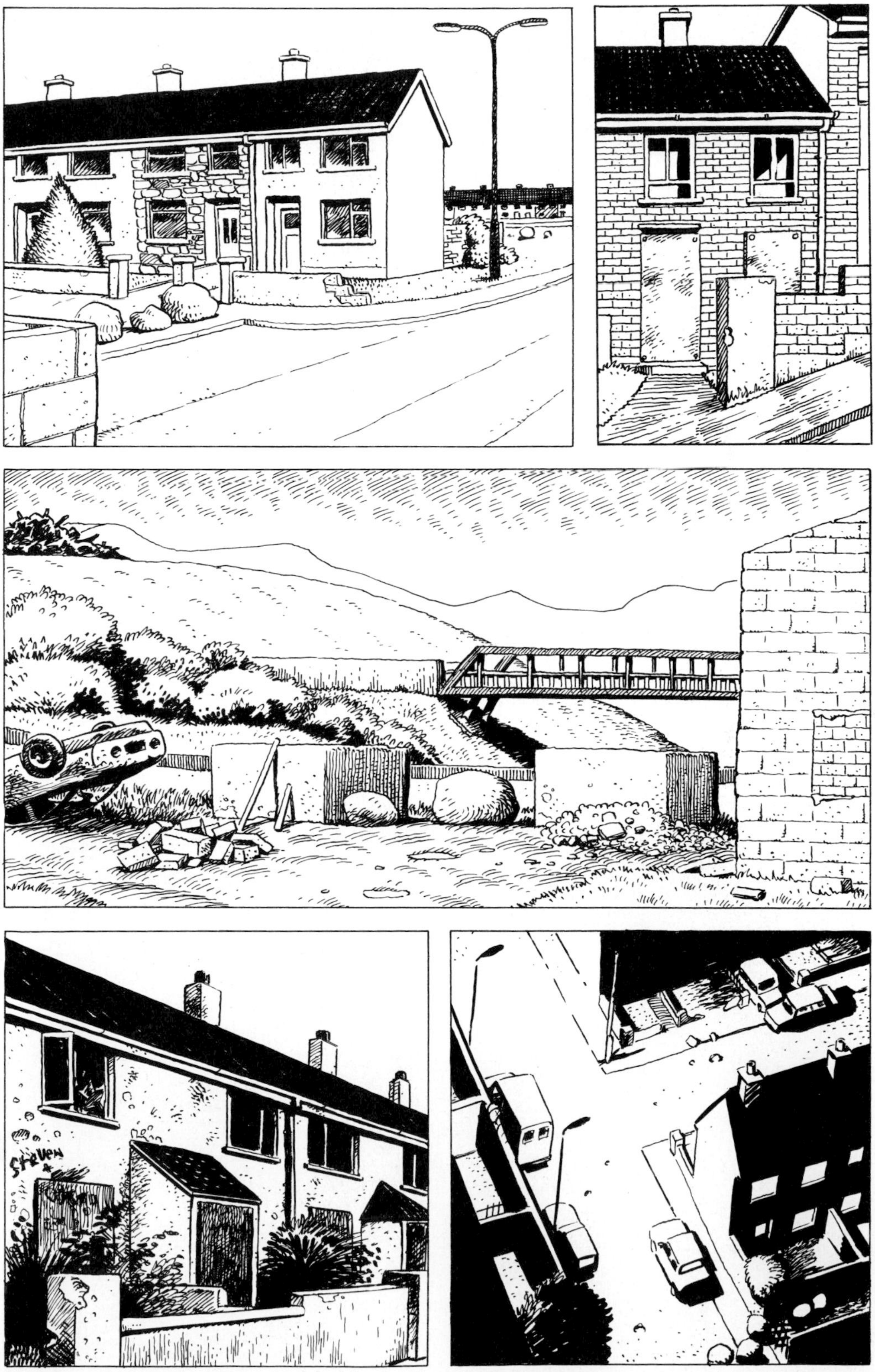
STEVEN &

MEET DE CREATORS

DECLAN SHALVEY

...thinks he's some fancy pants because he's drawing a critically acclaimed graphic novel series called *INJECTION* with Warren Ellis. He's also drawn *MOON KNIGHT*, *DEADPOOL* and *ALL STAR BATMAN* and thinks he's a big deal now because he's writing *DEADPOOL VS OLD MAN LOGAN*. What a gobshite.

PHILIP BARRETT

...is a comic artist, illustrator, live-drawer and a total legend to boot. He's been self-publishing his comic Matter since 2001, that's like before the internet and everything! He's also illustrated the book series 'WHERE'S LARRY?' which is gas craic.

JORDIE BELLAIRE

...is a two-timer Eisner-winning colourist for acclaimed projects such as *VISION*, *THEY'RE NOT LIKE US*, *PRETTY DEADLY*, *INJECTION*, *AUTUMNLANDS* etc. as well all mainstream hits like *BATMAN*, *SPIDER-MAN*, *DEADPOOL*, *MOON KNIGHT* and *HAWKEYE*. She is also the writer/co-creator of *REDLANDS*. Christ, that's a lot of comics, isn't it?

CLAYTON COWLES

...is the letterer of books like *THE WICKED + THE DIVINE*, *BITCH PLANET*, *BATMAN*, *VISION*, *STAR WARS* and *REDLANDS*. Christ knows how he lettered all the nonsense in this book, fair play to him like.

EMMA PRICE

...is a graphic designer and illustrator from... ugh, England. She has weaved her designy magic for books like *CRY HAVOC* and *ANGELIC*.

SEBASTIAN GIRNER

...is a freelance comic book editor, (whatever that's supposed to mean) for books like *DEADLY CLASS*, *SOUTHERN BASTARDS* and *THE GODDAMNED*. He's also the writer/co-creator of *SCALES & SCOUNDRELS* and co-writer/co-creator of *SHIRTLESS BEAR-FIGHTER!* Jaysus, is everyone on this book a bloody writer all of a sudden!?